LUKE RHINEHART

Adventures of Wim

GRAFTON BOOKS

A Division of the Collins Publishing Group

LONDON GLASGOW
TORONTO SYDNEY AUCKLAND

Grafton Books
A Division of the Collins Publishing Group
8 Grafton Street, London W1X 3LA

Published by Grafton Books 1987

First published in Great Britain by
Grafton Books 1986

Copyright © Luke Rinehart 1986

ISBN 0-586-06752-3

Printed and bound in Great Britain by
Collins, Glasgow

Set in Palatino

PREFACE

It will naturally be asked why we need another book about Wim. Scott Twain once quipped that without the subject of Wim the publishing, film and stereokinetic industries of the twenty-fourth century would have had a serious unemployment problem. Yet as the sage M. T. Soss has said: 'Each generation – aye, each man – must create its own Wim anew. The last thing he would want would be to be stuck with just one life.'

So I present here my personal 'Adventures of Wim'. It consists of selections from a few of the classic books about Wim, ranging from the bitterly disparaging *Fact Sheets on Wim* (edited by Dr Wilhelm Einrecher Bost, *et alii*, 218 volumes, Pantheon Press, New York, 2028) to the idolatrous and somewhat fanciful hagiography *The Book of Chances* (Children of Chance Books, Orient, New York, 2016).

Fact Sheets, of course, is the mammoth scientific effort to explain all of the unusual and even miraculous phenomena which accompanied Wim's extraordinary life. It is a tribute to the energy and tenacity of numerous twenty-first-century sociologists and psychologists that the work runs to 218 volumes. The reader will, however, be reassured to know I have used it sparingly.

The Book of Chances has been dipped into both for some of its many supernatural tales about Wim and for its selections from 'Fragments of Wim' – the hundred pages of actual autobiographical fragments written by Wim before the age of eighteen.

For most of the narrative of Wim's early life I have used the delightful *Memoirs of an Old Liar* by Wim's Montauk mentor, Grain-of-Sand (Pauper's Press, Montauk, New

York, 1996), and a few scenes on videocassette wafer from the ancient Paramount film *Adventures of Wim* (2002).

For R&R I have used the rarely reprinted classic *The Gospel According to Luke* by the twenty-second-century satirist Luke Froth (Magpie Books, London, 2121). Froth's *Gospel* is the first narrative of Wim's life to try to tell the story with the exaggeration and playfulness with which I imagine Wim himself might have written it.

Finally, I have, on random occasions, seen fit to print on the left-hand page one of the *Sixty-six Parables of Wim* (Random Press, New York, 2000). These parables, dramatizing Wim both as seeker and as sage, provide the flavour of his teachings, and no book about Wim should ever be printed without a few. Readers who for optical reasons are unable to read both left- and right-hand pages at the same time will, of course, miss the art of my book and will have to create their own version of *Adventures of Wim* by interspersing the selections from the left when they feel like it. But as the wise literary critic Vladistovik Ruskolni has said: 'Each reader creates his own book anyway. Why writers bother I can't imagine.'

Deya, Mallorca
August, 2366

ADVENTURES OF WIM

WIM LEARNS CHESS

'When I first began looking for ultimate truth,' explained Wim one day, 'I always thought that when I'd lost a game of chess I'd failed.'

'That's typical of all of us,' said one of his disciples.

'After going to the Himalayas and meeting the great Yogi Mayarishi I learned that when I *won* the game I had failed.'

'I see.'

'And then after staying with the monk Brother Bobo for a few months I came to realize that when I lost but still felt good about losing I had failed.'

'That's very good, Master, very good.'

'A few weeks later when I finally managed to locate the great Sufi Sage Narsufin in Harlem I learned from him that when I won but felt guilty about it I had failed.'

'That's tremendous, Master, tremendous.'

'Finally, I discovered ultimate truth.'

'What happened?'

'At last I learned how to develop my pawns.'

– from *Sixty-six Parables of Wim*

1

from the Paramount film *Adventures of Wim*, 2002,
screenplay by Olly Hart, pp. 3–8

FADE IN

EXTERIOR – GARDNER'S BAY – DAY – FULL

On a sunlit summer day a wide mirror of blue water
stretches away from Long Island. A few scattered boats are
sailing or motoring. The nearby shore is the lush green of
spring. The whole scene is idyllic.

Seagulls sweep down along the water making an occasional
distant raucous cry.

As a single fishing boat ploughs through the water, the
fishermen throw overboard the junk fish to the delight of
some scavenging gulls.

After establishing this peaceful modern sea scene the
camera slowly zooms in to a single old and beatup rowboat,
aboard which are two Indians, GRAIN-OF-SAND, who is fishing
from the stern, and WIDE POOL, who is rowing from slightly
forward of amidship.   .

GRAIN-OF-SAND is an old, bronze-skinned Indian, vigorous
and no-nonsense, with alert and piercing eyes. He is
wearing tattered jeans and a dirty sweatshirt. He holds an
old fishing rod, the line trailing out behind the boat as he
trolls, bright-eyed and totally engrossed.

WIDE POOL is a pretty young Indian girl, still in her teens but
immensely pregnant. She is wearing a voluminous old
brightly-coloured maternity dress. She is pulling gently on

the mismatched, unpainted oars, her pretty face showing tense concentration, half on the rowing, half on the child moving within her.

INTERCUT SHOTS OF GRAIN-OF-SAND AND WIDE POOL

Establishing the peacefulness of the present scene, but with the tension of the expectant fisherman and expectant mother-to-be. Sounds of water lapping and distant gulls.

Suddenly Grain-of-Sand's line goes taut, his rod bends sharply: he has hooked a fish.

CLOSE SHOT – WIDE POOL

At the same instant Wide Pool feels the first powerful pain of labour – almost as if the hooking of the fish and her beginning to birth are connected. Her face at these first pangs is a mixture of pain and joy.

CLOSE SHOT – GRAIN-OF-SAND

His face too is filled both with tension and excitement as he begins to struggle to land the fish.

> GRAIN-OF-SAND
> Watch your stern!

Wide Pool grapples with the oars to adjust the boat as Grain-of-Sand ordered, then releases one to hold her stomach and grimace with pain.

> GRAIN-OF-SAND (O.S.)
> Oh, what a fighter! Steady there!

Wide Pool grabs the oars again and begins rowing, her face still a mixture of pain and increasing joy.

Grain-of-Sand, battling with his fish, is now kneeling in the stern, his back to Wide Pool.

More to port!

As Wide Pool continues to struggle with the oars she begins to slide forward off her rowing seat on to the bottom of the boat. Nevertheless, her face is now becoming more purely ecstatic, her eyes aglow, her mouth open in joyous awe at what is happening.

Grain-of-Sand too is becoming more and more excited and happy. He is standing now, battling as the fish seems to be moving in an arc behind the boat.

GRAIN-OF-SAND

Oh, my God, what a beauty! *(pause)* Forward! Faster!

Wide Pool is now slumped totally off her seat and lying in the bottom of the boat between the two seats, her back up against the one she had been sitting on, her legs spread, her face aglow. She is gripping the oars with iron will, in seeming obedience to Grain-of-Sand, trying to row but flailing uselessly across the top of the water.

Grain-of-Sand, standing, is staring down into the water, his face at a pitch of ecstatic excitement.

GRAIN-OF-SAND

He's coming!

EXTERIOR – ROWBOAT, GRAIN-OF-SAND AND WIDE POOL AS SEEN FROM OFF TO ONE SIDE AND AT WATER LEVEL

Grain-of-Sand, straining as much and almost as ecstatic as Wide Pool, at last lifts his sharply bending rod up and swings a large fish, alive and beautiful, shimmering and quivering, up out of the water and then down and out of sight into the middle of the rowboat between himself and Wide Pool, whose head, facing Grain-of-Sand, is just visible amidships.

He is grinning madly.

GRAIN-OF-SAND
We did it!!

CLOSE SHOT – WIDE POOL

Her face, still glowing, is now at peace – the serene rapture of after-the-orgasm, after-the-birth.

Grain-of-Sand, still standing, looks skyward, and, holding the now tensionless rod in one hand, lifts the fist of his other and shakes it triumphantly as if to the gods.

GRAIN-OF-SAND
Thanks, fellas!! One of your better days!

He then turns to squat down to look into the centre of the boat.

His face goes from its happiness to confusion to stunned bewilderment.

GRAIN-OF-SAND
What happened to my fish!?

Wide Pool, still lying in the middle of the boat between the two seats, at last releases her grip on the two oars and slowly struggles to push herself back up into a sitting position and look forward between her legs.

There, lying neatly and quietly between her legs in the shallow bilgewater of the leaky rowboat, is a beautiful BABY, a baby somehow more glowing, more alert, more alive, more peaceful, than a normal just-born infant. His eyes are open and twinkling.

Wide Pool stares at her baby with unalloyed love.

Grain-of-Sand stares at the baby with stunned bafflement. He slowly kneels forward in front of the baby and lowers his rod on to the seats on one side of Wide Pool.

> GRAIN-OF-SAND
> Where's my fish!?

He leans forward and picks up part of Wide Pool's long skirt and peeks under it – no fish.

He gently moves the baby to look under Wide Pool's seat – no fish. His face looks more and more gravely puzzled.

Wide Pool reaches forward to gently touch her baby, caressing it softly.

> WIDE POOL
> (softly smiling)
> It's a boy.

> GRAIN-OF-SAND
> (nodding)
> That's jimdandy, but I still want to know where it went.

He takes the fish line that comes out of the end of his rod and begins to trace it down into the bilge of the boat where he sees it disappear under one side of the baby.

When he tenderly traces the line up to the baby he sees his lure with one of its hooks firmly implanted in the baby's right side.

REACTION SHOT – GRAIN-OF-SAND

Pure amazed awe.

He looks up at Wide Pool who returns his gaze with serene joy.

Then he looks at the alert baby, who gazes up at him with open, seeing eyes and smiles.

Grain-of-Sand then tensely but tenderly unhooks the lure from the baby's side, noting with amazement that the hook comes out easily with no trace of blood. He looks again at the baby, who gazes back at him.

> BABY
> (gurgling)
> Thanks.

REACTION SHOT – GRAIN-OF-SAND

His mouth falls open, and he stares in awe again at Wide Pool, who leans forward and takes the baby into her arms to cradle it at her chest.

> WIDE POOL
> (smiling serenely)
> Will you name him for me, Grain-of-Sand?

Numbly Grain-of-Sand nods, then looks up towards the sky.

> GRAIN-OF-SAND
> (gravely)
> Iskabee mora ... Wim.

> WIDE POOL
> Wim ... Wave-Rider ... Oh yes, Wim.
> That's a beautiful name.

The two of them gaze at the beautiful WIM, who smiles happily up at his mother.

> WIDE POOL
> Aren't you pleased, Grain-of-Sand?

Grain-of-Sand squats back on his heels and folds his arms across his chest, looking now dignified and stern. He nods gravely.

Grain-of-Sand very pleased.
(pause)
But you should have seen the one that
got away.

2

from Grain-of-Sand's *Memoirs of an Old Liar*, pp. 3-15

Well, you've heard of him I suppose, the usual lies anyway, but that ain't going to stop me from telling you *my* lies which, since I knew Wim from before he was born, are a lot more interesting than yours. At least to me.

To you he was just a crazy little Indian who parlayed a good passing arm, dark eyes and his nuttiness into some mass hysteria, a few TV appearances, and a new religion. But for me the last thing he wanted was to create a new religion, so the half million or so Children of Chance running around now would probably make Wim turn over in his grave, if he didn't enjoy lying still so much, and if he hadn't been cremated and his ashes scattered to some dumb seagulls in Gardner's Bay which makes turning over tough.

Wim was born on an incoming tide in the late afternoon of a blustery April day. The legends claim he emerged freshly born from the sea, swimming into Maganansett beach with a modified backstroke and being adopted by the Indian woman Wide Pool who happened to be clamming when he come cruising ashore.

That's not the way it happened and I was *there*. Fact is, Wim was born in a rowboat. Wide Pool had been pregnant for nine months, and since she had no money and no husband she was out fishing with me when Wim set to kicking up a fuss inside her. I had to give up a good bluefish to try to help out, but before I could get her to shore out he popped. To us Montauks it seemed a decent enough trade – Wim for a three-foot bluefish – though Sitting Cow claims I never did stop complaining that the Gods might of let me have both. And I suppose the legend about Wim's birth got started when some people begun saying that I *hooked* Wim and reeled him in – 'put up a helluva fight', they said. This version turned out to be too unromantic for humans, so it soon got changed to Wim's swimming in from the sea from another solar system. But Wide Pool says just what I says here, and she can no more tell a lie than I can stick to the truth.

My name is Grain-of-Sand. When Wim first swum into view I was already fifty years old and the official navigator of the Montauk nation. Now 'navigator' is my translation of the Montauk phrase that means 'He-who-can-read-the-stars-and-waves', and the phrase comes down to us from the ancient navigators who got us to Long Island from the South Pacific two thousand or so years ago. Being navigator of a whole nation is a pretty big deal, even if the Montauk nation at the time of Wim's birth consisted of only twenty-seven Montauks and a couple of hundred other assimilated Montauks who would occasionally pretend to be real Montauks to pick up a buck.

The navigator was the official historian, storyteller, poet, and geographical and spiritual guide. He wasn't the same as the chief. The chief was the judge, general, president and legislature. If a Montauk had a problem with a neighbour he went to the chief. If he had a problem with the universe he went to the navigator. I got to know Wim real well over the years.

I suppose I should fill you in a little on the Montauk Indians. Now everyone knows – meaning most humans think – that the Montauk Indians became extinct in the late nineteenth century, and that crazies like me who claim to be Montauks are charlatans and liars. Well, we're charlatans and liars all right, that's how we survive , but we're still Montauks, at least when we feel like admitting it.

Fact is, until the white man come over here we Montauks didn't have a history. Although we'd existed for thousands of years, the oral tradition handed down by our navigators was that 'Nothing ever happened', 'Tide rises, tide falls, fish bite at dusk'. There were no battles in our history or, if there were, they were considered no more significant than a March nor'easter or a summer thunderstorm. We've recorded no great chiefs or great warriors, at least in the usual human sense. When Wim asked me once why the Montauks had never had any great chiefs or warriors, I told him our truth: 'Our Great Chiefs kept us out of battle. Good at doing nothing. We had many great chiefs before white man come: that's why nothing ever happen.'

But when the first white men come stomping ashore about four hundred years ago, the Montauks began to have a history. According to tradition the first chief of the sad period when 'Things began to happen' was Little Pebble. It was him who was forced to negotiate with John Holcombe, who wanted, on behalf of the village of Southampton, to buy land that we Montauks had lived on for close to two thousand years. Holcombe first offered for the five thousand acres we were living on three purple rags, two pink rags and two dozen metal trinkets that mostly resembled bent nails. When the chief declined, Holcombe upped the offer to an even dozen coloured rags and four dozen bent nails.

'No,' said Chief Little Pebble. 'Prefer five thousand acres.'

Holcombe then made an offer the chief couldn't refuse.

'Well, chief,' he said to Little Pebble, 'you get your fucking Indians off that land or we'll kill you all.'

Chief Little Pebble was one of our great chiefs. He looked Holcombe right in the eye and without flinching said: 'We move.'

Holcombe thought he'd got himself a deal, but Little Pebble fooled him: he *gave* the whites the land. He refused the coloured rags and the bent nails and didn't sign a thing.

18

Holcombe and the other whites were forced to take over the land free, and Little Pebble and his people moved to lousier land. That was the history of all Indian nations, but the difference with us was that we never fought, never sold and never signed. We made a religion out of retreat.

And in the nineteenth century our great Chief Waterdrop thunk out the strategy that saved our nation. While thousands of other Indians in the West were being massacred or herded on to reservations, the chief came up with the trick used by all real Montauks ever since – invisibility. Thanks to his far-sighted policy, by 1900 we Montauks were declared extinct. That's the way, unlike all other American Indians, we managed to avoid massacre, assimilation and the reservation.

The speech Chief Waterdrop made to his assembled retreaters back in 1876 or so when a delegation of Suffolk County businessmen and US Infantry come to buy the last twenty-two acres of our land, is memorized by every Montauk child. Several retreaters said that we should break tradition and fight rather than give up the last of our land. A few said we should sail back to the South Pacific. Others said just leave the land and get some cheaper land someplace else – the way we'd been doing for two hundred and fifty years. The chief answered them all.

'No matter how bravely we fight, the white man will kill us. No matter how far we sail, the white man will follow. No matter how shitty the land, the white man will someday want it. Montauks will never again fight. Never again own land. Today we Montauks resign from the human race. Today we begin to disappear. If Montauks have nothing, white men can't steal from us. If we don't exist, white men can't kill us. Today we bury ourselves so that we can live for ever.'

And that's what we did. From that day on we broke up into tiny tribes of sea gypsies, living in small boats, camping on unused beaches, sailing from Greenport to Gardner's

19

Island to Montauk Point down to Cape Hatteras and back again, as wind and whites permitted, eating shellfish, clams, fish and wild berries, learning to dress like white fishermen, talk like white fishermen, lie like white fishermen. When caught trespassing we didn't resist, just served time in county jails and then returned to invisibility.

To confuse the white men Waterdrop ordered every Montauk to give his or her name as Gene or Jeanne Smith. Since Montauks always pretend they can't read or write, on that glorious day the entire Montauk nation of over two thousand souls all became Gene Smith. For fifty years the human beings cursed and fumed and swore, but every last Montauk they talked to claimed to be Gene (or Jeanne) Smith.

But you can't outfox the Gods for more'n a few seconds: they got too much free time on their hands. In 1942 tragedy struck.

The US government Selective Service somehow called up 'Gene Smith', and with one stroke of the pen the entire Montauk nation was wiped out – drafted.

Well, our Chief Shallow Well thunk awhile and then come up with the policy Montauks been following ever since. That night every last Gene Smith had a heart attack and died, and the next morning every Montauk had a new 'white man's name' and changed it every single day ever after. Since no Montauk had ever been to a hospital or seen a doctor, none had a birth certificate. Since none had ever been on welfare or worked for a white man except under the table, none had a social security card number. Since none had registered for the draft except that one renegade who messed us all up, they had no Selective Service number. So we managed to avoid World War II after all and kept up our record of never being in a winning battle. 'Course since between 1880 and 1942 every time a Montauk was arrested he'd give his name as Gene Smith, that poor guy had the longest criminal record in US history.

The new policy of always giving a different name – usually one whites didn't take to, like George Washington Mud or U. R. White Shit – broke down in '67 or so. That same US Selective Service, Suffolk County branch, hearing rumours there was over a hundred thousand renegade Indians living along the water in the county, ordered the police to round them up so they could defend the country from the threat of invasion from North Vietnam.

Now the idea that there were so many of us come from all the names we'd bandied about over two decades. Actually there were only about a hundred of us then, and since none of us had been massacred or herded on to reservations, I guess I better explain how we went from two thousand in 1880 to only a hundred just eighty-five years later.

The secret is standards. Practising our ancient birth-control technique, Montauk women usually have only one child. If the kid is born crippled or sickly the navigator may let the mother give him back to the Gods and try again. You can figure for yourself that with that kind of birth-rate our nation tends to get at least halved every generation. Actually we don't decrease that fast because we've always accepted a few human beings into the tribe.

I know that don't make much sense. When I was a boy, I used to wonder why Montauks let themselves be burdened and contaminated with humans. And I suppose now you probably wonder what in hell any decent human being could possibly find in a tribe of people who have no money, no land, no houses, no jobs and no prospects. The answer is two things: freedom and sex. I don't expect you to understand what we mean by freedom, but sex you can figure. Fact is, Montauk men and women are beautiful. You've seen pictures of Wim and know his dark hair and those big dark eyes and that golden bronze skin, and that powerful little muscular body of his were pretty striking.

21

And 'course Dawn too was a knockout, the sort of gal who caused more traffic accidents than drunks.

Human beings've had hard-ons for Montauks ever since Sir John Gardner sailed into our bay, and every now and then, with the permission of the chief and the navigator, we adopt one into the tribe. It's kept us humble and made us realize, as Chief Leaf-Fragment said: 'Even a human being can become a Montauk.'

It kept our numbers up, too. Since we turned down about four out of every five humans that wanted to join and only accepted the best, we kept our standards.

All in all we lived a pretty good life. As Chief Waterdrop's grandson Bird-Feather said: 'Montauks some lucky Indians. We never born and so we never die. No own land and never get foreclosed. We no vote for President and never feel stupid.'

But back to Wim. I helped Wide Pool take him home – a partly sunken coal barge with the wrecked cabin of an old Chris-Craft on the deck. Wide Pool had lived there since she'd come back to the traditional Montauks from her renegade mother when she was thirteen. The sunken barge was one of the better Montauk homes: waterfront, plenty of fresh air, automatic sewage disposal and no danger of sinking.

For a bed Wide Pool had an old mattress raised on a platform of a half-dozen abandoned fish crates. She was still pretty blissful – though pooped – when she stretched out to rest and give her kid his first meal.

I was feeling strange. I'd begun remembering a Vision I'd had so many years before I thought I'd forgotten it. So seeing the kid enjoying his chow time I left to get my sister, Sitting Cow, and do some thinking.

When we got back to the barge, Sitting Cow went straight to Wide Pool and the baby and touched them both and pronounced the baby beautiful. I shuffled forward, my already wizened face crunched into a scowl, and squinted down at the infant. Taking my first careful look I saw an unusually small kid with a full head of black hair and large, wide-open dark eyes, and a perfectly formed body – even at less than a day old, active and alert. Fact is, he was staring up at me, bright-eyed and smiling.

'Hi,' he said.

Now I'd been feeling nervous enough ever since the birth without some showoff baby trying to start a conversation. I just stared back at him for a minute, glowering I imagine, and then looked up at Wide Pool, who lay on her foam mattress and looked back at me respectfully.

'Where'd he come from?' I asked sharply, scowling at Wide Pool, because I was beginning to be pretty certain this baby was someone special, 'Hi' or no 'Hi' – in fact the Special Being that our myths and my Vision had told me was one day to come.

Both women looked at me uncertainly.

'What do you mean "Where'd he come from?", you old fool,' Sitting Cow snapped. 'He came from Wide Pool's belly.'

'Who's the daddy?' I continued, still scowling, knowing from my Vision that the Special Being would have no earthly father. Wide Pool looked a little teary and picked up Wim to hold him to her breast.

'He had no father,' she replied in Montauk.

I felt my knees go weak.

'You never been screwed?' I asked her, speaking in English since I weren't certain I'd understood her Montauk reply. My own Montauk wasn't too hot – I'd only learned to speak it after getting back from a four-year stint with the US Marines during a wiseass period when I thought I wanted to be a human being.

Wide Pool repeated her words in English.

'I thought so,' I said, looking up with a fierce excitement. Sitting Cow was frowning and glaring at me.

'Do you mean the father was a white man?' she asked Wide Pool. 'A human being?'

'No,' she replied softly in Montauk. 'He had no father.'

'Course he had no father,' I said triumphantly. 'I knew that the moment I saw him.' I now looked again at the beautiful baby in Wide Pool's arms, and he was smiling at me again. I smiled back.

Then I stood up as straight as I could and raised my arms high above my head and spoke in the kind of thunderous Montauk we navigators specialize in.

'This child is called Wim!' I boomed out into the little cabin. 'He who rides the waves ... He's been sent to us by the Gods on a special mission ... one only he will some day know ... He's the last hope of the Montauk nation. Bury him.'

And without another word I drew my cast-off L. L. Bean windbreaker around me and turned and shuffled out.

Well, I may have been the navigator of the entire Montauk nation, but it don't mean I could speak the language real good. Like most of us, I'd gotten side-tracked into English for a couple of decades, and the fact is I said, 'Wagah tossomy balaska,' which Wide Pool understood to mean, 'He is our last hope, bury him.' 'Course I'd meant to say 'Wagah tossomy malahka': 'He is our last hope, hide him,' but the US Marines and too much TV had just about done in my Montauk. And the Gods, always on the lookout for some fun, twiddled my tongue.

After me and Sitting Cow left, poor Wide Pool was stuck with the horrible command to bury her child – even though he was the last hope of the Montauk nation. So she hugged Wim and sobbed out her love for him, begging his forgiveness, but sure that if I told her to bury her son then it must be the will of the Great Spirit.

She bundled Wim up in an old blanket and, feeling a little wobbly, staggered back down to Gull-Tamer's old rowboat. Like in all our traditional burials she stuck Wim in the bow, clear of the water awash in the bilge, and begun chanting the ancient Montauk burial chant. The tears were streaming down her face like to sink the boat, but when she finished, she pushed the boat out into the bay. The barge set on a salt marsh open to the southern end of Block Island Sound, and slowly but surely the wind and currents sucked the boat away from Wide Pool and out into the vast expanse of open water.

Well, seeing her baby riding away into the sunset made Wide Pool feel on the dismal side, and with a good healthy scream of anguish she turned away and run stumbling back to her barge. She threw herself down and sobbed, tore at her hair, ripped her last good sheet, and generally acted like gals do on such occasions – although she didn't once say bad things about me or the Great Spirit. She was a Montauk, that gal, through and through.

At dusk, still lying in her bed, she heard a strange light bumping at the seaward end of her barge, as if some floating object were gently knocking. She pulled herself up outta bed to go take a look around. It was now high tide, and when she peeked over the side, there, gently nosing the barge like a piglet at a sow, was Gull-Tamer's rowboat, and in it, awake and smiling up at her, was Wim.

'Hi, Mum,' he said.

With a muffled cry of joy she stumbled down to the boat and knelt in the bilge to hug the little fella to her breast. Even as she rocked back and forth in blind happiness in the rowboat, Wim nosed around until he had broken through the buttoned blouse and found a nipple and begun sucking. Wim always was one for snacking whenever he got the chance.

But Wide Pool knew that if I said bury her baby then she had to bury her baby, no matter how stupid and horrible a thing it was to do. After Wim had tanked himself up pretty good and fallen asleep, she again wrapped him in the old blanket, placed him in the bow, and, after chanting once more the Montauk burial chant, pushed the boat out to sea. When she trudged back to her bed that second time she felt even worse than she had the first.

But at dawn twelve hours later damned if something didn't begin bumping her barge again. She rushed out and saw that at the new high tide the old rowboat had come moseying back with Wim. By now poor Wide Pool didn't know whether to laugh or scream, but she gathered the little fella into her arms, carried him back to her cabin on the barge, and said something like 'Fuck this!' or 'Enough is enough' or probably something more delicate, her being Wide Pool. Anyway I guess she figured that though the Gods had returned Wim twice, she weren't about to see how absent-minded they might be the third time around. Instead she sang the Montauk birth song, crawled back into bed, give Wim her tit, and decided Wim was growing up, navigator or no navigator.

Later that morning me and Sitting Cow come by for a visit. Wide Pool, a trifle fearful about disobeying, hid Wim deep under her one blanket.

'I been thinking,' I said to her, pulling up a wooden box to sit next to Wide Pool, who was sitting in an old wooden rocking chair. 'Where you been burying Wim?', meaning, of course, 'Where you been hiding him?'

The poor girl stared at me with fright and confusion.

'In the rowboat,' she finally answered, being unable to lie.

'In the rowboat!' Sitting Cow exclaimed.

'Yes ...'

I nodded my head. 'Good ... good,' I said absent-mindedly. 'If the humans ask, tell them you lost the baby.'

Wide Pool nodded uncertainly.

'The baby's in the rowboat *now*?!' Sitting Cow asked, still looking shocked.

Wim began crawling under the covers in order to find his mum and, when he reached the edge of the bed, continued on with a thump to the barge's wooden deck. We all turned to stare at him as he continued crawling towards Wide Pool. He looked to me, I remember, like a large bare-assed mouse.

'He won't stay buried,' Wide Pool explained softly.

'Buried!?' Sitting Cow screamed, finally realizing the problem.

'I keep burying him in the rowboat, and the Gods keep sending him back.'

Well, I was still confused about the distinction in Montauk between the words for hide and bury, so to cover my confusion and avoid having to look at Sitting Cow who looked like she was about to explode, I sat up straight and pronounced loudly, 'Wave-Rider is the Montauks' last hope, we must bury him.'

'HIDE him, you moron!' Sitting Cow shouted at me. 'You mean she must *hide* him!'

'Exactly,' I said with that serene dignity that made me our navigator. 'Hide him. I'm glad you understand.'

3

The Inimmaculate Conception

from *The Gospel According to Luke*, pp. 18–19

And it so chanced that there lived in the town of Maganansett, on the shores of Block Island Sound, in the County of
Suffolk, on the island named Long, in the State of New
York, in the nation of the United States, on the planet
Earth, of the solar system Irradius, of the galaxi Ipplebaum,
of the subuniverse number 33,176f, a young girl named
Wide Pool, who happened to be a virgin, of no other special
attributes except that the Royal Roll of the Divine Cubes
had chosen her among all those capable of bearing children
to be visited one night in the year 3,176,487,277 (subuniverse number 33,176f) by one of the Gods, who did come to
her bed at night and did come into her, and then she was
visited by another God, who did come to her bed that night
and did come into her, and then by another God, and then
yet Another, until on that Glorious Night of the Inimmac-
ulate Conception it did come to pass that each and every
one of the Gods of the entire universe did visit her and did
come into her and did deposit their Spirits within her. And
lo, the Spirits of each and every one of the Gods did swim
up the Great Virgin River and did arrive by Chance at the
exact same instant at the Great Virgin Egg, and Whammo,
that Great Virgin Egg did receive into itself against all the
laws of Cause and Effect, each and every one of the Divine
Spiritozoa, so that the Child so conceived was not single
and self-confident but was multiple and confused. 'Wim'
was he to be named, He of Many Chances.

4

from *Fact Sheets on Wim*, vol. I, pp. 234–6

The Montauk Indians were probably the smallest and least significant Indian tribe in the whole of North America, a tribe noted only for its cowardice and cultural backwardness.[65] According to their own far-fetched legends the Montauks had arrived on Long Island at roughly the time of Christ by boat from the South Pacific. This legend has, of course, no historical merit whatsoever. The fact that the Montauks are the only Indians in this hemisphere to use catamarans, the only ones to orient their lives exclusively to the sea, the only ones whose myths and traditions all involve water and sailing, is mere coincidence. In all other respects they are so similar to other North American tribes that these chance characteristics can be dismissed.[66] Their closeness to and respect for nature, their social organization, their indifference to the ownership of land or things, their inability to respect white civilization – these traits they share to a large degree with other Indian tribes. We can assume they created their sea myths as a way to justify their failure to be successful hunters or farmers. Their tendency to build catamarans identical to those found in the South Pacific may be explained by their needing the fastest available means for their innumerable cowardly flights from the white man. In any case their claim to have sailed in open boats the ten thousand miles around Cape Horn and up the Atlantic to Long Island with no navigational aids and fifteen hundred years before white men so marvellously began exploring the oceans can be dismissed *ipso facto*.[67] And even if they did, it was just luck.

Although the earthly Montauks were 'of Comely Appearance'[68] and 'Manly Vigour', they were, unlike some early Indians, innocent and honest to the point of childishness. Robert Gardner reported in 1673 that two Montauk Indians swam across two miles of the (now Gardner's) Bay to return a shirt he had inadvertently left on the beach during a visit earlier in the day. He notes derisively that the Indians returned an essentially worthless shirt 'soaked in Salte Water and decorated with an Abundance of Kelp.'[69]

In addition to their simple-mindedness the Montauks were also noted for being total incompetents at the 'Arte of Battle',[70] choosing to run and hide rather than confront their enemies like men. The only white man known to have been killed in battle with the Montauks was Roger Backman, who drowned when his canoe overturned while he was firing at a suspected enemy enclave.[71]

Nevertheless, the Montauks at first caused trouble for the early white settlers by being located on land Divinely Appointed for the white man. The Montauks were originally settled in what is now Southampton and Easthampton, rich farming and socializing country, but through persistent persuasion were moved continually eastward over the next century until finally they lived on sterile sand and useless saltwater bogs more suited to their primitive life style.[72] From thenceforth the Montauks slowly but surely disappeared from history until the fraudulent Wim claimed to be a Montauk eighty years after all authorities agree the tribe was extinct.[73] In Volume III of this study we will examine *why* Wim chose to make this false claim, but for now ...

5

from Grain-of-Sand's *Memoirs of an Old Liar*, pp. 62–9

Well now, we Montauks aren't too enthusiastic about human beings, so for the first seven years of his life little Wim was pretty much hidden from the human race. He spent most his time with his mum or me or the little girl Dawn. With Wide Pool he learned to clam and fish and to know which berries, grasses, vegetables and fruit to pick or steal for food. His mum took him with her wherever she went – when she could find him.

Wim also began getting lessons from me, mostly in the Montauk martial arts. A nation don't survive free and independent for more than two thousand years, and more than a hundred years longer than any other Indian nation, without having mastered techniques of warfare. I begun teaching Wim running, retreating, ducking, hiding, disguising, pretending, faking death and surrendering.

I taught him navigation too – on the seas of water and the seas of life. Not long after he was weaned I ordered Wide Pool to let him sleep in the forward hold on a catamaran I built for him with webbing between the hulls. Since the barge had holes in it, when the tide was high, Wim's bed would float around inside the huge dark hold like a cork on the ocean. At low tide it would rest on the bottom. I made a skylight for the huge hatch so Wim would have light in the day and be able to study the stars at night. The little fella passed his exam in astronavigation when he was only five – the second youngest Montauk ever.

From the earliest age a Montauk is taught to swim and to sail, and by the age of three Wim could swim across the half-mile channel to Gardner's Island and sail a little six-foot homemade catamaran as if he were born on it. Maybe starting life in a rowboat has its advantages.

Wim was special from the first. He talked a blue streak from the time he was a week old and crawled and walked and swam before most kids can sit up. And he had a strange way of being over-polite. All Montauk children are taught to respect their elders, but Wim seemed to respect everybody. Here was a kid who could soon out-talk, out-learn, out-run, out-hide, out-pretend just about everybody less than three times his size, and yet he always acted as if the other was superior. At first I thought he must have been faking all his 'Yes, sirs', and 'No, ma'ams', and since pretending is only allowed with human beings and not with other Montauks, I was worried. But after a while I came to see that it was just the way he was: a little strange.

But in other ways he was so advanced that if I hadn't known from my Vision that Wim was a Special Being, it would have been downright scary. I remember once I was walking along the beach one wintry day and saw swimming along about ten feet from the drift ice along the shore a big, plump, white grouper. Now we Montauks ain't made it into the twentieth century without improvising, and any live edible fish within a stone's throw of a live edibling Montauk had better say its prayers. I nonchalanted myself to a halt and looked around for the nearest weapon which, unfortunately, was only my hands. I wandered slow as a senile snail out into the water towards that big white lazy grouper chanting the Montauk hunting song. The water was so cold my feet felt like they were being electrocuted, but I kept easing myself forward. After about two minutes I'd gotten within four feet of it and was leaning over with a gleam in my eye and my talons tensed when 'splash!', that grouper broke the surface with a big grin and said 'Hi'. Naked as a babe, three-year-old Wim was out for what he said was his morning swim.

I suppose things like that didn't help none suppressing the legend about his swimming ashore at birth.

Fact is, Wim at three could hold his breath longer than any Montauk I ever knew, and after I gave him the traditional training in playing dead, he doubled even that. By the time he was four and a half he could swim across the channel underwater, 'so as not to scare my mum,' Wim explained, Wide Pool not being too hot about her baby swimming across the bay.

'Course the other reason he swam underwater was to avoid being seen by human beings. Both the parents' and the navigator's biggest job was teaching all the young ones how to avoid being seen. Hide 'n' seek was the favourite Montauk game, some playing Montauks and the others playing humans. We taught them to avoid being seen as a game. They weren't to fear humans; they weren't to hate humans; they weren't to despise humans – only avoid being seen by them.

I remember the time I first took him to peek at humans. He was only about four then, and as I walked with him along the beach and then up the bluff he scurried after me in his tiny frayed shorts and grubby T-shirt like a precocious dwarf – exceptin' he was too pretty to be a dwarf. I was dressed in my usual outfit of old pants and sweatshirt – this one reading 'Only Brave Men Run'. I lectured him as we hiked, and he listened as careful as if I were one of the Gods. Made me feel brilliant and forget the danger of what I was doing.

When we got to the top there was a bunch of scrub oak, but after I'd led him through that we come to the top of a rise. There, spread below us about two hundred yards away, was what the humans had done to Montauk land: a large shopping centre with supermarket, department store, Cinema Sixteen and stuff like that. A big parking lot was filled, and humans were milling about everywhere, looking like a colony of unemployed ants.

'Wow,' said Wim, looking awed and frightened.

'Yep,' I said.

I could tell by his expression that seeing those hectic, dull-eyed, irritated and giddy humans rushing about like they was in a keystone cop comedy was the scariest thing the poor kid had ever seen.

'What ... what are they doing?' he asked in a tiny voice.

'They're being human,' I said.

'Wow.'

'Yep. It's tough. But they work at it every second.'

'And ... and they're the enemy?'

'Didn't say that. Just that you got to avoid them.'

Wim looked awed.

'But ... why?' he asked.

'Well,' I said, 'for the same reason you avoid skating on thin ice or sailing near land in a storm.'

'They're dangerous?' asked Wim.

'Yep. Only difference is that while you know how broken ice or a bad storm can sink you, you're never sure how a human being is going to do it.'

'But –'

'Only that they will.'

Well, Wim he stared down at that parking lot with a funny wistful expression – as if it were the promised land instead of purgatory.

'They don't look scary,' he said in a low voice.

'Nope. It's not so much what they do to you, as what they end up making you do.'

'What ... what's wrong with them?'

'Well, nothing, I suppose,' I replied. 'Any more than there's anything wrong with fog.'

'Fog?'

'Humans make it tough to see things clearly.'

'But how?'

'You'd have to live in their fog for a while to understand,

34

and that's too dangerous. Montauks that tried it tend to get lost and never come out again.'

'But you made it out again,' Wim said, remembering my stint in the Marines I'd told him about.

'Well now, I'm a navigator ...'

'When I grow up I'd like to become a spy on human beings,' he said, looking up at me cheerfully for the first time that day. 'Do you think I could?'

I shook my head and turned back towards the beach.

Fact is, he hadn't reacted to seeing humans in the flesh the way I thought he should: he seemed to be attracted to 'em. And I wondered if the problem weren't his little friend Dawn.

She was the daughter of a rich human lawyer and his young Montauk wife Pond-Lily. Though Dawn always lived in a regular house, when she was young – the early seventies it was – her daddy was feeling liberal and thought it would be something he called 'groovy' to let her be brought up Montauk.

Anyway, she was the only Montauk kid close to Wim's age, and they hung out together. She was taller and skinnier than most and Wim was small and packed. 'Course from the first Dawn was ridiculously beautiful. She had large, almond-shaped blue eyes that gazed at you so directly and purely whenever you looked into them you seemed to remember every one of your sins. And she had fair skin, long blonde hair, and the face, I'd say, of an angel – if I hadn't a known so many homely angels.

But their being pals was always sort of strange to me, since Wim always liked to do things that no one else in his right mind wanted to do, and Dawn was so straight and obedient and moral she would have made any parent proud and anyone else annoyed, and she did. But no matter what far-out thing Wim did, Dawn always seemed to tag along, usually lecturing Wim every step of the way about how what he wanted to do was impossible, wrong or stupid, and usually all three. Dawn would chat away about his error, and Wim would nod and frown and go ahead and try to do whatever it was anyway. I think the reason she stuck with him was that with her moral outlook, the only way she could have fun was to let Wim lead her astray.

And 'cause he knew Dawn was half-human – at least by birth – I think he figured humans couldn't be as bad as I was making out.

I remember a year or so later lying in the sand one evening next to a little fire of driftwood and listening to Wim and Dawn. They were chattering away about the trip I'd let them take through the shopping centre in the afternoon, part of their lessons in learning how to pretend and be among humans without being noticed. In the darkness I think they must of thunk I was asleep.

'Why do you think humans need so many *things*?' I heard Wim ask Dawn, who was cooking some marshmallows for them over the fire. Her being older and having a human daddy made her an expert.

'My mum says that for humans things are like clothing,' Dawn said in that soft musical voice of hers. 'She says people need things to show who they are.'

'Huh,' said Wim. 'I guess that means me and the other Montauks are nobodies.'

'Well, sort of, maybe.'

'Who's your dad?' Wim asked.

'Well, he owns a house and a big boat and a Cadillac – I think that's who he is.'

'Who's your mum?'

'She's a Montauk,' Dawn said. 'For her things don't count.'

'Is she a nobody too?'

I could hear the fire hiss and spit a bit before Dawn answered.

'I don't know,' she said. 'My dad gives her lots of things,

but she only keeps them because it's nice of daddy to give them.'

'And why do humans like those green dollars so much?' Wim asked next in a whisper. 'Grain-of-Sand says dollars are too rough to wipe his behind with, and too loose to use as cards, and too crowded to use as writing paper. Why do you think humans like them so much?'

'Mum says dollars are just hidden things,' Dawn explained.

In the next silence I could hear the water lapping at pebbles a few feet away.

'When you grow up are you going to be like your mummy or your daddy?' Wim asked with a sudden intensity.

Dawn was silent again and a damn mosquito come and begun buzzing me for an attack.

'I'm going to be like mummy,' she finally whispered back. 'I'm going to marry a rich human so I can live in a nice house and have hot baths, but I'll stay a Montauk so I can keep seeing you and Grain-of-Sand.'

Well, Wim thunk about this one so hard the grinding of his brain drowned out the mosquito.

'Are you sure that isn't cheating?' he finally asked.

'Oh, no. Grain-of-Sand says it's all right to take hot baths as long as you don't own the bathtub.'

Wim was quiet again.

'You're going to marry a human being?' His voice sounded kinda worried.

'Maybe,' Dawn said. 'If I find one that's good ... and kind ... and lets me use the bathtub.'

Well, later, after Dawn had to go home, I roused myself so I could eat a marshmallow. Wim let me have the last of his and asked: 'Is it OK for a Montauk to pretend to be a human in order to get married?'

The marshmallow was burnt.

'Well,' I said. 'Humans always disguise themselves in order to get someone to marry them, but Montauks who marry Montauks never do.' It still tasted good, though. ''Course every now and then a Montauk gets the hots for a human and has to lie and pretend like every other human – like Dawn's mum did with that human she married.'

I knew what Wim was thinking about so I went on.

'Dawn's sort of special,' I said. 'She's half the time a Montauk and the other half a human. You thinking of marrying her?'

'Not for a while,' little Wim announced.

'Good,' I said. 'Marriage got a better chance if you wait 'til you're nine.'

It was getting late, so after we put out the fire Wim and I walked slowly back to his barge. As we got near we heard a loud burst of a man's laughter come from Wide Pool's cabin. We stopped in the moonlight, and before I could give him a boost up on to the deck he turned to me with a puzzled frown.

'But what about my mum?' he asked very softly. 'She spends a lot of time with humans. If ... if they're so dangerous then ... then what about her?'

'Well,' I said, 'Wide Pool's a good pretender. As long as you're pretending you still see what's really going on. Humans never see what's really going on.'

'Then ... she'll be all right?' he persisted.

'Sure,' I said, lifting him up and swinging him up on to the barge's high deck. 'Now jump down into the bilge and get some sleep.'

Well, Wim went to bed, but the fact is I was getting worried about Wide Pool. She'd always been shy and withdrawn, and finding herself the mum of a kid as strange as Wim didn't help none. Fact is, in the last year she'd begun to have a lot of boyfriends.

She was a small, slender, dark-haired girl, and like all Montauk women pretty. As she struggled at bringing up

Wim, a lot of volunteer help, mostly male, begun showing up at the sunken barge. At first I didn't think anything of it, but lately I'd begun to notice that most of the time it seemed to take all night to give Wide Pool the advice she needed. And the men weren't only Montauks, but were mostly human beings, both renegade Montauks – who are actually humans no matter what the colour of their skin – and the white-skinned kind. It seemed half the village of Maganansett was beginning to find its way to the sunken barge on the bay.

And they were giving her gifts – fishing poles, old oars, broken TVs, boxes of golf balls, lottery tickets, boxes of cereal, car radios, cartons of old cigars – the sort of stuff that might get left behind after a week-long jumble sale. Most of the gifts were broken or useless human things that we Montauks never use. But Wide Pool was a good Montauk, and if something was given in a real spirit of giving then she kept it, no matter how useless. And from what I was hearing she was taking a lot of the other gifts, no matter how valuable, and letting Wim take them out into the bay and sink 'em.

Now we Montauks aren't exactly tough on sexual morality. Generally speaking the chiefs and navigators down the years haven't said much about it. The most famous saying about sex is probably the answer Chief Little Pebble gave to the question his teenage son asked about what kind of sexual relations were permissible.

'If it fit, OK,' the chief advised.

Same way with girls. The great navigator Birdseed, who was a woman, had similar advice for her daughter.

'If Great Spirit not approve of sex,' she once said, 'She create us with corks.'

And because of our unique birth-control method handed down through the centuries, a method that accidentally seemed to protect us from all venereal diseases as well, even the youngest girl knew how to avoid pregnancy. So sleeping with a lot of men wasn't bad, it just wasn't usual. Most all Montauks pair off into stable couples and only play around on special occasions – religious festivals, harvest time, orgies: times like that. But Wide Pool's situation was worrisome because her men included mostly human beings – even if some were disguised as Montauks. A traditional Montauk might sleep with a human being, just to see what it's like, but when he or she did, he'd keep himself invisible – pretend to be other than he was.

But Wide Pool, despite her training, seemed to stay Wide Pool whether she was with Montauks or humans. Since as navigator I was responsible for the spiritual health of the nation, I finally decided I'd better question her.

The old barge then was a lot different than it had been when Wim was born. There was junk all over, inside and out: old fish-traps, netting, overstuffed chairs, broken clocks, old magazines and paperback books, broken TVs, radios and computers, a life-sized statue of Arnold Palmer in the middle of his backswing, used clothing of all sizes, styles, and shapes – a regular junk yard. It didn't seem a healthy place to bring up a kid – all those *things*. Still, Wide Pool loved Wim like no mum I ever saw, and Wim sure loved her, so I wasn't hot on interfering.

'Why you let humans come here all the time, Wide Pool?' I asked her. We navigators don't beat around the bush but call a spade a shovel right off. She was sitting in the same rocker she always sat in when I visited, and I was perched on a big TV console.

'For Wim, Grain-of-Sand,' she answered, rocking gently, her girlish bright eyes looking at me with that wide-eyed innocence that had a lot to do with the horniness of the local male population.

'How does having humans over here help Wim?' I asked. 'It's dangerous.'

She looked at me steadily, still rocking slowly.

'It's to protect him,' she said.

'How's that?'

'You've taught me yourself, Grain-of-Sand,' she answered, her eyes glistening. 'If there's a way to hurt you, humans will find it. Sooner or later they'll steal him from me.' She paused, her chin high but the hint of tears brighter in her eyes. 'When that time comes I want to have friends among the humans.'

I scowled, knowing she was right. Though Wim was a good hider and pretender, and a straight-A retreater, I knew there was no way we could keep him invisible for ever. Sooner or later they'd drag him off to their schools. No way we could prevent that. It was even part of my Vision.

'Humans can never be friends,' I said. 'You know that.'

'Yes, but I mean that ... when Wim ... is taken, I want to have ... some power over humans.'

I nodded and frowned at the same time. Montauks have always had to manipulate humans a little in order to survive – that's what lying and pretending are all about – but having *power* over humans was not something we ever wanted. The only power we wanted was to be able to avoid 'em.

'What you mean, "power"?' I asked.

'Just ... that they not turn him into a human being.'

'And how you think these humans you sleep with can do that?'

She hung her head and I saw the damn tears wetting her cheek.

'I don't know yet,' she said in a whisper. 'I only know that someday they'll steal Wim, and then I'll need their help.'

I shook my head. 'They'll never help you.'

She just hung her head and let the tears come. But I was tough.

'And what about Wim?' I asked, scowling as fiercely as I could. 'He keep himself invisible?'

Wide Pool looked up with a sudden small smile.

'He's the best hider ever,' she said proudly. 'Human beings have come into the room unexpectedly when Wim and I are together and he disappears so fast even I don't know where he's gone.'

'Well, that's good,' I said, nodding. 'But I bet he sticks around to spy on the humans.'

Wide Pool blushed. 'Oh yes. He loves to listen and watch.'

I kept nodding. 'I suppose the only danger there is he may learn some of the human's bad habits in love-making.'

'I keep us covered with a blanket.'

'If he asks if that's the way it's supposed to be done, you set him straight. Get a real Montauk over here and show him what's what.'

'Yes, Grain-of-Sand.'

''Course no sense hurrying it. Usually don't show our kids sex until they're eight.'

'Yes, Grain-of-Sand.'

'And you keep me posted on his disappearing. He got a ninety-eight on his last disappearing quiz, and I want to be sure he's really able to use it in real life.'

'Did you know he's been sitting behind that TV set you're sitting on since you entered?' Wide Pool asked with a shy but proud smile.

Well, I turned around and looked down behind that thing I was sitting on and there, so close he could of bit my ass without moving his head, was ... no one. I caught a brief glimpse of something – kind of a bright furry glow that sort of whooshed away the moment I looked – but no Wim. 'Course if Wide Pool said he'd been there, then he'd been there.

''Course I knew,' I said with a flush. 'Just testing to make sure he wouldn't give himself away.' And with that I walked with dignity from the room.

So the humans continued to come into Wide Pool and her house, but since humans are usually pretty harmless when they're rolling around inside a nice lady, I figured Wide Pool could handle them. And as for Wim, well, all the training and love in the world weren't going to save him from what sooner or later had to happen.

6

from *Fact Sheets on Wim*, vol. I, pp. 169–70

The myths surrounding Wim's early years, myths that seem to emerge about the life of any religious fraud, can be dealt with in short space. First, of course, his followers had to create a myth to explain how the mother of their 'Beloved Wim' could be, to phrase it delicately, a whore. We know, from overwhelming testimony, that his mother, when Wim was still quite small, began to accept into her bed a seemingly infinite succession of men, to receive them at a rate most scientific observers have estimated at an average of one man a week for eight years or so, or, as Professor Hineman of MIT informs us, a probable total of four hundred and fifty-seven (457) men.[21] Moreover, we know that this woman received 'gifts' from a vast majority of these men, and in only a small percentage of cases appears to have dispensed her 'favours' free of charge. Her association in later life with the Women's Freedom Society[22] does not, despite the efforts of some apologists, justify her earlier behaviour as 'Striking a blow for the freedom of women to sell their bodies as they please'.[23]

The plain fact is that little Wim's mother was, to state it neutrally, a slut, and she differed from other such women primarily in that she degraded her own home with her activities, exposed her own son to her sordid customers, and somehow escaped the necessity of having, to phrase it clinically, a pimp.

The claim that her sexual avidity arose from a deep longing to recapture the divine and divinely inspired rapture of the night of Wim's mythical conception is patently riddled. The claim presupposes that Wim was conceived by a – to use Professor Gurdner's phrase – 'Gangbang of the Gods,'[24] and is, on the face of it, disputable. No matter how fast they worked, could over two hundred thousand Gods really enjoy one woman within a nine-hour night? Professor Kleggle of the California Institute of Technology and Repairs has demonstrated beyond all scientific doubt that this is physically awkward.[25] Moreover, could all two hundred thousand spermatozoa arrive at the 'Divine Egg' at precisely the same instant? Professor Richardson argues forcefully in his books on the subject that the statistical probability of such an event is – to quote directly Professor Richardson – 'small'.[26]

The efforts of the myth-makers to describe Wide Pool as 'The Eternal Woman' are at best a sick slur on our fair sex, whose inferiority should never be mocked. No, the plain, unglossed and embarrassing fact still stands: Wim had a minimum of 457 fathers, most all of them, we will prove in sections 8 to 10 of this volume, demonstrably human...

7

from Grain-of-Sand's *Memoirs of an Old Liar*, pp. 53–61

From the time he was knee-high to a flea Wim couldn't get enough of peeking at humans and asking questions about them. And though he was good at pretending, one day I found out he had a fatal flaw that doomed him to be drug into the human web.

When Wim was about seven we was walking along the beach with Dawn, having one of our chats. The seagulls were squawking, the water sloshing and the horseflies biting, and I was giving one of my brilliant lectures, when I mentioned that the Montauk Indians they knew might be real Montauks or might have turned into human beings.

'How do you tell?' Wim asked with a puzzled look. He and Dawn were holding hands the way they always did, him wearing some oversized cast-off shorts and beat-up sneakers and Dawn a nice dress and carrying some fancy-looking shoes.

'Well,' I answered, 'the human beings don't *see* you. They're sort of like machines: they don't play, can't stay still, can't *be* with you.'

'But ... but one of my daddies, he's ... he's very different from most,' Wim said. 'I mean, he sometimes reminds me of *you* ...'

I cleared my throat a couple of times and pretended to be studying a piece of junk in the sand. Fact was, Wim was getting into advanced philosophy – stuff we usually didn't try to teach until the kid was eleven or twelve.

'Yep,' I finally said.

'But ... but does that mean that some white men might be Montauks in disguise?' Wim asked, the question making Dawn look frightened.

I knew the truth was dangerous for a youngster and I didn't want to scare Dawn any more than she already was, but I had to say it.

'Yep,' I said.

'Wow. How can this be?'

'I don't know. I only know I've known white men who see me, who play, who can be still, who were with me.'

'Their skin was real white?'

'Yep.'

'Then I can't tell a Montauk by the colour of his skin?'

'Nope. A Montauk may take on many disguises, may hide under many colour skins.'

'But ...' began Wim, 'but ...' (It was the little fella's favourite word for many years) 'but we Montauks are supposed never to lie to each other, only to humans.'

'That's right. To protect our invisibility and pretend to be humans we got to lie. 'Course that means when you're with humans you'll be lying most of the time.' I paused and got off a good shot of spit at the pebble I aimed at. 'But that's OK. They'll be lying too. To be a human is to lie.'

Wim stopped next to the water and was so interested he even let go Dawn's hand.

'But what if I don't know someone is actually a Montauk in disguise, and I lie to him?'

'Oh, you'll know,' I said. 'A Montauk is anyone you can't lie to.'

Wim was suddenly staring at the ground with the darndest expression I ever saw on his face. Damned if it didn't look like guilt.

'Grain-of-Sand,' he began in a low voice. 'There's something I been meaning to tell you.'

'Well, go ahead. You look like whatever it is, it weighs a ton.'

47

'Grain-of-Sand, I ... I can't lie to human beings.'

'What!?' I exclaimed.

'I can *pretend* with humans, but whenever they ask me a question I find I always want to tell the truth.'

'No, Wim, no,' I said, shaking my head and both arms and wanting to shake my legs too, but since I was standing, all I could do was sort of a hiccoughy dance. 'You can't be a Montauk if you don't lie to humans! They'll eat you up and shit you out so fast you won't know what hit you except that somehow they've turned you into dung.'

'I know. I know. Whenever I'm pretending and some human asks me a direct question, I want to say something that keeps up the pretence. I *know* it's what I ought to do, but I can't get the words out. I just can't. All I do is run away.'

'That's the sickest thing I ever heard,' I said firmly. 'And you got to get over it.'

'But I've tried!'

'Well, you keep trying. We'll have to cut you off from all human contact if you can't lie. You'd be a goner. We can't have it.'

'I'm sorry, Grain-of-Sand.'

'And you so good at hiding and pretending and retreating and you can't even lie. Why, human beings can't even recognize the truth if you hit 'em over the head with it on a shovel. It's wasted on 'em.'

'I know. I know. I try.'

'Next time you see a human being I want you to go up to him and say "Hi, my name's George." Just that. A nice clean lie that couldn't hurt a flea. You understand?'

'Yes, sir.'

Well, I didn't see Wim for a couple of days after that, and when I finally did I didn't have to have 20-20 vision to see he didn't look too happy.

'Well, son,' I said to him. 'How'd the lying go?'

He hung his head.

'I said how'd the lying go?'

He raised his eyes and looked up at me bravely.

'I went up to a human being,' he said in a low voice, 'and I said to him, "Hi, my name is..."'

When Wim stopped, I waited, but that was it.

'Well?' I asked.

'That's what I said to him,' Wim answered.

'That's all?'

'That's all that would come out,' Wim said, looking puzzled. 'The name George was banging around in my mind to beat the band, but I couldn't get it out. My tongue wouldn't do it.'

Well, from that moment on I knew Wim was doomed. Weren't no way in the world a Montauk could survive among human beings without lying. That night I prayed my darndest that the Great Spirit would free Wim's tongue from its horrible enslavement to truth, but it didn't do no good. Wim had many fine traits and great skills, but lying was never to be one of them.

A week later they got him.

It was his dog Arf that done him in. One of Wim's daddies, a former circus-owner, gave the dog to Wim's mum as a present. He claimed Arf was a genuine spanther, a cross between a cocker spaniel and a panther. They say that panthers can't mate with dogs, and it's true Arf was shaped mostly like a cocker spaniel, but his coat was spotted with light and dark dots, like a leopard, and he couldn't bark a lick, but instead – even when he was only a three-month-old puppy (or cub, as the circus guy called him) – made a loud, deep, scary growl that sounded like a charging wounded tiger.

But even with his tiger-roar Arf wasn't too brave. After Wim was forced to go to school, whenever anyone was beating up on him Arf would be sniffing at some telephone pole, or if the fight was real rough, he'd disappear underneath a girl's skirts. Arf never got near any of those bullies until after a fight was over. Then he'd trot up with his tail wagging and lick poor Wim's battered face and, to make sure there weren't no misunderstanding, he'd lick the feet of the bully usually standing over Wim. Arf, like all Montauks, wasn't too aggressive, and he only seemed to roar when he was sleepy – a sort of unique yawn.

Anyhow, Wim loved Arf and took him everywhere, even when he was spying on human beings. And one day he and Dawn were lying among some shrubs watching a group of boys play football on a field only a few hundred yards from his barge. Wim was explaining to her how the game worked – he'd figured it out from all his watching – when the game ended and the captain of the losing team began to walk towards where they were hiding. As he and Dawn began to hide, Wim noticed the boy had tears in his eyes from losing.

Now all his life Wim was a sucker for tears, and so was Arf. We navigators know that tears from a human being have as much value as salt water in the ocean, but neither of them ever learned that. Fact is, Wim had watched this particular kid play so often he thought of him already as a friend, even though the kid had never even seen Wim. Anyway, Arf wandered out towards the boy, wagging his tail and making a low sound that came out mostly like 'meow'. The kid stared down at Arf without really seeing him until Arf began licking his foot. Then, when the boy knelt down and began patting Arf kind of absent-mindedly, Wim couldn't resist. He done the thing that doomed him: he stood up and walked forward. Dawn, like a good Montauk, stayed hidden.

'Who are *you*?' the boy asked, quickly standing and brushing the wetness from his face with the sleeve of his blue windbreaker. Fact is, this boy was Billy Best, that sort of all-American human being who was to become Wim's best friend and chief rival. And like the cocky guy he always was he asked right off 'Who are *you*?' as if Wim was showing a lot of nerve just existing.

'I ... I'm Wim,' he said.

Well, that was it. The rest is history. No Montauk in almost four hundred years had ever told his true name to a human being, and Wim in one disastrous moment broke the mould.

'What kind of name is that?' Billy asked with his usual snottiness. He was a strong, good-looking boy even then, and he towered over Wim.

'It means Wave-Rider,' Wim said hesitantly, hoping that was a fair answer.

'You an Indian?'

'Yes, sir.'

'How old are you?'

'Almost eight.'

'How come you're so small?'

'I don't know. I guess I was born that way.'

'You a mon ... mongoloid?' Billy asked next.

'No, I'm a Montauk,' Wim answered promptly.

'A Montauk? What's that?'

'The name of my nation.'

Now Billy had obviously been embarrassed at being seen with tears in his eyes and was just tossing questions to keep Wim from saying anything about his crying, but Billy was bright and he saw right away there was something special about Wim.

'You're weird,' Billy said.

'I guess so,' said Wim.

'And so's your dog.'

'I know,' said Wim. 'Were you crying after the game?'

'Crying!?' Billy said with a sneer. 'You got to be kidding. I got sand in my eyes on the last play.'

'Oh,' said Wim. 'But I notice you don't like to lose.'

'Who does? My father expects me to be the best at everything.'

'Really? Grain-of-Sand says it's important only to play at everything.'

'I *am* the best at everything, so it's a real drag when I lose.'

'If you'd like,' said Wim shyly, 'I might be able to help you win the next game of football you play against those big guys.'

'You!' Billy sneered. 'They'd make mincemeat out of you.'

'What's mincemeat?'

'I'm not sure, but that's what they'd do. You're too small.'

'But I'm fast and I can dodge.'

'You are, huh?' Billy said, already chomping on his next victory, and smiled for the first time. 'I'll race you to those far goal posts.'

Well, after Wim agreed, Billy said 'Get ready, get set, go,' and even though he lit out on the words 'get set' and Wim didn't start 'til 'go', it weren't even close. With Wim's little legs whirling away making him look like a miniature eggbeater he cruised past Billy as if the bigger boy were wallowing through molasses.

'Course Billy explained his loss by saying that Wim had an unfair advantage because his tiny size cut down his wind resistance, but he knew a good thing when he saw one. Next afternoon Wim got to play his first game of football – as a running back for Billy's Blazers.

Dawn told me all about it the next day. Seems that, like Billy, most of these boys were a couple of years older than Wim. They were all at least twice as big and wearing helmets and pads and fancy uniforms. So when Wim came wandering out on to the field with that funny little rapid walk of his and wearing nothing but short pants and a dirty T-shirt, they thought Billy was making some sort of joke – excepting Billy Best never joked about nothing in his life.

Well, when Billy's team kicked off, Wim zipped down the field faster than anyone to tackle the guy with the ball, but instead they run over him like a herd of elephants over a paraplegic rabbit. Wim never was much good on defence.

By the time Billy's team got the ball, Billy had begun to think he'd made a big mistake in his recruiting, but I suppose he figured he might as well get Wim kilt and get it over with, so on their first play he told Wim to run the ball through the middle.

Well, at the sight of little Wim standing back there in his short pants, all two foot ten inches of him, with his big wide eyes looking excited and determined, the boys on both teams began giggling. And Billy, though he hated being laughed at and was scowling and wishing he could shrink out of sight, still began to bark out the signals. A second or two later he handed the ball off to Wim – had to lean down to do it – and Wim ran into the middle of the line and was buried.

Dawn says she never saw such a pile of bodies as Butch's Bums made on top of where Wim disappeared into the line. She thinks even most of the Blazers piled on top too – just for the hell of it – all except Billy, who just stood staring at the pile and muttering at his stupidity.

Well, slowly but surely the boys began to unpile, laughing and joking and wondering how deep Wim was sunk, when a little voice shouted from the end of the field behind them.

'Hey fellas! Whatcha doing!?'

There, standing on the Bums' goal line, hugging the ball to his chest, looking more like a baby holding a balloon, was little Wim.

Well, that was it. The humans had been given their first sight of Wim's zig, zag and zip. And Wim had earned the everlasting enmity of half of the toughest jocks in the county.

Billy Best jogged down the field to clap Wim on the back (and cause the first of Wim's many fumbles). Wim had a grin on his face almost as big as Billy's.

'Not bad,' Billy said. Then he asked a fateful question. 'How come I never noticed you in school?'

And Wim's smile slowly faded into his usual look of

confused dismay. He knew right then and there that he'd gone and done a stupid thing and that he was a goner.

Well, after Billy's Blazers had gone on to clobber Butch's Bums 66 to 24 and Wim had run for eight touchdowns and showed he could throw the ball fifty yards and knock his receiver's helmet off nine times out of ten, it weren't more than a week before all the boys and half the parents knew there was some weird Indian who could run circles around Road-Runner living on a barge on the bay and being forced to sleep in the bilge. At the end of the second week the first social worker showed up to question Wide Pool. And, of course, two days later they ordered Wim to school.

8

from *The Gospel According to Luke*, pp. 53–61

Although Wide Pool had been preparing all of Wim's life for the day when he'd be captured, when the fatal day actually came she barely managed to get together a lunch consisting of a mussels, kelp and acorn sandwich, a handful of blackberries, six chocolate chip cookies, and a corked coke bottle filled with water. She put them into a rusty metal lunch box engraved on the side with the words 'Beat the Japs', and knelt in the sand beside her Beloved Wim.

She adjusted his shirt and short pants – the only kind small enough to fit him, but not exactly in style in the late 1970s – but was too numb to think of anything to say.

Dawn was waiting a few yards off to the side. She'd insisted that she be allowed to go to school with Wim, claiming that he needed her moral guidance and that it was time for her to develop the human side of herself. Her Montauk mum hadn't much liked the idea, but Dawn's dad had outgrown his counter-culture stage and was tremendously relieved that his precocious daughter was finally going to get some decent schooling, even if it was because of her association with her funny little playmate Wim.

Wim's face had the same expression of surprised dismay that it had shown when Billy asked him about school. He was still trying to grasp the connection between being nice to a human being (Billy) and being forced to do what his mother and navigator had warned him was the worst thing that could befall a Montauk. When Wide Pool finally released him from her warm, tight embrace and handed him his lunch box, he found he couldn't turn away.

'I'm sorry, Mum,' he whispered.

'Just do your best to pretend,' she responded, trying to force a smile. 'And pray to the Great Spirit to teach you to lie . . .' But she trailed off, shaking her head with a sad smile at the slim chances of Wim's getting the hang of lying.

Wim leaned forward to rub his nose briefly against hers and then turned and walked away. As he reached Dawn he took her hand, and together they marched off towards the enemy.

But he stopped after a dozen steps and turned back to Wide Pool.

'I won't become a human being if it's the last thing I do,' he announced defiantly, and Wide Pool smiled and waved and, as he marched off with Dawn, finally let herself cry.

When Wim and Dawn arrived in the schoolyard they made an odd-looking pair: Dawn tall, slender and pale, with long blonde hair down her back and a cold, proud gaze, and Wim short, round and bronzely dark, with his large black eyes gazing out with his usual bewildered innocence. At eight, Wim was still smaller than the smallest kindergartener, and his having led Billy's Blazers to four straight victories did not endear him to Butch Messmire and several of his friends.

So as he and Dawn, still hand in hand, began to walk up the main drive to the suburban Maganansett elementary school, the children on either side stopped to stare at the newcomers, some in stunned silence and a few with snickers and laughter. On the steps, Butch and his sixth-grader friends looked down first with envy – it was the first time they had seen the beautiful Dawn – and then relish, as they saw their tiny cowardly enemy. They knew from their encounters with Wim on the football field that although a slippery son-of-a-bitch, he *could* be taken, and his confident showoffy march up the sidewalk with that tall skinny blonde angel at his side made Butch know that this had to be one of those times.

When Wim was about thirty feet away and saw what was waiting for him on the steps, he released Dawn to let her be taken in hand by a few comforting girls. Then he walked on alone, his rusty lunch box – looking next to his small frame like a large rusty suitcase – swinging less and less confidently at his side.

When his advance had brought him to within fifteen feet of the steps, Butch led his six or seven boys in a loud charge down the steps directly at Wim and almost immediately he was overwhelmed. For several seconds, amidst the happy shrieks of some girls and the triumphant yells of the boys, Butch and his gang pummelled at something in their midst until one by one they broke off to gaze in confusion around at their feet in search of their victim, who, however, was now mounting the steps, his lunch box again swinging handsomely. For better or worse, Wim had arrived at school.

9

from *The Gospel According to Luke*, pp. 97–100

'Your mother's a whore! Your mother's a whore!' Billy Best and Butch Messmire and Sally Hope and several other boys and girls yelled enthusiastically at Our Beloved Wim. Wim's next three days of school went this way every time upon his arrival in the morning and at break.

'Mummy, what's a whore?' Wim asked Wide Pool on the evening of the third day.

Wide Pool was sewing up a pair of Wim's trousers, while one of his daddies was seated in the rocker reading an ancient issue of *Sports Illustrated* by flashlight. He was a small man in his forties who worked occasionally as an auto mechanic. Wide Pool, who had been impressed how easily Wim seemed to be taking the shock of living among human beings, slowly lowered her sewing into her lap and sighed.

'Why do you ask, my Wim?' she said in her soft melodious voice. The auto mechanic yawned and took a swig from his bottle of warm beer.

'The kids at school keep yelling that you're a whore, as if that were bad,' Wim explained.

The daddy glanced once at Wide Pool and burped.

Wide Pool frowned and looked down at the floor.

'It's because different men come to visit me and spend the night,' she said in a low voice. 'Some people think that's bad and they call such a woman ... a whore.'

'Bullshit!' exclaimed the daddy complacently. 'Don't you listen to 'em, kid. Your ma's no whore. Mary here wouldn't take money unless you told her it was coloured toilet paper.'

'Then why do Billy and Butch and a lot of the other kids yell that at me?' Wim asked with a puzzled expression.

'They're just being kids,' the daddy answered. 'They're just testing you to see if you can take it like a man. Tell 'em to shove it.' He laughed, and reburied his nose in the magazine.

'If you want me to stop having visitors, I will,' Wide Pool said quietly to Wim, who still looked puzzled.

'Oh, no,' said Wim. 'That's all right. I like my daddies. I just have to figure out what to do.'

The next day at noon recess, with a group of about twenty boys and girls surrounding him and shouting about his mother's purported method of earning a livelihood, and another thirty children looking on, Wim fought back. He raised his little arm for silence and shouted as loudly as he could: 'The sky is falling!'

There was a momentary surprised silence, and several children looked upward. Wim took advantage.

'Who pays your allowance?' he abruptly shouted at his tormentors.

'Daddy,' several replied.

'Who pays for all the presents at Christmas time?'

'Daddy,' said some.

'Santa Claus,' said others.

'What's Christmas?' asked another.

'Who bought your bicycle?'

'Daddy!' most of them cried.

'And how many daddies do you have?' Wim asked.

'One,' shouted most, although several answered 'two' or 'three'.

'Well,' said Wim, swaggering his little shoulders. 'I've got hundreds.' And he began to saunter – as well as a three-foot-tall child can saunter – out of the circle.

'Hold it!' cried Billy Best. 'How do we know your fathers really pay you an allowance or buy you a bicycle or Christmas presents?'

'Easy,' replied Wim, looking up at the much taller Billy. 'Does your father do this for you?'

'Sure,' answered Billy.

'And how about your father, Butch?'

'I guess so.'

'Sally?'

'Naturally.'

'Jack?'

'That's my business.'

'The rest of you?'

'Yes!' most of them shouted.

'Well, then,' said Our Beloved Wim, puffing his bony chest out as full as it would go (a quarter inch), 'my fathers do too, since my fathers and your fathers are the same.'

For a moment there was a silence and the other children all looked bewildered.

'What do you mean?' Butch finally asked.

'Who do you think my daddies are?' said Wim.

Plumpish Sally Hope piped up in a voice that showed pride in having found the right answer: '*Your* daddies are *our* daddies!'

'Right!' said Wim. 'Only I've got at least a hundred of them, and you've only got one or two.'

'Come, children,' came the voice of Miss Lunnigan, their teacher, 'it's time for social studies.'

'My mother collects fathers,' concluded Wim triumphantly, 'while yours only collect grocery coupons.'

10

from 'Fragments of Wim', pp. 21–4

I was born, probably. I don't want to claim anything that isn't true, but I assume I was born. After that though, things get murky.

All my life I've been small. As a full-grown teenager now I'm still only five feet two in my stocking feet, and that's wearing three pairs of socks. I still weigh less than a hundred and twenty-eight pounds. Being small is nice unless you begin to live near people who enjoy squashing things.

I can see now that I lived in a kind of paradise until they made me go to school. With my mum, life was easy and fun. I could go wherever I wanted and do whatever I wanted, as long as I kept hidden from humans and followed the principles Grain-of-Sand was teaching me. I loved to swim and fish and play games, especially with Dawn. Sometimes when I'd swim across to Gardner's Island she'd agree to ride on my back, and whenever I wanted to sneak into Maganansett Village to spy on the human beings she'd tag along to make sure I stayed invisible.

When we went to school we stuck together there too because we were both outcasts. I was an outsider because I was me, and she was one because even though she came from a good middle-class human family and didn't look Indian, she voiced her high moral principles to anyone who wanted to listen and to quite a few who didn't want to. That wasn't too well received by third-graders. She wasn't taunted or bullied like I was since she was taller than most of the boys in her class and had a terrific right cross. After she'd used it a few times after we first got to school, the other kids tended to listen to her until she was out of range.

Although I sensed from the first I was different from most people, until I went to school I thought it was other people who were strange. When I was three I can remember wondering to myself, 'Gee, why is everybody so *slow*?' When I first spied on human beings at the beach I wondered, 'Gee, why do they swim on *top* of the water?' And whenever I thought about my size I wondered why other children were so oversized and clumsy, and felt sorry for them. And I was also surprised that other people didn't like to play games all the time, and ask questions, and pretend, and sleep on a boat in a bilge, and have long talks with Grain-of-Sand. Of course, when I finally went to school the humans taught me that it was me that was strange.

Although I spent a lot of my early schooldays running and hiding, my life wasn't all trouble. Whenever Billy Best was involved in a game he would refuse to let me be used as the ball because he insisted I be on his team and help him win. As long as I was scoring points or, better yet, helping him score points, Billy was the best of friends. Of course his interest waned a bit when the game was over, and he didn't always notice the bullies who decided to make up for lost time.

But I still spent a lot of time with Billy because he was the only boy I knew who could think up as interesting things to do as me. And he turned everything into a game just like Grain-of-Sand said I should, although Billy always wanted to win. But in most ways we were opposites. Even as a fifth-grader Billy was steady, reliable, mature and consistently good in everything he did, while I was always erratic, undependable, and unpredictable – great one minute and terrible the next. No one ever laughed at Billy, but everyone was always laughing at or making fun of me, including Billy. Billy was always serene and confident because he knew he'd always be the best at whatever he did and would never fail – or if he did, he'd be able to come up with a good excuse. On those few occasions when I was serene, it was because I'd failed so often and gone from brilliant to stupid so erratically that I decided I hadn't the foggiest notion of or least control over what was going to happen next and I might as well relax and enjoy it.

But from the day I walked into school I felt out of place. Because I was so small I always had to take two steps to cover the ground covered by one normal step, and with my large hands and feet I felt like a character out of some old silent movie: while I was running around puppet-like from one place to another, the rest of the world had graduated to talkies and slower motion, and moved leisurely all around me...

ABOUT WIM'S NAME

One day Billy Best asked Wim: 'How come you have only one name, Wim?'

'Why?' Wim replied. 'How many do you have?'

'I have three. My name is William Oliphant Best.'

'Why?'

'Why what?'

'Why does everybody have three names?'

Billy Best thought about this for several minutes before answering.

'A first name for friends, a middle name for the Internal Revenue Service and a last name to give to your wife.'

Wim frowned.

'So why do you have only one name, Wim?' repeated Billy.

'Well,' Wim suddenly decided, 'when I grow up I'm going to settle for only having friends.'

– from *Sixty-six Parables of Wim*

11

from *The Gospel According to Luke*, pp. 83–98

During the first two years of Wim's schooling the human beings tried six hours a day to make him realize the importance of success and self and spelling and winning and knowing all about human history and rock and roll and subversive enemies and proper hairstyle. Then two or three hours a week Wim would walk along the beach and let Grain-of-Sand try to teach him the worthlessness of success and self and spelling and winning and knowing all about human history and rock and roll and quite a bit else the school felt was important. It was an uneven battle.

First they put Wim into the kindergarten. When he began answering many of the questions before the other children even knew a question had been asked, they decided to promote him to the first grade. Things went well enough there for a few weeks until Wim began to correct the teacher's spelling. The teacher put up with this for a while – Wim was quite polite about it – but when he began answering the question how much is 7 plus 7 by saying 'the square root of 196', and the teacher had to go all the way up to the sixth-grade maths teacher before she found someone who knew if the answer was correct or not, Wim was promoted to the third grade.

Dawn was already in the third grade, so Wim decided he'd found his right level. But his reputation as weird and smart and helpless led many of the other children to decide that fate had kindly given them a new toy. When the middle-aged dumpling of a teacher would ask through thick glasses 'Who can tell me what a verb is?' the class's blank expressions indicated she might as well have asked them to explain Einstein's theory of relativity. So when Wim tentatively raised his hand to volunteer an answer, and the teacher turned her back to write the answer on the blackboard, many of the other children expressed their appreciation of Wim by pelting him with a barrage of spitballs, erasers, chalk, pencils, paper airplanes, abandoned tomato sandwiches, rotting hard-boiled eggs, ink, toilet paper, frogs, toads and dead fish. By late afternoon the area around Wim's desk looked like the New York City Sanitation Department had just made an emergency dump.

To decrease the effect of missiles incoming on Wim the teacher soon set him near the back of the class. Unfortunately, when he stood on his chair or desk to see the blackboard she concluded he was hacking around and ordered him to stand in the corner facing the wall. In his six years at school Wim never was to see much of the blackboard.

And Wim's reputation wasn't helped by his mind having an unpredictable way of being brilliant one minute and numbskull the next. One day he might know that 7 plus 7 equalled the square root of something, but then the next not be able to tell the exact result of 2 plus 2. He could sometimes spell some of the words his teachers called him, like 'incorrigible', but then be baffled at the trickiness of spelling 'cat'. And because he'd never watched television or lived much among civilized beings, he was ignorant about all things American. He not only didn't know the name of the President of the United States but, even more disastrous to his reputation, hadn't heard of someone named Michael Jackson – a person who, Wim reported to Grain-of-Sand, was famous for looking like a Montauk wearing white gloves.

And Wim's questions in class didn't help matters either. His classmates began to realize that whenever Wim would stand up on his desk and raise his hand almost anything could happen. He might ask Miss Lunnigan something obvious like 'Who's Ronald Reagan?' or 'Why do we have to wear clothes?' or something trickier like 'What's a Christian?' or 'Since everyone hates the Russians, does that mean they're all Indians or blacks?'

And because of his smallness even some of his friends whispered that he still wore diapers. The girls in his class liked to hold him in their laps and pretend he was their doll. That was all right until they began dressing him in their dolls' clothes and were careless with pins.

Outside of class a small group of bullies got the idea it would be fun to use Wim as their football. Wim went along for a while, but when they wanted to kick the ball, he decided it was time to zig, zag and zip. So the bullies ended up each break and lunch hour buzzing after Wim like bees after a mouse soaked in honey. Wim discovered it was convenient to shimmy up the school flag pole and eat his lunch there, but he didn't always make it. Although Wim was a good runner, his zig, zag and zip didn't inevitably come out right. Every now and then some bully would accidentally be standing right in the way of Wim's zag. When Wim's forty-pound body crashed into the eighty-pound bully the results, Wim reported to Grain-of-Sand, stunk. And then his ability to resume his zig, zag and zip was hampered considerably by having a bully's hands round his throat.

But even then Wim couldn't stop being polite. If he accidentally stepped on someone's toe while being roughed up, he invariably apologized. Naturally, this too was held against him.

Although Wim never fought back, he'd sometimes daydream of revenge. And one time he even made the mistake of trying it.

He trained Arf to make his growl whenever Wim scratched his own left ear. Then he brought Arf for the first time to school.

'You see this dog?' Wim said to Butch, as the sixth-grader and a few members of his gang came happily up to Wim to say good morning and perhaps play a little pitch and catch with Wim's body. Other children stopped to watch the beginning of the morning's fun.

'Yeah, I see the dog, peanut prick, so what?'

'This dog is part panther and has a lot of leopard and tiger in him too.'

Butch looked down at little Arf scratching a flea, and though Butch was not weighted down with the size of his brain, he knew a harmless creature when he saw one, even if it did have spots. After he'd stopped laughing he said to Wim, 'I'll take my chances. Which side of you do you want to pretend is the laces?'

'Just as a warning,' Wim said, 'I'm going to show you how fierce this dog can be.'

'Go ahead, I'm ready for another laugh.'

When Wim scratched his left ear, Arf, still working on his fleas, let out a tiger's roar that shattered two mirrors in the west-wing boys' room and sent all the children except Wim, Dawn and Butch screaming away almost as fast as Wim usually ran. When the school building stopped shaking, Butch said uncertainly: 'That's quite a dog.'

'Yes, sir,' Wim said proudly.

'You a ventriloquist?'

'Oh, no, sir. Why, even if I keep my mouth completely –'

'Mind if I test?' Butch said and picked Wim up, pinning his arms to his sides and covering his mouth. Arf looked up and, sensing trouble, wagged his tail faster.

'Now let's hear the tiger roar,' said Butch.

'Mmmmmmm,' Wim said through Butch's fingers.

'Shit, that's nothing,' said Butch. 'I'm gonna see how good a spiral you can make.'

He lifted Wim in his right hand, faded back three steps and threw him towards the school sandbox. Wim didn't

68

spiral too well, mostly because he was desperately scratching his left ear, and when he plopped into the sandbox, Arf came racing up with wagging tail to lick his face. Arf hadn't made a sound, so Wim stood up and began tearing at his left ear and shouting, but Arf just slunk silently away with his tail between his legs.

Although Wim couldn't stay angry at Arf, he did give up trying to teach him tricks. He decided he had enough trouble with bullies as it was.

Perhaps because he was such a complete outsider, after four months of school Wim was still pretty much Wim: not much humanness had rubbed off on him. And since a large black boy named Rocky Peters had become his friend he wasn't getting pelted or bullied as much. A few children would still chase him or try to give him a hicky, but only to keep up appearances.

However, when reports began reaching the authorities that Wim was disrupting his third-grade class, encouraging innocent children to violence both in the class and on the playgrounds, and usually not handing in his social studies homework, they knew he must be a deeply disturbed child. And when they heard that this poor retarded Indian was being locked up by his mother at the bottom of a sunken ship and forced to breathe through an old garden hose, a social worker named Miss Fraggett came to visit Wide Pool.

Miss Fraggett, a tall, slender woman dressed in a grey suit, marched on to the barge and tried not to scrunch up her nose at the heavy seaweed smell. She saw at a glance what a pitiful environment Wim lived in. Inspecting the wrecked cabin with Wide Pool and Wim, she frowned. When she questioned Wide Pool about all the strange and varied and mostly useless things scattered around the barge and learned that they were 'presents', she concluded that Wide Pool had too many boyfriends, and their presents could hardly be a good influence on the poor Indian boy. Wim's being small might mean a case of malnutrition. His eating a lot of chocolate chip cookies was certainly a compulsive intake of sugar. His always asking weird questions indicated emotional problems. His failure to fight back against bullies twice his size showed a lack of healthy masculinity. His showing so much love for his mother might mean he was upset by all the rival fathers.

So it didn't take Miss Fraggett long to decide that Wim would be much better off in a normal environment. After peering with a grimace over the side of the barge and seeing the seaweed and flotsam there, she turned to Wide Pool.

'But you're eligible for welfare,' she repeated. 'And with public assistance you could afford a decent home for your son. This place is a disgrace.'

Wide Pool glanced down at Wim, who was looking wide-eyed at Miss Fraggett.

'This is Wim's home,' she replied simply.

'A child needs a room of his own, electricity, running water ...' Miss Fraggett went on.

'We have plenty of running water all over the place,' said Wim.

'Where does the poor child sleep?' the woman asked, ignoring Wim.

'On his catamaran in the bilge,' Wide Pool answered calmly.

'In the bilge!' Miss Fraggett exclaimed, clutching her clipboard to her chest as if in protection.

Wim himself ran proudly forward to the large open hatch on the seaward end of the barge and was followed by the social worker and his mother. Miss Fraggett stared down at the small six-foot catamaran sloshing peacefully back and forth in the water inside the barge. A sleeping bag was folded neatly across the canvas trampoline.

'There!?' she asked, feeling frightened for the poor boy.

Wim glanced fearfully up at his mother and then at the increasingly fierce-faced Miss Fraggett.

'It's the biggest room in the house,' Wim suggested tentatively.

Miss Fraggett frowned further, keeping her eyes on Wide Pool.

'Solar heating ...' Wim continued hopefully. 'Plenty of fresh air ...'

Miss Fraggett, lips tight, shook her head.

'I thought ...' Wim tried again, 'I thought humans liked waterbeds?'

'I suggest,' the social worker said quietly to Wide Pool, 'that you place Wim in a foster home.'

Wide Pool returned Miss Fraggett's gaze with outward calm, although her heart was shuddering.

'No,' she answered in a whisper.

'But this environment is destroying the poor child!' Miss Fraggett said.

'How?' Wide Pool asked politely.

'By coddling him so he's always playing and not studying. By having so many different men around giving him treats but making him jealous. By feeding him chocolate chip cookies until he's no larger than an erect rabbit!' Miss Fraggett blushed. 'A rabbit in a standing position,' she added hastily.

'No,' Wide Pool whispered again softly. 'I am Wim's mother, and I'll never give him up to anyone else. I may not be educated in your human ways and may not be rich, but Wim is happy, and until he isn't, I want him to be with me.'

Miss Fraggett turned for the first time to smile down at Wim.

'Wouldn't you like to live in a house with television and a refrigerator and a regular bed?' she asked.

Wim, wide-eyed, simply shook his head no.

'A house that would be warm in the winter?' Miss Fraggett continued with her hopeful smile. 'Where you'd have electric lights to read by, and a toaster?'

Wim hesitated.

'Maybe,' he said. 'As long as I can bring mum and some of my daddies.'

The social worker shook her head sadly and turned back to Wide Pool.

'I'm afraid if you hope to keep your son, you'll have to cease having men visiting you all the time,' she said.

'All right,' Wide Pool replied quietly.

Wim looked up at the two women without understanding.

'If forbidding all men means that your food supply is reduced,' Miss Fraggett went on firmly to Wide Pool, 'then you must accept public assistance – food stamps.'

'We'll make do,' Wide Pool said softly.

Miss Fraggett looked at the Indian woman and shook her head sadly. Then she smiled down a last time at the beautiful Indian boy, ruffled his hair with her free hand, and left.

In the next week, after Wide Pool had informed the men of Maganansett of her decision to become a fit mother, part of the town was hit by so much drunkenness, fist-fighting, and conjugal rape that it seemed a plague had struck instead of simple withdrawal symptoms. The gifts stopped coming, and Wide Pool refused to register for the food stamp programme, but the authorities decided that even were Wim to die of starvation, at least his mother could be proud, knowing that she had become a fit mother for her dead son. And the overall effect on Wim was the best the authorities might have hoped for: he was lonely and unhappy.

Wim missed his daddies. Even if most of them were human beings, having one around the house was like having another dog that he could pet and tease and play with. The old barge seemed empty without them. When he'd get home from school there would be no one to go crabbing or fishing with; no one to discuss spelling and maths and social studies with; no one to scare shitless with Arf's roar.

His mother tried to play ping-pong with him, but even when he hit the ball right to her she usually managed either to miss it or hit it into the bilge. They tried playing tic-tac-toe together and crazy eights or even 'war' with cards, but Wide Pool just wasn't interested in winning at anything. If her ace of spades captured his king at 'war', it didn't matter to her. And in tic-tac-toe she found crooked lines just as good as straight ones. Wim had the same tendency, but he usually worked up a temporary interest in aces and straight lines and the flight of a ping-pong ball, and she didn't. After a while he pretended he didn't like games any more.

But Billy Best loved playing games and winning, and so Wim began to go over to Billy's barn after school instead of back to the barge. Billy lived in a huge mansion overlooking the bay, and, on a side lawn big enough to land a B52, there would usually be a game of touch football or keepaway or hide-and-seek or a trampoline or, on rainy days, all sorts of card games in the barn.

And according to Wim, playing card games with Billy was interesting because as soon as Billy's opponents would learn to play a game as well as he could, Billy would invent a new game, one whose rules he understood better than anyone else and one whose strategy he could figure out quickest. Wim loved these new games, although it got a little annoying sometimes to think you had won a game and then learn of an obscure rule that had been hidden in small print on the bottom line of the last page of Billy's mind that made you lose. Still, it was more challenging than playing tic-tac-toe with his mother.

Although Wim liked these afternoons at Billy's better than the loneliness at home after his daddies had all gone on vacation, he began to feel confused and sad. This was the way he was supposed to feel according to humans but not what a Montauk would feel. So by Wim's second year in school Grain-of-Sand knew he had to do something.

WHY WIM RUNS FAST

One day a disciple asked Our Beloved Wim: 'How is it, Wim, that you've always been able to run so fast?'

Wim frowned a moment and then answered: 'When I was born I made a desperate effort to race back up inside my mother,' he said. 'But at the last second they caught me and dragged me back.' He paused and then smiled. 'From that moment on I vowed never to be tackled from behind again.'

– from *Sixty-six Parables of Wim*

12

Well, throwing Wim in with humans was like throwing a ragdoll to crocodiles: the crocodiles didn't really enjoy munching on the ragdoll, but they sure didn't do it no good. When he first begun telling me the shit the other kids were throwing at him and how dedicated all his teachers were to cure him of being a Montauk, I felt like crying, except navigators never cry. We just sort of scowl.

Social workers are good enough as people go, but when humans get the hots for doing good to Indians, we know it's time to run for cover. But it weren't just the problem with Miss Fraggett that made me decide to pull up my breeches and set to work. Over the years about half us Montauks would get killed off in school and emerge as human beings whether they ever got waylaid by a Miss Fraggett or not. Fifty per cent of your nation is a lot to lose when at the time we only had eight kids overall.

And Wim was in a specially precarious spot because even when he managed to force himself to tell a lie, it weren't much better than a half-truth and so exhausted him that the next thing he always said was the whole truth. Lying ain't much use if the best you can do is only one.

So it weren't the bullying or teasing of Wim that worried me, or the teachers treating him like a moron, it was his seeming to have no sense of the importance of remaining a Montauk, and no sense of his being Somebody Special.

Now it ain't the navigator's job to say straight out to someone 'You're Special, you better get your ass moving because Big Things are expected of you.' Navigators are sometimes given a Vision that lets them know this, but the job of letting someone know he's a Special Being is up to the Big Beings in the sky who sent him down here in the first place. All we navigators can do is try to open the channels of communication. I was trying to do that with my teaching, but against eight hours of school and two or three of Billy Best, I didn't seem to be doin' too good.

And then, to make matters worse, it began to look like the humans were out to rope in Wim completely.

The health department suddenly discovered that Wide Pool's barge, which had been settin' in the mud for thirty years, and her in it for ten, had holes in it. Even worse it suddenly appeared it didn't have no proper outhouse. And belonged to the Pittsburgh Coal Company. Miss Fraggett got herself a local judge to issue a court order to enjoin 'Mary' from living on the barge since said barge was a health hazard, was polluting wetlands, was improperly parked, was trespassing on private property, hadn't paid land taxes in thirty years, and besides she didn't own it.

And Billy Best was also working on Wim to move. He went to ask his dad to let Wim come live with them in order to help Billy become an even greater football star than he already was.

Billy's pop was a big deal human – Dr Humphrey Best – a chubby man with the smile of a dentist about to pull a tooth, and he liked to come out on the lawn or into the games-room to urge the other kids to try their best to beat Billy because they couldn't possibly do it, and their trying would make Billy even better than he already was, and their losing would be good for their souls. Then he'd disappear back into his office. He was a rich doctor specializing in problems with the liver, the bladder, and other obscure things they'd found around in there. He had a lot of rich patients so couldn't spend more than a couple of minutes a day urging on the other kids to lose to Billy. Wim looked like a good loser, so Dr Best said 'fine' to his son.

Billy began telling Wim all about soft beds, eight kinds of breakfast cereals, a room filled with train tracks, VCRs, hot tubs, TV games, and a year's supply of chocolate chip cookies, but Wim just kept saying 'no'. He admitted to me that once he weakened just enough to ask if his mum couldn't come live at Billy's too, but by this time Dr Best had learned about Wide Pool's long guest list and said it was no deal.

Finally, after Dr Best began to throw his weight around, they evicted Wide Pool and Wim from the old barge.

Now Montauks don't make any big fuss about getting evicted – it's been our national fate since humans arrived – so Wim built himself another catamaran, and he and Wide Pool sailed off to find a new home across the bay. Gardner's Island is what human beings call a nature preserve – meaning they've decided not to ruin it. That means they keep humans off it. 'Course we Montauks been living on it for two thousand years now, but since we leave no more trace than geese in the sky, no one's noticed. Wim and Wide Pool set up a shelter in the woods near the water and, as far as the humans were concerned, disappeared from the face of the earth.

That weren't exactly what Miss Fraggett and Dr Best had in mind when they got Wide Pool kicked off the barge. Dr Best hired a private detective to find Wim, but after a week of talking to the stupidest bunch of Indians he'd ever heard of – namely us – Dr Best was out three thousand dollars and the detective was close to a nervous breakdown. Dr Best decided that if things kept up the way they were going it would be cheaper and a lot less fuss to sign a top-draft choice of the NFL, so he give up.

And Wim's school decided they were free of their number one nuisance and told the social services and truant officer to limit their search for Wim to the bar of the local Holiday Inn.

Wim began living again the good old-fashioned Montauk life, where nothing much happens and one day blends into the next like sea into sky. He swam and fished and picked berries and helped Wide Pool make snail salad with seaweed and marsh grass, and he sailed and, of course, he begun seeing me again regular.

It took me a month or two before I realized that Wim weren't Wim any more. He weren't happy. He missed Dawn. She'd been forced to stay in school by her human daddy, who'd become a judge and a republican and now realized that most Indians – including his own damn wife – were uncivilized heathens and a bad influence on rational men. But Wim also missed – Lordie, how it shames me to remember – he missed human beings. He missed Billy Best and pass patterns and zig, zag and zip and card games whose rules unfolded with the game itself and car crashes on the TV and breakfast cereals he'd snacked on in Billy's barn that were ninety-nine and forty-four one-hundredths per cent sugar, and he missed something called PacMan. He began to stare off across the bay at the mansions of Maganansett like a sick cow.

It near broke my heart. Here was the last hope of the Montauk nation already deteriorated into a human being. Most Montauks survive years of school, but Wim appeared done in by barely two.

I'd been thinking of moving the whole Montauk nation down to Cape Hatteras from the day they first captured Wim, and now I knew I got to do it. Along the Outer Banks there were three or four times as many sunken barges and abandoned fishing shacks and other first-class Montauk houses, and a lot fewer humans.

Thing was, though, we'd been living here for two thousand years, and though we'd sometimes wintered down on the Outer Banks we'd always felt that the south fork of Long Island was our home. Still, owning land was for humans, not Montauks. When I saw it was either give up our ancient homeland or lose all the Montauks to the humans, I called the nation together and announced we were sailing off to Cape Hatteras. They all looked at me for a few seconds and then began packing.

'Course packing ain't the right word for it since most Montauks didn't have enough belongings to fill up a medium-size garbage bag. Sweepin' up is really what most 'em done. Leaving the land the way they found it. Poor Wide Pool had the most work to do. She had to sneak back to the mainland and arrange to clear off her old barge of seven or eight years' worth of accumulated shit. She had a jumble sale that had human folks drooling for miles around. What she did was put everything for sale and tell the folks they could take whatever they wanted and pay whatever they thought was fair. Since Wide Pool weren't going to touch the money anyhow – she was letting a black gal friend of hers have it all – Wide Pool got her yard picked up for free. They say Billy Best picked up the life-sized statue of Arnold Palmer in his backswing paying three dollars and later sold it for five thousand to some Easthampton millionaire telling him it was an original Rodin.

Anyway, in about a week the Montauk nation had cleaned up and was ready to leave. But every day nearer to the time for setting sail, Wim's face got longer and longer and more and more human. Me and Wide Pool and the other two dozen Montauks were all bustling along the beach on Gardner's Island, me telling everybody which catamaran they was supposed to be on and who was supposed to steer and things like that, and Wim is standing there big-eyed and stupid and just totally lacking in that bright-eyed innocent love of everything that I thought of as Wim.

Well, I was mad. I drug him up the beach aways and reminded him of all the stupid things human beings done through the centuries and all the cruel things they done to him in just two years, but after about ten minutes of probably the most brilliant talk I ever give anybody, I see that for Wim all the past sins of the human race were nothing compared to the opportunities at Billy's mansion. So I stopped.

Wim just stood there with his head hanging down staring at a fiddler crab out for a stroll. When he finally looked up at me, he looked like he'd just had a great philosophical insight.

'I ... guess I like humans,' is what he said.

Enough to make a man puke.

'Why?' I asked, feeling the lines of my face furrowing yet deeper and wanting to stomp something.

A kind of puzzled frown clouded up his face, too.

'I ... I guess they're interesting,' he said. 'Billy does so many different things ... and Dawn ... I ... I like pretending to be a human.'

'But they ain't pretending,' I snapped back at him. 'It's no game to them. That Billy'll knife you someday like he'd never known you.'

Wim didn't bat an eyelash.

'And here ... nothing happens.'

'Nothing's supposed to happen. Getting knifed – that's a happening. Getting cheated – that's a happening.'

'I'm sorry, Grain-of-Sand,' he said, hanging his head again like the guilty boy he was.

I nodded. Navigators know when they're beaten.

'Do you want to leave your mum?' I asked.

'Oh, no,' Wim answered. 'It's just that ... I'm lonely here.'

'You want to go back to school?'

He looked confused. 'I don't know. I guess I don't much like school, but there are things to do there ... and books ...'

Well, I turned away and stared out across the water. Wim had always been strange and unusual and unpredictable and annoying, but his sudden failure to be happy as a Montauk was the surprisingest and most depressing thing that had ever happened since he first began flopping around in the bilge of that old rowboat. My Vision hadn't made it clear exactly how Wim was the last hope of the Montauk nation or how he was a Special Being, but it didn't make much sense to me that living with human beings was part of the path. 'Course I knew that Wim always seemed to take the hard way. And, of course, it was the first principle of all Montauk navigators that the Gods never made much sense.

'Well,' I said, testing the feel of my arthritis to see if the frightening conclusion I seemed to be reaching might somehow be the right one, 'if you feel you got to go back and play at being human, then I guess maybe you better not come with us.'

Wim looked up at me, surprised.

'But ...'

'I've had enough of your "buts" to last me two lifetimes,' I said irritably. 'I'll talk to your mum and tell her that I think the Gods got it into their heads that you got to live with the humans.'

'But where will I live?' asked Wim.

'That's none of my concern,' I shot back. 'A navigator only points the way. You got to do the hiking yourself.'

'But I can't leave my mum,' he said, beginning to look frightened.

'The humans don't want just part of you, they want all of you. Ain't no way they're gonna let Wide Pool come with you.'

'Then I'll go with you,' he announced. 'If I can't be with –'

'Well, make up your mind,' I interrupted, turning to leave. 'The Montauk nation is heading south, but we ain't taking any humans.'

'But I don't know what I want!' Wim cried, running up to me and grabbing my arm.

Well, that stopped me dead in my tracks. Wim had just used the exact words that Montauks know define a human

81

being: 'He who doesn't know what he wants.' Wim was already lost. Whether he lived with his mum and us or not made no difference. I turned back and gave him my number one high-powered glare.

'Go,' I commanded.

'What? I don't understand. You –'

'Go. You ain't a Montauk any more. You got to go and live with your own kind.'

'But Grain-of-Sand, please –'

'Go play your human games. I done what I could. When the Gods want to use me again, I'm sure they'll let me know. But for now I have nothing more to teach you.'

'But I love you, Grain-of-Sand, and I want to be a good Montauk.'

Well, I cringed at the phrase 'good Montauk'. There were only Montauks and non-Montauks – good or bad's got nothing to do with it. Still, this poor lost being was a former Montauk and one that somehow, someway, sometime might possibly be the last hope of the Montauk nation.

'Go, child,' I repeated in a more gentle voice. 'My spirit and Wide Pool's spirit will always be with you, no matter how far you travel into the human darkness.'

Well, the little fella's eyes filled with tears, but much as I loved him I wasn't gonna be suckered into that whirlpool.

'I have to go back to the mainland?' he asked brokenly.

'You *want* to go back to the mainland,' I said, looking down with that special controlled dignity I used to practise in front of a mirror before I become navigator. 'It's your way – a crooked way, a baffling way, a stupid way – but it's yours. You're the last hope of the Montauk nation – which puts our hopes about knee-high to a turtle – but I see you got to stay behind here and make a fool of yourself...'

I marched up the beach away from him and, shouting, ordered the two Montauks I'd put on a boat with Wim to get into the big catamaran I was navigating. Then I ordered everyone to hoist sail and cast off for Hatteras.

Four of our five catamarans began to sail out into Block Island Sound, while Wim, alone, ran to the boat I'd left for him and jumped on. The wind picked up the minute we were out on the water and pushed us east like crazy towards the open sea. Wim was raising his sail to come after us when something strange happened. The wind, which was blowing us east, seemed where he was – only a hundred yards away – to be blowing west. He tried to tack against the wind, but every time he'd begin a tack, the wind would push him towards the mainland, and when he'd come about, it would shift again, always blocking him.

When Wide Pool saw what was happening she grabbed the tiller of the boat she was in and tried to turn back to get to her Wim, but the same thing happened to her. The wind was blowing Wim and the Montauk nation farther and farther apart.

Well, I just sat there with my hand on the tiller of the main catamaran and shook my head. I knew the Gods had went and made another of their Mistakes. Weren't the first, wouldn't be the last. But navigators got to have faith, and I did. I figured that sooner or later the Gods would decide They needed me again for Wim and send for me in one of their Stupid Ways and I'd be able to get Wim back on the Montauk path.

'Course, then again They might not. As far as I could see, nothing They did in connection with Wim made the slightest bit of sense, so I'd have to be pretty stupid to think They would suddenly change their Policy and begin doing things reasonable.

The last I seen of Wim that day – the last I seen of him for four years – the wind had tore a hole in his sail you could drive a pickup through, his mast was broke, and he seemed about to go on the rocks of Maganansett Beach. For the Gods, it seemed about par for the course.

13

from the Paramount film *Adventures of Wim*, 2002,
screenplay by Olly Hart, pp. 34–6

EXTERIOR – MANSION AND GROUNDS OF DR BEST – DAY – FULL

A large two-storey brick house with stately lawns and
formal gardens in front, with a long driveway running up
to a circle under an impressive portico with towering white
columns. A large Cadillac enters the driveway and proceeds
towards the house.

INTERIOR – MOVING CADILLAC – THE BESTS AND WIM – P.O.V. WIM

Past Wim's head we see DR BEST driving, and MRS BEST, a
nondescript woman of middle age totally eclipsed by her
ambitious husband, in the passenger seat beside him. BILLY
is seated in the back with Wim. (After Wim's P.O.V. is
established, all of this sequence is shot as if the camera were
the eyes of Wim.)

EXT. – P.O.V. WIM – DRIVEWAY, GARDENS, MANSION AND BARN

Through the rear window Wim catches his first glimpse of
his new home.

After surveying the mansion his eyes are drawn to an old
barn a hundred feet off to one side and linger longingly on
it as the car draws up to the front steps of the mansion.

The car halts, and the rear door is opened by a SERVANT,
whose face is cold and indifferent. Wim gets out, and almost
immediately sees

A LARGE DOBERMAN, teeth bared, fierce eyes fixed directly at the camera. SOUND OF DEEP MENACING GROWL, followed by a brief vicious ROAR OF BARKING.

CAMERA TRUCKING, moves past the dog whose bared teeth and growl continue and whose fierce eyes follow Wim's P.O.V.

> VOICE OF DR BEST (O.S.)
> Easy, Panzer, easy. We'll feed you later.

CAMERA TRUCKING – Wim follows the three Bests through the large front door into the main hallway, where the SERVANT takes Dr Best's coat and Mrs Best's hat.

Wim looks first into a large lush living-room on one side and a large, lavishly furnished formal dining-room on the other.

A matronly black MAID appears and smiles down in a warm motherly fashion at the camera and Wim.

> VOICE OF DR BEST (O.S.)
> Watch yourself, Bertha.

REACTION SHOT – MAID

Her motherly smile is instantly erased and replaced by a look of stern disapproval, which she directs vaguely off nowhere.

Billy then turns to Wim and motions for him to follow up the stairs.

INT. BILLY'S BEDROOM – BILLY AND WIM

Billy is motioning Wim to enter through the door into an exceptionally large bedroom. On one bureau are a half-dozen tiny trophies, presumably already won by the eleven-year-old Billy. Scattered about the room are: a coloured TV set with VCR, a computer, a set of weights, a large stereo system, and even a tiny 'bar', from which Billy can serve cokes. His bed is huge, and in the open closet hangs a multitude of clothing.

Wim's eyes travel slowly around this world of opulence.

His eyes are wide with wonder, but his face shows neither envy nor sadness.

Billy then motions Wim to follow him again and they head out the bedroom doorway.

CUT TO

INT. BEST LIVING-ROOM - DAY - DR AND MRS BEST - CAMERA TRUCKING

Following Dr Best, who is leading his wife across the living-room, talking half to her and half to himself.

> DR BEST
> Billy wanted a computer, I got him a computer.
> He wanted a VCR, I got him a VCR ... He wants
> a live-in running back, he's now got a live-in
> running back ...

INT. WIM'S SMALL BEDROOM - WIM AND BILLY

Again Billy is motioning Wim to enter a bedroom, this one clearly intended for Wim. It is a quarter the size of Billy's and is furnished simply with a tiny cot, an old oaken desk and a single small bureau.

REACTION SHOT - WIM

Again his eyes are wide, but his face shows no other emotion but wonder.

BILLY
Pretty soon, Wim, you'll be able to forget all about
your past and become just like us.

Wim's expression slowly changes from wide-eyed wonder
to sadness and dismay.

14

from *Fact Sheets on Wim*, vol. III, pp. 234–7

We must now assess the four years of Wim's life when he was given so much help, training, and caring to assist him in becoming a serious and productive member of the human race. Living those four years free from the primitive influences of his Indian mentor and mother, living in the cultured, comfortable home of Dr Humphrey Best, attending the fine schools of Maganansett Township, Wim had every opportunity to develop into at least a normal human being. Yet at the end of these four years, when Grain-of-Sand and his mother returned, Wim fell immediately and catastrophically back under their influence. Within days of their return he foolishly sailed off on a 'Vision Quest' and, upon his return, began those years of exotic, extravagant and ridiculous actions which the myth-makers claim are all connected with his 'Great Quest for Ultimate Truth'.[36] From our more scientific point of view we must sadly conclude that a potential human reverted to his primitive origins.

However, in this volume we will delineate the ways in which Wim manifested several desirable human traits during this period.

First, he showed a healthy interest in competitive sports, in particular scholastic football, at which he achieved a certain amount of local fame as both a 'running back',[37] and a 'passer'.[38] Although his skills at this sport were highly erratic, it seems clear that Wim was permitted to skip most of two different grades of school solely so that he might begin playing varsity football at the same time as Senator

William O. Best (then known more commonly as 'Billy').[39] Senator Best was fourteen years old and already sexually mature[40] when he began starring as a 'wide receiver' for the Maganansett High School Gulls, but Wim was promoted to the freshman class and began playing varsity football when he was only twelve years old.[41] Dr Hans Doppleganger of the Department of Human, Animal and Vegetable Sexuality at the University of California at Malibu Beach indicates that this early exposure to older and sexually mature men may have frightened the young Wim and thus brought about his relatively late sexual maturation at the age of almost fifteen.[42] Certainly Dr Doppleganger's explanation makes more sense than the one offered by the myth-makers that we will examine in volume IV.[43]

Secondly, thanks to the precocious influence of Senator Best, Wim also began to manifest a healthy interest in money. Over the years Wim lived at the Bests he and the Senator engaged in a wide variety of business enterprises, all created by the Senator.[44] Although they began simply enough with enterprises such as lawn-mowing, leaf-raking, chain-sawing, window-cleaning and painting, by their junior year in high school, when Billy was seventeen and Wim approaching fifteen, Senator Best had diversified them into videocassette rentals,[45] home security systems[46] and personal messenger service,[47] the last, of course, to take advantage of Wim's speed. It is estimated that at the age of sixteen the Senator had already accumulated a personal fortune of close to sixty thousand dollars, and his chief employee and partner, Wim, almost nine thousand dollars.[48] The disparity in their savings is explained both by Wim's incurable habit of giving things away and also by those words from the Bible that Senator Best so loved to quote: 'By those who hath, more shall be taken.'[48]

Thirdly, Wim began to make human friends. In addition to Senator Best, he spent much time with Dawn Holt, the only daughter of Judge Robert B. Holt,[49] who in 1998 handed down the controversial decision (later overturned by the Supreme Court) declaring that children were unconstitutional.[50] Wim also had many football player friends, especially the gigantic young negro, 'Rocky' Peters, later to become an all-American fullback at Michigan and founder of Indiantown, the well-known home for orphaned Indians.[51]

The young negro had apparently befriended Wim originally by walking up to a student named Butch Messmire and saying simply, 'I like Wim.'[52] Although Mr Messmire already weighed at the age of eleven almost a hundred and sixty pounds,[53] Mr Peters, also at that time eleven, already weighed over two hundred pounds, and when Mr Peters spoke, everyone listened. The evidence is that from the day Mr Peters announced 'I like Wim,' the bullying of Wim effectively ended.[54]

Nevertheless, with all the advantages that Senator Best and his family were able to give him, many reports we will now examine indicate that during this period Wim continued to have a disturbing tendency to remain Wim ...[55]

THE SEE-SAW

Wim once saw two boys rocking up and down on a see-saw.
First one boy went zooming upwards and then the other.
  'Which one of you is higher?' Wim yelled with a smile.
  'I am!' cried one boy.
  'I am!' a moment later cried the other.
  'That's the way it goes,' said Wim to himself.
  'And which is lower?' he asked.
  'He is!' cried the first boy.
  'He is!' a moment later cried the second.
  'That's the way it goes,' thought Wim.

– from Sixty-six Parables of Wim

15

from *The Gospel According to Luke*, pp. 88–95

Wim was lonely, missing his mother and Grain-of-Sand even more than on Gardner's Island he'd missed Dawn and Billy and human things. He wrote both of them long letters all through the first three months and mailed them to 'Montauk Nation, Outer Banks, N.C.' with the right zip code, and later, on Billy's advice, to 'General Delivery, Cape Hatteras, N.C.', but, after a while they all were returned to him one by one by the post office. Just before Christmas he received a single postcard from Grain-of-Sand with a picture of a seagull on a beach. The postcard said:

> Montauk nation fine. Your mum loves you and would write every day except she don't know how to write and I won't help her.
>
> The Gods are silent.

> Grain-of-Sand

> P.S. I left a lure next to the green rock at Little Pebble's Point. You might find it and save it for me.

It was after this that Wim decided he might as well stop writing and let himself become human.

The trouble was that even when he enjoyed being human, Wim wasn't usually too good at it. He received a lot of advice from everyone, but it mostly made him confused. Billy was always telling him that the secret of success was to make everything into a contest and to win every one. Wim liked competing, but it usually bored him after a while. Billy would be scratching for the last extra inch even with his team ahead by thirty points, but Wim would lose interest. Instead of throwing a pass to Billy as the play called for, he might try to knock the helmet off the opponent's middle linebacker.

And no matter how much Billy lectured him, he still couldn't get the hang of lying. He sometimes liked to spend money and was learning to like material things, but he still enjoyed giving stuff away, which Billy said in the US was illegal.

And Dawn was always giving him advice too. She introduced him to laws and social customs and moral duties that even Billy never knew existed. And just when he thought he finally knew how to avoid a no-no while pulling off some trick on some adult or bully, Dawn would giggle and giggle but then come up with some obscure rule previously hidden in an appendix of her mind that would make what he'd done slightly wrong after all.

And soon after he arrived at the Bests and was about to begin the sixth grade, Wim was called out on to the stone patio where Dr Best took his afternoon scotch. The doctor then gave him a long lecture about success in education. As human lectures go it made a lot of sense.

'First of all, Wim,' Dr Best said, leaning back in his lounge chair and cradling his glass of scotch, while Wim stood attentively nearby on the stones, 'I want you to remember that an "A" is a grade given to a student in recognition of the student's ability to manipulate and con the teacher, and is hence a valid measure of intelligence.'

Wim was a bit surprised, but realized that this might explain why he had such trouble ever earning an 'A'.

'I expect you, therefore,' Dr Best continued, 'despite your habitual laziness, to try to uphold the Best name and get high "B"s in all your work – Billy, of course, must get all the high "A"s. To come to me later this year and tell me you only received a "C" or a "D" because the teacher doesn't like you is to admit failure to achieve. It is your scholastic duty to see to it that the teacher likes you. That is what American education is all about.'

'Yes, sir,' said Wim politely, feeling that it sounded suspiciously difficult since he had not once found a teacher who liked him.

'In athletics, however,' Dr Best went on, cheerfully clinking the ice-cubes in his glass, 'your behaviour may be somewhat different. In sports you do not have to please the coach, only score points. Coaches who don't like you will curse you, hit you, penalize you, but, if you score points, play you. Coaches, unlike academic teachers, are forced to keep in touch with reality, and if the reality is that you're running for touchdowns and hitting eighty per cent of your passes, then you will play no matter how totally you fail to bullshit the coach.'

'Yes, sir,' said Wim politely, feeling that it sounded suspiciously like the way Billy picked boys to play on his Blazers. It seemed that every bully that had ever picked on Wim was welcome on the Blazers, providing they could bully the opponents even better than they had Wim.

'In the classroom, however, ability is a minor matter,' Dr Best went on, smiling amiably with that warm love he always had for himself. 'What counts is your staying in touch with your teacher, making him or her believe that you *care* that the capital of Singapore is Bangkok, or if it isn't that it's a personal tragedy that you got it wrong. In my junior year algebra class I was very seldom able to determine the value of "X", but after the teacher showed me my mistakes I *cried*, and she knew that I cared and gave me an "A".'

'But, sir,' Wim finally protested, 'isn't it important to learn a few things about geography or maths or English?'

Dr Best rocked forward and reached out a chubby hand to give Wim a friendly tap in the belly.

'Son,' he said benevolently. 'Does it make any difference to the final score of one of your football games whether you know O. J. Simpson's passing statistics in 1954 or the correct grammatical construction of the sentence you use calling for Billy on the fly pattern or the location of the Los Angeles Coliseum?'

'No, sir.'

'Well, it's the same with your work in high school,' Dr Best concluded, leaning back and idly patting Panzer who had wandered over with a fang-baring growl to say hello. 'If you score a high grade average, you're a winner, and if you score low, you're a loser. Knowing that Joyce Brothers wrote *Ulysses* or that the Vikings sailed to Minnesota a year before Columbus got to Ohio is irrelevant.'

'I see,' said Wim, feeling sure that this wasn't at all the way Dawn would see it.

'Which brings us to cheating,' continued Dr Best. 'Billy tells me that you do not like to cheat. Is this true?'

'Yes, sir.'

'I was afraid of that,' said Dr Best with a frown and pushing Panzer away. 'Again, the way to see things clearly is to think of a football game. When a player holds or throws an illegal block it is considered part of the game. If he gets away with it, he helps himself and his team. If he is caught he is penalized. So too with cheating. Successful cheaters are both improving their grade average and preparing themselves for adult life. When they are caught, they are penalized. When they are not caught – which, thanks to our splendid educational system, is seldom – they are rewarded. Do you see now how simple it is?'

'I suppose so,' said Wim, frowning and not daring to say more with Panzer still only a dozen feet away.

'As long as you remember that the American way of life always focuses on winning and success and not the means of getting there, and certainly not on the losers left behind, you'll be fine.' Dr Best leaned back contentedly and finished the last of his drink. 'However,' he concluded, 'your failure to cheat is a sign of your lack of seriousness, a lack that I fear will doom you to perpetual failure.'

As Wim looked off across the endless lawn towards the distant bay, Dr Best cupped his glass in his hands and smiled.

'Well, Wim,' he said, 'tell me honestly what you think of my advice.'

Wim turned to look at Dr Best with an expression of horror.

'B-b-b-beg pardon?' he asked.

'Tell me honestly what you think.'

Wim's expression went from horror to innocent determination back to horror. Finally, he spoke.

'Well,' he said in a tiny voice, 'I guess I find most of what the teachers and Coach Cannonball and you have to say to be ... to be ... a crock.'

Dr Best's mouth fell open. For a long moment he tried to absorb what Wim had said.

'A ... crock?' he asked doubtfully.

'A crock of shit,' Wim explained more loudly, gazing steadily and honestly and hopelessly at Dr Best. 'It's a phrase Billy taught me.'

'You find my advice a crock of ... shit,' Dr Best said in a dull voice, his wide eyes fixed incredulously on Wim.

'Yes, sir,' said Wim. 'Which makes it tough for me to take any of your words seriously.'

Dr Best lowered his glass to the table, and his face became red. He glared at Wim and then swung his head to the right.

'Panzer!' he screamed. 'Dinner!!!'

Wim's face collapsed into fear, and he wheeled to race off towards the distant bay. The Doberman, roaring and growling and drooling away with total happiness, galloped gracefully after him in hot pursuit.

There were other lectures later, but the fact is that after less than a year at the Bests, Wim discovered that it was almost impossible to please Dr Best and thus not really important to listen to him. Dr Best was a strict father. He believed there was a right way and a wrong way to do things, and he could infallibly tell which was which by seeing what Wim did. Wim's way was the wrong way. It simplified the moral universe considerably to know that whatever he felt like doing was bound to be wrong, but it somewhat dampened Wim's enthusiasm for Dr Best.

In any case, within three years Wim had managed to settle into being a typical high school student – or as typical as he would ever be. Wim had to admit he didn't like high school that much. He supposed it was teaching him a good deal: the fact that all Gaul was divided into three parts, the way people in Spain asked one another to open the door, the slot formation option pass to the weak side, the spelling of 'changeable', the reasons *Silas Marner* was a great novel, seven card stud, how to say 'hello' to MHS girls in such a way that they'd say 'hello' back to you, the relations of certain congruent triangles, and other things that he could never quite remember.

Wim had to admit that it didn't teach him boredom though, since he'd already learned that in elementary school. But boredom seemed to be its primary lesson, and it impressed him to realize the complicated and ingenious devices the teachers had developed to create it. Mr Horner managed over two years of algebra to make 'x', which Wim had always felt to be the most exciting concept in the world, as boring as old 'a' and 'b', which, of course, were always known.

English class wasn't much better. Wim had always enjoyed writing but often gave in to the impulse not to complete his sentences. He also developed the theory that readers are able to grasp meaning without good grammar: 'witness American Presidents.' Spelling, too, he felt was overated or overrated – he was never sure which. As for literature, he concluded that a good book is a joy for ever –

until it gets into a high school English programme. He believed that it was possible that English 10 with Mrs Moribund could make *Catch-22* seem like *Ivanhoe*. The desire and talent were there anyway.

Science was sometimes interesting but only because Mr Jamison and Mr Lucky were always trying to demonstrate some known physical or chemical law by experiments. In chemistry, for example, Mr Lucky once demonstrated clearly that sulphuric acid, when spilled on his suit jacket, eats through the cloth to the skin, where it causes pain. Another time he proved conclusively to every student's satisfaction that if hydrogen chloride is mixed with sulphuric acid at a ratio of two to one at a temperature of 180 degrees Fahrenheit when Rosie Myers's blouse has just been torn in half by an errant nail in the woodwork, the results will not be remembered. His famous melting ice experiment demonstrated beyond reasonable doubt that a glass containing ice-cubes filled to the brim will overflow into a lap when struck by an elbow. In brief, Wim learned in chemistry that Accident influences all and he who tries to deny it often gets wet pants.

Throughout all his school years Wim had a normal progressive sexual education. In the third grade he had watched a cartoon film about an adventurous tadpole sperm named 'Teddy' who with great difficulty outdistanced his rivals and made it up the rapids to meet and meld with a bashful spherical glob called 'Nan', a film that indicated to Wim and most of the other third-graders that boys should be good swimmers and that shy chubby girls could still find a husband who, however, might look like a tadpole.

In the fourth grade Wim was offered a documentary entitled 'The Fallopian Tube: A Survey', which taught him and his classmates the basic geography of a country apparently located in Asia and governed by officials called hormones and under the influence of a religion which believed in the significance of the phases of the moon. The film hinted that the girls of the class might when they grew older be captured by these officials and tortured on a monthly basis, but it all seemed far-fetched.

The fifth-grade programme presented another documentary, this one showing a woman going through twenty minutes of great pain before having a difficult bowel movement, which turned out to contain a baby, apparently a pleasant surprise for all concerned.

The sixth-grade annual sexual education programme was shocking. The cartoon film dramatized the life of a shy penis named 'Dave' who grew up and investigated a cave named 'Doris'. It was never made clear what Dave was looking for in Doris and all Wim was able to learn from the film was that when he grew older he could investigate caves but would shrivel up afterwards.

In the seventh grade Wim and Billy and Dawn saw a full-colour half-hour documentary of real people engaging in an act of sexual intercourse, a film that made considerable use of slow motion, instant replay and a voice-over narration that sounded like the commentator intoning before the Superbowl. From this Wim learned that the thing his mother did in her bedroom with his fathers involved serious and formal slow-motion callisthenics, quite similar to the yoga he'd read about in Patanjali, only callisthenics centred around a penis much larger than Wim's and which kept growing and shrinking and moving in time to background music that Billy identified as identical to that used on the weekly TV show 'NFL in Action'.

In the eighth grade a film entitled 'Methods of Contraception' took Wim and his friends back into Asia and the Governing Hormones, but now showed his old friend 'Teddy' turned into a bad guy to be kept away from the jolly blob 'Nan' at all costs. Germ warfare – called simply and menacingly 'The Pill' – had apparently been developed to keep Nan from growing each month, and there were two or three tragic scenes in which Teddy made it up the rapids only to find nobody home. In other skirmishes in which The Pill seemed to have been outlawed by some sort of Geneva Convention, the defenders built a small, tricky dam across the rapids so that Teddy ended up beating himself to death against it whenever he tried to make it up to Nan. It was all sad and depressing, especially when the defenders threw a film-like balloon over Dave, Teddy's home, so that even though Dave got Teddy right up close to Nan, when he rushed out to play with her he was trapped inside the film and died a slow horrifying death only millimetres away from his goal.

The only time during the whole film that the seventh graders showed any emotion was when the film showed Teddy and a few of his men breaking through the end of the balloon and beginning to swim up the rapids. The whole auditorium broke into cheers and the cry of 'go go go', but it all ended sadly when the enemy poured in some different kind of germ warfare that wiped out Teddy and all the others before they could make it to Nan. For days afterwards Wim moped around depressed, daydreaming compulsively of ways of blowing up the tricky dam or stopping the mysterious and evil Pill from bribing the Hormones to assassinate Nan, or slipping Teddy his boy scout knife so he could break through the rubber film and out into the rapids to Nan.

By the ninth grade Wim was also getting occasional sex education lectures from Billy Best and Rocky Peters, but that year's programme managed to outdo all the others in bewildering Wim as to the nature of sex. That year, on the first day of spring, the students filled the auditorium for the annual sex education programme. First there was a short documentary film consisting of an interesting lecture by a former prostitute on the evils of associating with prostitutes. Wim learned that it was foolish of a man to pay a woman just to obtain her diseases since her diseases seemed to be more trouble than they were worth and besides could be gotten free from other women.

Then Mr Thompson, the sixty-six-year-old biology teacher, introduced the main part of the programme: a naked man and woman – the woman looking suspiciously like the one on film who had given the lecture – performing fellatio, cunnilingus, masturbation, anal intercourse, soixante-neuf, and sexual intercourse in thirty-seven different positions. At the end of the eight-minute live demonstration, Mr Thompson, who had guided it all using a long wooden pointer tipped with Vaseline, concluded with a few admonitions on such things as brushing one's teeth before cunnilingus, not eating cabbage prior to anal intercourse and doing deep-breathing exercises prior to position nineteen and soixante-neuf.

There followed a brief period of questions from the students, most of which turned out to be on such matters as the spelling of 'fellatio', the type of toothbrush the school recommended, and whether one had to use all thirty-seven positions every time one did it. At thirteen and not yet sexually mature, Wim was baffled and depressed by the enormity of what he had seen. Determined nevertheless to do his best, he asked what turned out to be the last question.

'Sir,' he said, standing on his chair as usual and trying not to notice the girls all staring at him.

'Yes, Wim?' said Mr Thompson genially.

'What's the homework assignment?'

16

from *The Easy Climb to the Top: the Autobiography of Senator William O. Best*, Harper, Row, Morrow, Random House & Schuster, New York, 2029

The big thing in high school though was sports, and in sports Wim, while naturally overshadowed by me, was nevertheless a standout, especially in football. At five feet tall and a hundred and twenty-eight pounds he was not exceptionally big or heavy, but he was fast and he had great moves. When Wim faked left and zipped right, the lineman who had dared confront him would hang like the leaning tower of Pisa to the left and, after Wim raced by him on the right, topple in a slow heap behind him like a crumbling building.

And of course he was a fine passer too. His hands were large for his tiny body, and he once completed twenty-two straight passes, the twenty-third attempt being thrown over the stadium roof.

And I'm afraid it was Wim's tragic inability to maintain consistency which always flawed his otherwise fine play and made him the failure he eventually became. The sad truth is Wim never lived up to his potential. For example, his famous fake left, zip right. About a quarter of the time it seemed, Wim would make his famous fake left and then get an irresistible impulse to *zip left* as well. The result would be that he would pile his one hundred and twenty-eight pounds into the infinite belly of some stunned but ecstatic two hundred and eighty pound middle guard.

Our coach, Mr Earnest E. Cannonball, would patiently explain to Wim that he was too small to run over opposing linemen and ought *always*, repeat *always*, fake one way and zip the other. But Wim never seemed to learn. Or care. Or be strong enough to resist the impulse to do the opposite of what he usually did.

And his passing was equally erratic. He once threw nine interceptions, including six in a row, which is still the world record. When Coach Cannonball was asked after that game why he hadn't sent in another quarterback, he'd sighed and answered: 'Wim doesn't throw interceptions because he's *bad*, he throws them because he's *Wim*. After his first five interceptions he was just as likely to throw five straight touchdown passes as he was more interceptions.'

'Isn't there any way you can prepare for Wim's having this kind of day?' a reporter went on to ask. Coach nodded gloomily. 'Certainly,' he replied. 'I drink a half quart of scotch before each game.'

Some people claimed his inconsistency as a passer was caused by his extreme smallness, and for three or four games Coach Cannonball thought so too. But in our fourth game, at my suggestion, the coach developed a unique passing attack based on Wim's standing on Rocky Peters's broad shoulders while Rocky held his feet, and passing from there. Wim's accuracy from ten feet was no better and no worse than it had been at five feet, but when Wim failed to throw a pass and poor Rocky Peters began a shuffling scramble to elude the thundering rush of the opposing front four, sometimes, when Rocky was tackled, Wim, carrying the ball, would land on his feet and continue the run from there, a tactic so resented by opposing teams that the Suffolk County Association of Interscholastic Athletic Institutions unanimously passed a new local football rule forbidding the throwing of a football from more than seven feet nine inches from the earth, thus ending our highly publicized piggyback offence.

And Wim's play calling was a source of great distress too. If Coach Cannonball tried to send in a play, Wim might or might not call it. Since Wim was such a sensational runner and brilliant passer, and since we usually, no matter how erratically, *won*, Coach Cannonball had no effective threat against him. We all knew that an undependable, inconsistent, lunatic Wim was, in football at any rate, preferable to no Wim at all.

But his play calling and inconsistency upset everyone. A fullback never knew as he barrelled towards the line of scrimmage to take a handoff whether he was going to be handed the ball or not. And I can remember one Saturday after Wim had been studying probability theory in maths class all week, he called R-23, Rocky Peters to run the ball straight up the middle fifteen consecutive times.

By the fourth or fifth time in a row when we came out of our huddle we could see on the faces of the opposing linemen a deep *angst*. Wim had called the same play five straight times and warned them in advance and yet and yet … They all instinctively knew what Wim had told me he'd been learning in probability theory: that when tossing coins, six consecutive heads does not alter the odds of fifty-fifty that the next coin will fall tails. But was football the same? Was Wim as reliable as a Lincoln penny? The opposing linemen couldn't be certain, but it seemed doubtful.

'OK, Rocky, let's try it again,' Wim would say, or 'Hit in there hard, Rocky Baby,' and to our right tackle, 'Move that guy out of there this time, Sam. Move him out. Twenty-two, fifteen, eight, hut hut hut hut.' Two-yard gain.

By the fourteenth play two of their linebackers were crying and we had fourth down and inches on about their twenty-yard line.

'Once more to the breach, Rocky, just an inch or two, kid. Twenty-two, fifteen, nine, hut, hut.' Wim faked the ball into Rocky's belly and slid along the line on a bootleg, and everyone in the stadium was watching Rocky smashing his brains out against their *angst*-filled line except for their defensive left end, but Wim gave him a zig-left zag-right and he toppled Wimless to the earth, and Wim ran twenty yards downfield all by himself, no one even looking at him except some drunk in the stand who didn't understand football. But near their goal line Wim stopped and, holding the ball in the air, began walking back towards the pile-up at the line of scrimmage.

'Darn it all, Rocky,' he shouted at the top of his lungs. 'You forgot to take the ball.'

For about five seconds all twenty-one of us other players just stared at him a little numb, and then their three linebackers recovered and tore down to blast Wim, caused him to fumble and, well, we went on to lose the game.

Wim apologized afterwards, and for three weeks Coach Cannonball benched him every game until we would fall behind and need him, but none of us ever really understood *why* Wim would do the strange things he did.

The only thing that made the players forgive him was his creation of his famous play that we came to call 'X-X-X on the third'. It was Wim's own play, and it wasn't until the seventh game of our junior season that Coach Cannonball even knew about it. I personally remember the impact it had on all of us the first time Wim called the play.

We were driving downfield using good running plays and short passes when Wim knelt down in the huddle and said something like: 'OK, on three, everybody do his thing, on three, break!'

When Wim said 'Break!' we all shuffled up to the line of scrimmage trying to figure out what he meant. Some of us assumed he wanted us to run the same play we'd just run; others were still leafing the pages of their play book in their mind when the ball was snapped and poor Rocky Peters got the ball from Wim and was overwhelmed for a four-yard loss.

'OK, now look, you guys,' Wim said when we'd shuffled uneasily back to the huddle, each one of us feeling personally responsible for the failure of the play, 'Let me make this play clear: I want everyone to pick a play in your own mind and then execute your assigned role with all your might, on three – that's the only part of the play we all should try to do together – although of course I won't insist even on that. Ready? On three. Break!'

So we all went back to the line of scrimmage confused but anxious to obey our quarterback. I decided to run a turn-in pattern. Rocky later told me that he decided to run a draw play to the right side. Our guards blocked for an off-tackle plunge; our wide receiver decided it would be a run and he could loaf; the centre blocked for a roll-out; while our halfback decided it was a quick-kick, himself kicking.

Wim apparently called for himself a pass to the wide receiver on a fly pattern and faded smartly back to pass. He says he was a little annoyed to see his wide receiver take two or three steps downfield and yawn, and baffled to see Bob Lanson, our halfback, going through the motions of punting. Rocky came barrelling by Wim and tried to take the ball from him for the draw, but Wim held on and faded deeper. He saw his two tackles moving off to the right to block for a screen pass and looked for a receiver there, but there was no one there except the two tackles and two of Northport's linebackers, looking confused and frightened: both were sure they'd missed the play.

The fake quick-kick and fake draw and fake plunge up the middle totally confused the passrush so if Wim had seen anyone to pass to, he had the rest of the afternoon to do it. But I was the only eligible receiver downfield and totally covered. He pumped once in my direction and then remembered he had a yawning wide receiver on the opposite side of the field, and without looking, lofted a pass over the confused mêlée of players to the precise spot he recalled seeing Tom standing and yawning.

Tom told us later that after he had taken his three steps downfield and yawned, he looked over to see how well the run was going. He saw Wim fading to pass and Bob quick-kicking and Rocky groping for a handoff on the draw and wondered who the two tackles were screening for and thought it was the prettiest and trickiest play he'd ever seen us run. He was thinking how wide open he himself was, when he felt something hit him on the helmet and saw a football bounce at his feet.

I had played football for four years before that play and played six more years afterwards, but I don't think I have ever returned to a huddle when the players have been so fired up with enthusiasm. Even though the play had only resulted in an incomplete pass we all saw how confused and demoralized the Northport players had been, and each of us felt we knew exactly what would work against their confusion. There was so much noise in the huddle that Wim had to call a time out to get us to quiet down.

'Call that one again!' Bob Lanson kept pleading and others were shouting the same, but Wim was firm.

'We don't want to settle into any patterns and we don't want to use our best play all the time. I'm calling twenty-three on two, Rocky off tackle, move 'em out, on two. Break!'

But later he called his 'special', but to vary it he said, we'd do it on 'one' this time instead of 'three'.

I won't bother to detail how each of us acted on this play, but will note that tackle Ed Peters ran twenty-seven yards after taking a handoff from tight-end Barry Plume. The next time Wim called it, Bob Lanson quick-kicked Rocky Peters's helmet fifty-four yards downfield and out of bounds on their six-yard line, while guard Timmy Stew was throwing a screen pass to Wim, who scampered ten yards before lateralling to guard Jerry Rigoorowski who fumbled.

Coach Cannonball kept asking us what play that was when – but we all answered vaguely. Since we were winning the game and had totally demoralized Northport, he was too jubilant to press us.

In the long run, of course, Wim's 'X-X-X on the third' cost us much more yardage than it gained since most of our completed passes were called back because of illegal receivers downfield, and several of our good runs were marred by fumbles because the runner, one of our guards or tackles, was still inexperienced. But the lift to team morale was incredible. Our linemen and backs began to fear that Wim wouldn't call the play unless they did well on other plays, and since we all looked forward to 'X-X-X on the third' we really hustled. Coach Cannonball's nationwide fame as 'United States' most imaginative high school offensive coach' (*Time* magazine) rests, of course, almost entirely on Wim's 'X-X-X on the third' – even though, paradoxically, Coach Cannonball spent most of the year trying to figure out a way to get us to stop running it.

17

from *The Book of Chances* . . .

Wim was he called, Wim was his name, He of Many Chances. Born of Mary, she of many husbands, she who all her life tried to recapture the divine ecstasy of her Night with the Gods.

Raised was Wim by not-raising, educated by not-schooling, formed by unforming: a man before he was a boy, a child when he had matured to manhood, Wim was he called, He of Many Chances.

And in the beginning the people reviled him for his low birth and dark skin and small stature, reviled him for his mother and for his bedraggled socks, reviled him for not wiping his nose or brushing his teeth, until, lo, he developed tricky moves and a forward pass and the revulsion disappeared. A sign.

And the wonders he began to work on the playing fields of Maganansett were as nothing to the wonders he began to perform in the high school. There did he rise up one day at the age of fourteen in the class in physics and did say: 'There is no Cause and Effect: all is Chance in the best of all possible worlds.'

'Ah, my son,' said the teacher, 'but if I release this eraser from my hand, where will it fall?'

'I don't know,' answered Wim. 'Chance will take it where it will.'

'No, my son,' replied the old teacher. 'This eraser will fall to the floor. For forty-one years I have been releasing this eraser in the third week of freshman physics and every damn time it has fallen to the floor. That, my son, is cause and effect.'

'Still,' said Wim. 'That's the past. We can't predict what Chance will bring today.'

'Cause and effect will take the eraser to the floor,' said the old man.

'We'll see,' said Wim.

The old teacher ostentatiously held the eraser high up over his head and, looking gloomily out at his thirty students, suddenly released it.

The eraser started to fall to the floor, hesitated a moment halfway down, and then swooped along the blackboard to the far corner of the room, made a right turn and continued in a systematic sweep all the way around the room, until, with a soft explosion of chalk, it dropped to the floor at the teacher's feet.

The thirty students stared wide-eyed at the old teacher. He looked down for a long moment at the motionless eraser and then looked up at his class.

'Although I admit there was a struggle,' said the old professor gloomily, 'notice that in the long run cause and effect won.'

18

from Grain-of-Sand's *Memoirs of an Old Liar*, pp. 89–98

In North Carolina nothing much happened, which meant it was a good time for the Montauk nation. 'Course I worried about Wim a few seconds a week, but a navigator knows not to rush things.

Fact is, the fishing was damn good off Hatteras. So many ships been wrecked there that fish from all over the Atlantic come to live in the apartment complexes the humans planted for them.

Wide Pool was doing pretty good too. She was a Montauk. That meant that she loved Wim as much as it's possible for a mum to love her kid, but that like me she figured Wim was somehow special and for us to try to run his life was almost as stupid as Wim himself trying to run it.

It was September, a little more than four years since we sailed away from Long Island, when the Gods farted. What they done was cook up a hurricane. Winds come across the sand bar where the Montauk nation was squatting with hundred m.p.h. winds. That hurricane did five million dollars' damage to North Carolina the radio said, but it didn't even mess the hair of the flimsy structures of our twenty-seven Montauks – except for two: mine and Wide Pool's. The shack I built and the shack she built were each picked up and transplanted to the State of Virginia.

Well, in the dictionary of navigators that's known as a Hint. A Hint is when the Gods do something that implies maybe you ought to think. Chief Froth-on-the-Wave said it best six hundred years ago: 'When the sky falls and it hits only you, maybe time to re-examine your position.'

Then the Gods sent me a dream. You can always tell when a dream has been sent by the Gods rather than by something else because you wake up all tingly. That kind of a dream is a Hint too, but generally considered a smaller Hint than a waking Hint. I dreamed of being out in the ocean sailing on my catamaran, and there, surfing down the wave ahead of me in his little cat, was Wim. We was both sailing to beat the band, and it felt terrific the way the water sizzled away beneath our boats. I was feeling real good until Wim's boat began to tear off directly out into the ocean while mine began to veer back towards land. I felt kind of sad about this, but in the dream I could see that Wim was wide-eyed and enthusiastic and heading where he was supposed to go.

Well, now, two Hints makes what navigator tradition calls a Nudge. If a navigator neglects a Nudge he's in danger of receiving a Poke, and a Poke from the Gods is likely to leave you a cripple or a loony, so we try to take action at the Nudge stage.

Fact is, the moment I woke up from that dream I knew that I got to send Wim on a Vision Quest. Traditionally if a youngster seems to have the stuff for a V.Q. we usually try to send him off when he's about thirteen years old and about to become a man (or gal as the case may be). We usually have him build his own catamaran and sail it out into the Atlantic Ocean a couple hundred miles without food and water and see what happens.

Usually something does. Sometimes, of course, the youngster never returns. We figure the Gods know what they're doing and simply decided to cut their losses. Most of those who do make it back (and it took one kid four years – he sailed to England) have some sort of vision or other. 'Course occasionally a boy comes back all hepped up and bursting with himself and announces he's had a vision, a vision that the Raiders are going to beat the Cowboys in the Superbowl by two touchdowns. It's tough to convince the kid right off that he might have had a more productive vision, so all the navigator can do in a case like that is bet a bundle on the Raiders and chalk the kid off as probably doomed to become a human.

Other kids come back with visions that they can't make head nor tail of and it's up to the navigator to interpret them. It's a tough job. It takes practice and patience and centredness and spirituality and the ability to really throw the bull. In the twenty years I was navigator before Wim went on his Vision Quest I only knew two or three Montauks who the Gods said anything special to or gave interesting tasks. One had a vision that said he was to spend his whole life creating beauty and, by gum, he's doing it. You may well have seen his work, but of course you didn't know it at the time. He just goes around the world rearranging things a little wherever he goes so that things are in a bit better balance, more harmonious. He straightens pictures on walls, tears down ugly posters and ads, picks things up off the sidewalks and stuff like that. Creates more beauty in a day than some artists do in a year.

Anyway, I knew from the two Hints that Wim needed to go on a Vision Quest. 'Course I figured Wim was no longer a Montauk, and I'd never sent a human being out on a Vision Quest, but I knew now that that's what I had to do. I didn't know what would happen or what he'd find, but I figured I had to risk it before he became hopelessly human and beyond seeing visions.

The morning after my dream I told Wide Pool we were sailing back to Long Island to see Wim. She nodded and went to prepare for our long sail by borrowing a bathing suit. The Gods naturally hadn't touched my catamaran with their hurricane, though they turned all the other Montauk boats into kindling wood. So by mid afternoon we'd loaded up the boat and I'd given some sound spiritual advice to the remaining Montauks. It took me about an hour, but essentially all I said was the old Montauk

114

philosophy passed down since forever: 'Whatever you do, don't do anything.' They all nodded and yawned, and then Wide Pool and I cast off.

Three days later we pulled in next to her old barge.

And there was Wim.

He rushed out into the water and hugged his mum and hugged me and, like a typical human, began blubbering and laughing and generally acting as if something were happening. He was dressed in nice neat jeans and a football jersey with 'Gulls' on the front and '6' on the back. He'd growed quite a bit in four years. He must of been about five feet high though still shorter than his mum, but he looked big to us. He still had those large pool-like eyes, and even if he was a human he hadn't lost that strange glow about him.

Well, Wim claimed he hadn't been back to the old barge in two or three years, but 'just felt like it' that afternoon. 'Course, his being there was what we call an Accident. An Accident is an accident or coincidence that smells fishy, or 'goddy' as Little Pebble called it. Two Hints and an Accident is getting dangerously close to a Poke so I took Wim aside as fast as I could and told him he was going on a Vision Quest.

It took me a while to explain about sailing out into the Atlantic without food or water to see what would happen, and when I finished he wasn't looking too cheery.

'What will happen is that I'll starve to death,' he finally said.

'Could be,' I said. 'But you got to give it a try.'

'You're sure?'

'Yep.'

'I don't think Coach Cannonball will let me miss this Saturday's game.'

'Yep. Fuck Coach Cannonball.'

'And I've got my first physics test next week.'

'Yep. Fuck physics.'

'I have to go?'

'Deep down, so far out of sight neither of us can see it right now, you're a Montauk, and the Gods just ordered you to report for duty.'

'Wow. I never thought of it that way.'

'Yep. Now go get to work on your catamaran.'

Well, it took him a few hours, but by then I could see he was pleased as a seagull behind a garbage barge about going on a quest. He still loved to build boats and loved to sail, and, being human, he didn't have the foggiest about how serious this Vision business can be. And he had no more fear of sailing out into the Atlantic on some flimsy homemade boat without food and fresh water than a flea does on the backside of a bull.

It's up to the seeker to decide how to build his own catamaran, but for most of two thousand years we been building them of wood and fibre and hemp and animal skins stitched together with rat-gut. But poor Wim, after four years at the Bests, even though tradition required that he couldn't buy anything, went and built a twentieth-century catamaran out of junk.

For his two hulls he lashed sixteen empty beer kegs together with wire and aluminium bars from old deckchairs and some old iron bars from a jungle gym. To hide the mess and muffle the racket the beer kegs made when sailing he wrapped them in the rubber undermatting of some old carpet. He used two old cast-iron plumbing pipes three inches in diameter for his two crossbeams to join the two beer-keg hulls. Billy Best let him have a worn trampoline canvas for his platform, and he borrowed his high school flag pole for his mast, staying it with telephone wire, the telephone wire having been carelessly left between two poles. He used a torn parachute for his spinnaker, an old shop awning for his storm jib, and sewed together a lot of nylon and polyester pieces of clothing he'd noticed in the Bests' attic as his mainsail.

Four days later when he was done he showed it to me.

It was the most disgusting catamaran I ever saw. I figured the whole south shore of Long Island was doomed since when the Gods got a good look at that contraption sailing out on their sea they would surely cook up the biggest hurricane in history and turn Wim's catamaran into the rubble it once was.

So I wasn't feeling too cheery when I went down with Wim to the bay the next day to see him off. Fact is, I was ready to tell him that the Vision Quest was cancelled, that I'd gotten new orders from the Great Spirit that he was to spend the rest of his life on land. But when that thought came to me the arthritis in my knees exploded into pain and I knew the damn Gods were bugging my thoughts. When the Gods got something they think they want you to do there's not a thing you can do about it except take a crap and get down to business.

'Wim,' I said, 'may the Great Spirit guide you and bless you with a great vision.'

'Thank you, Grain-of-Sand,' he said, looking up at me bright-eyed and raring to go. 'I can sail any place I feel like?'

'That's right.' Knowing Wim I figured he'd probably head for Antarctica, that being the farthest and least desirable place I could think of.

'I wish you could come with me,' he said, looking just a touch sad.

'Now that's a nice thought,' I replied, thinking it was the most horrifying thought I'd heard in years. 'But the Great Spirit has to test you alone. What's that you got under your windbreaker?'

'Oh, that,' said Wim, flushing, and for a second I thought he might be trying to sneak some food aboard. 'That's my social studies homework for the next three months. Mrs Stockman was nice enough to give it to me and wish me a long voyage.'

'You got to leave that human stuff behind,' I said sharply. 'Ain't no way the Gods going to give you even the smallest

Peek if you're carrying along a lot of crap about how Columbus discovered America and the Indians created turkeys so the white man could have Thanksgiving and watch the Green Bay Packers play the Lions ...'

'I'm sorry,' Wim said and pulled out a bundle of papers and a book and handed them to me.

'You got to remember you're gonna be a Montauk again, not a human, and on this voyage – the Gods willing – you'll see you weren't put on this earth to play football and learn the multiplication tables.'

'Yes, sir.'

He looked so ashamed of himself I felt a little guilty and so I leaned over and gave him a hug. 'Well, time to see if this junkheap floats. Get aboard and I'll push you off.'

The thought of sailing cheered him up immediately and he leapt on to the trampoline, grabbed the oar handle that was his tiller and looked back at me with a smile.

I frowned. When he went forward and raised his awning jib and patchwork mainsail I scowled. When the wind caught the sails and pulled the damn thing off the shallows and away, and the beer kegs began clammering I put wrinkles on my scowl. Then something whizzed past my legs and splashed into the water and I saw his damn dog Arf paddling away like a drowning rat out towards the slowly sailing catamaran. Wim saw him and looked at me guiltily when he slowed the boat and helped Arf up on to the trampoline. I consulted my arthritis and it seemed that since Arf wasn't human he was permitted to go along.

Damned if Wim's contraption didn't sail to beat the band. The last thing I saw of him he was seated up on the starboard beer kegs, clothesline in his teeth to control the jib, another around his wrist to control the mainsail, one hand on the tiller and the other trying to keep Arf from sliding off, and that old catamaran was sizzling through the water like the Gods were towing it behind one of their speedboats. The last thing I heard was the loudest most dismal most despairing roar of a wounded tiger I ever heard. And then they were gone.

Shuffling back up the beach I thought that the Gods surely had a funny way of running the universe and began to examine the horizon to see when the hurricane would be coming.

WIM AND THE WHITE MAN'S BURDEN

They will call it lies, but every word of these stories has been passed down from generation to generation, each story kept as sacred as the stool of the Gods. That many are true even the liars admit.

Wim we call Him, Wim we have always called Him, He of Many Chances, He who freed us from the white man's burden.

My mother told me stories of Wim before I was old enough to walk. My father, Run-of-the-Mill, told me stories of Wim whenever we would go hunting together for a used car or a second-hand refrigerator, and my grandfather, Pete Smith, would every Saturday gather around him outside his shack off the Sunrise Highway all the children of the neighbourhood and tell us of his own adventures with Wim and teach us some of Wim's games that would permit him to win pennies from us.

For me Wim has always been freedom, and because he is freedom the human beings have always condemned all stories and legends and facts about him as lies. For we non-humans this condemnation is reassuring. What conflict we would face if Wim were accepted too by our enemies. We would then fear we had been tricked again.

– from the preface to *Sixty-six Parables of Wim*

19

Our Beloved Wim had no idea what to expect sailing around Montauk Point and out into the Atlantic on his vision quest. After the first exhilaration of being out on the sea had worn off he began to have all the worries any ordinary human would have about sailing out into the ocean alone without charts, radar, Loran, depthfinder, auxiliary power, ship-to-shore radio, short-wave, fishfinder, refrigeration or reliable crew. His supplies were limited too, being without food and water. He also found the idea of a vision quest a little weird. What was the star quarterback of the Maganansett Gulls doing sailing out into the Atlantic? Billy hadn't found it a very reasonable thing to do, especially since the only reason Wim could give was that an old Indian said he should.

He was glad to have Arf aboard as someone to talk to, but Arf didn't look too happy, so he let him eat the six Reggie bars Billy Best had talked him into sneaking aboard, and when it rained – as it did each morning between seven and eight for the entire time he was at sea – Wim let Arf have first sip from the trampoline where he captured what water he could.

The wind blew him out the first two days when he was supposed to sail directly out and then, when he was free to sail where he wanted, it shifted a hundred and eighty degrees and began blowing him back towards land. By this time Wim was excited and afraid and determined to do just what Grain-of-Sand expected. That meant drinking only if the Gods saw fit to send down some rain and eating only if they saw fit to let him figure out a way to catch fish or seagulls.

He had discovered a new method of navigation more accurate than Loran since Arf's nose always – rain or shine, fog or night – pointed directly back at Maganansett Beach.

But that's not where the wind seemed to blow him or where he found himself wanting to go. Instead he went more to the west, and on the fourth day awoke at dawn to see huge buildings poking up at the sky and big freighters all around. He knew from watching television that this was New York City and was excited that the Gods were sending him to such an important place. Since he'd caught plenty of fish and it kept raining he hadn't had any visions yet. Arf didn't like fish and seemed to be having plenty of visions if his moans when sleeping were any clue. Wim guessed Arf's visions didn't count though.

They sailed right past Manhattan and up the Hudson River. Wim found he just didn't feel like landing. Or rather the one time he did – he decided poor Arf had to have something to eat before he either starved or visioned himself to death – and steered his boat towards shore, the wind shifted and made it impossible. His boat was very fast, but whenever he tried to go to land the beer kegs would get to vibrating so much he was afraid the boat would break apart. So he sailed on.

He sailed a whole day up the Hudson, and he'd never seen anything so beautiful. The mountains to the west sometimes came right down to the river and the colours of the autumn leaves were almost as spectacular as his mainsail. He even liked the occasional train on the railroad tracks along both banks of the river: it seemed so puny from the middle of the water that the mountains seemed even grander. Arf seemed to feel better now that he could see land, even if every time Wim tried to steer towards it the wind would shift and blow them back.

On the afternoon of the second day up the river, when they were in a lonely, narrow stretch where the wooded hills came right down to the water, big blubbery black clouds began to roll in, darkening the sky. The wind began to gust, blowing them towards the western shore. Though Wim tried to keep his boat headed up the river the wind was too quick and too smart. It kept pushing his little boat towards the rocky shore. Rain began pelting his face, his mainsail began flogging so badly he had to lower it, and an aft beer keg broke loose and floated away. He was beginning to feel frightened when, several seconds after a brilliant white flash of lightning, he heard the thunder speak.

A long, heavy, carefully worded rumble of thudthud-thuds tumbled along the top of the world, and Wim, kneeling on the trampoline of his cat as it neared the shore, suddenly had a frightening feeling that the thunder was trying to speak to him.

Fearful and uncertain, he let his boat be blown on to the rocky shore. When it had scrunched and clonked to a halt and he had tied down the sails, Wim jumped off and waded ashore, Arf following. He stood for a moment under the turbulent hissing leaves of the big maples that lined the bank, listening for the next loud announcement from the sky. Zzzsst!! went the lightning and then BOOM!! tumble rumble bump bump boom thudda boom thudda boom.

Although he didn't quite understand what the words were saying, the thunder *was* trying to speak to him. He was sure of it.

As Wim huddled down in the fallen leaves beside the trunk of a tree, Arf slithered along under the leaves to huddle next to him. But noise wasn't a vision, was it? Wim wondered. Was it possible the Gods might speak instead of show?

Wim slowly stood up, brushed off a few leaves, stared up at the big, dark bulging clouds which tumbled across the sky above him, and waited for the next call. Arf pushed his nose out from the leaves, looked longingly back at the catamaran, and then disappeared again into his camouflage. A great flickering of white light filled the afternoon gloom for several seconds and then vanished. Five seconds later the call came: bump bump rumble thudda dhamada tathata boom bump.

Whatever the thunder was trying to say Wim couldn't yet understand, but he felt that if he could get nearer he would. His ninth-grade teacher had once told him that the thunder was actually the noise made by men bowling in the mountains, but Grain-of-Sand once told a story that said it was a God trying to clear his throat.

In any case Wim began climbing, but after a few steps stopped to call his faithful dog. Arf poked his nose out, looked around and finally began moving, but so close to the earth and with such a covering of leaves balanced on his back that Wim could see no more of him than of a snake slinking along. The only flaw in the mobile leaf-pile was a six-inch spotted tail suddenly emerging straight up and oscillating back and forth twice before sinking again beneath the sea of leaves, like a submarine's periscope withdrawing.

As they climbed up through the woods Wim looked back and saw far below the silver-grey Hudson and his little catamaran nudged into the shore. Although it made him feel sad and frightened to leave it, he kept walking on. A heavy cloudbank had settled around the mountain he was climbing so that its highest parts were obscured. Even as the wind began to blow in angrier bursts and rain to fall and the thunder to speak yet more loudly, Wim walked determinedly upwards towards the sky, Arf slinking along a few yards behind.

They hiked for at least an hour, Wim sliding and slipping on the mud hidden under the cover of leaves, water pouring in cold rivulets down his face and back. The lightning was exploding in terrific flashes, followed immediately by the DHAMADA BAM DAAM Boom DAMmadamboomduddaboom, loud and fierce and seemingly only a few feet away, but still not quite saying anything Wim could understand. Tired, Wim finally stopped in a little clearing. Zzzzztcchowww!! went the lightning and DHAMADA BAM Tathata Boombumpadumbuddaboom went the thunder, and even as Wim strained all his energy on hearing, he saw standing in front of him a giant bear. The bear – like Winnie-the-Pooh only about thirty-six times larger – was looking down at him like some vaguely disapproving father.

Wim believed that the secret of dealing with animals, a secret he had learned from Billy's comic books, was not to seem afraid. He stood before the bear with as much imposing dignity as he could marshal and said as casually as he could: 'Hi. My name is Wim.' He had never seen a bear in the rain before, and though it looked as big as he had imagined bears to be (rather bigger, in fact) it looked a little bedraggled, its fur matted with mud along its right leg and side.

'And this is my faithful dog Arf,' he added and turned to indicate Arf, who was, however, invisible and motionless someplace beneath the leaves. The bear didn't deign to glance towards where Wim indicated but instead lumbered in rolling strides towards the little boy, reached down with his gigantic paws – like those of King Kong, Wim noted with increasing fear – and picked up Wim bodily eight feet into the air, holding him opposite the bear's nose.

'I'm light,' Wim said, trying to act calm and not frighten the bear.

'And bony,' he added when he saw the bear's teeth suddenly emerge from between the parting red lips like white cannon appearing abruptly in the side of a pirate ship.

The bear frowned and then drew Wim right up against

the tip of his nose so that Wim's eyes were staring into the fierce red eyes of the bear only four inches away.

'I'm trying to find the thunder,' Wim continued desperately. 'You don't happen to know where it is, do you?'

The bear again frowned as if in concentration. A flash of lightning sheeted the sky behind him, and after two or three seconds the thunder rumbled out its message: Dhamadatathatadumbuddhadumbuddhadumbumboom. The bear, as if still in deep thought, slowly lowered Wim to the earth, loosened the grip of his claws and, with his ungainly lumbering wobble, began moving away from Wim into the forest, shaking his head as he went.

Wim swayed in place for several seconds and then toppled sideways, evoking from the leaves the despairing helpless roar of a wounded tiger. The familiar sound of Arf reoriented Wim, and Wim's turning out to be only Wim revived Arf, and they spent the next minute hugging and licking each other respectfully.

When Wim finally stood up again, the storm was moving off, and the words of the thunder were becoming more muffled. With the sun setting behind a distant range of mountains and the rain beginning to fall harder, Wim was cold, wet and hungry. After hiking back down the mountain for half an hour he noticed a boulder jutting out over a ledge to form a small cave. He and Arf crawled under the shelter, curled up together on some dry pine needles back against the deepest part and, shivering, stared out at the retreating storm and gathering night. They stared and shivered and stared and shivered until blackness and silence drowned them both. They slept.

'Potato chips, Sonny?'

The voice came so much as part of his dream world that Wim found himself staring at the old man squatting in front of him for at least fifteen seconds before he realized that he was probably awake.

'Beg pardon?' asked Wim, lifting his head off the pine needles.

'How long you been here?' the man asked, scratching his chest right through the long full beard which sprouted downwards from his chin like a white mop.

'Last night, I guess,' Wim replied, stretching a leg and sitting up against the boulder. The sun was shining, and the only sign of the storm was the drip drip drip from the top of the ledge on to the rockface and pine needles beside him.

'Potato chips?' the old man asked again, stretching forth with his bony fingers a torn and seemingly empty cellophane bag.

'Er, no thanks,' Wim replied. 'I'm not supposed to eat between meals.' He didn't think he should mention fasting.

'Nice storm, wasn't it?' the old man went on. He was dressed in patched and tattered clothing, and as he talked he nibbled on the tiny crumbs he seemed able to dig out of the cellophane container.

'It was loud,' Wim answered.

'Thunder gets that way when it's trying to say something,' the old man said, chewing. He had to wipe his mouth with the back of his hand, and Wim noticed potato chip crumbs in his beard.

'It *does*?' Wim asked, sitting up straighter and putting a hand on Arf, who had awakened and let out a long, low tiger-growl.

The old man squinted at Arf for a moment and then turned back to Wim. 'It was a real chatterbox last night.'

'You heard it speaking?'

'Yep.'

'What was it saying?'

The old man wiped his mouth and then spat sloppily off into the pine needles to his right. 'Don't really know,' he said, looking back at Wim. 'Damn thunder spoke in Sanskrit.'

'Beg pardon?'

127

'In Sanskrit. It's a language you don't hear bandied about much any more. Can't say I ever picked it up.'

'But ...'

'Learned a few words once in India, that's how I knew what the thunder was doing, but damned if I could put it all together.'

'In sandspit,' echoed Wim doubtfully.

'Only words I was sure of were "Tathata" and "Dhammada".'

When the old man spoke the words they both sounded just like the sounds Wim remembered hearing in the thunder the night before. 'I see,' said Wim, not seeing. '"Tathata" and "Damdaddy".'

'Yep,' the old man sighed. 'And the thunder sure did repeat himself last night.'

'But what do the words mean?'

The old man stopped nibbling on the potato chips and set the empty bag down between himself and Wim. He turned to look out into the forest. 'Yep, yep, all right,' he mumbled and, turning back to Wim, said: 'Well, they sorta mean somepin like "Ultimate Truth" and "Quest".'

Wim looked blankly at the old man. A wind came up and made the pine branches sigh. 'I see,' said Wim.

'That sorta means ... "what's what" and "having a good look around".'

'I see.'

'Together they sorta mean "have a good look 'round for what's what".'

'I see.'

'"Course, damned if I can remember if they actually came together.'

'Look around for ... for Ultimate Truth,' Wim repeated carefully.

'That's good, Sonny. You gotta good mind.'

'I get "B+"s in maths,' Wim said.

'Well, guess that 'counts for it.'

'Did ... did the thunder seem to be speaking to *you*?' Wim asked.

'Oh, no,' said the old man. 'It spoke to me once or twice about sixty years ago, but ain't even bothered to swear at me since.'

'Who ... who was it talking to?'

'Yep, well, I don't know. But somebody around here. Thunder don't get ka-booming about with all that fuss in these hills unless it's talking to somebody mighty close.'

'I see,' said Wim, feeling very pleased and honoured. '"Look around real good for Ultimate Truth",' he repeated.

'Yep,' said the old man.

The two of them sat in silence for two or three minutes until finally Wim said politely: 'But it doesn't *mean* anything.'

'Bit abstract, gotta admit,' said the old man.

'*Does* it mean anything?'

'Oh, well, couldn't say. Old Ultimate Truth doesn't mean anything. It's something you sorta *see*.'

'But ...' began Wim uncertainly, frowning and scratching Arf's ear absent-mindedly. 'But ... but why should I go on a quest to find Ultimate Truth? What good will it do me?'

The old man leaned back on his haunches and frowned, his crooked teeth wet with saliva. 'That's what they all ask,' he said.

'I mean you seem to be saying I should start spending my life looking for old Ultimate Truth and then some day I'll see it and what will I have? Nothing!'

'That about sums it up, I suppose,' said the old man gloomily. 'But look, Sonny, people been setting off looking for Ultimate Truth for thousands of years, and when some of 'em found it, they seemed to feel it was a big deal.'

'Maybe it was just their long looking that made it seem important,' suggested Wim.

'That's pretty good, little fella, pretty good. But that ain't quite all there is to it.' The old man didn't go on, but sat staring directly with large watery eyes at Wim.

'Well then,' said Wim bravely, 'what else is there to it?'

The old man stared at him fiercely, his hand trembling as he raised it to wipe saliva from his lips and beard. Finally he leaned forward until his red eyes were only a foot from Wim's.

'It's a secret,' he said in a hoarse whisper.

Wim stared back defiantly.

'Big deal,' he said. 'I don't believe you.'

The old man blinked once and sniffed. 'Well,' he said in his soft, hoarse voice, 'if you don't believe me I suppose it won't do no harm to tell you.' He glanced sharply over his left shoulder into the woods and then lowered his face yet closer to Wim's.

'Ultimate Truth is the only cure,' he whispered in a voice so low that only its fierce intensity let Wim hear it. The man's eyes were now just inches from Wim's and seemed in the cloud-like haze of the old man's face like two huge disembodied planets burning redly.

'Cure for what?' Wim whispered back, feeling for the first time frightened.

'U.T. is the only cure for what we all got,' the old man whispered sharply.

'Wha ... what we all got?' Wim whispered back.

'The sickness,' the old man hissed.

Our Beloved Wim felt himself tremble violently as if he'd been shocked by an electric current. Bravely he still stared into the red-rivered planets of the old man's eyes.

'*What* sickness?' Wim whispered.

'What we all get the moment we're born,' the old man answered hoarsely. 'The sickness ...'

'But *what* sickness?' Wim insisted again, shivering with cold and fright.

'*The* sickness. The only one we got, the only one we need to have to ruin everything.'

Wim stared in silence at the glimmering red eyes inches

away from him. 'The sickness ...' he echoed hollowly, feeling a strange gloom.

'And Ultimate Truth is the cure,' the old man said less intensely, as if satisfied that Wim finally understood. 'The *only* cure,' he added.

'Have I got the sickness?' Wim asked abruptly, feeling a rock jabbing into his back where he was pressing away from the old man against the cave wall.

''Course you do,' the old man answered softly. 'You're human, ain't you?'

Wim flushed. 'I'm not sure,' he said. 'I guess so.'

'Well, you are,' the old man said confidently.

Wim brooded on the implications of all he was hearing. 'But then everybody's got the sickness,' he finally exclaimed. 'Even Montauks.'

'Shh,' hissed the old man. 'I told you this is all a secret.' His bony fingers were clutching Wim's arm at the wrist.

'But ... but ...' Wim began uncertainly. 'Why ... why is it a secret?'

'Part of the sickness is not knowin' you're sick,' the old man said softly.

'Wow,' said Wim.

'Yep.'

'But ... what are the symptoms?' Wim asked.

The old man looked nervously over his shoulder.

'Human behaviour,' he replied.

'But ...'

'You seen a man get a bit testy ... a woman bitchy?'

'I guess so.'

'The sickness ...' the old man whispered confidentially. 'You seen a boy get mad 'cause he didn't win?'

'Sure. Why, Billy –'

'The sickness. You seen a daddy be unfair and nasty?'

'Why, I got hundreds –'

'The sickness,' concluded the old man, and he leaned away from Wim at last. 'Wars, hatred, greed, bitchiness, starvation, unfairness, cruelty – you name it – just another symptom of the sickness.'

'Wow,' said Wim. 'But still, what *is* the sickness?'

'Well, if we knew, we'd cure it,' replied the old man amiably. 'But we don't know, so we just die of it.'

Wim sat silently for several minutes, idly scratching Arf's ear and eliciting a low purr. What the old man was telling him didn't make life seem too good.

Then the old man lowered his head again and whispered intensely: 'You find Ultimate Truth, you find the only cure.'

Wim stared at him.

'And then I could save everybody!' he exclaimed.

'Didn't say that,' replied the old man. 'Just said it's the only cure.'

'But if I get cured and I know what the cure is, then I can become a doctor and at least try to save everybody.'

'Oh sure. Almost everyone who finally bumps into U.T. and gets cured comes back and tries to help others. It's one of the symptoms of being cured.'

Wim sat still for a long time thinking of all that the old man had told him. His life that had seemed so lazy and fun with his mother and so confused and troublesome in school seemed now to be exciting and purposeful. He supposed this must have something to do with his Vision Quest and felt that this was an important moment in his life, equal to the time last month when he had scored six touchdowns against Babylon.

'My name is Wim,' he now announced with dignity to the old man. 'What's your name?'

The old man shook his head. 'Damned if I know. I forgot mine eight or nine years ago.'

'But everybody has a name.'

'I know, I know, but once you get used to being without one it's sorta nice.'

'I like being Wim.'

'That's fine. Don't blame you one bit.'

'What do your friends call you?'

'Yep. My friends aren't very talkative. They just sorta don't call me anything.'

'Huh,' said Wim.

'Yep.'

'My mother has a name.'

'Don't blame her one bit.'

'And so do most of my daddies.'

'Good men, every one, I'm sure.'

'Can I call you something?' asked Wim.

'Well, now, I don't know ...' The old man scowled. 'It might not hurt too much, I guess, but ...'

Wim thought very hard.

'Hank!' he announced.

'Hank!' the old man snorted back. 'Great jumpin' thunder, a million names to pick from – Krishna, Lucifer, Siddhartha, Lao-Tse, Tonto, billions even – and you fix me with "Hank".' He seemed quite upset.

'But ... but "Hank" ...'

'Shit!' the old man said loudly. 'You ought to be careful before you nail a name like that on to a body.'

'I'm sorry.'

'Well, pull it out, it hurts.'

'Beg pardon?'

'Take your "Hank" and put it back where it came from.'

'I will. I'm sorry.'

The old man stood up. His bony fingers trembled and he was chewing now on his beard.

'Seven, eight years I been walkin' free as a bird, and then you come along and ... "Hank!" Oh Lordy, Lordy.'

'I've taken it back!' Wim said, feeling almost like crying.

'Don't do no good. It's stuck in too far.' He groaned once and then with a limp moved off into the forest, leaving only the empty cellophane bag behind.

Wim shouted after him, 'I'm sorry!' but the old man was gone.

WIM NEEDS TO GO

One of the unusual characteristics of Wim's ashram after he became a teacher was that he always encouraged his disciples to challenge him. Wim felt that only by such continual prodding could both he and others stay free from religious humbug.

One day he was visiting some new buildings in a new centre. At one point as he was wandering down a hall alone he was forced to ask a disciple: 'Where can I find a bathroom?'

'O Wise One,' answered the disciple with a smile. 'Merely look within the astral plane and you shall surely see.'

'I have looked,' Wim said promptly. 'And I assure you there are no bathrooms on the astral plane.'

– from *Sixty-six Parables of Wim*

20

from Grain-of-Sand's *Memoirs of an Old Liar*, pp. 188–96

The day Wim got back from his Vision Quest he scrunched his junkheap catamaran back up on the beach and rushed to tell me all about the bear and the thunder and an old man who'd told him some wild story about a god yelling at him in Sanskrit.

Well, as navigator I know young Montauks have had a lot of fishy visions over the centuries, but I never knew one that claimed the Gods spoke in Sanskrit. Gods have spoken Montauk since the first day of creation and it didn't seem likely that they'd switch now. As for going on a quest for something called ultimate truth, I was sure it was a misunderstanding or a trick. First of all there aren't any words in Montauk for 'ultimate truth' or enlightenment or salvation or things like that: those are all words made up by humans. Montauks might go on quests for a vision or a swordfish or a deer or a lost stone, but for ultimate truth? Montauks don't take much stock in things you can't see and smell and touch and eat.

'Course all that business about the sickness weren't nothing new. Montauks have known about the human sickness for three thousand years, but as far as we've been able to tell there ain't no cure. Every now and then a human has a spontaneous remission of his symptoms and becomes a Montauk, but we've never been able to see why it happens.

So I made Wim tell his story again and again, figuring the Great Spirit must have had something in mind and it was my job to figure out what. The bear shaking his head was clearly a big deal but I couldn't quite get my fingernails on what kind of a big deal. The potato chips were certainly important – them you could eat – but Wim didn't think so. The fact that Wim named the old man 'Hank' must have meant something, but damned if I could figure what.

So Wim told and retold his story that afternoon, all the time itching to get at his search. And I pondered and thunk and hemmed and hawed, wanting to lasso in his blind passion for searching for ultimate truth, but I just couldn't come up with nothing. I thought of making up some crap about Dhammada actually being the Sanskrit word for 'Beautiful Lie' so Wim would get back to working on his being able to fib, but I couldn't do it. I finally decided if Wim thought he was supposed to search for ultimate truth – and I couldn't see what else his Vision Quest meant – then the Gods must have wanted him to go on a wild goose chase. I figured it must have something to do with tricking Wim into becoming a Montauk again. The search seemed a waste of time and talent, but one thing I've learned over the years is that when the Gods got something really important on their Minds, you can be pretty sure it'll seem stupid to most humans. And sometimes even to navigators.

And so Wim started his big search for u.t. He didn't have too clear an idea what his ultimate truth would look like but seemed to feel that if he was lucky enough to stumble on it he'd know. He figured it would have to be something he hadn't seen before so he began by checking out the junk in the Bests' attic. Scrounging through the things that had been stored there over the years, he found a great many things he'd never laid eyes on before, and he asked himself about each one: 'Can this be Ultimate Truth?' Under a dusty curtain he found an empty birdcage and stared at it, his brow etched with its two exclamation marks of concentration, but nothing clicked. From an old trunk he pulled out thirty or so back issues of *Life* magazine, old razors, rusty coathangers, sieved sweaters, odd slippers, an old potty and a small barbell, but none of this junk seemed to qualify as ultimate truth either. He found an old photograph book with pictures of buffalo being marched into a building and coming out the other side as blankets and mink coats, some reindeer antlers with paintings of Niagara Falls on them, some postcards with naked men and women wrestling, a man's hairpiece, four old transistor radios and three comic books.

Wim's first big run at u.t. came grinding to a crawl on page one of 'SuperAvenger and the Masked Neutron-Man', and was totally stuck by the time he'd finished 'The Incredible Hulk Meets the Red Sky-Rider on the Gravity-Free Planet Urlh'! Next thing he knew, Wim told me, he was making himself a sandwich and was deep into a long fantasy about becoming the world's first gravity-free human by living on an exclusive diet of peanut butter and jelly and helium. When he realized how he'd failed the thunder, he wanted to march back to look into some more trunks but decided he really ought to know a little bit more about what he was looking for. Maybe if he learned Sanskrit and saw what the Sanskrittens had had to say about the size and colour of ultimate truth, he might get some hints. He licked the last of the peanut butter off his chin and proudly put the 'Incredible Hulk' in the waste basket. The next day he would ask his Spanish teacher to begin teaching him Sanskrit, and if she couldn't do it, he'd go to the very top – the Latin teacher.

Well, going to humans in a quest for anything is always a dumb thing to do, and I discouraged him every way I could. But you know Wim: if there was a weird way to do something, he always found it.

And those first days he was so hot for finding his ultimate truth he could no more listen to me than if I were an announcer on the TV talking about deodorants. Enough to give a man a 'feriority complex.

And over the next few months he had his big wide dark innocent eyes so zeroed in on old u.t. he couldn't see elephant poo in front of him if it were dumptruck high. Ain't no wonder then that during this time he got a lot of you-know-what on his shoes.

21

from The Gospel According to Luke ...

Thanks to Wim's remarkable facility at learning new languages, within a month he had read twenty or thirty of the ancient vedas, the *Upanishads*, the *Bhagavad-Gita*, and Patanjali's Yoga Sutras, and thus had begun to see clearly that ultimate truth was obscure and a tough thing to find. When he'd told his Spanish teacher he wanted to learn Sanskrit she had referred him to the French teacher who had referred him to the librarian who had referred him to the social worker who had told him to stop playing games and get back to learning 'Buenas tardes, niño'. It was Billy who told him that if he wanted to read dirty books the place to go was the library at the university in Southampton. There, a mere ten-mile hike, Wim found a librarian who found nothing startling about a small quarterback wanting to read Hindu classics in the original.

So he began. Unfortunately, the more he read the less he remembered about *why* he was reading. It seemed the Sanskrittens had a lot of trouble seeing u.t. clearly too, so had developed all sorts of yogas to help their eyesight. The Buddhists seemed to do the same thing. Although most of what he read was rather blurry and boring, Wim was fascinated by Patanjali's sutras on yoga, which seemed to promise all sorts of powers if he could just do a few tricky things to his mind and body. Although a lot of this was tough to translate, such discipline seemed to involve things like breathing in slow motion, standing on his head, scratching his left ear with his right big toe, licking the tip of his nose with his tongue, flexing his anal muscles and

139

concentrating his mind on one of seven centres that seemed to be scattered up and down the body like Christmas-tree lights.

After he'd worked hard for two weeks Wim was able to develop himself to the point where he was able to breathe only once every eight and a half minutes while standing on his head scratching his left ear with his right big toe while licking the tip of his nose with his tongue and flexing his anal muscles concentrating all the time on a spot south-southeast of his liver, but it was tough. And it didn't seem to have too many immediate practical uses.

And there were a lot of other exercises he couldn't do. He couldn't break a two-by-four with his 'abdominable muscles', nor stand erect on one toe for more than eleven seconds, nor twist his body and neck around so that his head and feet were both facing forward while his belly button was aimed to the rear, nor reach his tongue to his anus in order to cleanse it after a bowel movement.

Wim feared that it might be these failures that were blocking both his search for u.t. (on those occasions when he remembered it) and his development of those extraordinary powers which Patanjali hinted at. Wim was particularly interested in being able to levitate, so that he could sleep in mid-air and feel almost as nice as when he used to sleep on his catamaran in the bilge of his mum's barge, and thus not even have to make up his bed in the morning. He also wanted to be able to read another person's mind so that he could get the answers to all questions on tests in school simply by tuning in to either the teacher or Billy Best, and in being able to exude an odour of roses like the great yogi Yaniprajna, so that Dawn would like him better than Billy, who she said smelled like lemonade.

But things never quite worked out right for Our Beloved Wim. He did reach the point where he could levitate his whole body about nine inches off the ground, but he found that when he fell asleep in that position he immediately crashed to the floor. Worse yet, on at least two occasions when he had managed to raise himself up nine inches and was concentrating ferociously on getting higher, he suddenly fell to the ceiling, crashing there with tremendous force, and thus lost his concentration and fell back eight feet to the floor. Nine inches seemed to be his safe operating limit. Though he could hold the position for hours, he found trying to sleep that way was chilly unless he pulled a blanket over himself and then if he fell asleep he collapsed anyway.

Wim also managed to develop the ability to pick up other people's thoughts, but in class he found that the only pupils' thoughts he could read were those of students who still got 6 when they subtracted 9 from 17, and who recognized New York as the capital of the nation. He could read his teacher's mind too, but whenever she'd give a test he discovered she would be thinking about some man named Brad and his Corvette and underclothing and a lot of boring body stuff that didn't even identify Washington, D.C.

When he finally began to put out an odour just as Patanjali promised, it smelled awfully nice to Wim but not quite like a rose. When he asked Dawn about it she said she thought his smell came from his sleeping with Arf after the dog had gotten into some decomposing fish.

After a while Wim dropped his passionate search for *power* and had begun to try for sunyata, the void. According to the sutras, if he just meditated correctly he would be able to know the Void or Emptiness, which sounded suspiciously at times like a disguise for old ultimate truth. The Sanskrittens were often fuzzy in their use of terms, and Wim was never clear about the differences between dhammada and tathata and sunyata and prajna, certain only that they were all good guys. Sometimes after reading a long sutra filled with such terms he'd feel as if everything – all the terms and even everything he'd seen in the attic –

everything was Ultimate Truth if he'd just look at it right. But he just couldn't seem to get the hang of looking.

Of course, Wim tried to hide his obsession with u.t. from the Bests and his school and his friends, but it was tough. When he would stand up in biology class and ask 'What is life?' it seemed to old Mr Thompson that the question was no more out of left field than the previous year's question of 'Why are snails snails?' His American history teacher found his quest-produced question 'Why don't politicians care about truth?' no more relevant than his asking in September: 'How come the Battle of the Little Big Horn isn't a national holiday?' His maths teacher found 'How can I get to infinity?' on a par with Wim's earlier 'How can I programme a heart into my Commodore 64 computer?'

Wim also decided that to concentrate on u.t. he'd have to give up football. It was a tough choice, since he'd found that football players tend to attract friends, while pursuers of ultimate truth tended to repel them, but he decided that he had to do it.

When he informed Coach Cannonball of his decision the Coach indicated he felt Wim's decision might possibly be unwise.

'You get your fucking ass to practice this afternoon or I'll tie your legs together and have every defensive lineman on the squad key on you every play until you find your u.t. as ridiculous an idea as every other red-blooded man finds it.'

Wim decided that under the circumstances he would continue football for a while, but on the football field his play became a little more erratic than usual. Still, having Wim throw three straight interceptions was a hazard Coach Cannonball had long before resigned himself to in order to savour the look on the opposing coach's face when Wim would zig, zag and zip for two or three minutes behind the line of scrimmage and then loft a seventy-yard pass to Billy Best who had snuck into the left corner of the end zone after the defensive backs had gotten bored of running in circles.

Ultimately, of course, Wim couldn't keep his quest from Billy. Billy had first hoped that Wim was finally getting interested in girls and was thus studying Sanskrit in order to read the unexpurgated *Kama Sutra*, and was doing a lot of pretzel-like callisthenics in order to build up his body for sex appeal, but when Wim started turning down chocolate chip cookies and talking about losing being a way of overcoming winning, Billy knew Wim was in trouble. The poor kid was beginning to act as weirdly as he used to before coming to live with Billy.

And then one day in football practice Wim, as quarterback, ducked in under centre to call signals and went into a meditative trance. The poor linemen and backs, including Billy, were forced to remain frozen in their three-point stance for so long waiting for Wim to start the play that by the time (five minutes some claim) Coach Cannonball realized that the play was a little slow getting off, half the offence had developed back problems. When Billy was driving Wim home that afternoon, he insisted that Wim explain what was going on. After ten minutes Wim finally caved in and poured out the whole story of his quest.

'Ultimate truth, huh?' Billy commented when Wim had finished. He had parked on a pulloff on the beach road along the Atlantic Ocean. 'But what's it got to do with life – with football and SATs and net income and getting laid?'

'It's the *cure*,' Wim said enthusiastically. 'U.T. is what will cure the sickness.'

'What sickness?' Billy asked, leaning forward to turn on his tape-deck and listen to Dolly Parton belt out '9 to 5'.

'The one that makes human beings so unhappy.'

'Who's unhappy?' asked Billy, taking out a pack of cigarettes. 'Only the losers.'

Wim stared at Billy, stunned by his suggestion, but then brightened.

143

'But that still means almost everyone except you!'

Billy stopped in the act of striking a match.

'I never thought of it that way,' he said. 'I suppose "losers" does pretty much summarize most of humanity.' He made the match explode into life and took in a deep pull on his cigarette. 'But how will u.t. turn them into winners?'

'I don't know,' said Wim. 'But the old man said –'

'And what's Sanskrit and yoga and meditating got to do with u.t.?'

'They're sort of ways to try to open my eyes so I can see it.'

Billy watched the surf breaking in orderly runs along the beach in front of them and wondered why he was sitting here with Wim and not with Sara Tillman or Beebee Culpepper.

'But what good does u.t. do *you*?' he asked.

'I'm sick too.'

Billy exhaled a symmetrical flow of smoke.

'Oh. Yeah.' He turned on the ignition and began to back out of the pulloff. 'Well, I guess u.t. can't actually hurt you,' he concluded. 'But I think the guys would appreciate it if you'd hold up on your quest during football practice.'

'I will, Billy,' Wim said quickly, nodding. 'I'm sorry about today.'

'Yeah . . .' Billy said and burned rubber as he pulled out on to the Montauk Highway. As the car settled into a steady sixty he went on: 'I'll tell my dad that all the weird things you're getting into are part of a mind and body building programme recommended by NASA. As long as he thinks you're pursuing success he'll be happy.'

'Thanks, Billy.'

'As for me, I like your going after u.t. When I sense you're getting close, then I'll join in and see if I can beat you to it.'

'I don't think it works that way, Bill.'

'Hey, man, if u.t. exists, then ol' Billy Best can be the first guy to get to it – that's a truism.'

'I guess so.'

'They haven't created the game I can't win.'

'Maybe, Billy,' said Wim, 'but all the books say that with U.T. you've got to learn to lose in order to win.'

Billy laughed and floored the Mustang to pull past a pickup.

'Hey, Wim baby, I guess that means you got a chance!'

Wim smiled too.

'That's right!'

When Wim told Dawn about his quest she was very proud of him. After they'd talked awhile she decided that Ultimate Truth was God and goodness and sunshine and Love. When Wim asked her to be more specific she claimed Ultimate Truth had to be vague and unspecific – otherwise it wasn't Ultimate Truth. 'If you can see it and touch it,' Dawn insisted, 'then there wouldn't be anything ultimate about it. It would be too ordinary. It's got to be the most special, tremendous, inconceivable thing in the universe, which is why you should always capitalize Ultimate Truth.'

Wim wasn't too sure about Dawn's theories since he knew that his quest was to *find* ultimate truth, and he was sure you couldn't find anything as vague as Dawn thought it was. He was hopeful u.t. was something a little less tremendous, something you could pick up and touch and feel and maybe show off to your girlfriend and the guys.

22

from *Fact Sheets on Wim*, vol. III, pp. 133–7

Wim's extensive study of Sanskrit in his junior year managed to go on for several weeks until his social studies teacher accused him of swearing at her in Sanskrit, and his football coach, Mr Earnest B. Cannonball, B.S., complained that Wim had begun calling plays in Sanskrit. Both threatened to resign unless something were done.[71] As a result Wim was forbidden to choose for his optional book reports the Sanskrit originals of the *Upanishads* or the *Bhagavad-Gita*, but was assigned instead reading more appropriate for his age level and physical size: the advanced honours class versions of 'Hiawatha' and 'The Pit and the Pendulum'.[72]

How extensive Wim's knowledge of Sanskrit became in his five months of study is unclear. His followers, of course, claim that he learned it thoroughly.[73] Dr Iniru Smoo of the University of Calcutta claims, however, after an extensive examination of the surviving fragments of philosophical speculation, personal notes to friends, descriptions of football plays, homework assignments and other scattered pieces[74] that Wim's work in Sanskrit at that time, while impressive perhaps for an American high school student, showed at least four grammatical errors[75] and is, stylistically, well below that of the *Bhagavad-Gita*.[76] Professor Smoo does admit that Wim's Sanskrit style is an improvement over most of the vedas, but notes that Wim had the advantage of reading Professor Smoo's books on the vedas.[77]

In any case, Wim's active interest in the Sanskrit classics was effectively curtailed by the combined efforts of his teachers, the school principal, the social worker, Coach Cannonball, and the school psychologist, Mr Henry Little,[78] who wisely convinced Wim that he would remain small, would in fact stop growing completely if he didn't give up reading Sanskrit...

We must now deal too with those alleged miracles associated with his study of yoga and Hindu classics. Far-fetched as most of these miracles may appear, many have a certain superficial basis in reports from normally reliable sources.[91] We may divide the miracles of this period into five general categories: levitation, psychokinesis, hatha yoga, olfactory productivity and 'emptiness' or invisibility.[92]

The alleged miracles of levitation are most easily dismissed. Shams, frauds, fakers and magicians have been using such levitation tricks since Jesus of Nazareth pulled it off in front of his disciples after his beautifully staged resurrection.[93, 94] Wim, totally lacking in the 'big scene' mentality of Jesus, never used his levitation tricks for anything except the most trivial effects.[95] In fact, there are only four events substantiated by enough personal testimony to warrant our examining them at length. The rest we have happily relegated to a five-hundred page appendix to volume VI.[96]

The first is the alleged 'Miracle of the Dangling Dunce'.[97, 98] On 7 April 1986, when Wim was two-thirds through his junior high school year, Miss Mulberry (or Ms Mulberry as she is called by radical historians) became exasperated by Wim's again sitting in a meditative trance during the first three hours of school and thereby enticing other students to shoot assorted projectiles at his head, pour ink down his shirt back, urinate in his shoes, drop chairs on his toes, and do other things that tended to distract the students from a history of American democracy at work. She therefore banished Wim to a far corner of the room by lifting him up, carrying him there, wrenching his legs out of the lotus posture and into a vertical position, and then leaning his stiff body at an angle of thirty-two degrees up against the wall with a dunce cap (in fact a converted nosecone of a large missile which Wim had been ordered to construct earlier in the year[99]) placed on his head.

The other students were encouraged to cease hitting Wim with spitballs, erasers, magnets, ink bottles and frogs by Miss Mulberry's promise that if they behaved they could take Wim outside with them during recess.[100] When someone (Senator Best has assured interviewers it was not he) suggested the possibility of exploring Wim's utility as a dive bomber from the top of the jungle gym, all the students began listening respectfully to Miss Mulberry's discourse on the great opportunities for labour created by the imagination of nineteenth-century thinkers like Jay Gould.[101]

As she continued her talk, which was apparently a reading of pages 73 and 74 of the social studies textbook *An Honest Look at Why America is Great*,[102] most of the students seemed to be listening, until Miss Mulberry suddenly shouted: 'Get down from there!'

According to the reports of Miss Mulberry and several of the students since interviewed by our staff,[103, 104] Wim had drifted to the ceiling, still stiff in his trance and still at an angle variously estimated at between thirty and forty degrees,[105] with the tip of his dunce cap just resting against the wall a few inches from the ceiling,[106] his feet approximately eight feet from the floor.[107] Wim failed to accede to Miss Mulberry's request and the students, according to their teacher, appeared highly upset, the girls giggling hysterically and the young men glaring in apparent jealousy at Wim's elevated position.[108] Miss Mulberry reports that having determined Wim's recalcitrance she quickly and efficiently filled out a requisition form to obtain a ladder . . .

23

from *The Gospel According to Luke* ...

The trouble with u.t., Wim decided after a while, was that it kept itself hidden all the time and promised so little to those who finally managed to find it. Patanjali promised levitation or reading minds or smelling like a rose. And when some zen and taoist books promised that he might be able to become invisible, it looked a lot more definite than old u.t. Supposedly relief from his confusion of human desires lay in the strange idea of 'Emptiness'. One obscure passage indicated that if he could just meditate hard enough and discipline his desires he might achieve Emptiness and simply disappear from the face of the earth – become invisible. The idea of emptying himself out so completely that all his conflicts and confusions would disappear and he'd become invisible immediately fired him with an enthusiasm far greater than any he'd felt for dull old u.t. except in the first few days after getting back from his Vision Quest. Montauks had always quested for invisibility, although they meant only disguises and blending and hiding, and since living with the Bests he couldn't even do that.

So soon Wim was spending all his spare time and a lot that wasn't exactly spare in his new kind of meditation. Especially during the more boring of his classes. Especially during Social Studies. Mr Hoelter had been warned about Wim by Miss Lunnigan, Miss Mulberry, and seven other teachers, so when he noticed Wim's trance-like immobility, he figured he should feel thankful Wim wasn't standing on

149

his desk or floating to the ceiling. Thus he didn't bother him until it was time to close and lock the classroom, at which time he came up to him and shouted in his face: 'GET OUT!!!' thus successfully terminating Wim's meditation.

On his way home from school that afternoon Wim told Dawn all about his new ambition. Of course it was hard to explain to someone who wasn't unhappy and didn't feel like disappearing, but Dawn listened.

'You want to become invisible,' she said when he'd finished. They were sitting on the cement base of the big cardboard sign that proclaimed 'Park Garden Forest Lake Bay Estates: An Esteemed Residential Community. Inquire Within'.

'I want to become invisible,' agreed Wim.

'But that's immoral,' announced Dawn, munching on a cracker left over from her lunch.

'Why?' asked Wim.

'Disappearing is running away from life,' said Dawn. 'It's a person's moral duty to be visible.'

'But why?' he asked again. 'Being invisible doesn't hurt anyone.'

'But it doesn't help anyone.'

'But maybe ... maybe I could still help people even after I become invisible.'

'How?'

'Well,' began Wim, frowning. 'I could still pick up candy wrappers off the sidewalk, wipe my feet before I come into the house, take out the garbage, wash my hands before dinner, brush my teeth – do all the things the Bests want me to.'

'You could,' said Dawn after thinking about it for a while, 'but if you were invisible it wouldn't count.'

'It wouldn't?'

'No. Being good means being seen,' said Dawn with her usual certainty, taking out another cracker and offering half of it to Wim. 'Whoever heard of a good man sneaking around closing doors when no one was around or helping an old lady across the street when she wasn't looking?'

'But ... but there must be *some* sneaky good people.'

'No there aren't. If they were sneaky good it would mean they were immoral.'

'But why?'

'Because they'd be setting a bad example.'

'If they're invisible how can they set a bad example?'

'By not showing their goodness,' said Dawn, looking down firmly at Wim and wagging a finger like Miss Lunnigan used to.

'Does Billy Graham hide his goodness?' she added.

'No.'

'Does President Reagan hide his?'

'I guess not.'

'See. The Bible says you shouldn't hide your light under a bushel basket, and all my father's friends don't even *own* a bushel basket. If they need one they borrow it.'

'But ... but ... if a person does invisible good we wouldn't hear of him. If he kept hiding under his basket he wouldn't get on TV.'

'If we haven't heard of him he can't be good,' Dawn announced.

'But ... but my mother hides her goodness,' said Wim cautiously.

'She does?'

'Every day she used to do nice things for my daddies, but she never advertised on TV.'

Dawn flushed. 'That's different,' she said.

Wim was feeling bewildered and a little depressed by the sudden intrusion of moral duty into the discussion, since all he really wanted in becoming invisible was just to be left in peace, and maybe sneak around and peek at his friends. But somehow, whenever he got into a discussion with Dawn, there seemed to be ways of looking at whatever Wim felt like doing which made things much more complicated than they were when it was simply a case of feeling like doing it. Still . . .

'I don't care,' said Wim decisively. 'I like you, Dawn, and I have nothing against moral duty, but I want to try to become empty and invisible. It's part of my quest.'

'Well, you can *try*,' decided Dawn. 'And I won't try to stop you.'

'You won't? That's swell. But how come?'

Dawn hesitated a long time and then flushed.

'It sounds like fun,' she said with a shy smile. 'If you find out how to do it, will you let me do it too?'

'I will, Dawn, I will.'

'But when we've both disappeared,' Dawn concluded, 'don't expect me to approve.'

And so began Wim's magnificent effort to empty himself of all ego, of all grasping, of all pride, and thus merge with the Void and become invisible. It was to be only the first of dozens of titanic struggles with the forces of maya and samsara and cause and effect, and in some ways his most remarkable.

He knew from his reading that the essence of emptiness was to rid himself of all of his basic cravings. To begin with he knew he would have to give up chocolate chip cookies. And re-reading carefully, he saw that peanut butter and jelly would have to go too. And hot chocolate. NY Mets bubble-gum cards. Making Coach Cannonball tear his hair. The Incredible Hulk. Playing card games with Billy. Lolling in the bathtub. Building catamarans and sailing. Not handing in homework.

In fact the more Wim thought, the more things he had to add to his list of basic cravings. After three hours he'd reached a total of seventy-two and was pooped. But the next day when he talked his list over with Dawn she further depressed him by helpfully making him add another one hundred and eighty: climbing trees, swimming, surfing with Billy, hiding Dr Best's newspaper, pretending to Arf that he (Wim) was dead until Arf howled like a wounded lion, flying kites from the bluffs, speaking in Sanskrit to his teachers – it soon seemed to Wim that the only thing that limited Dawn's list of additional basic cravings to a mere hundred and eighty was that she had to get back home for dinner.

Still, as Our Beloved Wim thought of each one he realized that each was, in its own way, a basic craving, and for him to obtain Emptiness it would have to go. It was a little discouraging to realize that once he had eliminated these two hundred and fifty-two basic cravings he would be left a rather empty life. As far as he could see all he was now permitted to do was arise when the alarm clock went off (basic craving number sixty-one had been to stay in bed for ten minutes after alarm went off), get dressed (but not with sweatshirt emblazoned 'Montauk Marauder' – basic craving fifty-one), eat breakfast (cold oatmeal – all the others being classified as basic cravings), walk (riding in the car with Billy not allowed) to school, talk to Dawn briefly before their first class (he had suggested that his enjoyment of talking with her was a basic craving, but Dawn had argued successfully that since she was good, talking to her could only be good), paying attention in all his classes (basic craving number one hundred ten: not paying attention in any of his classes), standing mute against a wall during recesses (basic cravings 133 to 136 involved footballs, frisbees, tennis balls and bull-sessions), do homework during study halls (no more making mazes to challenge Billy), and return home after school to meditate and try to become invisible.

Wim did most of his meditation in his bedroom standing on his head. Of all the traditional asanas, he found standing on his head made it easiest for him to empty his mind of thoughts: by counting the dog hairs in the rug a few feet from his nose all thoughts tended to disappear. But despite his efforts, after three days of complete dedication to his programme of invisibility, as far as he could tell – he always propped a mirror up against the wall opposite him – he was still just as full of Wim as ever.

Wim's strange appetites (or lack of usual appetites) and refusal to play the games that he and Billy so loved soon came to the attention of Dr Best, who, two days after learning about the reason behind all of Wim's oddities, called him into his study for a conference. When he asked Wim to explain his newly strange behaviour, Wim, unable to lie, told Dr Best the entire truth. Having already heard most of it from Billy, Dr Best took it all in his stride, nodding benevolently through Wim's whole fantastic narrative. When it was over, Dr Best sighed heavily.

'First of all, Wim,' Dr Best said, chewing contentedly on a long unlit cigar and tilting back in his study chair, 'I want to congratulate you on your desire to become invisible.'

'Really?' said Wim, looking up with a surprised and tentative smile. 'Thank you, sir.'

'You appear to have come to realize your limitations. Your desire to become invisible strikes me as a kind of *reductio plus ultra* of your well-deserved humility, a desire to be a kind of "nobody minus", a "less than zero", an aspiration I find eminently worthy of your talents, and not so pretentious as aiming at a full "minus one".'

'Thank you, sir,' said Wim, with something less of a smile. 'I'm glad you approve.'

'On the other hand,' Dr Best went on with a stern frown, 'your behaviour lately is something of an inconvenience to the entire Best family, and I want you to know that the only reason your foster-mother and I will tolerate it is that we feel this may be the only chance for you ever to make something of yourself. Since you're too small ever to be a professional athlete like Billy and too dismal at snowjobs ever to be a successful college student, we feel that the only alternative to your ultimately being tempted to go on welfare is that you somehow sell your freakishness. A midget that can become invisible while speaking Sanskrit standing on his head is, Mrs Best and I both feel, enough of a fresh angle to permit us to let you go ahead.'

'I appreciate that, sir.'

'Now, you tell me that despite giving up all your known basic cravings and despite meditating from 5.20 when you get home from school until 6.58 when Mrs Best makes you come down to dinner, and from 7.52 after you've finished eating and washing the dishes and brushing your teeth, until 9.58 when Mrs Best makes you wash your face and go to bed, you nevertheless retain your basic visibility.'

'Yes, sir.'

'There are three possible explanations. Number one, becoming invisible is not, in fact, possible.'

'Oh, no.'

'This possibility we reject because then the only alternative would appear to be your going on welfare.' He paused, placing his fingers in a respectful cathedral in front of his nose. 'Secondly, you may not yet have discovered the correct method.'

'Oh, no, sir,' said Wim firmly. 'I've read seventeen books on the subject. I'm sure I'm doing it right.'

'Good, good. We reject explanation number two. Thirdly, then, you may not be trying hard enough.'

'But, sir, I …'

'Considering your habitual laziness, your consistent failure to concentrate, and your obvious genetic deficiencies, this third explanation is clearly correct.'

Wim hung his head, feeling anger and doubt and gloom. 'I'm … not trying hard enough,' he echoed softly.

'I have noticed that whenever a human being fails to achieve success in any endeavour it inevitably can be explained by either his lack of effort or by his failure to cheat.'

'I ... I'm not becoming invisible because I'm not trying hard enough,' Wim said again thoughtfully.

'Exactly. Were you really to give your full one hundred per cent effort, "POP!" you'd disappear. And then, as soon as you relaxed your effort, "POOP!" you'd be back again.'

'Wow,' said Wim, momentarily brightening. 'And if I kept really trying I could be invisible all during school.'

'Absolutely. Or, more practically, you could remain invisible during the half-hour television documentary on your miracle which we would sell to CBS for three hundred thousand dollars.'

'But how can I try any harder?' Wim abruptly asked with a groan. 'My teachers and Mrs Best won't let me spend any more time meditating.'

'Mothers and teachers are never against genuine achievement,' Dr Best said, reaching out a heavy hand to pat Wim consolingly on the shoulder. 'Were you to remind them of the low level of all your abilities and the hope you have of earning your foster-parents money by becoming the Invisible Midget, I'm sure they'd relax some of their rules.'

'You really think so?' asked Wim hesitantly.

'Absolutely. You can do completely without dinner – fasting is always a safe hedge in the miracle market – and I'll get Billy to wash your face and brush your teeth while you're standing on your head. As for bedtime, I see no reason to compel you to sleep at all. Real strivers seldom sleep much. Look at Macbeth. We'll take care of school too,' Dr Best went on, enjoying the sound of his voice.

'I don't have to go to school?' Wim asked tentatively.

'No, no, of course you must go to school,' Dr Best countered emphatically. 'The example you will be setting for the other probable nobodies must be set. We'll simply ask your teacher to set you up on your head in a corner and then go on with the usual lesson plan.'

'Wow! That would be swell.'

'There may need to be a curtain for a while so you don't distract the other students, but Mr Hoelter can now and then check to see whether you've melted down or not, and at the end of the day turn you right side up so you can walk home.'

'Thanks, Dr Best.'

'But remember, effort is all. And to encourage your trying I'll do you a favour. Let's agree that if you haven't achieved invisibility within one week, you'll have to mow our lawn, shovel all snow, take out the trash, empty the garbage, put away the dishes, and repaint the barns each summer from now until you're eighteen – almost four years. That should help your effort.'

Wim stared wide-eyed at his foster-father.

'But –' he began.

'Goodbye and good luck.'

Wim first realized that perhaps he was making progress even though he wasn't aware of any when Mrs Best asked him one morning at breakfast (cold oatmeal for the tenth straight day) where he had snuck off to the night before. Wim replied that he hadn't snuck away anywhere; he'd been meditating all night except for one brief period of six hours when he'd been daydreaming of scrambled eggs and sausage. Mrs Best announced that Wim was a liar. Dr Best asked what else was new. Billy Best verified that his mother and he had entered Wim's room at nine o'clock, and then he himself at nine-twenty and ten, and Wim was not there. Wim stared at them.

'Then I must have done it,' he said softly.

'Nonsense,' said Mrs Best. 'If you did it we would have seen you, that is, we would have ...' She trailed off.

'I did it,' Wim repeated in an awed tone to himself.

'If you did, you'd better practise some more,' said Billy, 'so you can do it when someone besides you is watching.'

'I did it,' repeated Wim.

'Nonsense,' said Dr Best. 'If it actually happened, *we* did it, and if it hasn't happened yet then it's because you're not trying hard enough.'

WIM AND THE BEE

One day Wim got carried away speaking on the theme of rising above all of the dualities: of living beyond success and failure, life and death, pleasure and pain ... Surrounded by a dozen worshipful disciples he was preaching with unaccustomed eloquence on flowing above all the dualities when a bee stung him on the nose. He leapt up screaming and ran in a circle twice around the room.

When he had reseated himself and assumed a position of dignity there was an embarrassed silence. Finally the youngest disciple dared to speak.

'O Master,' he asked. 'What is the lesson to be learned from this event?'

'It's simple,' said Wim, frowning sternly. 'To rise above pain one must be very detached, and very careful about bees.'

– from *Sixty-six Parables of Wim*

24

from *The Gospel According to Luke*, pp. 186–94

One day, even as he was working hard on his invisibility, Wim stumbled across a twenty-year-old issue of *Time* magazine that reported that high school students were using marijuana, LSD, mushrooms and a lot of other strange chemicals in order to discover ultimate truth. He was stunned. The article indicated that the students also discovered sexual pleasure, terror, kicks, insanity, good vibes and addiction – no one finding all seven of these, but everyone apparently managing to find at least one.

He found out that back in the late sixties and early seventies old ultimate truth was reasonably respectable in some quarters. People had often gotten their heads together and dropped everything or dropped something and looked around for it.

But in the eighties, Wim knew, u.t. was held in very low esteem. President Reagan himself had announced only a month earlier that as part of his budget cuts no more government money would be spent on research into ultimate truth. This would save taxpayers $4,120.22, enough money, the President bragged, to buy six-and-a-half boxes of carbon paper for the Department of Defense.

Reading about why people used dope back in the sixties confused Wim, since now – in the mid eighties – for Billy and Rocky and most of Wim's other friends, dope was something you used for good sex, instant ego and escaping from parental hassles. If you met ultimate truth under the influence, the cool thing to do was ignore it. Only guys like Ram Dass and Chogyam Trompa and a few fat Indians with tough names were into Ultimate Truth, and at MHS everyone Wim tried to talk to about Chogyam Trompa thought he was some big dumb Polish defensive lineman for Babylon High.

In any case, Wim asked Billy where he could get some of this magic stuff that had led some people to u.t. Billy laughed and said there was a big senior at Westhampton Military Institute named Oscar Broom who'd first introduced Billy to dope a few years earlier. Wim remembered that weekend. Billy had smoked his first couple of joints and it had made him feel 'different', which Wim now decided might be as close to u.t. as a person like Billy was likely to get. Later Rocky Peters had reported that when he'd taken three tokes from one of Oscar's hash pipes he'd felt 'spooky,' and 'the sky got bluer'.

A month later Billy had announced that Oscar had sold him a capsule of mescaline and that it had made him see surrealistic paintings where before he'd only seen *New York Times* photographs, and that a peach he'd been looking at had turned into a female breast and winked at him, and that a five-minute sequence on television's 'NFL in Action' had turned unexpectedly into an incredible homosexual orgy. When Wim questioned Billy about that time now, he reported no sign of Ultimate Truth.

When Rocky had dropped a tab of acid he'd 'flown, man, really flown'. He'd gotten divided up into six people, four of whom he didn't like, and all of whom looked like fragmented Picasso nudes descending a staircase. In the park where he'd been the trees looked like huge gobs of green cotton candy and the lake like a pool of crank-case oil. The noise of autos passing by was like a hacksaw going through all thirteen ribs at once. Although Rocky now remembered that he'd 'flown, man, really flown,' the trip had not, then, been totally smooth, and if Ultimate Truth were there it had hidden.

But despite these negative reports from his friends, Wim decided to go see Oscar Broom and request something that might have a bit of u.t. hidden inside. Oscar was a gangly slump-shouldered young man with sad eyes. He took one look at little Wim and announced he didn't sell nothing to no third-graders. When Wim persisted and mentioned the possible purchase of tabs of mescaline or LSD, Oscar smiled and sneered and said he wasn't in the business of corrupting infants and sent him away with nothing. As Wim continued to press his friends about the superpowers of pills, Billy announced that the ingestion of speed over a four-day period had made him feel that his greatness had reached such heretofore unscaled heights that his wisdom, athletic prowess and personal charm threatened to unbalance the stability of the universe. If ultimate truth existed, Billy reported feeling, it was undoubtedly Billy Best. On the fifth day, without his speed, Billy felt considerably different about everything, becoming so depressed that he seriously considered the possibility that there might be other human beings as great as he.

Rocky said that sniffing cocaine made his penis grow two inches, a Budweiser beer taste like the most delicious liquid in creation, and the touch of the pigskin of his football a caress beyond imagination. If ultimate truth existed, he said, it lay somewhere between the football and the beer.

By now Wim was convinced that at least one of these substances must have something to do with his quest, and he went again to Oscar and demanded four tablets of speed and a spoonful of cocaine. Oscar was not noticeably moved by Wim's demand and merely replied with a scowl, 'Stop hassling me, man, you want to get me busted? Selling to minors is bad enough, but to kids still in diapers it's likely maybe even to get me arrested.' Wim assured Oscar he didn't want to get Oscar either busted or arrested since he was the only potential supplier of u.t. that Wim knew, but that Wim's quest for u.t. was serious. Oscar declared that as far as he knew his supplier didn't handle U.T. but he'd check.

When Wim returned three days later, Oscar shouted at him to go away, stop bugging him, that there was no U.T. on the market, hadn't been for years, that Wim must mean STP or DMT or PCB or BLT, but he couldn't sell him any of these either and to get out. But Wim would no longer take no for an answer. When Oscar locked the front door of his small house, Wim climbed in the bathroom window and, planting himself firmly in front of the toilet, declared that he wouldn't budge an inch until he had been given *something* which would help him with his search for u.t. Oscar, swearing and crying and laughing and blustering, three times threw Wim down his front stairs only to find him standing again near some window he had snuck in. Finally, tears in his eyes and mumbling incoherently, Oscar reached into his pocket, groped around, and then held out his large sweaty palm towards Wim.

'Here,' he said.

Our Beloved Wim, flushing happily but with dignified restraint, advanced five feet and asked politely: 'What is it?'

'It's pot,' said Oscar.

Wim stared at the apparently empty palm of Oscar's hand. 'Where is it?' he asked.

'Here!' said Oscar, stretching his hand way down to place it under Wim's nose, and looking offended.

And there, so tiny it had become almost buried in the deep crease of the lifeline of Oscar's palm, was a single seed.

'That ... that's pot?' asked Wim fearfully.

'Yeah,' said Oscar. 'Not a full ounce maybe, but a seed. A seed you can plant and make grow, and when it's big you can pick it and smoke it and live happily ever after until you make your next score. Go ahead, take it.'

Gingerly, so as not to frighten it back deeper into the crevice in which it was embedded, Wim reached into the palm of Oscar Broom's hand and removed the seed. It was brown and hard and moist from Oscar's sweat.

'How much do I owe you?' asked Wim, holding the seed gently between two fingers of his left hand while removing his wallet with his right.

'Forget it,' said Oscar graciously. 'When the seed's grown a big plant, you can give me half.'

'Thank you,' said Wim.

'One thing though,' said Oscar. 'You gotta have good soil and plenty of light and water and fertilizer, and above all else you gotta give your seed *love*.'

'Love?' asked Wim uncertainly.

'Yeah, love,' said Oscar. 'Pot that's grown from unloved seeds don't give anywhere near the high as loved pot.'

'Yes, sir.'

'Light, water, manure, and love: in three months you'll be getting stoned and have all the old U.T. you'll ever need.'

And so it came to pass that Our Beloved Wim did possess his Seed and did plant his Seed. Because it was already early December he used a small dixie cup for his pot and earth from the Best flower garden for his soil and excrement from his own bowels for fertilizer and water from the bathroom sink and a thirty-watt desk lamp for light, and love. Billy Best rented him an old, dog-eared thirty-page pamphlet entitled 'On the Cultivation of Cannabis in an Artificial Environment', published and distributed by the United States Department of Agriculture and co-authored by Timothy Leary and Richard Alpert. He also informed Wim that Dr Best strongly disapproved of all stimulants or hallucinogens that contained less than eleven per cent alcohol, and that since Wim was incapable of lying, if he were ever caught by Dr Best with a pot plant and asked whether Billy knew about it, Wim was to commit suicide.

Wim felt that was an extreme remedy but promised to give up his life before implicating Billy and retired to his room to read the pamphlet. He soon read that he could grow his seed indoors even in the winter as long as he watered it regularly and fertilized the soil and gave it plenty of light. It didn't say anything about love, but maybe the pamphlet was out of date.

Wim planted his little seed on Sunday night, 14 December, and all that evening until he fell asleep he sat on his bed in the lotus posture and sent out love to his seed. When he awoke the next morning there, like a green angel with outspread wings, was a three-inch high plant with two serrated leaves arching in lovely symmetry on either side. Wim read rapidly again through the pages of the Department of Agriculture pamphlet and discovered, as he feared, that the seed should not sprout until four or five days after it had been planted. Already, after only one day, he must have done something wrong. Still, all he could do was try to give it the necessary fertilizer, water, light and love, and hope for the best. Reluctantly he went down to breakfast and off to school.

When he returned in the afternoon the plant seemed just as he'd left it – it hadn't grown at all. Discouraged, Wim rushed to the bathroom and forced out another bowel movement, planting it snugly around the base of the little green sprout. He watered it and then went marching around the house collecting all those lamps that he hoped wouldn't be missed. Soon he had eight different lights blazing away in a circle around the plant. Finally, deciding that more than two bowel movements a day might be dangerous for both himself and the plant, and guessing that five hundred and fifteen watts of light was probably adequate, he concluded that all he could do was love. So he sat down again on his bed and concentrated on love.

When he awoke the next morning his plant had leapt up during the night another three inches and had sprouted two more leaves. It was leaning towards Wim as if bowing good morning. Wim danced down the stairs to breakfast.

There he was greeted by a Dr Best whose glower at Wim's appearance seemed even darker than usual.

'So now you've taken to stealing lamps,' he said to Wim by way of good morning. He lowered his cup of coffee with menacing dignity.

'No, sir,' Wim replied, glancing quickly at Billy, who was eating his bacon and eggs with unusual attentiveness. 'I was borrowing them.'

'And why, may I ask, did you steal them?' Dr Best countered easily.

'It ... it's part of an agricultural ... project,' Wim whispered, the only truth he could come up with that wasn't a full confession.

'You lie!' shouted Dr Best. He leapt up as fast as his corpulent body would permit, grabbed Wim by the hair, and began marching him back up the stairs.

The top of Wim's head felt as if it were on fire, and his eyes were filled with tears, especially when Dr Best swung open the door of his room and saw the circle of lamps all shining on his lovely green plant.

'Ah ha!' snapped Dr Best, releasing Wim's hair and striding up to the helpless plant. 'This is no agricultural experiment. It's grass, and you know it.' When he turned to dare Wim to deny it, Wim simply lowered his head.

'Exactly,' said Dr Best and reached down and picked up the dixie cup, wheeled back out of the room and down the hall. 'Follow me,' he commanded.

When he arrived in the bathroom Wim saw him tip the dixie cup upside down and spill his plant and its soil into the toilet bowl. He then triumphantly flushed the toilet.

'This is what happens to all bad and dirty things,' Dr Best announced as he and Wim watched the tender plant swirl prettily for several seconds and then disappear. After the last gurgle he turned to Wim. 'Do you understand?'

'Yes, sir,' Wim answered in a whisper. He wondered with

a hint of hope whether that meant someday it would happen to Dr Best.

'And you'd better be careful,' Dr Best concluded as he marched past Wim to return to breakfast. 'You're small enough.' Wim heard a happy chuckle as his foster-father disappeared.

So it was with a feeling of tremendous loss that Wim trudged off to school that day, finding it hard to understand how his dream of growing his own Ultimate Truth could be so quickly dashed. He dawdled back from school, refused to play any basketball with Billy, refused to feed the birds with Dawn, and finally just lay down on his bed and felt utterly alone. He didn't even feel up to bothering to try to become invisible.

But when he went to the bathroom just before dinner there in the middle of the toilet bowl, somehow standing straight up and looking as good as new, was Wim's beloved plant. Wide-eyed and grinning, Wim picked it up, rescued the same dixie cup from the wastebasket, and prepared to get new soil to fill it.

But if love was what made the plant grow then this time he wouldn't let it be in the Bests' house. He'd take it to the old farmhouse his mother was now living in and start growing it there. Wide Pool had more love in her little finger than Dr Best had in his whole belly put together. And so after a dinner in which he pretended gloom and shame to Dr Best's cheerful preaching, Wim hid his plant in a pocket and hiked the mile and a half to his mother's farmhouse.

When he left there an hour later with Wide Pool's kiss still wet on his cheek, Wim was again smiling. Since he'd finally gotten his seed and begun growing the plant, he was even feeling interested again in u.t.

25

from 'Fragments of Wim', pp. 98–101

Trying to become invisible is almost as depressing as trying to please Dr Best, but at least I know that becoming invisible is possible. Wanting to spend all my time on my meditations and taking care of my strange plant means I'm having trouble doing what my teachers and Dr Best want me to. One of the things I find I don't like about life is all the things that people seem to feel I *have* to do. Like writing an essay on Benjamin Franklin. Washing the dishes. Making my bed. Running twice around the track after practice. Sometimes even having to look for old u.t. And especially taking out the garbage. The moment one of the Bests orders me to carry the garbage from the kitchen to the trash can to the kerb, I feel an overwhelming lethargy. The garbage suddenly looks incredibly heavy. The distance from the kitchen to the kerb only slightly shorter than that from Moscow to Siberia, and a trip about as pleasant. The fact that I have to do it makes it a horrible task. Usually I *like* walking, like lifting things, even like *garbage*, but combine these three nice things with a command 'do it' and suddenly it's work. Things I *have* to do are things I never want to do.

It seems my only escape is to disappear. I sometimes wonder if that's why some taoist didn't discover how to become invisible: he hated having to take out the garbage.

But I worry about myself. Sometimes I seem to be trying for invisibility not because it has something to do with u.t. but because I want to escape from and get revenge on Dr Best.

I want to learn to become invisible but never let him know about it. I daydream about sneaking around and when he's playing bridge slip his opponents the best cards, and when he's playing golf run ahead and stick his ball in a rut or nudge his putts just off line so his ball won't sink into the hole. When he isn't looking I'll sprinkle too much salt on his food and put urine in his bourbon.

I've developed a long fantasy about a big dinner party with dozens of his rich friends. After Dr Best opens the wine I'll substitute another wine bottle with urine. Dr Best will sniff it and say what a great bouquet it has and everyone's glass will be filled, and Dr Best will propose a toast to money and success. Then with great dignity and sophistication all twelve of them will take a drink. After a brief pause their smiling faces will freeze – until all at once and all together they'll spit the wine out all over each other. I'm getting a lot of mileage out of this fantasy, but I'm not sure Grain-of-Sand would approve.

And I get the feeling that the more I hate Dr Best and want to become invisible the less chance I have of doing it. I know the key to becoming invisible is emptying myself of all desires, and if I desire to get revenge on Dr Best then I'm full. I want to get back to just wanting to become invisible because, like growing my plant, it's got something to do with my quest for u.t., but it's tough. I sometimes think that deep down inside I'd rather see Dr Best spit urine than find u.t.

It seems a little unfair that the reason I'm going for u.t. is to cure my human sickness, and that the reason it's almost impossible to find u.t. is I'm so blinded by my human sickness. Do the Gods always rig things so much against the person given a quest? I asked Grain-of-Sand this question and he just nodded, grinned, and said: 'Yep. Every time.'

'Why?' I asked.

'Beats me,' he said. 'Only thing I can figure is they get bored and set up impossible quests to keep themselves amused.'

I think Grain-of-Sand is a cynic.

I think if I keep trying for u.t. I may become one too.

26

from Grain-of-Sand's *Memoirs of an Old Liar*, pp. 234–41

When I first saw Wim's plant it was more than four feet tall and growing out of a rusty garbage can in his room in the dilapidated farmhouse where his mum was living. When him and I come in I noticed that the plant seemed to sway towards Wim as if bowing a greeting. Most plants are supposed to grow towards the light, but darned if this plant only grew towards Wim. Seems if he fell asleep too long giving out love, when he woke the plant would be pretty near breaking its stem leaning towards him so far. Naturally this got Wim a bit worried, so by the time I come he'd rigged a hammock along the ceiling so if he stayed overnight he could sleep above the plant and help it grow straight up. Trouble was the plant seemed to be growing about eight inches a day and there weren't that much room up at the ceiling. He'd also found he was running short of his own shit and sort of wondered whether I'd let him have some of mine.

All I knew about pot in those days was that it gave a nice sort of feel to a woman's tits and that a lot of kids were using it like beer. I couldn't see that it had much to do with ultimate truth, but I figured it couldn't hurt any more than reading Sanskrit. Trouble was, though, I was a bit constipated. Dawn came in about then, and Wim told her about growing his seed and asked her if she'd mind giving some of her 'output' to help the plant, but she didn't respond too good.

Fact is, all she knew about pot was what her daddy had explained to her: pot was synonymous with sin, orgies, addiction and psychosis, that it led to opium, heroin, LSD and sunflower seeds, that it was illegal and always got you twenty-five years in jail.

So when Wim asked for some of her shit for his pot plant she hit him over the head with her social studies textbook and ran out the room. Wim ran down the stairs and got her back, but she weren't too happy.

'You're evil!' is what she screamed at him.

'I only wanted a *little* bowel movement,' Wim said, holding on to her arms.

'It's not that,' Dawn said. 'It's growing that horrible plant.'

'What horrible plant?' asked Wim, looking around as if some poison sumac might of sprung up beside his bed.

'You *know!*' she said, and pulled away to run, but he grabbed her again.

'Tell her it's part of my quest, Grain-of-Sand,' Wim said to me.

'It's just a living thing,' I said to her, not wanting to say one way or another that pot was part of his quest.

'But . . . it's illegal,' Dawn insisted.

'No it isn't,' said Wim. 'It won't be illegal until it flowers.'

'Then you're encouraging it to become illegal,' she shouted at him. 'And worse yet, if I gave you my . . . what you asked for, I'd become an accessory to . . . the encouragement of illegalness.'

'I don't know about all that,' I said, getting annoyed at being stuck in a conversation with humans. 'But seems to me that Wim loves his plant and the plant seems to love Wim. I can't see where there's much room for evil to sneak in.'

'Then it must not be a marijuana plant,' Dawn said.

When she said that, Wim looked at her hopefully.

'Then maybe you could like it until we find out what it turns out to be,' he suggested.

Well, I guess Dawn decided to give the plant the benefit of the doubt. Soon she and Wim were holding hands again, and a bit later I noticed Wim crumbling up some turds around his plant and Dawn looking suspiciously proud. And the fact is the darn plant seemed to have a mellowing mood on not only her but me too. Love seemed to fill the room: Wim for his plant, the plant for Wim, and, after Dawn had contributed her bit for the plant, the love of her and Wim for each other.

Dawn kept chatting away as if the pot plant were some sort of ceremonial flower, apparently having convinced herself that since she loved the plant it couldn't possibly be illegal. I suppose that made her life free of guilt for a while – until seeing everybody's getting zonked when they just got close to the plant began to make her wonder whether Wim might have managed to trick her into something she should have known was wrong.

About a week later Billy warned Wim he was going to be busted for his pot plant. Seems someone named Butch had started rumours that the men always visiting Wide Pool were all scoring dope. Well, Wim immediately told his mum and his mum had a chat with one of Wim's fathers – who didn't happen to love cops – and the three of 'em come up with a plan.

Two days before Christmas four narcs and three drug-sniffing dogs busted into the old farmhouse, and all hell broke loose. First off Arf got all excited and let out one of his wounded-tiger roars that was heard in Queens eighty miles away, and it sent those drug-sniffing dogs out the front door so fast dragging the poor narcs that one guy broke his nose and another an arm. This kinda start didn't make 'em feel any more friendly towards Wim and his mum, and they threatened to shoot Arf if they didn't muzzle him and lock him up. Two of the dogs had had some sort of nervous breakdown or something and at first couldn't be dragged back into the house, but the narcs came back in and began ransacking the house.

While Wim's daddy that week sat puffing a pipe in front of the Christmas-tree, they destroyed several television sets, tore up all of Wim's stuffed toys, broke down a wall and discovered a hidden room that no one knew existed, let their dogs so frighten Mary's senile ostrich that it had a stroke and got paralysed with its head in the down position, and emptied every bureau in the house of the masses of rags that Wide Pool kept in them. They didn't even find a single joint.

By this time they'd managed to get all the dogs back in the house, and the dogs kept returning to the Christmas-tree, whining and moaning and lifting their legs to pee on everything near it as if Jesus himself must've been buried there. Well those agents were smart fellas, so they opened all the presents around the tree – Wide Pool and Wim had already been given more than sixty from his daddies – but damned if they found nothing illegal except three stolen tapedecks, two electric blankets from a stolen shipment, a case of smuggled liquor, and twelve cartons of untaxed cigarettes. Since they were narcs and their warrant only said illegal drugs, they began to brood a bit about their failure and drunk two quarts of smuggled scotch and borrowed the rest to check it for illegal substances, and decided to take the cigarettes to make sure they weren't hash, and asked if they could borrow the three tapedecks for a decade, and pretty soon were feeling nice and cheerful. So, leaning all the doors they'd broke down against walls, they left with a wave and a smile.

Well, poor Wim, shaking and blinking back tears over the damage they done to his plant, rushed to remove the bulbs, tinsel and Star of David, and did his best to build splints for the bent and broken branches. Then he carried the wounded plant back upstairs to his bedroom and replanted it in the garbage pail and set about tending it with love.

But it seemed to me he was always worrying. Two days later he told me he had to saw a hole in his bedroom ceiling so the plant could keep growing up. He figured in another week or two he'd have to saw a hole in the attic roof. Billy was telling him it was growing like no pot plant Billy ever heard of, and that at the rate it was going Wim's mum might have to live in a skyscraper.

Next thing I knew he was telling me the farmhouse weren't big enough. He was gonna have to transplant to the old barn on the far side of the Best estate where Dr Best never went except to stand against the weatherbeaten boards to have his picture taken holding a hoe. So he and Billy and Dawn and me snuck it in there one day and dug a big hole in the earth floor and planted Wim's strange plant.

Now that plant, though it was only a youngster, somehow had us getting all giggling as we worked, something a navigator don't do except on special occasions. Wim said it was a contact high from the love of the plant.

The old barn was over forty feet high in the middle, and though Wim had to adjust a few branches around the lower beams, when he set the roots into the hole the plant looked real content. Wim poured in some soil we'd gotten and poured in a couple of pails of water. It looked for a second that he was going to ask us to make another personal contribution of fertilizer, but I gave him a fierce look and he didn't say nothing. Finally he strung a hammock from the barn roof so that if he slept out in the barn the plant would keep growing straight up.

Though it looked like clear growing for a month or so, Wim still worried. Some book he had said that it ought to be grown in temperatures of forty degrees or more, and the temperature in the barn that day was cold enough to freeze snot. So using some torn-up floorboards for wood, Wim and Billy built two fires on either side of the plant and then went and got a bunch of old blankets out of the attic and three electric blankets Billy borrowed from a closet and used them to protect the plant from the cold. Wim figured that them and his love would pull his plant through. That night he snuck out of the Bests' house and slept in the hammock and concentrated on love, and the next morning that plant was not only healthy but had grown another foot.

Well, we Montauks aren't big on vegetables – we eat mostly things that swim and crawl – but I got to admit that I got a kick out of watching that plant grow and poor Wim try to keep up with it. Wim ended up piling on more blankets than I'd seen since I last slept at the Salvation Army, doing his damndest to fit them on the branches. When he weren't running with a blanket he was bringing firewood to feed the fires that he had to keep going all the time. No matter how hectic it got, Wim seemed to be as happy as humans ever get. I figured it was the love he was giving the plant, but had to admit I was feeling pretty jolly whenever I was there, and Billy and Dawn did more giggling every day than I'd seen either of them ever do. The tree was blooming out sideways every which way, its green branches getting bigger and bigger until a few were already longer than a man.

'Course as a navigator I spent a lot of time trying to figure out what the hell it all meant. As usual I couldn't see what growing this plant had to do with u.t., but I had to admit there was something weird about the way just being near the darn thing made me feel. Peaceful like. As if the sun were shining and all the mosquitoes were taking naps and there weren't any humans. When I was away from the barn I couldn't make head nor tail of what Wim and his plant were all about, but when I was at the barn I didn't give a damn.

I decided I better not visit it too often: navigators can't afford to forget mosquitoes and humans.

27

from *The Gospel According to Luke*, pp. 122–7

When Our Beloved Wim finally became invisible it didn't happen at all the way he thought it would, and wasn't quite the solution to his problems that he'd daydreamed about. And the way he finally did it was totally unexpected. For five weeks he'd been trying with (for him) remarkable consistency to give up all his two hundred and eighty basic cravings, even though each of them seemed to be definitely basic. And he meditated during school and dinner and while sending love to his plant and even during Coach Cannonball's pep talks before games. Coach Cannonball wondered why, after one of his long tirades about the value of violence in a valueless world, he would look from one player to the next and see each face suffused with anger, hatred and the determination to kill or at least maim several of the opponent's players and then come to Wim's face which would be blank-eyed and smiling as if he'd just smoked two kilos of pot.

At home Wim practised meditating standing on his head all the time. The top of his head was becoming so flat that while he was sitting in a meditative trance at breakfast Billy would sometimes do his maths homework on it. And Wim's digestive system was getting so fouled up from his upside-downness that whenever he sat on the toilet and had a bowel movement the stupid turds would sometimes come out of him and fall to the ceiling, making Mrs Best call him disgusting and other adjectives. In school Mr Hoelter had taken to placing a gigantic wastebasket over him so that his standing on his head not doing geography wouldn't distract the other students. There's no circulation under an upside-down metal waste basket, and sometimes Butch or another boy would put glue in the bottom of it so that when Mr Hoelter picked it up to release Wim his feet would stick to the bottom and he'd rise with the basket. Mr Hoelter would then accuse Wim of hiding and trying to fake disappearing when it was really only Butch's glue and Wim's exercising his toes.

So Wim had been undergoing what he considered to be hardships – eating only two meals a day, both always of things he didn't like – and not having any fun at any time except when visiting his plant, and always *trying* to become invisible as Dr Best advised.

Then one night in his room at the Bests, after he'd been standing on his head for five consecutive hours, and there was so much blood in his head his eyes saw the sheets on his bed as pink, all of a sudden he thought to himself that there was one basic craving that he hadn't eliminated: the craving to become invisible.

Wim felt suddenly confused. He was so confused he uttered the first word aloud he'd ever said while meditating.

'Huh,' he said.

It seemed to him that the books had said that to become empty and invisible he had to free himself from *all* cravings, and all cravings would include his craving to be invisible. But if he ceased to desire to become invisible, then he wouldn't have any desires left at all. He'd be nothing, a blank, nobody, empty …

Empty! It was his *trying* to become Empty that kept him filled! If he could just turn off the faucet of his trying to be invisible then there'd be nothing left and he'd … disappear!

It was confusing but it was funny too. The harder he tried to become invisible the fuller he'd get with desire and thus the more visible he must have become. But if he let go and stopped trying … Wow! Wim started laughing and laughing – which is tough standing on your head – and the next thing he knew Arf was licking his face and he was reading a Spider Man comic book on his bed. He knew he must have gone 'pop!' the moment he stopped trying and started laughing.

But he wasn't sure he'd gone 'pop' at the time. In fact, he soon discovered that one of the problems of becoming completely empty and invisible is that whenever he went 'pop' and disappeared, at that very second he seemed to lose all awareness of past and future and self and Emptiness and thus didn't notice that he'd gone 'pop'. One moment he'd be standing on his head staring at himself upside down in the mirror trying as hard as he could not to try to become invisible, and the next moment – three hours later perhaps – he'd be sitting at his desk making a super maze to frustrate Billy. And the only way he'd know he'd been invisible is that Dr or Mrs Best would later complain that he'd snuck away and hid someplace to get out of doing something they wanted him to do.

Wim discovered that the Invisible Man doesn't *feel* invisible. Wim felt his same little old Wim self except a little lighter maybe, and suddenly people might be bumping into him and shrieking. He came to sympathize with Casper the Friendly Ghost.

And other problems developed, especially after Dr Best learned that he could do it. Billy had reported to his father that he'd been watching through the keyhole while Wim stood on his head and he'd seen Wim go 'pop!' and disappear and later go 'poop!' and come back again. After this report, Dr Best called Wim into his study.

'Son,' he said – when he used that word Wim knew that somehow against all the odds he must have done something right – 'Billy informs me that you've been doing good work and are now able to turn yourself on and off like a lightbulb.'

'Oh, no, sir,' Wim replied quickly. 'It's not that easy at all. I can't –'

'Nonsense,' said Dr Best jovially. 'Now let's see you do your stuff. Disappear.'

'But I can't disappear right now, sir,' Wim said desperately. 'It doesn't seem to work that way. Whenever I –'

'Nonsense,' said Dr Best contentedly. 'There's no sense in hiding your light under a bushel or, in this case, hiding your invisibility under a bushel. Melt.'

'I'd like to please you, sir, but it takes me a long time to –'

'Nonsense,' said Dr Best evenly. 'Where there's a will there's a way. Evaporate.'

'But you're making me try and I've found the harder I try the visibler I get. I've got to be relaxed and laughing and –'

'Nonsense,' said Dr Best irritably. 'The harder you try the quicker you'll disappear. Try! Quit standing there making excuses. Go pop!'

So Wim tried. He stood there and strained with all his might to become invisible, knowing that it never worked that way, but trying harder than he'd ever done before.

'Nonsense!' Dr Best shouted angrily. 'You're going the wrong direction! You're getting brighter and bigger or something. Stop *shining* at me! Disintegrate!'

Wim felt tears come to his eyes. For two minutes he just stood in front of Dr Best trying to blink them away while Dr Best's face went from purple to red to pink to yellow to white.

'Go to your room,' Dr Best finally said in a quiet, cold voice. 'And don't you dare show yourself before me again until I can't see you.'

And there was something else unexpected about becoming invisible. After all his elaborate daydreams of what he would do to Dr Best and Butch and several other people, Wim found that only when he laughed at his hating Dr Best could he become invisible, and then he didn't have the least interest in hurting anybody. When invisible, his fantasies of

181

revenge seemed trivial and unimportant. He found he *liked* Dr Best. In fact, all he felt like doing when he was invisible was nice things: putting extra money in people's wallets, candy in kids' desks, moving out of the way things people were about to trip over, steering Dr Best's putts so they went in the hole or putting a little bourbon in his coffee to put him in a better mood. The moment he felt angry at Dr Best, Wim would go 'poop!' and be visible again, often frightening Dr Best considerably which was nice, but not letting Wim do anything else revengeful.

After a while Wim decided that becoming invisible might not be worth all the hassle even though it did seem to solve all his problems. Whenever he was invisible, he was light and happy and everything seemed exactly as it should be. He even found that most of his two hundred and eighty basic cravings were actually rather uninteresting and unnecessary, and the rest he found he could enjoy without becoming visible. The Bests seemed nice human beings, and instead of wanting to defeat or trick Billy, he felt warm towards him and wanted to help him come to enjoy losing. Wim even found that as soon as he was invisible, taking out the garbage was one of the best experiences life had to offer.

But there were always new problems. Whenever Dr Best saw the garbage going out to the kerb all by itself, or the dishes washing themselves and putting themselves in a neat stack to drain, he would come running over and shouting, 'Son, son, that's magnificent! We're rich! Just show yourself to me for thirty seconds and then disappear again.' He would be holding a portable video camera which would be grinding away at the self-washing dishes.

Well, when Wim was invisible he loved Dr Best and wanted to please him, but of course there was no way he could go 'poop!' and appear, because there was no 'I' around to do it.

So as he remained invisibly washing and stacking the dishes, Dr Best would whirr away with his camera and shout and swear and get red in the face waiting for him to go 'poop!', and then Wim would feel so sorry for him he'd go and stroke his arm or back and Dr Best would shriek and run away.

And when he went to school invisible it didn't work out too well either. The teachers couldn't see him when he raised his hand to ask a question, and all the tricks he'd thought he'd play on the teacher and certain of the more obnoxious bullies when he daydreamed about being invisible didn't interest him in the least. He spent his time reading and watching people and being ridiculously good. Dawn would have been proud of him if she hadn't been ashamed of him for doing good without people being able to see him.

Later, back in his room, and back to his old mixed-up highly visible self, he'd be annoyed that the invisible Wim hadn't done any of the marvellous things the human Wim thought up to baffle and embarrass his enemies. He was certainly happy when he was invisible, except that he wasn't there to enjoy it. The Gods seemed to have put one over on him again.

So he finally went to see Grain-of-Sand to tell him what he'd been doing and the problems he'd met.

Grain-of-Sand listened and scowled and listened and laughed and then sighed.

'Beats me,' he said. 'We Montauks believe in invisibility in order to hide from humans, and your method seems to work real good – almost as good as the one old Chief Little Speck used to use. But when you're visible, instead of being a Montauk you go right back to being a human being, right? Something's missing.'

'I know,' Wim said, 'but what?'

Grain-of-Sand sighed again.

'You still haven't found old u.t.?' he asked.

'No, Grain-of-Sand,' Wim answered, feeling ashamed as usual. 'I haven't.'

'You still looking?'

'Of course. I think becoming invisible has something to do with it and so does my plant, but I still haven't *seen* anything.'

'Yep. Well, all I can say then is keep at it. Looking for ultimate truth don't make no sense to me, but this much I'm sure of: it's your quest and until you've fulfilled it you're going to be stuck. I figure it's got something to do with your being the last hope of the Montauk nation, though if it does I don't plan to be betting much on the Montauk nation. Anyway, visible or invisible, you got to look.'

'I will, Grain-of-Sand, I really will.'

'All I know is that a human being never has a quest. It's what makes him a he-who-doesn't-know-what-he-wants. But I can't say I see what becoming invisible has to do with your u.t.'

'I ... want to become invisible,' Wim said tentatively.

'I bet you do. You just want to escape your troubles every now and then. 'Tain't the same thing as looking for u.t. I don't give a fart for what you think you want. What you need is to finish your quest.'

'But I don't know where to look,' Wim pleaded, 'except where the Sanskrittens and the Buddhists and the other guys who have found it say to look.'

'Well, I guess I can't help you much with the looking,' said Grain-of-Sand, standing up with a grunt to end the conversation. 'Ultimate truth don't mean a thing to me. It ain't my quest. It's yours. Just keep your eyes and ears open and the Gods will begin to give you hints. That's their style. Just when you think your quest is hopeless they'll plant a little clue on your dinner plate and get you moving in a better direction. All you got to do is keep seeking.'

'I don't know, Grain-of-Sand,' Wim said doubtfully. 'Sometimes it just seems hopeless and I lose interest.'

'Well, you're human now and can't expect to focus all the time on much of anything. But give it a try.'

'Yes, sir.'

'And I wouldn't worry too much about that invisibility stuff,' concluded Grain-of-Sand. 'Until you're a Montauk again and have finished your quest and found your stupid ultimate truth, it don't make a bit of difference if anyone sees you or not.'

Grain-of-Sand then marched off down the beach. The trouble with a navigator, Wim found himself thinking, was that he had the answers, but all Wim got to do was try to prove him right.

BYE-BYE FROM U.T.

'Knock, knock,' suddenly came from within the soul.

'Who's there?' asked Wim uncertainly.

'Ultimate Truth,' replied the voice.

'Thank God!' exclaimed Wim. 'I've been looking for you for ten years.'

'That's nice,' said Ultimate Truth. 'So long.'

'But ...'

And there was silence.

– from *Sixty-six Parables of Wim*

28

from *The Gospel According to Luke*, pp. 211–17

It was a day, Wim was to think for a long time, that would live in infamy. It struck with the suddenness and devastation of a Pearl Harbor and marked the beginning of a long war.

It happened in the dead of winter, a thing so sudden, so unexpected, and so terrible it transformed his life. One morning he woke up and found that his voice had overnight changed from its usual soprano squeak to a deep rich scary baritone. Black hair had sprouted in his armpits and above and around his genitals; his face, which had been as smooth and soft as a baby's behind, was suddenly bristling with tiny sharp black quills that demanded shaving. And, worst of all, his balls, which had always been nicely tucked up out of the way, had now dropped down and were banging away between his thighs, and his penis – his good old innocuous penis, whose sole previous claim to fame or interest had been its ability to piss further than Billy's – suddenly overnight had grown two or three inches, thickened, and looked suspiciously like an angry red, one-eyed mouse.

Wim had become a man.

And he was totally unprepared.

He was unprepared despite his faithful attendance over the years at his school's annual sex education classes, despite his observing during his childhood numerous couplings of his mother with a father, despite, being Wim, his having asked Wide Pool and his fathers hundreds of questions: why one of them had done a certain thing, what it felt like, what it was supposed to mean, and why did people bother at all. And Wide Pool had always answered fully and clearly and gently until by the time he was fourteen and standing horror-struck in front of the mirror looking at this grisly hairy body he suddenly found himself with, Wim knew everything there was to know about human sex.

But when he went to school that morning all his knowledge didn't do him the least good. He discovered to his horror that almost all the girls in the school had been reincarnated overnight as lascivious, creamy-skinned, sweater-bursting, lip-licking, tongue-teasing, eye-flashing, butt-twitching women. Any one of them could with a glance, a smile or a yawn cause his peewee, against all of Wim's rational commands or personal desires, to go berserk. It would unaccountably harden, lengthen, and leap up to a two hundred and twenty-five degree angle, stretching underwear, threatening to split pants, making all locomotion uncomfortable, and there it would bob and throb like a mad terrier straining at his leash to get at a cat. Later, equally unaccountably, it would yawn and shrink and rest between his thighs like an innocent child.

Everything that had interested Wim up to then became in what seemed a single day utterly uninteresting. He found that his two hundred and eighty basic desires had been reduced to only one. His entire universe began to consist solely of the eyes, lips, hair, skin, legs, breasts and movements of girls, and the resulting panting and pulsating and pelting and prying and pinching and probing and prowling and ploughing and partying and popping of his unmanageable yo-yoing prick. Everything he had learned about sex from a loving mother, bragging fathers, a dedicated school system, and bullshitting guys became utterly useless.

And although Wim didn't notice it, those around him were suddenly aware that little Wim, the runt of the Suffolk County school system, that scrawny little weirdo that made it so much fun to be a bully, had suddenly become as solid as a cast-iron fireplug. His shoulders and chest had broadened, his arm and thigh muscles thickened, and the body that could throw a football seventy yards and hit a thimble nine times out of ten, and zig and zag and zip until opposing linemen had to see psychiatrists, suddenly *looked* like such a body.

And Wim's face, which had all his life just been big-eyed and innocent, suddenly was dark and brooding, with thick curly black hair, a straight nose and firm chin, and dark piercing eyes that one girl soon described as like black stars. And though he still moved through the hallways of the school like a tiny frightened puppy in a world of giant adults, the bullies who continued casually to give Wim a shove to send him crashing into lockers or bouncing off some screaming girl found that trying to shove Wim was like pushing at the side of the Empire State Building, and that if he happened to notice that you had tried to shove him and shoved back, you were likely to go through the wall. So though there was a great deal of giggling about the tendency of Wim's prowler to be pounding at the door to his trousers like an irate bill collector, the boys of the school unanimously decided that giggles was as far as it was safe to go.

And if Wim's life was suddenly filled with girls, the lives of a few girls became filled with Wim. Little, adorable, harmless, innocent Wim had suddenly become a shy, dark, brooding Byronic hero – even down to the limp, caused, however, not by a club foot, but by his usually ill-positioned pulsator. And though the ninth- and tenth-grade girls talked mostly of Wim's eyes, or thick, curly black hair, or his biceps or thighs, the more mature girls spoke in hushed tones of the prancing panther between Wim's legs bursting to get loose.

Wim totally forgot all about ultimate truth. The letters 'u.t.' became fuzzy in his mind. He dimly remembered they meant something, but what that could be he couldn't quite

189

remember. Although he still occasionally tried to become invisible it was only so he might sneak into the girls' shower for purposes which apparently the taoists didn't approve of. Anyway, he found overnight he had lost his ability to become invisible.

He didn't abandon his plant since whenever his pirate would curl up in his underwear and take a nap, Wim still had enough love left for his plant to trudge over to the barn and water it and zap it with a little love, but as soon as his puncher woke up he'd have to rush away to obey its commands.

So the next few weeks of Wim's new life were filled with awkward words and silences, inaccurate kissing and groping, blind passion followed by bewildered indifference. When the girls in the books Billy kept showing him got kissed by the hero they immediately began saying things like 'Oh yes yes yes' or 'Fuck me fuck me fuck me,' but Wim soon discovered that the girls he managed to kiss tended to say things like 'Careful of my braces' or 'I bet you ate hamburger tonight'.

Wim soon discovered that he and his pendulum often had differing opinions about girls. Wim wasn't at all interested in a plump freshman who had only recently learned to read and whose conversational repertoire consisted of 'Oh wow' and 'Far out'. But his pecker took one look at her bouncing buttocks and yanked Wim around to set him traipsing after her. Wim still thought that Dawn was the prettiest girl he'd ever known, but his poker inevitably greeted her tall stick-like body, flat chest and rump, thin lips and austere critical eyes by shrivelling up to the size of a small caterpillar, and sometimes threatened to disappear entirely.

Of course his friendship with Dawn was strained. Dawn's strict morality, although always secular and humanistic rather than religious, nevertheless found Wim's unpredictable prober a bit much. Her father's sexual code for women was on the strict side: in his old age he had come

190

to believe that St Augustine was the last word on the subject. As a result Dawn pointed out with some vigour that Wim's piercer seemed to 'have no respect for the individual', to show 'a complete disregard for intellectual compatibility', 'to ignore disparate interests', and to have a tendency to prefer 'quantity over quality'. Wim agreed that everything she said was brilliant and true and relevant, but found his pouncer had its own programme. Worse yet, his plunger had so many friends throughout his body that when it came to a vote, Wim's head tended to get out-voted three or four hundred to one, and his body would go marching off after another girl with a thirty-eight-word vocabulary and a thirty-eight-inch bust.

But although his imprudent proboscis always knew what object it wanted, it was strangely unable to control entirely Wim's brain and tongue. After pushing and hauling Wim up close to a girl, his passionate pisser couldn't get him to say the things that might have led the power to the glory.

The fact was that girls frightened Wim. When one would brush a plump braless breast against his elbow, he would be apt to spend the next three days thinking about it and wondering what he should have done about it or what he now should do. After taking a girl to a movie and with more courage than he thought humanly possible managing to hold her hand for fifteen seconds, Wim would afterwards find himself able to talk only about the movie, analysing it from thirty-three different points of view. The girl, whether her IQ was thirty or a hundred and thirty, would end up rushing for home like a man fleeing a life-insurance salesman.

Wim tried to learn how things were done from bullsessions with Billy and Rocky. Now that Wim was as obsessed with girls as they were and built like a small tank instead of a stuffed Snoopy toy, the other boys accepted him as an equal. They all agreed that their confrontations with girls were a game more exciting, intellectual and exhausting than their Saturday afternoon football games. Analysing these contests became more interesting than talking about sports. The three of them would sit for hours discussing pass patterns that might work against Tanya Culpepper, Vera Watts' poor blocking pattern on attempted plunges up the middle, Joani Kobalewski's upcoming defensive plan, Tina Smart's inspiring audibles, the scoring possibilities against Margie Topp's weak zone defence, Mary Umbrage's fly pattern, the disturbing tendency to fumble it all away when Ann Moppit began using her hands on defence, or the possibly illegal efforts of Olga Retch to signal a change of play whenever the line of scrimmage reached within inches of her end zone.

The discussions were immensely informative to Wim, but they didn't seem to do him much good. He still couldn't figure out what to do when Joani Kobalewski seemed to want to spend an entire date talking about Newton's law of gravity while she sat on the rug playing with Arf. Or how to avoid what happened to him with Olga Retch. Olga seemed to like him a lot and invited him over to her parents' house when they were away and greeted him wearing a low-cut blouse without a bra that had his peter solid as a rock. She let him cook her a delicious steak dinner, bake her an apple pie, and fix her three drinks. She then suggested they watch an R-rated video in front of a fire she had him build. When she went off to take a bubble bath she asked him to change the sheets on her bed, and when she came out, she asked him to help her change into something 'more comfortable', a something that couldn't have weighed more than two ounces and was so flimsy it made mosquito netting look like chainmail. Then she announced that she felt tired and had a headache and that it was time for Wim to ride his bicycle home.

And he didn't have much better luck with Vera Watts. According to Billy, Vera was as close to a sure thing as the Gods had given to the menkind of Suffolk County. In her parents' basement she acted in the most seductive and affectionate manner, reaching the point, in fact, where she was wearing only earrings and an ankle bracelet, when Wim suddenly emitted a body odour of such overwhelming power and such nauseating stink that she was forced to flee naked from the room, 'lucky,' as she later told all five hundred and three students at Maganansett High, 'to escape with my life,' since four goldfish and a hamster in the room were killed outright, and several others died in long-drawn-out agony. Wim himself was unaware of the odour – although he had been practising Patanjali's odour-producing mantra earlier in the evening – and attributed Vera's sudden retching and running away to her disappointment at seeing the size of his penis.

And occasionally Wim would be disappointed in its size too. Although when thinking about dating Margie Topp his powerpack had been bulging in his jeans with the size and hardness of a bowling pin, when Margie ended up naked in bed with him and had totally abandoned her weak zone defence, neither she nor he could find Wim's pathetic pleader.

'I can't even *see* it,' Margie complained.

'It's there! It's there!' cried Wim desperately.

'But I can't *find* it!' shouted Margie.

'I know it was there half an hour ago,' moaned Wim. 'Keep looking.'

'I need a magnifying glass,' sobbed Margie.

And the trouble with this 'now you see it, now you don't' policy of his yo-yo peewee, was that whenever it happened, the girl would immediately begin crying, claiming that Wim wasn't attracted to her because of her pimples, or body odour, or breasts being too big, or her folks being democrats, or her pubic hair the wrong shade, or the shape of her toes, or the wrong kind of fillings in her teeth, and so on. Wim hated to make girls unhappy even more than his

193

poolcue didn't give a fuck, but try as he did to assure the girl that it was all his crazy popcorn's fault, she brooded.

And of course sometimes the damned thing would get too big. One time he dated Mary Umbrage, a nice shy innocent virginal sort of wanton who might have been quite unable to resist Wim if his pointer was reduced to nil. But that night his perambulator swelled and swelled until he had to grab it and pull it in against his body in order to stop knocking lamps off tables as he chased poor Mary fleeing shrieking through the house, complaining that if she'd wanted to be split she would have gone to a sawmill.

Or that time with sweet Tanya Culpepper, the nicest girl he knew except for Dawn. Out under the stars on a warm spring night after Wim had scored three touchdowns in spring practice and given the game ball to Tanya she was dreamily lying on her back and had let her skirt and panties move south three feet and absent-mindedly spread her legs into an amazingly wide V. Wim knelt gently between them and would have entered her but found that he wouldn't fit. Instead of his usual modest six inches and normal circumference his palpitator had shrunk to four inches long but four inches wide, an inconvenient shape to say the least.

And even on those occasions when his penis was otherwise behaving in a scientifically reliable manner, he often found that in its blind pursuit of its goal it would often go into one of its epileptic fits midway through a date and lose all interest in the girl. Wim ended up trying to make conversation and apologies to someone he found himself with only because his prodder had prodded him there against his will.

And it made him sad to become indifferent to a girl just because his pumper had changed its mind. He was usually more polite and considerate after his pelican had shrunk to a peanut than he was when it was banging away at his fly, but he still usually wanted to go home.

194

Of course, on those rare occasions when his penis would curl up and take a nap, Wim was able to tend his plant, make perfunctory stabs at invisibility, do his maths homework, or talk to Dawn. Although Wim still thought Dawn's face was the most beautiful thing sent to earth since waterlilies, it was clear that physically she hadn't had the horrible thing happen to her that had happened to him. Nevertheless, he liked to take her to movies or on walks or out sailing, and on these dates she assured Wim that she understood all about his problems and forgave him his frequent bouts of madness, saying that it was a stage everyone had to go through. She knew he was too good a person to hurt any of the several dozen innocent girls he grovelled after each week.

Wim suggested he wasn't so sure the girls were all that innocent, but Dawn insisted that, being young and female, they were by definition innocent, and he, being male, was by definition guilty. Wim nodded, since he knew that if he'd been able to tell one-tenth the lies his pasta had urged him to cook up on just a single date, he would have lied more than the entire Montauk nation had in three thousand years. His popper had no morals whatsoever, and so Wim figured guys must deserve all the blame they usually got. But he was glad Dawn was still his friend and even gladder his propeller hadn't yet noticed her.

Dawn liked to have him kiss her on their dates and he liked it too, but his penis would stay curled up in his underwear sound asleep, often even emitting a rhythmic low humming sound that Wim soon realized must be its snoring. So Dawn and Wim would chat about the day's doings, and she would lecture him, and they would kiss and whisper the same childish words of affection that they'd exchanged when they were six. Wim would feel at peace and at home and happy because Dawn seemed to give him the only rest he could find from the mad bomber between his legs.

Thanks to not being distracted, Wim even figured out once when he was with Dawn what u.t. must stand for. It stood for 'ultramarine tooth'. Now all he had to figure out was why he was on a quest for an ultramarine tooth.

ON NOT BEING DISTRACTED BY A QUEST

One day Wim went out to the long stretch of sand where Grain-of-Sand often strolled and finally found him.

'I'm afraid I've got a really serious problem, Grain-of-Sand,' he said. 'I seem to want to make love to almost every girl I meet. I'm constantly being distracted from my quest for ultimate truth.'

'That's a biggie,' Grain-of-Sand said, frowning one of his fierce frowns. 'And a lot of Montauks have had that problem. Unfortunately, there's only one solution.'

'What is it?'

'You gotta try to make love to every gal you meet.'

'But Grain-of-Sand –'

'But be absolutely sure you're not distracted by getting the hots for ultimate truth.'

'But –'

'Yep,' said Grain-of-Sand.

– from *Sixty-six Parables of Wim*

29

from *The Gospel According to Luke*, pp. 231–40

In the spring of that fateful year Our Beloved Wim was to have no peace. Not only did he have two hundred and sixteen problems at Maganansett High (there were two hundred and sixteen girls in Maganansett High), but there were suddenly a multitude of problems with his beloved plant.

First of all, the plant kept growing and growing and growing like no plant of any species in any book either he or Billy could dig up. By early April its top was nearing the barn roof, and its branches were now twenty and thirty feet long and filled the whole building. The lovely green serrated leaves were now up to five feet long. In a desperate effort to find peace from his impossible pecker Wim began to sleep up in the plant, using one leaf as a mattress, a second as a top sheet, and strapping on blankets above and below. The limb would sway gently as he crawled out on to it, and when he stretched out, the leaf seemed to fold in around him like a cocoon. He felt it gave him the nicest rest since he'd had to give up sleeping on his catamaran in the bilge, and lying on one of the leaves was even softer than levitation.

But the problems kept coming. The sad truth is that Billy Best had acquired a fifty-one per cent interest in Oscar Broom's half-interest in the fruit of Wim's seed. Moreover, since Wim had told everyone that Dawn and he were partners and that she was as much the owner of the plant as he, this meant, so Billy informed Wim in a carefully typed letter, that he, William O. Best, was the majority owner of 'said plant', since Billy owned 25.5 per cent, Wim and Dawn 25 per cent each, and Oscar Broom 24.5 per cent. The letter made it clear, however, that Mr Best's 25.5 per cent of the plant included none of those portions of the plant which might be illegal under the NY State penal code, all of which, the document stated: belonged to Mr Wim. As the major owner Billy had begun organizing formal tours of the barn and plant, charging twenty-five cents to enter and see the plant, fifty cents to climb it, and a dollar to lick it three times.

These tours depressed poor Wim since he soon noticed that many of the less scrupulous students were breaking off tiny pieces of the leaves or digging their fingernails into the soft green trunk of the tree and scratching out as much of the resin as they could surreptitiously acquire. Wim begged Billy to do something, and finally he agreed. He raised prices across the board – 'to drive the riff-raff out'. But the despoliation continued.

Then Billy discovered that everyone felt so mellow around the plant that if he put out a plate and asked only for 'contributions' he ended up making more money than he could with established fees. But the despoliation continued.

And the growth of the plant gave Wim no peace either. When the top of the plant reached the barn roof, he, Billy and Dawn had to decide whether to open up the top of the barn and begin exposing the upper leaves to the outside world, or to bend the tip of the plant or even break it off so that the rest of the plant might grow. They all agreed that it would be wrong to bend or break the tip, so they sawed and chopped a large hole in the very top of the barn roof through which the green tip of the plant seemed to leap towards the stars. To try to hide it from possibly disapproving neighbours, Wim and Dawn and Billy and some of his employees built a square topless wooden shelter around the opening so that the only direction from which the plant could be seen was from above. As the days passed and the plant bloomed towards the sky, they had to add to the wooden shelter. After a week it looked as if the barn had a gigantic, growing wooden chimney in its exact centre, purpose unknown.

Which produced the problem of Dr Best. The doctor was categorically, unequivocally and absolutely opposed to all illegal drugs. Then Billy explained to him the profit potential of a possibly two or three thousand pound pot plant with pot selling at one hundred and fifty dollars an ounce. Dr Best hesitated.

Billy then suggested that it was only fair that the current owner of the barn share in the profits. Dr Best began to sweat. To eliminate the risk to Dr Best, Billy proposed that he sell the barn either to Wim or Billy himself for several thousand dollars so that should a bust occur, Billy or Wim would be legally responsible.

Dr Best began to believe that categorical, unequivocal and absolute principles were not all they were cracked up to be. Billy went on to explain that the effect of the plant was to make everyone mellow and loving and giggly and giving, and that if Dr Best were to route his patients past the old barn, they might pay their bills on the spot no matter how extravagant. Dr Best fought back a smile.

Then Billy pointed out that since no marijuana plant had ever grown forty feet high or developed a trunk almost two feet thick, this plant couldn't possibly be marijuana even if it was so powerful that people got stoned simply staring at it.

Dr Best finally nodded.

'If you'd like to continue your agricultural experiment,' he said cautiously, 'in *Wim's* barn, then I would be happy to let you do so. All I ask is a modest fifty per cent of any profits that in some unlikely case may ensue.'

'Twenty per cent,' said Billy.

'Forty.'

'Twenty-five is tops.'

'I couldn't conceivably give up my categorical, unequivocal and absolute principles for less than thirty-five.'

'Because you're my dad, I suppose I could let you have thirty.'

'Because you're my son I suppose I could accept a third.'

'After my expenses.'

'Sold,' concluded Dr Best, letting a grin explode across his face.

Which quickly became related to the problem of the shareholders.

Billy Best had gone public with a stock offering of a thousand shares in his 25.5 per cent interest in the plant, capitalizing at fifty dollars a share. Although it was later revealed in the invisible ink at the bottom of the contract, ink that became visible after thirty days, that Billy had retained four thousand shares for himself, the local boys and girls of Maganansett High School bought up the entire offering in three days. Since they were shareholders they were always trying to tell Wim what to do for the plant or with the plant and often simply trying to do it themselves. Many claimed the plant needed 'pruning', and until Billy helped Wim put a stop to it by setting up a round-the-clock security system, several shareholders armed with saws did some aggressive pruning. Billy tied his Doberman to the base of the tree, made a tape-recording of one of Arf's more impressive wounded-tiger roars, and changed the bylaws of his 'Maganansett Feed the Poor Agricultural Project Corporation' to stipulate that any shareholder caught 'pruning' forfeited his shares, shares which were then trading on the Over the Countryside Market at 17 dollars 50 a share – three times the offering price.

Unfortunately, the Doberman was so mellowed by the plant that his aggressiveness disappeared and he was no more dangerous than a kitten. In fact, Panzer spent most of his time licking cats whose fur had gotten dirty or helping kittens across the main thoroughfare to the plant.

And then there arose the problem of the barn. One morning Wim and Billy awoke to find it was much colder and windier than usual. When they looked down from their bedleafs they saw that during the night the whole barn had been raised right off its foundation a full foot from the ground. It was not a case of displaced levitation, but rather of the growing branches of the plant hooking under the barn beams and pushing in places against the roof and thus lifting the barn towards the sky.

At first Wim feared the strain might injure his plant, but Billy assured him that he had another pamphlet which declared that large marijuana plants needed such isometric exercises. Billy claimed the only problem was to disguise the rising barn from passers-by. So each morning before driving off to school he and Wim and Dawn and Billy's workcrews would patiently add a foot of old lumber around the two sides of the barn facing the rural road. By the time the plant finally flowered, the barn had grown more than twenty feet higher, but none of the people who drove past each day had noticed anything suspicious or out of the ordinary except that there seemed to be a lot of birds and animals lolling all the time around this interesting old barn which had a twenty-five-foot-high ten-foot-wide wooden chimney which, along with the barn itself, seemed to grow a foot or so taller every day.

And then there was the problem of money. Following Billy's advice Wim had over the previous two years invested money in the stock market with moderate success, especially so since his quest for u.t. had made him increasingly indifferent to money. But now, needing extra funds to buy the barn from Dr Best, and also to pay for his dates with MHS girls, each of whom seemed to discover some new ever-more exclusive and expensive restaurant, Wim had decided to make his own stock decisions. Somehow things hadn't worked out too well.

First of all, over Dawn's strong objections, he invested all his savings in something called Napalm Enterprises, a former producer of cigarette-lighters that had expanded into defence work. But the next day someone thoughtlessly blew up the main plant of Napalm Enterprises and the stock fell ten points. Disappointed in the stock's performance, Wim sold his shares at a loss of four thousand dollars, and invested what was left to buy two hundred shares of Kute Kayaks, Inc., agreeing with Dawn that Kute Kayaks had fewer enemies than Napalm Enterprises.

Unfortunately, the next day Kute Kayaks's only factory, located in the little river town of Peepsville, Georgia, was the victim of a freak tidal wave, unusual in inland waters, and was totally destroyed, cutting the value of its stock in half.

Wim then invested what remained of his money in Good Guy Hamburgers Shoppes, telling Dawn that distributing food was a reasonably moral thing to do, even for a profit, and telling Billy that Good Guy Hamburger Shoppes, being widely dispersed over the entire United States, had a better chance for survival than did his earlier investments. The next day the *New York Times* had a splendid article reporting that all the meat used in Good Guy Hamburgers was not beef or meal or innards of horsemeat as in most pure American hamburgers but was reprocessed cow dung of limited nutritional value. This report had an adverse effect upon the public image of Good Guy Hamburger Shoppes, and the value of its stock fell from eight to one in twenty-two minutes. When Wim sold his shares he found he thus had only seven hundred dollars left of his original twelve thousand dollar investment, 'an off-week for me in the market,' he admitted to Billy.

At this point, Wim had a tragic brainstorm. Instead of buying a stock and hoping its value would increase, Wim decided to sell a stock short, thus earning a profit when the stock's value went down, which, on the basis of his previous stock selections, seemed a reasonably good bet. Wim chose as his 'victim', as he called it, since whatever stock he invested in seemed to be struck by lightning, the Durable Dirigible Corporation, a firm which specialized in the production and servicing of small family-sized vacation dirigibles. The stock had dropped in value over the years from a brief high of sixteen when Merril-Lynch, Pierce, Fenner & Goof had told its twenty-seven million investors that low-cost dirigibles might be the thing of the future, to its 10 April price of three when many investors had come to believe that the company's yearly price-earnings ratio of infinity was a bit high. Also, in the course of its eight years' existence, the company had produced and sold only eleven dirigibles to low-income families looking to get away from it all.

Wim sold short one thousand shares of Durable Dirigibles at three dollars per share, planning to buy the shares back after the price had dropped to one and a half or one, thus realizing a profit of between one and two thousand dollars. Wim apparently went to bed that night convinced that at last he had found a foolproof way to invest, but awoke to three-inch headlines which upset his calculations. It seems that the small, family-sized, vacation dirigible of a Mr and Mrs Otto Tuckle of Loop, Iowa, missing someplace over the Andes since October of the previous year, suddenly reappeared over Shea Stadium on Long Island during the third inning of a Mets game containing not only the Tuckles, their two children and a cat, all sun-tanned and healthy, but also six primitive Inca Indians from a tribe lost to civilization for two thousand years.

By that afternoon Mr Tuckle had sold the story of his adventures in his dirigible – adventures which included visits to Tahiti, Mt Fuji, Moscow, Santa's actual workshop at the North Pole, and the moon ('too damn rocky for my taste,' wrote Mr Tuckle) – to *Esquire* magazine for one hundred thousand dollars, and the stock of Durable

Dirigible, Inc., which had been at three dollars when Wim sold it short, had increased to one hundred and seventy-nine dollars per share, now that he had to buy it. Wim thus had a loss of about one hundred and seventy-five thousand dollars, 'an off-day in the market,' Wim admitted to Billy.

The next day Wim was ordered to 'cease and desist from trading in the stock market' by the Securities and Trade Commission 'for the stability and safety of the American economy', since by then brokers throughout the country had taken to watching which stock Wim was buying or selling in order to do immediately the opposite before the earthquake, tidal wave or news story struck.

It looked like Wim was going to have to declare bankruptcy, but since that would mean a lien on the barn, Billy Best raced to the rescue. He pointed out to the STC and Merril-Lynch, Pierce, Fenner & Goof that Wim was barely fifteen years old and was trading only because of derelict screening of customers by some unscrupulous broker. To avoid the negative publicity implicit in a fifteen-year-old losing his shirt and everything else, Wim's losses were quietly settled out of court, Billy getting ninety per cent of Wim's twenty-five per cent interest in the plant, and Wim being declared free of responsibility for the Durable Dirigible short sale providing he never buy or sell stocks again. He thus walked free, unburdened, like all Montauks, of the vicissitudes of money.

But it was a tough spring.

30

from Grain-of-Sand's *Memoirs of an Old Liar*, pp. 188–93

Wim was just gloomier than a turtle on an expressway. He come to me and talked about girls and Billy and money and his plant and I'm afraid it took me a while to stop laughing.

I told him I still didn't have the foggiest about his gigantic plant. We Montauks have legends about an Indian named Froth who once grew a giant pumpkin the size of a small house and lived in it one winter. And another Montauk a century or two later grew a cucumber the size of a small World War II bomber, but far as the legends say the only big effect either of them had was to make people hungry. The Montauks ate nothing but pumpkin mush one whole summer, and a century later they made a dugout out of the cucumber and sailed it halfway to North Carolina before it sank: seems some of the crew were snacking on their sailboat. But neither the pumpkin nor the cucumber had much effect on creatures' minds the way Wim's plant did.

I tried to answer his questions about sex but it didn't do no good. All the girls Wim knew were human beings which meant they were as screwed up as he was. There weren't no advice anyone could give him that would make his life any less laughable than it was. Montauks have a tradition that the Gods gave men pricks and gals pussies so that they'd never forget how funny and stupid and unserious life is, but somehow human beings have messed this up too. Where and when a guy gets to put his prick seems the most serious and important thing since the discovery of fire. And gals are just as bad.

Anyway poor Wim just couldn't get it out of his head that he was doomed to be a human being for ever. I kept saying that he no more had to be a human being than he had to be a turtle hiding under its shell all the time.

'But, Grain-of-Sand, how!?' he asked. We were strolling along the beach the way we usually did for important chats.

'Simple,' I said. 'Just stop playing at being a human being and begin playing a god.'

'But that would be pretending!'

'Pretending is what creation is all about,' I said.

'It's no use,' he said. 'I'm a real human.'

'Bullshit,' I said, speaking metaphorically of course. 'You only think you are. You're no more real than that island out there,' I added, pointing out to the empty open sea.

'What island?' he asked, not seeing anything.

'Exactly,' I said. 'You're only pretending to be a human. Try pretending you're a god. Notice the improvement.'

'But how do I go about pretending to be a god?'

'Well, the main thing is this: fake it,' I said.

He stopped and looked up at me with a wistful, amused smile.

'Second,' I went on, 'gods don't worry. You never catch one of them biting his fingernails. And since a god assumes he created the universe he doesn't waste any time standing around and complaining about it.'

'But –'

'I know all about your "buts" … let me finish.'

'I'm sorry.'

'Since a god is all-powerful he doesn't get all knotted up worrying about the future. He figures that though he doesn't quite remember what he had planned for the next minute it must of been pretty brilliant or he wouldn't a done it.'

'Wow, that's neat,' said Wim.

'Only if you think you're a god and good at pretending it.'

'What else?' Wim asked.

'Well, since a god is god he doesn't worry about how his hair looks or whether his jeans are cool. He figures that since he's god, the way he's parting his hair and wearing his jeans is *the* in way to do it.'

Wim was looking down at the sand now, frowning, but nodding his head in agreement.

'And lastly, since a god is everywhere and also everyone,' I went on, feeling in pretty good form, 'he don't waste energy getting pissed off at any of his other selves. If someone bugs him, he just relaxes and gives the guy a friendly right cross.'

When I paused, Wim looked up at me.

'It must be pretty nice being a god,' he said with a faraway look in his eyes.

'You *are* a god,' I shot back. 'All you got to do to prove it is start pretending.'

He stared at me blankly a second, smiled uncertainly, scowled, then looked up gloomily.

'But what should I do?' he asked.

'Being a god, you do whatever you feel like doing.'

'But what about good and evil?'

'Being god, whatever you do is good, and what you don't do don't matter.'

'But that means I can do *anything*.'

'Sure,' I said, but squinting down fiercely at him to make him see my next point. 'But that's the pretend human speaking. When you begin pretending to be a god you'll do some things and won't do others. Don't ask me why.'

'I don't know, Grain-of-Sand,' he said, shaking his head and looking down again. 'If I'm pretending then everything I do is a sort of illusion.'

'Don't worry about it. Being god, everything you do is, by definition you might say, reality.'

'But ... but what about other people?'

'Being god, you *are* other people.'

'But how can I pretend to be other people?'

'The same way you're now pretending to be only yourself.'

A few days later he came out to the sand dunes along the bay for another chat.

'I pretended to be a god,' he said to me gloomily.

'What happened?' I asked.

'Butch Messmire hit me in the mouth and knocked three of my teeth loose.'

'Mmmmmm,' I commented.

'It ... it was ... magnificent.'

'Of course it was.'

'Poor Butch didn't even realize that it was really *me* who was hitting me in the mouth.'

'You get the idea.'

'I laughed and laughed,' said Wim, smiling.

'Good.'

'Still,' he said after a long pause, and beginning to frown. 'Dr Best says I've got to earn the money to pay the dentist.'

'Don't worry,' I said, patting him on the back. 'Remember, you're the dentist.'

Well, he had as tough a time as most humans remembering that he was the dentist, and by the end of the week I could see he wanted to give up pretending to be a god as a lost cause. Claimed that he was a human and there was nothing he could do about it. I tried giving him the same brilliant lecture but I think I may have gotten some of the key ideas wrong and 'course it didn't do no good. He was still too young.

Well, I finally decided, this too shall pass. One of the ways humans get themselves stuck is to become convinced they can't help being humans, so they try to relax and enjoy it. It always works for a while – I know, I tried it – but sooner or later, especially if you're a Special Being – and Wim came to say we're all Special Beings – the Gods will figure out a way to wake you up again.

31

from 'Fragments of Wim' ...

I'm depressed at how much I've changed in the last three months from the innocent boy who went on a vision quest for Grain-of-Sand. In those days I had such determination and faith I meditated, learned Sanskrit, and even levitated, sometimes getting nine feet up. Now it's all I can do in the morning just to get out bed, much less above it. Then I managed to become invisible. Now, no matter how hard I try – or don't try – I stand out like a sore thumb. Back then, looking for ultimate truth seemed for weeks at a time the most beautiful and important thing in the whole world. These days, after I've read a book about zen or Tibetan yoga or the sufis, I may get fired up, but then an hour or two later I'll meet some girl who has a shy smile and 'whoosh' – all the air goes out of my interest in ultimate truth.

Billy knows with total certainty that he has to be the best at all he does, and he also knows that only things like grades and sports and money and girls are important, but I keep wobbling. There are dozens of things I find important, but I can never stick to one for more than an hour or a day. When I'm surfing with Billy and catch a big one just right and come sliding down the face like a jet on skis, *that's* the most beautiful thing in the world. Or when I've known a new girl for a while and we go out and talk and laugh and play, and somehow the words I say are just right, and where my hands go is just right, and she's shy and excited, and so am I, and it all comes together and we make it, and afterwards she doesn't tell me something like I was the only one in our class she hadn't made it with before but instead says she likes me a lot and is glad we made love – well then *that's* the most beautiful and right thing in the whole world.

Or sometimes in a football game I'll weave my way through the forest of hulks like a jackrabbit in a maze. The moment when I break clear and pull away and everyone else is being dragged backwards and I'm floating over the earth is – just terrific.

And reading tales of zen masters or sufis will sometimes remind me of how I feel with Grain-of-Sand. I'll want to go see him, want to work on finding ultimate truth, knowing it's something near me, knowing it's right here if I could just see – but this mood, like all the others, dies.

I can never stick to just one thing: the most beautiful, important and right thing in the whole world one day may be like having to take out the garbage the next. All the happy unity of my early years is gone now in the confusion of flirtatious girls and virtuous Dawn, Coach Cannonball's sermons on the value of humiliating the enemy and my love of sometimes looking at the way the clouds tumble across the sky, in the alternating pulls of my quest and the strange beauties of everyday life.

Sometimes I feel I'm an alien from outer space assigned to earth on some big-deal mission about which, unfortunately, no one has briefed me.

Grain-of-Sand keeps trying to tell me I'm special, but that only makes things worse. The responsibilities of being special are too much for my fragmented character. I don't like it when having to find ultimate truth begins to feel like having to take out the garbage.

Other questers have other jobs, I guess. Some have to become strong, others go on great journeys, some have to love, others to preach, some have to be killed. But my job seems to be to find ultimate truth. And though every now and then old u.t. seems fascinating, most of the time it seems a bore compared to Boston cream pie, a girl with a shy smile, a good novel, a backhand volley past Billy or the right wave. Ultimate truth lacks character. I find it easy to climb a mountain for Boston cream pie or Dawn or any of those other things, but my legs get heavy when I have to climb for u.t.

Let's face it, I'm in danger of becoming a healthy, normal, well-adjusted jerk. People are even beginning to accept me, even pretend to like me – as a normal human weirdo, I guess. At parties guys shout my name and call me motherfucking bastard in a friendly way. Successful quarterbacks are sometimes seduced by high school girls who are into being gotten into by successful quarterbacks. Teachers assume my failure to turn in homework is a mere oversight which, though I've been doing it for three years, will momentarily end and thus can be overlooked.

The only way I'm not a healthy human is my quest. For reasons I don't understand some god has given me an important assignment, and until I do it, everything else I do is only a distraction.

But I sure do love the distractions.

WIM AND THE PSYCHIATRIST

'So you feel you have many personalities,' the psychiatrist said cautiously to Wim.

'Yes, we do,' Wim replied cheerfully.

'And do the voices of these other personalities speak to you?'

'We talk to each other sometimes.'

'Do some of your other selves frighten you?'

'Of course not,' said Wim.

'Which of your selves do you like the best?'

'Each of us likes himself the best.'

'But which do *you* like best?' insisted the psychiatrist.

'Me.'

'Who's "me"?'

'Me-here-now,' said Wim.

'What's "me-here-now" like?'

'He's like only him-there-then a few seconds ago. Now the one I like best is the new me-here-now.'

'I see,' said the psychiatrist, frowning and scribbling rapidly. 'Don't you feel any continuity between your consecutive selves?'

'Oh sure,' said Wim. 'We all think our predecessors are fools.'

'What do you want to do with your life?'

'Whose life?'

'The lives of yourselves.'

'Oh, we all have different plans,' said Wim.

'Well, what determines which one of you acts at any given moment?'

Wim smiled. 'Ignorance and Chance,' he replied.

– from *Sixty-six Parables of Wim*

32

from *The Gospel According to Luke*, pp. 256–63

It happened one day during Wim's seventh period biology class with old Mr Thompson. On that day, at exactly 1.52 in the afternoon, Dawn's body, which had been lean, hard, straight and unutterably dull, suddenly became lithe, soft, supple and curved. Her hair, which for fourteen years she had worn short, suddenly tumbled to her shoulders and lay there bunched in soft curls like scoops of warm vanilla ice-cream waiting to be eaten. Her eyes, which had always been cold and distant, suddenly became dizzying pools of electricity which short-circuited the thought processes of all who dared to look within.

But that is not what caused the riot. What caused the riot was that Dawn had dressed that morning for her old body, so that the tiny training bra she'd been wearing for four years in desperate longing and her formal white blouse were both blasted to smithereens by her suddenly exploding chest. Her blue jeans split down the middle as if an earthquake had struck rather than the sudden ballooning of her buttocks into round globes that left the boys of Biology 11-C gasping. Girls began running from the room screaming and guys were moaning and groaning and squirming at their desks and clawing at themselves with one hand and at Dawn with the other, and old Mr Thompson began staggering after her, mumbling about biological improbabilities and median durational period of adolescence and incredible knockers, grabbing his Vaseline-tipped wooden pointer as he went.

Wim's panter, which had been snoozing all during biology class, leapt to life, ripped through Wim's jeans and burst up at attention like a missile at the launching pad. Wim covered it as best he could with his baseball cap, but a single twitch of Wim's powerpack sent the hat sailing across the room like a frisbee.

Meanwhile, poor Dawn was blushing and crying and trying desperately to cover two square feet (actually rounded feet) of chest with one square foot of material and not succeeding. She managed to ask the drooling Mr Thompson if she could be excused to go to the girls' room, but he was in no condition to speak. The only thing that saved her was the bell that ended the period. Since none of the males were in any condition to leave, Dawn was able to escape.

From that day on everything changed for Our Beloved Wim and his beloved Dawn. Dawn herself, who up to then had seemed to feel that all pleasures were intellectual and all athletics a waste of time, soon, for reasons that baffled Dawn and terrified Wim, began insisting that she be permitted to play in their touch football games, and then, worse, became interested in making the games *tackle*. And whenever Wim tackled her, it seemed that the only parts of her he could get a hold of, no matter how purposefully he tried to avoid them, were those new incredible protuberances of flesh at heart and rear that made Dawn seem so strange, electric and frightening. Nothing he had learned from any of his seven annual sex education programmes, from Billy, or from any of his dates, prepared him for the overwhelming dynamite of a single wrestling of Dawn to the ground on a warm spring afternoon, though if Dawn's chest came crashing down on his nose, his reaction was to faint, leading to an unjust penalty of fifteen yards against Dawn's team for unnecessary roughness.

It didn't take more than a week before Billy Best, wise beyond his years, realized that something had to be done.

They were all sitting around in Billy's recreation room typing up Coach Cannonball's final phys. ed. exam they were to take the next day, when Billy let Rocky bring up the subject of their new number one opponent: the formidable, offence-minded, superbly equipped, marvellously padded, terrifying Dawn.

'I think Dawn's become a girl,' is the way Rocky began the discussion.

Wim looked up as if Rocky had announced his mother's death.

'Don't say that,' he whispered hoarsely.

'When I tackled her in our little pickup game yesterday,' Rocky went on, 'I noticed.'

'Yeah, me too,' said Billy. 'What's worse, she knows she's a girl.' He'd recently taken up pipe smoking, partly because he'd promised his father he wouldn't smoke cigarettes until he got a full-tuition football scholarship to a Big Ten school and partly because hash and grass smoked easier from a pipe. He let a cloudful of smoke into the room.

'Yeah,' said Rocky.

'And what bothers me even more,' continued Billy, 'is that I've heard that Roger Clout plans to ask her out.'

Both Wim and Rocky looked appalled.

'I don't believe it,' said Rocky.

'I'm afraid it's true,' Billy said soberly. 'And I fear that Dawn might do something on a date with him she might regret.'

'And that *Roger* might regret,' said Rocky, banging his huge black fist down on the table.

'What worries me,' said Wim, frowning down into his glass of ginger ale, 'is that maybe it's our job, our responsibility as her . . . older brothers so to speak, to speak to her and warn her about . . . about . . .'

'About us,' said Billy.

Wim flushed.

'About the fact that men sometimes, guys sometimes –'

219

'Usually,' said Rocky.

'Guys usually ... they usually when they date a girl as beautiful as Dawn, want to ... want to ...'

'I think she knows already,' said Rocky gloomily.

'I know,' said Wim, frowning. 'That's what worries me.'

'Why?'

'Because she seems to know, but instead of defending herself she ... she –'

'Seems to want to help the ball carrier make his score,' concluded Billy.

Wim nodded mutely.

'It's my feeling,' Billy said, standing up and confronting his two young friends, 'that we ought to have a heart-to-heart talk with Dawn about sex, warn her of the dangers, and then treat her with all the consideration, intelligence, dedication and competitive spirit with which we treat every other girl.'

'No!' said Wim.

'Why not?' Billy asked. 'We are all working within the free-enterprise system, the best in the world, and Dawn is inevitably part of the system. Were we to try to protect her, it would be a kind of socialism, an act my dad would never permit me to engage in.'

'But Dawn's our friend,' protested Rocky.

'*Was* our friend,' Billy corrected. 'On the afternoon when she suddenly emerged from that biology class looking ... with those incredible ... on that afternoon,' he concluded after Wim had recovered from a brief faint, 'she lost her right to be our friend.'

'I'm confused,' said Rocky, frowning and stroking his fuzzy cheeks. 'On the one hand I feel towards Dawn the way I do towards you guys, but on the other I feel towards her now the way I do towards –'

'Vera, Olga, Joani ...' Billy concluded.

'Yeah.'

'Exactly,' said Billy. 'Our duty is obvious and we can't shirk it.'

'What do you mean?' Wim asked, looking at Billy fearfully.

'Dawn is *in* the game. She has become, with the recent and sudden emergence of her goal posts, an opponent, and we must respond to the challenge.'

'What the hell does that mean?' asked Rocky.

Billy puffed wisely and thoughtfully on his pipe and then replied: 'We must begin dating her.'

For several minutes all sat silently, two of them contemplating ravenously the almost unbelievable glories that lay potentially before them on such a playing field, and the third half-ravenous and half-horrified: how could one lust for one's moral conscience?

'But,' Rocky began uncertainly, staring down at Coach Cannonball's phys. ed. exam as if it were the problem, 'but a Dawn that *fucks* wouldn't be Dawn any more.'

'Whatever Dawn used to exist,' Billy said philosophically, 'was exploded out of existence in that biology class at the same time and for the same reason as her blouse.'

'But –' began Wim.

'If it's not one of us, it'll be Roger Clout or some asshole like that,' Billy said firmly.

'Oh, no,' said Wim.

'Better an asshole like us,' said Rocky.

'Exactly,' said Billy, tapping his pipe with dignity on the arm of his chair. 'Our course is clear. We begin immediately. It must be one of us.'

'Oh, no,' said Wim.

'Let's agree that whoever has the best day in this Saturday afternoon's crucial baseball game against Babylon High gets the first chance to date Dawn.'

'But couldn't … shouldn't Dawn remain a virgin?' Wim asked tentatively.

'Impossible,' Billy replied. 'You've heard Mr Talis speak of Manifest Destiny. A recent *Playboy* survey indicated that in our modern rational era a girl loses her virginity on the average eleven point two days after her first date, and at an average age of thirteen point eight. Dawn, it appears, has matured much later than the average girl, perhaps because of a series of only mediocre biology teachers. Nevertheless, the unpleasant fact is that soon she may have a date with Roger Clout and the countdown has begun. It's either us or them. One way or another Dawn's Manifest Destiny is ... to be just like all the others.'

The three young men all stared gloomily at Coach Cannonball's phys. ed. exam.

'It doesn't seem fair,' said Wim.

'It's the way the world works,' said Billy, puffing again on his pipe. 'Read your Plato and Hugh Hefner.'

33

from *The Gospel According to Luke*, pp. 288–92

For the first time in the brief history of his young manhood Wim's penis and the rest of him were in complete agreement: Dawn was the most beautiful and desirable woman in the world. Wim could now walk through the halls of Maganansett High and have girls wink, smile, slink, sway, brush breast, thigh, hand or lip against him, and his once outrageous member wouldn't budge an inch, but would remain curled up in his shorts like a hibernating bear cub. But should Wim see or talk to or even think of Dawn – whammo! His perker would twang to attention so stiff and hard it would sometimes bend the metal athletic cup he'd taken to wearing to cut down the sewing his poor mum had begun to have to do on the crotches of his blue jeans.

But unfortunately it looked like maybe Dawn was going through the stage he'd been going through for the last few months. She seemed able to look at Billy and Roger Clout and Rocky the same way she looked at him: which was enough to erect a Sears Skyscraper, much less a mere penis.

And he was afraid he didn't have too good a chance in the big baseball game to win the right to date Dawn, which depressed him. The only thing more frightening than Wim's having to date Dawn, was having someone else date her. And baseball wasn't exactly Wim's strong suit.

It so happened that he'd begun playing baseball for the first and only period of his life this spring, baseball being, he soon concluded, the single most boring national pastime in the history of western civilization. It came as no surprise to him that the game was invented by a schoolteacher, Abner

Doubleday. As he told Billy, 'Old Abner invented baseball as an ingenious way to keep guys bored even when they *aren't* in school.'

And Wim really wasn't very good at it. He first began playing centrefield because of his speed, but after shagging a few flies like a tiny jet-propelled wastebasket on wheels, he was abruptly shifted to second base when in the eighth inning of a tie game he ran back beautifully for a long fly and then stopped to pick two wildflowers he noticed growing in the grass. Coach Cannonball decided that wildflowers didn't grow too well in the dirt around second base, and if Wim played there the worst a wildflower could cost would be a single.

But Wim found playing second base very boring. About once every forty minutes or so someone might kindly hit a ground ball somewhat in his direction or pop a fly that he would feel vaguely responsible for, and every thirty minutes or so he got to bat. But Wim was a bad hitter (two hits in twenty-one at bats over his whole brief career), his only asset being that because he was so short he walked about half the time and then stole second and third bases if they weren't already occupied, and sometimes even if they were.

In brief, it seems that beginning in the third varsity game he played in, Wim began to go into meditative trances, which, no matter what their spiritual value might be, seemed to Coach Cannonball suspiciously like sleep. First on the bench waiting to hit (Rocky would nudge him when his turn to bat came), and then at second base. We mean a deep meditative trance. A meditative trance that might include snores. Wim would assume his infield crouch, hands on knees, and would begin chattering encouragement to the pitcher, usually Billy Best, with what he told his friends was his baseball mantra: 'AttababyBillbabykidbaby letsgokidbabykid.' After a while he would close his eyes and, his mouth still typewriting along loudly the baseball mantra, he would go into a trance, lose consciousness, dream even.

It is a tribute to the nature of baseball that although Wim slept solidly the entire last four innings of his first game, no one even noticed except Rocky and Miracle High School's second baseman, who would, in a sportsmanlike gesture, tap Wim on the shoulder at the end of each inning so that Wim could sleepjog in to the bench and continue his trance there. When tapped Wim would immediately cease shouting 'AttababyBillbabykid', trot off the field and continue to rest on the bench, shifting there to baseball mantra number two: 'GetaholdofoneRockybabykid blastherbabykid youcandoitRockybaby' until Rocky would wake him to bat.

Legend has it that a ground ball did travel through the infield about ten feet to Wim's left for a single in the sixth inning and several teammates wondered at the time why all Wim did was remain in his crouch shouting encouragement to Billy Best, especially since for the last two innings the Maganansett pitcher wasn't Billy but a left-hander named Timothy Droot. Nevertheless, Wim continued loyally to the very end to shout encouragement to 'Billbaby' even after Billbaby was back in the locker room smoking a joint.

In the fourth game Coach Cannonball had begun to notice that Wim seemed to have rather limited range on ground balls (he only fielded those that happened to hit his glove and wake him up) and ordered the shortstop to throw stones at Wim every pitch or two, and to shriek if a pop fly or ground ball seemed heading Wim's way. It didn't do much good. Since Wim wore dark glasses and kept up his chatter it was hard to tell when he was asleep, and the usual effect of a shriek was to send him running over to the shortstop to see what the trouble was. Nevertheless, since Wim averaged two walks and three stolen bases per game over the first five games, Coach Cannonball was reluctant to remove him from the lineup.

But Wim's baseball career was a short one, and it came to a dramatic end in the big game against arch-rival Babylon High, which, as usual, was far better than Maganansett.

Because which boy dated Dawn hung in the balance, Wim stayed solidly awake during the first three innings, but after Billy got a hit and he and Rocky didn't, he began going into his trance in the fourth. When by the sixth inning his team was behind 5-1 and Billy had gotten another hit, Wim was solidly asleep on the field and on the bench.

When Wim came to bat in the last inning of the game, Coach Cannonball looked grim. The score was five to two and there were already two outs. Wim, shouting encouragement to Billbaby, walked on five pitches and, forgetting that he shouldn't take chances with his team behind by three runs, stole second and third bases on the next two pitches to the next batter, who eventually walked.

Meanwhile, on third base Wim scampered up and down the line menacingly, but when the pitcher began working out of a stretch, Wim knew he couldn't steal home and so just stood five yards off the bag and began to feel bored, and when Billy Best began fouling off pitches, Wim – we report it with shame – at last and without excuse, again fell solidly asleep. In an alert crouch, hands on knees, head slightly inclined towards home, he slept.

The rest is history. After Billy walked to load the bases, Rocky Peters came up and worked the count to three and two, the huge Maganansett crowd shouting and cheering in a frenzy of hope and anguish. And then Rocky did the horrible thing which wrecked Wim's promising baseball career.

He struck the next pitch deep to left field, far over the left fielder's head, sending it rolling five hundred feet away up against the left rear tyre of Bud Foster's '63 Chevy. Maganansett's burly Bill Jakowski came steaming from second base, jammed his spiked shoe into the bag at third and chugged happily on for home. He told Coach Cannonball later that when he passed the frozen midget statue of Wim crouched on the third base line he had a vague feeling that something was wrong but felt his principal obligation was not to stop to inquire but to hurry home.

Billy Best tore around second base, flew towards third, cut sharply and competently around the bag, and zipped on purposefully towards home. He claimed later that he thought Wim was his team's third base coach that inning and felt vaguely annoyed that Wim didn't even have the intelligence to wave Billy home.

With two thousand Maganansett fans screaming deliriously, big Rocky Peters went running excitedly towards first base, wheeled gleefully to second, sailed ecstatically on towards third. He could see the left fielder still futilely chasing the ball, only now stooping to pick it up as Rocky stepped serenely on third, cut joyfully past the bag and began slowing up for his triumphant trot to home plate with the winning run. He raised both his arms high over his head with clenched fists to signal the magnitude of his happiness, and had trotted halfway down the line to home (and ten yards past Wim) when his big, open, glowing, friendly, appreciative, triumphant, modest grin began slowly with each stride to falter and be transformed into a big, wide-eyed, open, unglowing, unfriendly, unappreciative, defeated, selfish look of total terror, as (he reported later) the 'shock of recognition' (to quote Edmund Wilson) sunk in, and he realized that the statue back on the third base line was Wim, his beloved Wim, and that in passing him and reaching home plate first, all the runs that he thought they were scoring didn't count and the game was lost.

The rest is legend. The Maganansett fans were having epileptic fits of ecstasy, Rocky was being pounded on the back by half his teammates, his arms still raised, his fists still clenched, the look of shocked terror still total, and the Babylon players were trudging sorrowfully from the field, when at last everyone noticed Rocky's strange behaviour: he was standing immobile like some modern sculptor's frozen vision of The Last Judgement, arms up, fists clenched, eyes bulging, staring back up the third base line at the strange small silent crouching figure of Wim.

The crowd stopped epilepticking. The Babylon players stopped trudging. The backslappers of Rocky's back stopped backslapping. A silence descended upon the playing fields of Maganansett so total you could hear the termites at work on the visiting team's bench. Everyone (except the termites) turned to stare at Wim in his familiar alert crouch (to be the last familiar alert crouch of his brief but memorable career), hands on knees, head slightly inclined towards home plate.

Then the Babylon shortstop, who happened to have caught the baseball thrown in by the left fielder, walked over to Wim and with a malicious leer, touched him sharply on the shoulder with the ball. The silence which preceded this act was at last broken. Wim, hands still on knees, opened his eyes and shouted out enthusiastically: 'Come on Rockyba-bykidbabykid getaholdofone Rockykidbaby youcando-itRockyfellakidbabykid blastitbabykidbabyblastit ...'

34

from *Fact Sheets on Wim*, vol. III, pp. 334–5

We know that approximately two weeks after Dawn suddenly in her seventh period biology class gained 14.2 pounds in the traditional areas[14] and thus began to want to play tackle for reasons she was unable to articulate,[15] and only a few days before she first accepted a date with Senator William O. Best (at that time more commonly known as Billy), that on the weekend of 23 April, when her parents were on a holiday in Montego Bay,[16] she chanced to discover high in a closet among some golf balls and copies of *The Wall Street Journal*[17] a small collection of 8mm full-colour sound films, travelogue documentaries about various parts of the world.

We know that she was surprised to see, as the documentary 'China, Then and Today' unwound, two naked men moaning[18] and plunging[19] and tonguing[20] and mouthing[21] and mounting[22] a single plump moaning,[23] mouthing[24] girl.[25] 'The Adirondacks: Gateway to Paradise' reportedly presented a huge penis being devoured in monstrous full-colour closeup by a woman whose mouth and throat revealed an elasticity considerably beyond the statistical norm.[26] 'The United Nations: Spiritual Hope of the World' revealed one huge man[27] engaging in a variety of sexual acts[28, 29] with three imaginative[30, 31] women of different nationalities.[32] 'Incredible Journey: the Himalayas' portrayed two teenagers, one of whom looked to Dawn upsettingly like Dawn herself, engaged in a variety of sexual activities with three young well-endowed[33, 34] football players, all of them spurred on by the teenage girls' continual obscene verbal enthusiasms.[35]

Now the evidence is that Dawn, to a much greater degree than Wim, had remained to this age sexually innocent.[36] She had had the benefit of a superb public school educational programme regarding coitus and its accoutrements,[37] and of a mother who was liberal to the point even of occasionally voting Democratic.[38] But her distinguished father, Judge Robert B. Holt – who had undoubtedly been examining the pornographic films in connection with a court case – had seen to it that Dawn was unaware that she herself might enjoy sexual activity. By the end of that tragic weekend, Dawn, who watched each of the first three films two times and the last one about the enthusiastic teenagers five, was, in the words of Dr Hans Korp, who interviewed both her and several of her male acquaintances of that period, 'an electric-eyed, electric-bodied nervous wreck,'[39] who could see 'nothing but huge male members behind every pair of trousers'[40] and 'whose various orifices were inflamed for the food which all the women in her father's travel films seemed to obtain with so little effort and so much pleasure'.[41]

She had contracted what Dr Korp has diagnosed as a severe case of psychonymphomania, a condition which he describes as lasting for from ten days to two weeks,[42] and which normally has no lasting detrimental effects to either the patient or those she shares her disease with. The only known treatment, Dr Korp reports, is half-hourly application of the male penis[43] or a reasonable equivalent[44,45,46,47,48] to as many of the affected orifices as possible.[49]

In any case ...

35

from *The Gospel According to Luke* ...

'Tonight I want to rap about virginity,' Billy Best said to Dawn on the second date of her life three days after she had seen her father's provocative films. Billy had won the right to date her by being the only one of the three boys to get any *official* hits against Babylon High. He removed his pipe to look at Dawn with what he assumed were deep, mature and infinitely sexy eyes.

'Oh, really?' she said. The two were seated slightly apart from each other on the couch of the children's playroom in the basement of Billy's home. It was about ten in the evening, and his parents were out at some kind of spontaneous rally for Mayor Koch and not scheduled back until 12.18. Wim was up in his bedroom having a nervous breakdown.

'Yeah. What do you think?'

'I ... I guess I must be in favour of it,' Dawn replied, pulling nervously at the topmost of the three buttons on her low-cut blouse, which fit, but barely. She wished she hadn't agreed to date Billy and that he weren't so handsome and mature and sexy.

'I figured,' said Billy, frowning, trying to keep his eyes off everything but Dawn's elbows in order to avoid premature ejaculation. 'Why are you in favour of it?' he asked.

Dawn frowned in concentration, trying to ignore her awareness of Billy's biceps. 'I think a girl ought to remain a virgin ... not give herself completely to a man until ... until ...'

'Marriage?' asked Billy.

'Oh no,' Dawn said quickly. 'I'm too young to think about that.'

'Until she's definitely in love?' asked Billy.

'Oh no. I've been in love for years so that shouldn't be a factor one way or another.' She felt vague guilt about Wim but a brief montage of scenes from her father's films smothered it.

'Then I'm not sure I get your position,' said Billy, barely restraining himself from getting to her position.

The long habit of morality remained with Dawn even during these horrible days of her degradation and she knew she couldn't just go ahead and do what she so wanted to do unless she could find a moral justification. She frowned in intense concentration.

'I guess I believe that a girl should remain a virgin ... and not give herself completely to a man – I mean everything, you know, sucking and having a good fuck' (Billy suddenly grew pale) 'until ... until ... she's ...'

'Y-y-y-y-yes?' said Billy.

'Until ... until she feels sexual desire for a man.'

'And ... and that's *all*?' asked Billy, looking a little sick. 'You think a woman should remain a virgin until she ... feels sexual desire for a man?'

'And also –'

'Ahhh, I thought so.'

'Also the man feels sexual desire for her.' Dawn looked over at Billy feeling relieved with having established some sort of code of ethics.

Billy stared at her, his pipe pointing disjointedly down.

'It's ... it's in that sense you believe in being a virgin?'

'Yes,' Dawn answered. 'Of course, these are only general moral principles. It may sometimes be necessary to make exceptions.'

'I see.' Billy coughed and sputtered on his pipe smoke and tapped out the ashes ferociously into an ashtray.

'Uh ... lgh,' he began again. 'Do you ... do you ... feel ... er sexual desire?'

'I ... I think so, Billy,' Dawn said shyly, blushing, and the button she had been playing with on her blouse popped off on to the couch between them.

'I see,' said Billy, swallowing.

Dawn sat there smiling over at him, her lashes fluttering.

'I think I've felt desire ever since you and Wim made that marvellous gang tackle on me in that 33-27 game about a week ago.'

'I see,' said Billy. 'Well.'

'Yes?'

'I ... I find your position much more mature than that of most young women I encounter.'

'Oh thank you, Billy,' said Dawn, who was now rubbing between her fingers the second button of her blouse, which was, however, no longer attached to the blouse.

'It is, I regret to say,' Billy went on nervously, 'one of those insidious attacks upon the free enterprise system inspired by American labour unions.'

'What? *What* is?' Dawn said, pulling her skirt nervously up towards her upper thighs.

'Er ... virginity. I see it as a nationwide strike on the part of certain females for higher pay.'

'You do?'

'The refusal of women to work with men ... sexually, until a marriage contract, is a typical union ploy and works against the God-given moral right of every male human being to ... to –'

'To get laid?' Dawn suggested.

'To engage in social, political and other forms of intercourse without unjust limitation of contract.'

'Gee.'

'Thus, any girl who gives up her virginity is, in effect, striking a blow for the free enterprise system against socialism, communism and monopolistic labour union power.'

'I think that's wonderful, I guess,' Dawn said.

'I'm glad you understand,' Billy said, puffing on his pipe, although it had ceased to produce smoke five minutes earlier.

'I've been wanting to do something ... something *important* like that for ... for almost eight days,' Dawn said and took a deep breath and let out a long sigh.

'I see,' said Billy.

'Lately, Billy, I've been getting these silly overwhelming urges ...'

'Overwhelming urges ...' Billy echoed weakly.

'... To sort of rip off all my clothes and have some man do to me everything he might feel like.'

Billy found he couldn't swallow.

'Or to, well, rip off all your clothes and hold at last in my hands your ... your cock, is it?'

'Er ... yes. Or prick.'

'Or open my blouse and let you or Wim or Rocky suck at my breasts.' Dawn tugged nervously at her blouse, and the last button popped off.

'Mmmm.'

'It's all so strange. But I definitely believe that I *do* have some sexual desire.'

'True,' Billy replied, clearing his throat and adjusting his clothes. 'I ... I believe, then, that we understand each other.'

'Oh yes.'

'And you're aware that Roger Clout is a dangerous influence and ought to be avoided?'

'Oh that. But – but he's male.'

'He's dangerous.'

'So?'

'A fink.'

'His hands –'

'Look, Dawn, aren't you attracted to me?'

234

'Oh yes, Billy, yes, yes,' Dawn replied and threw herself on top of him. In an instant poor Billy was sprawled beneath her across the couch, his head jammed against volume IX of the Encyclopaedia Britannica which he had apparently been consulting earlier in the evening. Dawn pressed her mouth against his and her hips and belly against his loins. As they writhed against each other, Dawn moaned 'Oh yes yes yes,' and heard, as they briefly broke their kiss and she rhythmically pushed her pelvis against poor Billy, an echoing 'Oh no oh no oh no,' from Billy.

The next afternoon Billy Best puffed on his pipe, tipped back in his chair and gazed thoughtfully out the window. Wim and Rocky were leaning towards him, their mouths open and their eyes wide.

'And thus,' Billy commented on what he had already told them, 'although I had fumbled the ball at midfield, so to speak, I knew that it was only half-time.'

Wim and Rocky, who had a moment before looked somewhat relieved, now frowned and sagged in unison.

'Only ... only half-time?' Wim asked uncertainly.

'Exactly,' answered Billy, still gazing with philosophical detachment out the window. 'And I knew that my capacity to reorganize my offence was sufficient to mount another scoring drive after the usual fifteen-minute rest period.'

'I see,' said Wim, lowering his head gloomily.

'We can thus see why Coach Cannonball emphasizes the importance of conditioning,' said Billy soberly. 'As a matter of fact Dawn permitted no half-time rest – perhaps unaware of my fumble – and began as I lay on my back in comparative passivity, to tear from my body piece by piece every article of clothing I was wearing.'

'Jesus and Mary,' said Rocky with a moan.

'It was an unusual experience, I confess, one I have had on few previous dates. When she had me lying before her totally naked she groaned loudly and again threw herself on top of me.'

'Jesus, Jesus, Jesus,' said Rocky. Wim simply let his head fall lower to the floor.

'Although she herself remained more or less fully clothed, the experience of holding her against my bare flesh was an exciting one, and my offence quickly stiffened. Dawn seemed – I say this in the spirit of scientific objectivity – hornier than any woman in the history of the universe. She kissed my mouth, my eyes, my ears, my neck, my chest, my mouth, all the time moving her incredible left and right ends in rhythmic rush and back-pedal.'

Billy paused but neither of his two listeners seemed eager either to speak or for him to go on, both their heads hanging low. Billy puffed on his pipe and looked again out the window.

'The game was soon entirely over,' he went on neutrally. 'I realized after about five minutes of listening to her audibles and being pummelled by her end that I was nearing a second fumble and so I tore my mouth from hers and said with great passion and romantic fervour: "It's time to fuck!"'

'Her eyes were centred down on my mouth, but after I'd spoken they shifted up to mine. Her eyes –' Billy hesitated, staring out the window again as if searching for the correct words, 'seemed to be having some sort of orgasm, and she whispered hoarsely, "Oh Billy, Billy, how I want your … prick!" and then she drooled into my mouth.'

For several long moments Billy was silent, Rocky was quietly tearing the Suffolk County phone book into long thin thousand-page strips, and Wim was fighting back tears. Billy finally concluded: 'She then writhed two, three, four more times against my offensive alignment, leapt to her feet, and began to tear off her clothes.'

Here he again stared out of the window with that serene philosophical control so amazing in one so young.

'Unfortunately,' he went on, 'the effect of her climaxing eyes, her obscene words, her drooling mouth, her last writhing into my belly, the sight of her ... incredible breasts spilling out into the room as she began tearing off her clothes – the effect, I say, of all these offensive plays on her part was to lead me once more into an instinctive, uncontrollable premature spurt for a score, one which was, of course, immediately frustrated by the simultaneous withdrawal of the end zone, so that I was left holding the ... ah – or to try to stick to the metaphor, fumbling again at midfield. The next thing I was aware of was Dawn, two-thirds undressed, staring down at my second-half offence plunging away in helpless ineffectuality.'

The two boys looked up quickly and brightly at Billy Best, who stared out the window.

'You mean ... you mean ...' began Wim hopefully.

'She's still ... she's still –' began Rocky.

'She's still undefeated,' finished Billy Best and he sighed hugely for the first time and turned to face his two friends. 'The whole experience simply verifies what Coach Cannonball has been saying to us for the last year: "The best defence" – and clearly he was thinking of girls when he said this – "The best defence is a good offence." Of course, he also said that no defence is unbeatable.'

Wim and Rocky were now staring out the window, and Billy let his gaze return there also. He concluded with another sigh:

'But I bet Coach Cannonball never dated Dawn.'

'So tomorrow afternoon you're borrowing Rocky's car and taking her up to that cabin in the Catskills, huh?' Billy asked Wim a week later, leaning back in his desk chair and puffing on his pipe. They were in Billy's bedroom.

'Yes,' said Wim, seated nervously on Billy's bed.

'What about the floods?'

'Well, it's stopped raining and all the roads are still open,' Wim replied. 'Dawn says there's no more excuses; we can go this weekend.'

'And you believe that you can do what Rocky and I have in successive encounters failed to do?'

'Oh no,' said Wim shaking his head vigorously. 'Of course not. But ... but it's my ... duty to ... try.'

'Of course, yeah, you're right there,' said Billy sighing. 'We don't want Dawn to end up losing her first game to some dude like –'

'That's right,' said Wim, looking sad again.

'Unfortunately,' said Billy, 'you don't stand a chance.'

'I don't?' asked Wim, looking up hopefully.

'Not a chance.'

'But there must be some way to avoid what happened to you and Rocky.'

'I doubt it,' said Billy and he leaned back further in his desk chair to stare at the full-length poster of Joe Namath on his bedroom wall and consider Wim's statement. 'In the first place,' he went on, 'there are her eyes.'

'Her eyes?'

'Her eyes get so filled with electricity and ... ooze, that a guy loses even before he's gotten on to the field.'

'I'll *blindfold* her!' announced Wim.

Billy considered it.

'Well,' he concluded after a short pause, 'I suppose that might get you past the coin toss, but then you'd run up against the problem of her hands.'

'Her hands?'

'Her hands get moving over a guy's body so fast and with such uncanny accuracy that he loses all control of the game even before he's aware the ball has been hiked.'

'I'll tie her hands down!' announced Wim hopefully.

Billy puffed on his pipe sedately for several seconds and then nodded.

'I suppose that might do it, but then you'd still run into the problem of her thighs.'

'Her thighs?'

'Her thighs get pressing and squeezing and wrapping and rotating and plunging so sensuously that a guy fumbles before he even knows he's got the ball.'

'I'll tie down her legs!' announced Wim hopefully.

Billy puffed on his pipe for several seconds and then nodded.

'I suppose that might do it, but then you'd still run into the problem of her voice.'

'Her voice?'

'Even blindfolded and tied down, when Dawn begins calling out her audibles, they contain such a variety of moans and groans and whinnies of such horniness that a guy loses all control even before the play begins.'

'I'll gag her!' announced Wim.

Billy puffed.

'I suppose that might do it,' he said, 'but then you'd still have the problem of your eyes.'

'My eyes?'

'The moment Dawn begins to get into her full uniform she reveals a body so luscious, lithe, round, soft, creamy and honey-like, that a guy loses his offensive potential before there's even been any body contact.'

Wim stared at Billy wide-eyed and concentrating and then finally announced loudly:

'I'll blindfold myself!'

Billy puffed on his pipe for a long time before concluding with a long sigh: 'It might all work, but I'm beginning to think they haven't invented the game plan that will work against Dawn.'

'Then what can we do?' asked Wim.

'Ultimately there's only one solution,' sighed Billy.

'What?'

'Castration.'

36

from *Fact Sheets on Wim*, vol. VII, pp. 456–7

In dealing with Wim's alleged miracles it is important, of course, to seek for the natural scientific explanation for the phenomena that his followers claim to be miraculous. Thus in volume VI, section 13, we dealt at length with the alleged 'Miracle of the Immaculate Adolescence': the claim that Wim went through his entire adolescence without masturbating.[19] There we were able to demonstrate clearly that if the claim is true, and by its very nature the claim can never be proved conclusively, the explanation lies not in Wim's miraculous powers,[20] but rather in Wim's sick fascination with members of the opposite sex, a fascination that led him to express himself sexually only in the presence of girls, thus making him incapable of the healthy normal adolescent activity of continual masturbation.[21] Moreover, it is highly probable, according to Dr Rudolph Glick of the Manninger Institute of Male Studies, that Wim's failure to masturbate regularly may account for his incipient insanity[22, 23] and his sporadically small penis.[24, 25, 26] *

In this chapter, however, we must deal with the legend of Dawn's virginity, a legend given its most influential embodiment in the chapter 'How Dawn Became a Virgin' in the

---

* The fact that Wim's fully erect penis varied at times in length from one and one-half inches to eleven and one-half inches and in circumference proportionally, while fully documented by the dedicated research of Alice Tully, Jeanne Mason, Barbara Kelly, Ruth Smith and Janet O'Blittery,[27, 28, 29, 30, 31] also has a perfectly natural explanation refuting the absurd myth concocted in the alleged 'Miracles of the Multiplied Meat'.[32] It appears that the capillaries in Wim's penis ...

notoriously unreliable *The Book of Chances* and in the patently unreliable Paramount film *Adventures of Wim*.[33] We will demonstrate in these chapters that, contrary to the myths, Wim made a coldly calculated and brutal effort to rape Dawn, an effort involving binding her to a bed with heavy rope,[34] ruthless and painful gags and blindfolds,[35] and the use of a poisonous snake as a dildo.[36] Moreover, his rape even involved the traditional threat of 'your honour or your life', as was extensively documented by the witnesses from the Coosketoe Nursing Home for the Elderly, who so gallantly testified to what they saw.[37,38] It is our contention that the whole horrible experience froze the healthy sexual responses Dawn had developed from watching her father's educational films into a cold and sterile virginity inconsistent with the happiness of mankind.[39]

The legend, on the other hand, while acknowledging the rope, the painful gag, the snake, the obvious danger of death, attempts to give the whole sick story an entirely different colouring, tries to give to Wim an innocence totally out of keeping with his perverse character.[40] The myth claims that Wim and Dawn were heading towards a perfectly natural and mutually desired physical consummation of their love when 'Chance' intervened and gave to Dawn a sign that indicated to her a higher purpose for her body than 'mere ecstasy'.[41] In fact, it claims that she had a mystical experience while being 'baptized' in the holy waters of the Coosketoe River.[42]

This whole meandering and outrageous myth must now be examined and exposed . . .

241

37

from the Paramount film *Adventures of Wim*, 2002, screenplay by Olly Hart ...

(*These scenes from the film appeared in black and white with a speeded-up time frame. A piano musical score and subtitles were also used to create the illusion of a nineteen-twenties silent film. Mr Hart's screenplay has been edited here into novel form.*)

A battered old jeep is moving slowly along a muddy dirt road that winds through woods. The day is dark, and the road pockmarked with puddles from recent rains. Wim is seated up on top of several pillows driving, his face showing fierce concentration. He turns his head to the right and speaks.

'We'll be there in another five minutes.'

We see the back of Dawn's head, her long blonde hair flowing to her shoulders, a thin black bandanna around the top of her head.

'Mmmmmmmmmm.'

After we see again Wim's grim face he turns to his right, and we have our first frontal view of Dawn: blindfolded and gagged and wearing a shapeless burlap sack over whatever other clothing she may be wearing.

The car passes a detour sign warning of a washed-out bridge, but Wim turns up a dirt road to the right and, after a brief drive through the thick woods, he parks. Thirty feet away is a log cabin, and beyond it a raging mountain river.

Wim stops the car, turns off the ignition, opens his door, and slides off his pillows to get out. Then, stony-faced and mechanical – almost like a wooden puppet or Buster Keaton – he pulls out of the jeep a small suitcase that has been sitting between him and Dawn like some carefully constructed wall, closes his door, and marches around the front of the jeep to open the door for Dawn.

After she has climbed clumsily out, Wim pauses to put the suitcase on the hood of the jeep, opens it and pulls out a large asbestos glove which he puts on his left hand. He then takes Dawn's elbow to lead her across the muddy ground to the door of the cabin. He pauses to look apprehensively at the river that is lapping at the wooden steps of the cabin, then to look up the stream at the water rampaging over rapids towards them, down the stream where it flows smoothly away, and finally up at the sky, which is cloudy and threatening. At last he wheels and leads the blindfolded and gagged Dawn up the two steps into the cabin.

Inside she immediately tries to throw herself into his arms, but Wim protects himself with his suitcase and asbestos glove and speaks sharply.

'Don't try any funny business, Dawn! I know your tricks!'

Dawn's face appears agitated.

'Mmmm! Mmmmmmm Mmmm!'

Wim then leads Dawn further into the primitively furnished cabin, dominated by the bed – a giant, king-sized four-poster with a large inflated air mattress embedded into it. Wim puts his suitcase on an old wooden chair beside it and removes a white sheet which he spreads out over the air mattress, mechanically tucking it in on each of the four sides. Then, looking excited and uncertain, he points to the bed and speaks – not too confidently.

'On to the bed, Dawn.'

Dawn, looking for a brief instant coy, hops on to the bed and spreads herself out in the middle on her back. Wim turns fearfully away to his small suitcase on the chair, from which he withdraws the end of a long piece of thick rope. He moves quickly to the nearest post of the four-poster and ties the end fast with a large knot (which looks suspiciously like a bow knot), pulls a further length of the rope from the suitcase and makes a simple knot around the thin white wrist of Dawn. Back he goes to wrap the rope once around the same near post, then down to the foot of the bed where he ties another quick knot before proceeding to wrap the thick rope around Dawn's ankle, back to the post, across to the next post, down to the other ankle, and so on with increasing rapidity, all the time more and more thick rope emerging from the tiny suitcase until, when he has finished, the bed is encased in a spiderweb of the thick hemp and Dawn, spreadeagled, is bound by all four extremities to the four bedposts.

Without looking at her, his movements quicker now, Wim marches back to the suitcase and takes a large black blindfold and ties it around his own eyes. He then withdraws a second giant asbestos glove and a comically large pair of scissors. He turns to the bed and, leaning over it blindfolded towards Dawn, begins tearing off her clothes with wild abandon, ripping and scissoring and tearing and tossing fragments of sackcloth, slip, bra, panties, etc., over his shoulder like a mad doctor at an operating table. We see among the fragments being tossed the polka-dotted gag Dawn had been wearing around her mouth.

Grim-mouthed, Wim steps back from the bed, scissors held at port arms like a rifle, and stands momentarily still. Dawn is mostly naked, only a few chance fragments lying loosely on her bosom and loins preserving her modesty. A close-up shows her lifting her still blindfolded face and leering lasciviously in the general direction of Wim. She speaks.

'Oh Wim, you're rough, but I love you so much!'

Wim gives a startled jump, drops his scissors, removes his gloves, then his shirt, his boots, his socks, his trousers, and at last his underpants, until he is standing naked beside the bed, wearing only his blindfold. For a long moment he stands there, Dawn again lifting her head, until he abruptly wheels back to the suitcase from which, after raising his blindfold, he now extracts a washcloth, towel, hairbrush, toothpaste and toothbrush and marches away from the bed into a bathroom.

He swivels into the shower stall, closes the glass doors firmly behind him, and turns on the shower. As he begins to wash himself under the heavy rush of water, we see him singing loudly.

'Go, go, go, you amazing Maganansett Gulls!'

Wim washes and sings away until he notices that the drain of the shower must be plugged because two feet of water are sloshing around above his knees. With barely a break in his singing he stoops over and seems to be fingering away the pressed matted hairs, hairpins, gum and other debris around the drain, and, straightening, launches into fresh song.

'Oh come all ye faithful, joyful and triumphant!'

He seems to be well into the chorus and is rinsing off his back when he realizes the water inside the stall is now lapping above his groin. He seems to find this rather sensuous until he realizes that finding anything too sensuous at this stage is dangerous, and turns fiercely to grope for a plunger he'd noticed earlier in a corner of the stall. After pawing around under the water for a few moments Wim suddenly shows an expression of pleasure and triumph, and he straightens, holding in his right hand what turns out to be a fish. Wim holds it suspiciously in his hand a moment and then glances sternly at the shower nozzle above him. Dropping the fish, he opens the door to the shower, sloshes out and closes it quickly behind him, although the bathroom too is flooded. Irritably he ties a towel around his waist – it is immediately soaked – and quickly slides out the bathroom door and slams it behind him.

Fortunately, a hammer and nails are on the shelf just outside the door and he quickly pounds half a dozen nails into the door to make it fast, even though the viewer sees that the water in this part of the cabin is also above his waist.

At last, with a triumphant smile and the encouraging and playful words, 'Dawn! I'm ready!' he turns around and strides towards the bed, which, unfortunately, is in the process of floating out of the room into the flooded middle of the

Coosketoe River, the front wall and roof of the cabin having been already washed away. As Dawn, still spreadeagled on the bed, floats in stately grandeur away from him, Wim shouts: 'Dawn!' and we see her lift her head to reply: 'Oh Wim! Come to me! Come to me!'

Wim begins sloshing full-speed after the rapidly accelerating bed, his head barely above water, and shouts: 'I'm trying! I'm trying!'

He is, of course, a great swimmer, but in his excitement he is seen to be flailing like a submerged helicopter about ten feet behind the bed, keeping himself close and moving forwards but always with head beneath the water.

He finally makes it to the stern of the bed and for about fifteen seconds clings to the footboard with one hand, the rest of him dragging along underwater. After he at last manages to flail himself up on to the bed near the foot, he collapses, his head resting on the sheet exactly between Dawn's two knees.

'Oh Wim! I'm feeling such a rush!'

Beaten and bewildered, Wim flickers into momentary life and, teeth gritted, he manages to get to his knees and see the beautiful body of Dawn, still miraculously covered by tiny fragments at breast and loins. Wim looks both vaguely pleased with the prospect and also incredulous. As he sets his teeth again he notices something behind him and, looking, sees an alligator which is crawling up on to the bed exactly where he had crawled a few moments earlier. Wim leaps up and retreats to one of the bedposts at the head of the bed and watches in horror as the alligator, its jaws open as wide as possible, wallows forwards like a long green snowplough straight up the centre of the bed in the same direction and with the apparent same goal as Wim had just been taking. As the alligator's lower jaw begins to slide under Dawn's inner thighs she tosses her blindfolded head in apparent ecstasy, her mouth moaning out the words 'I want you!'

Wim races to the rescue, desperately pulling at the alligator's tail with one hand and holding on to his upper jaw with the other, face strained to the breaking point. Dawn's face is aglow with pleasure.

'Oh don't stop! Please don't stop!'

Wim is slowly able to pull the alligator back away from between Dawn's thighs, the long jaws closing just too late: only the hard green lips just brushing the blonde fuzz and white inner thighs as he withdraws.

'Oh yes! Yes!'

As the alligator turns fiercely to attack his tormentor, Wim breaks off the top of the left rear bedpost, and with a quick thrust fills the beast's mouth, jamming it open and sending the alligator sliding back into the water.

'Oh Wim! You're so big! So big!'

When Wim wheels back to Dawn he sees her clutching in her right hand, which she has somehow worked loose, a long thick slimy snake writhing on her belly where she holds it. As Wim screams, Dawn says: 'I'm sorry. I'll be gentle.'

Wim grabs the snake's tail and begins to pull, even as Dawn holds on to the snake firmly half a foot behind its head, which is only inches from her face. For several seconds they tug against each other until Wim finally shouts: 'Let go!!' and the snake, released, slithers over Dawn's tummy and breasts and abdomen and thighs until Wim, pulling it, is able to force it across the air mattress and into the water. Dawn's chest and abdomen seem to go through two or three spasms and with her face in ecstasy we see her cry out: 'Oh, Wim, I want you!'

But their bed-raft has just entered a series of rapids and Wim has to break off one of the two wooden slats at the rear of the bed to use as a steering oar, and for several seconds he has to struggle through huge boulders and waterspouts. After he has finally negotiated the incredible rapids he wipes his brow with a fragment of Dawn's bra, but continues to look harried and bewildered. His eyes move briefly to view Dawn and show hesitant pleasure, but when they move on to the surrounding water they fill again with fear and disbelief. Four or five sharks are now swimming in slow circles around the floating bed. As Dawn cries: 'Oh, please, Wim. Why are you wasting time?' Wim breaks off another bedpost and begins banging away at the sharks, who slam against the raft and flail and splash as Wim hammers his club against them. For several minutes the battle goes on, until the last of the sharks slinks away in disgust and Wim collapses in exhaustion at the front of the bed-raft. He stares in sad-eyed wonderment at the waters receding behind him and then again down at Dawn's beautiful writhing body.

'Where are you, Wim?'

Wim looks slowly and suspiciously but with increasing hopefulness first to the left, then to the right, and finally straight back to view what is behind; in each case he sees no new danger and his face brightens a degree or so at each glance. Almost smiling he gets to his knees and looks fully at Dawn for the first time, his eyes filled with love and tears and doubt. However, the camera then broadens its shot of his face to include first the bed flowing down the stream and then the river itself, which is carrying the raft with grand inevitability towards a gigantic waterfall. As Wim begins to crawl slowly towards Dawn we see his hopeful smile freeze as he begins to hear the tumult of the falls, and then his face again shows pained bewilderment. When he finally swings around he sees the bed only a dozen yards from the precipice.

SCENE TWO

Sitting on rocking chairs on the porch of the Coosketoe Nursing Home For the Parents of Senior Citizens, located on the ridge overlooking Infinity Falls, are Oscar Bibbs, Horace Applering and Josh Kloop, all watching through age-bleared eyes the passing flow of the Coosketoe. As the three old men sit and rock and sleep and spit there suddenly appears in the river some sort of floating raft on which the naked Wim is desperately trying to save himself and the naked Dawn from flowing over the falls.

'What's the river doing now?' asks old Mrs Higgins at work in the kitchen just behind them.

'Not much,' answers old Oscar Bibbs. 'Coupla young people going by.'

'Out sparkin' on the river?' asks Mrs Higgins.

''Pears so,' answers Mr Bibbs.

'Jesus!' comments Josh Kloop, as his eyes finally manage to convince his brain that they are seeing what he is seeing, and that he is still awake. The bed has reached the top of the falls, but Wim has saved the situation by grabbing an overhanging branch of a bankside oak tree with his arms and hooking his feet under the bottom slat of the foot of the bed, which is thus held out over the abyss.

'You want some cheese?' Mrs Higgins asks.

Horace Applering, who has been asleep and dreaming of watching his favourite TV programme, is awakened when Josh, seeing the raft dangling on the edge of the waterfall, exclaims even louder: 'Christ!!'

Horace looks out at the river through sleep-blurred eyes, at the naked man dangling from the branch, at the beautiful nude girl sprawled captive on the bed and says hoarsely: 'Turn the damn volume up!'

'Coupla young folks looking for thrills, I reckon,' says old Oscar.

Josh spits off the porch into the mud.

'Don't do their courtin' the way we used to,' he says. 'When we wanted to fuck, we fucked. These young shits got to go and make it a Cecil B. deMille epic.'

'Can't you turn the sound up?' Horace Applering persists urgently.

'That young fella got a lotta spunk, though,' says Oscar. 'You gotta admit it.'

'Shit, with that there girl,' replies Josh, 'I'd do it in a barrel going over Niagara Falls.'

'I've seen this one before,' comments Horace Applering. 'In 1926 – *Perils of Pauline*.'

As they watch Wim still hanging with both arms from the branch of the oak tree, Oscar says: 'Wonder how he's gonna get on his rubber.'

Josh Kloop spits into the mud.

'Don't need one these days,' he says. 'Gals all take pills.'

'After the commercial, the fire department arrives and rescues them,' says Horace Applering.

'Why that poor girl is helpless,' says Mrs Higgins, bringing out a plate of cheese to the porch.

'I suppose so,' says Oscar Bibbs. 'Still, it should be interesting to see how from that position the young fella's gonna get his end in.'

'The '26 version was censored though, I can see that now,' says Horace Applering, sitting more erect in his chair than he has in several decades.

'Looks like he's finally gonna get down to it,' says Josh Kloop with a tone of impatience.

And indeed, Wim, who has somehow managed – while supporting the end of the bed with his left foot – to poke upwards with his right foot a loose end of rope and tie it with one hand to the branch he holds on to with the other, is again crawling towards Dawn, the raft being barely held by this single piece of rope.

' 'Bout time,' comments Horace. 'Damn commercial due any minute.'

'Hope that girl's diaphragm warn't dislodged in them rapids,' comments Mrs Higgins.

The four old people watch as Wim throws himself on top of Dawn, but the instant he does, the bed topples over the falls and disappears from sight, being immediately replaced by a billboard which has floated down the flooded river and which lodges precisely where the bed had been a moment before, the billboard reading: FORD HAS BETTER IDEAS.

The four old people all get up in varying degrees of slowness and agility and crush together through the door back into the kitchen to get a snack before the commercial ends.

WIM JOGGING

One day Wim began jogging up and down a small hill outside a village. He would jog slowly up the hill and then lope down again. When out of breath or tired he would walk, up the hill and then down again. Finally a farmer who had been watching him for over three hours came up to him and said: 'Howdy.'

'Hi,' said Wim, jogging in place so as not to inconvenience the farmer.

'Hot day.'

'Yes, it is.'

The farmer stared off at the top of the hill towards which Wim was aimed and said: 'Doin' a bit of running.'

'Yes, sir,' Wim replied.

The farmer spit carefully off into the ditch.

'Goin' very far?' he asked.

'I don't know,' Wim answered. 'Grain-of-Sand says I'm already there.'

'Already made it, huh?' commented the farmer, watching Wim jogging in place.

'Yes, sir,' said Wim.

'Gonna wear out the road,' said the farmer.

'Well,' said Wim, 'I suppose you could say I'm planting pieces of sneaker along the road up this hill.'

'Planting sneakers, huh?'

'Yes, sir.'

'Don't know's they grow much. Macadam not too rich a soil.'

'Actually, I'm looking for ultimate truth.'

'Ultimate truth, huh?'

'Yes, sir.'

'Ever consider sitting?'

Wim stopped jogging.

'Good idea,' he replied, and sat down on the side of the road.

The farmer stared expressionlessly down at Wim for some time, chewing carefully on something in his mouth and then finally said: 'Looking for ultimate truth, huh?'

'Yes, sir.'

'Mmmmm. I see what you mean.'

'Sir?'

'Maybe you better start runnin' again.'

– from *Sixty-six Parables of Wim*

38

from *Fact Sheets on Wim*, vol. VII, pp. 344–5

(Being an interview with Dawn Holt by Dr Edgar F. Loon, chief psychologist at the Brookhavings Institute of Mental Health and Foundation Grants)

LOON: Go ahead, my dear, tell me what happened next. Don't be afraid.

DAWN: It was the most beautiful, most complete, most ecstatic experience of my entire life.

LOON: Wim had thrown himself on top of you and begun an act of coitus?

DAWN: Wim threw himself on top of me and we kissed, and the next seconds were the most exhilarating, joyful, beautiful, com–

LOON: Don't be afraid to give me the physical details.

DAWN: There were no physical details. Just this sudden feeling of floating in infinite space and then the experience of the explosion of white light and sound and cold shock ...

LOON: What was hap–

DAWN: And that's when I decided to become a virgin.

LOON: What do you mean, my dear? Hadn't Wim, I mean hadn't you and the young man already–

DAWN: Oh, no. Wim was just kissing me when we toppled over the falls and I had my ecstatic mystic experience. By the time we swam to shore I realized that no sexual experience could ever match what I had just felt, and that my third consecutive failure to give myself to a man must be a sign from heaven.

LOON: Didn't Wim renew his attentions when you were both safely ashore? After all, you were both still in a state of undress.

DAWN: Oh, no. Wim seemed tired and went to sleep.

LOON: But afterwards?

DAWN: When he woke up I told him that I had decided irrevocably that I was meant to be a virgin.

LOON: I see. And what was his reply when you told him that?

DAWN (frowning): He simply looked at me with an absolutely blank expression and said: 'Thank God'.

39

from Grain-of-Sand's *Memoirs of an Old Liar*, pp. 308–309

Got to say that in all the time I knew him I never seen Wim look so worried as those three weeks between the day Dawn became a gal and the day he took her out for a canoe ride on the Coosketoe River and got capsized.

So when I first seen him a few days after the river trip I was surprised at the change in him. He looked his old self: innocent, confused and happy. He and Dawn were walking hand in hand along the beach just like I'd seen 'em do now for more than ten years. 'Course Dawn had filled out a bit over that time – or at least in the last month – and Wim had growed too, but there was something nice about seeing them holding hands that did my old heart good.

Seems they'd come looking for me and here I was.

'We wanted you to be the first to know, Grain-of-Sand,' Wim said to me as we all stood not more than a hundred yards from the very beach where Wim was born. 'Dawn and I are engaged.'

'Engaged, huh,' I said. Montauks never have taken much stock in anything like 'being engaged': they either do it or don't, and live together as man and wife or don't. Long-range planning ain't our forte.

'That's right,' said Dawn, beaming and glowing like a gal that just won a beauty contest. 'I've promised my hand to Wim.'

'Your hand, huh?' I said, still a bit put off by their human ways, but not wanting to throw bilgewater on them.

'It may be a long engagement, though,' said Wim.

'Long one, huh,' I said.

'I feel we're still too young to marry,' Dawn explained, 'especially since my father disapproves of Wim.'

'Mmmm,' I said.

'And I realize that I really shouldn't let anything interfere with my quest for u.t.'

'Mmmm.'

'And once Wim finally finds his Ultimate Truth,' Dawn said, 'then I'll decide whether I'll marry him or dedicate my life to spiritual pursuits and remain a virgin.'

'Virgin for ever, huh.'

'We plan to remain celibate until I find ultimate truth,' said Wim.

'Yep, well,' I finally said, amazed at the delicious torture humans could create for themselves, 'ultimate truth better get on the stick then, 'cause there's nothing faster than a horny young boy when it comes to chasing after anything.'

'Thanks, Grain-of-Sand,' said Wim, and after another few minutes they went wandering down the beach by themselves, hand in hand.

Well, I can't knock it. The only folly humans got that makes Montauks a little envious is their blind, romantic, sex-postponing love. It looks like total madness, but damn, for a few hours or days or weeks they sure do enjoy it. 'Course then there's the rest of their lives.

40

When Wim lay back against the sand dune, Dawn cuddled up to him.

'I love you so much, Wimsy,' she said, kissing his fingers. 'I love the way you never know from one minute to the next what you're going to do.'

'I love you too, Dawn,' said Wim, putting his free hand in her hair.

'I love the way you leap into things before you're ready,' Dawn went on. 'And end up making such a fool of yourself.'

'I love you too, Dawn.'

'I love the way when you make a stupid mistake, you look up at me with your big eyes, the broken glass scattered all round you, and your face seems to say "Isn't it amazing the way material objects can disintegrate just because they hit concrete?"'

'Er, Dawn.'

'And I love the way when you get angry, you say stupid swear words that don't mean anything and generally act like a spoiled child having a temper tantrum.'

'Er, Dawn.'

'I love everything about you, even the way you grit your teeth and scratch away at your athlete's foot.'

'Er, I love you too, Dawn,' Wim said with a sigh. 'Especially the way you never criticize me.'

'My Wimsy.'

41

from *The Book of Chances* ...

And it came to pass that as Wim's Beloved Plant began to fill the barn the birds of the sky came in great numbers to sit on the barn roof and on the windowsills and door and on the bare branches of the two large oak trees growing near the barn and on the old shed between the barn and the mansion and on the grass and frozen earth nearby. The crow and the pigeon and the robin and the hawk and the pheasant and the chicken and the seagull and the sparrow and the humming-bird and the penguin and the osprey and the nightingale and the vulture and the owl and the albatross and the wood-pecker and the starling and the eagle and the cormorant and the bat did all come and did fly with one another and did sit with one another and there was peace.

And it came to pass that as Wim's Beloved Plant bloomed out its green garden of swaying softness the animals of the field did come in great numbers to sit on the cold earth of the back yard or in a comfortable hole in the foundation of the barn or around the shrubs and bushes and trees and rusting appliances and abandoned statues and other convenient objects. The cat and the dog and the rabbit and the fox and the fly and the spider and the hamster and the flea and the fieldmouse and the snake and the mole and the squirrel and the possum and the skunk and the horse and the mule and the bobcat and the deer and the sheep and the pig and the goat and the cow and the bull and the tiger and the raccoon and the hippopotamus did all come and did all sit with one another and there was peace.

And it came to pass that as Wim's Beloved Plant began to fill the old barn the fish of the sea did come in great numbers from the ocean to Block Island Sound to Gardner's Bay and did swim until they had found little Issiwawa Creek which ran past the rear of the barn through the cemetery, and to the tiny bulge in the creek nearest the barn they did come and there they did rest, the herring and the trout, the sardine and the flatfish, the porgie and the blue, the weakfish and the shark, the minnow and the porpoise, the blowfish and the eel, the kingfish and the snail, the shrimp and the whale, the codfish and the lobster, the jellyfish and the stingray, the one with the other, and there was peace.

And it came to pass that as Wim's Beloved Plant began to fill the old barn the boys and girls of Maganansett High School and of the Suffolk Military Academy and from all the other schools large and small in all of the area did come in great numbers to sit on the floor of the old barn and look at or climb into the sweet soft branches of Wim's strange green plant. The hippie and the square, the straight and the gay, the brain and the jock, the virgin and the easy lay, the ambitious and the lazy, the beautiful and the ugly, the radicals and the republicans, the phonies and the authentics, the loose and the uptight, the surfers and the studiers, the rock guitarists and the undeaf, the black and the white, the students and the dropouts, the boys and the girls, did all come and did be with each other and there was peace.

And it came to pass that the Beloved Plant which filled the old barn did at last blossom and bear fruit – gigantic symmetrical explosions of round green and then orange and finally red in the green forest of the Plant, and the plump round red fruit did grow as large as basketballs, and the birds of the air and the four-legged beasts of the field and the fish of the sea and the two-legged boys and girls did all rejoice, and there was peace.

42

from *The Gospel According to Luke*, pp. 344–53

Tomatoes! Big, balloon-size, red ripe tomatoes! Oh Jesus Jesus Jesus.

Billy had known for a long time that there was something fishy about Wim's plant but this was really too much. Wim might think it was a gas, but for Billy it meant a potential loss of millions of dollars.

Of course he'd had his worries all along. First, its sheer size. Then, even more, the peculiar powerful mellowness it produced in everyone just being near it. No buzz or blurriness or hallucinations, but a kind of debilitating good will that sapped Billy's desire to make money, win contests and re-establish every minute on the minute his superiority. Being near the plant tended to make him so unBilly-like that whenever he had any real business to transact, he'd taken to wearing scuba-diving gear into the barn so that he could breathe good clean artificial oxygen instead of the air contaminated by the plant that turned him into a hopeless Wim.

And he'd known that the plant had the same effect on others. When guys and girls were around the plant they didn't act the way they would in school or at a picnic or on a date. They were *nice* to each other. There wasn't any flirting or cockteasing or feeling up at all. Timmy Collins, the horniest, most lecherous, most one-track-minded individual Billy had ever known – even including Wim before Dawn had bloomed, and he'd fallen exclusively for her – Timmy Collins would wander around the barn and smile at girls and talk to them *normally*, as if they were humans instead of girls.

When Billy had questioned him just outside the barn Timmy had looked a little blank and bewildered and then said: 'You know, it's funny. When I'm here I'm no longer interested in a girl's ass or her titties. It's more ... it's more ... her *soul*, you know?'

'Her soul!!'

'Yeah, well, it's weird I can tell you. But nice. A girl's soul – they have them, they really do – a girl's soul is even better than ... her other things.'

And then to see big football jocks like Butch Messmire wandering around petting kittens, being nice to Wim, and helping girls with their knitting – it was unsettling.

And all the animals lolling around the barn and the side lawn, none of them chasing or eating the others, cats playing hide-and-seek with mice, dogs sharing their biscuits with cats, rabbits scratching for fleas while Panzer looked on zonked out of his mind.

And one day when the wind was blowing strongly from the barn towards his father's office in the house Dr Best had come out to Billy white as a sheet.

'What's wrong, Dad?' Billy had asked.

'I ... I ... I ...'

'What is it!?'

'Today, I ... I told all my patients that I've decided to lower all my fees by half,' Dr Best had said, blank-eyed and stunned. 'I told my secretary to stop billing Medicare triple, and not to bother to send out bills to any poor people who don't have insurance coverage.'

'Far out, Dad, that's great,' Billy had said, himself being zonked.

'Fuck far out!! Where's your scuba gear!?'

But Billy knew that he should have known he had problems

when he realized what happened when you smoked the plant.

As the chief owner and major shareholder Billy had taken upon himself the task of sampling the plant in order to determine its commercial value. He had shrewdly shared smokes on various occasions with selected shareholders and discovered that the effects were not those of normal pot. As far as he could now tell the effect of smoking the plant was to make the smoker even more of whatever he was. Since smoking it made Billy more ambitious, competitive and brilliant, Billy had at first figured he had a gold mine.

But when Butch smoked it, he became more stupid and aggressive. Tim Collins got sillier and hornier, and when Rocky smoked it, he got friendlier and gentler. Smoking the plant acted as a disinhibitor, but not of sexual inhibitions specifically, but of whatever it was that held you back from being more of what you already were. Billy figured that if Dawn smoked, now that she was back to her old moral, didactic self, she'd turn into Mother Teresa. Or if she'd smoked a few weeks earlier when she was dating, she might have ended up raping half of Suffolk County.

The only person he figured smoking the plant wouldn't affect was Wim. Wim couldn't be any more Wim than he already was.

So even before the disaster of the appearance of tomatoes, Billy was worried about how to market his plant. Finally he'd concluded that everyone naturally wanted to be even more of what he already was so that it would probably be a good seller even though it didn't give a buzz or so stone you that you didn't know whether you were here or there.

But the plant's final flowering into tomatoes: *that* was a blow. Billy knew immediately that if word got around that he was planning to charge one hundred and fifty dollars an ounce for ground-up tomatoes, he'd be in deep trouble. When he'd first realized that the growing green basketballs among the leaves of the plant weren't going to turn into pot seeds, he'd locked the barn and forbade even shareholders from entering. Then he'd rushed off to question Oscar Broom about the seed he'd given Wim six months earlier. Oscar admitted that it might have been a tomato seed. Jesus.

Nevertheless, standing in the barn staring up at the plant, Billy could only sigh. Some tomato plant.

When Billy announced to Wim that they'd have to harvest the plant, Wim was shattered. Two weeks after his life had begun to assume a certain degree of sanity – he still loved and lusted for Dawn, but she was as solid in her virginity as Plymouth Rock, and this gave him a strange peace – his sacred plant was going to be killed.

Billy went on in detail to describe how, using a chainsaw, they would saw off the major limbs first, then the trunk, sawing it all up into two-foot logs. Then they would split up the logs into kindling, and grind the kindling up into a sawdust powder to be sold for fifty dollars an ounce. Since the plant weighed, according to US Department of Agriculture estimates, more than two and a half tons, there would be something of a profit.

The leaves would be ground up in the seventeen blenders the stockholders had gathered, cooked in the eleven microwave ovens donated, packaged in the three thousand small plastic bags collected, and sold at a hundred and fifty dollars an ounce. All in all, the owners of the plant would gross a little over eight million, six hundred and eighty thousand dollars, which, after Billy had extracted his consultation fees, commissions, legal expenses, employee pension and retirement plans, withholding taxes, and extensive miscellaneous expenses, would net Wim and Dawn over nine hundred dollars each, which, he assured them, since Wim's total investment was apparently one hundred and one bowel movements, should seem to him a good profit. His shareholders, he pointed out, weren't getting any actual cash but were being paid in a generous dividend of sawdust.

But Wim didn't care about Billy's accounting methods. He wasn't interested in profit. Nor was he even interested in seeing whether by smoking his plant he could find Ultimate Truth, since his love for his plant and its love of him had eliminated his curiosity about Ultimate Truth. All he cared about was his plant, and he saw no reason just because it had flowered to have to give up the thing he loved.

And yet on that sad yet glorious day of the plant's blossoming, it seemed he had to. Dawn took him for a walk away from the crowds of people, animals and birds around the barn to explain to him that if he didn't agree to the chopping down and dismembering of the tree soon, or somehow make it disappear, then sooner or later – and with all the people always wandering zonked around the barn, probably sooner – the local authorities would raid the barn, and confiscate or destroy the plant.

That evening when Billy and his workers and his shareholders had gone – all having agreed on gathering the next day after school for the eight million dollar harvest, Wim sat under the leaves of the plant next to the Doberman and meditated, trying to see what he should do with his Beloved Plant. He had earlier made phone calls to find out how much it would cost to move his plant to some forest and transplant it there, but the two trucking companies he contacted said that they had no way of disguising a fifty-foot tree with branches extending twenty-five feet and furthermore such a tree couldn't be moved more than two hundred yards in the town of Maganansett without having to eliminate the entire telephone system.

The plant couldn't continue to grow where it was: already the barn was four storeys high where previously it had only been two, and there was a zoning law against structures more than four storeys high. Wim would die before he'd see it chopped up and put into blenders. He refused to see it confiscated by some narcotic agents no matter how nice they might be. He couldn't transplant it any place else. He could feel himself wanting to cry. Almost six months of dedication and love had – one way or another – to come to an end.

It wasn't until the next morning that he finally decided that the most fitting and loving death would be, in the traditional Montauk way, to bury his plant at sea. All he would have to do was dig his plant up by the roots, move it the fifty feet to the three-foot-wide Issiwawa Creek, somehow barge it down that to Gardner's Bay and to the ocean.

He began at once. Unfortunately after an hour of furious digging he had exposed only fifteen feet of one root which, from its six-inch diameter, looked like it must go out another forty feet from the plant. Without even considering the problems of hiring bulldozers and building rafts, Wim calculated that it would take him a minimum of a week just to dig up his plant, not mentioning moving it. Since he had only a few *hours*, he decided he needed another plan and went back to meditating. When he still came up with nothing he decided he had to see Grain-of-Sand.

The old man appeared almost the moment he'd decided to go see him, apparently on one of his periodic visits to see the plant.

'Billy says it has to be chopped down tonight,' Wim told the old man as they stood just inside the open barn door staring up at the plant that now completely filled the barn. With the coming of spring all the blankets and lights and fires were unnecessary, and with the late afternoon sunlight streaming in, the plant seemed more beautiful than Wim had ever seen it.

'Yep,' said Grain-of-Sand.

'I don't want it to be chopped down and cut up into pieces,' said Wim.

'Nope,' said Grain-of Sand.

'I think I should bury it at sea,' said Wim, glancing up hopefully at Grain-of-Sand.

'Yep.'

'But I can't figure how to get it down and away in only a few hours.'

'Nope.'

They stood for a while in silence.

'I need your help, Grain-of-Sand,' said Wim.

'Yep.'

Except for the soft twitter and cooing of a few birds and the refrigerator purring of several happy cats, the silence continued.

'I don't know what to do, Grain-of-Sand,' said Wim.

The old navigator looked up at the plant, at the slumbering and spaced-out creatures lolling on its leaves and in the nooks and crannies of the barn and felt a strange uneasiness. The thought of a lot of humans coming in and tearing the plant apart to divide it up to sell it and get drunk on it suddenly struck him as being as frightening and wrong as Wim apparently found it.

'Got to do something,' he said softly.

'I know, but what?' asked Wim.

'Yep.'

A single chipmunk walked lazily along the leaf nearest Grain-of-Sand, stared at him, yawned and went to sleep. Grain-of-Sand felt deeply that this plant was a bit out of his league, just as Wim was in some ways out of his league, but his whole body was telling him in no uncertain terms that Wim had to do *something*. Wim and his mum and maybe even Dawn might be able to handle it, but this plant was much too powerful for most humans. The thought of it cut up and spread out over the whole county was terrifying.

'What would the Sanskrittens do?' he finally asked.

Wim looked surprised, then frowned in puzzlement.

'I ... I guess they'd ... they'd burn it,' he finally answered. 'Make a funeral pyre and burn it.'

'Yep,' said Grain-of-Sand.

A robin flew in the barn with a fat worm in its beak, circled twice confusedly and then offered its worm to a big white cat. The cat raised its head and chomped on the worm idly from the bird's beak until it was eaten.

'You think we should burn the plant?' Wim asked.

'Don't know,' said Grain-of-Sand. 'It's your plant. Your special plant. Only you can know for sure what's right to do.'

Wim stood a long time in the barn entrance feeling the fading sunlight warm on his neck and then heard raucous laughter behind him and knew that the first students were arriving for the big harvest. Grain-of-Sand heard them too and felt a stab of fear knife through him sharper than anything he'd felt in years.

'Got to do something,' he said.

'Will you help me?' Wim asked.

Grain-of-Sand nodded.

Wim immediately felt that burning the plant was right. It was even a way of smoking his plant, but not in bits and pieces as Billy intended, but all at once, in a great big crematory blaze of extinction.

He quickly telephoned Dawn to tell her what he was going to do and was discouraged but not deterred by her belief that he only had the moral right to burn down his and Dawn's part of the plant and not that belonging to Billy, Oscar and the thousand shareholders. Nevertheless, she'd come over to help.

It was dusk when he left Billy busily phoning potential customers and snuck out of the Bests' mansion to meet Dawn inside the barn. He had to be careful not to step on any of the rabbits, pheasants, hamsters, mice, dogs, cats, rats and other animals resting happily in the spring grass. Although he felt badly about thwarting Billy's plans, he knew he had to go through with the burning, even if it took him a millennium to pay Billy back.

Inside, Dawn came up to him and gave him a little hug – actually it was hard for her to give a *little* hug – and then helped him gather kindling. When they'd gathered a lot, Wim climbed one last time up his beloved plant and out each of its limbs, saying a last goodbye. He discovered a boy and girl resting and snacking and licking on various leaves and told them it would be best if they'd leave. The pigeons and robins and bats, the only birds that seemed to come into the barn to rest, he had to carry down the plant and give to Grain-of-Sand and Dawn to put on the old well where there was still space. They seemed too spaced-out to fly.

He then knelt in the earth near the base of his beloved plant and prayed, asking the Great Spirit to forgive him for not making his plant into eight million joints and smoking some of them and thus perhaps getting closer to ultimate truth. He promised that as soon as his plant had smoked into the sky and joined the Great Spirit he would try to dedicate himself even better to the single-minded pursuit of u.t. Tonight, though, he had to destroy the thing he loved.

Wim prayed and cried and felt really good, while Grain-of-Sand stood by and watched and heard from outside the approaching sounds of more laughter. Then Wim took a candle to where they'd piled the old wood used for building up the sides of the barn each day and, using an abandoned paperback of *For Whom the Bell Tolls* as incendiary, he started the fire.

LETTING GO THE BIG FISH

One day Wim was fishing with Grain-of-Sand in the old duckboat the navigator had fixed up from a derelict. After Wim had tossed out a lure, the old man baited his hook with a worm and tossed the line in. After a while his thin bamboo pole began to bend, and as he reeled in his line, a large bass could be seen flailing away. Wim was pleased as Grain-of-Sand, smiling happily, reeled in the fish and gingerly removed it from the hook. Then, looking the bass right in the eye – it was the biggest they'd caught all summer – he said: 'Sorry, fella, you're too big,' and dropped the fish gently back into the water.

Over the next hour Wim watched Grain-of-Sand reel in and keep several small fish and medium-sized fish, but when he landed a second really big fish, he again happily returned it to the sea.

Wim cleared his throat and said: 'Gee, that's the second nice fish you've caught today.'

'Yep,' said Grain-of-Sand.

'Big enough to eat.'

'Yep.'

'Big enough to stuff.'

'Yep.'

Wim silently jigged his line for several moments, and then he finally said: 'But you threw them both back.'

'Yep.'

'Why?'

'The way I figure it,' Grain-of-Sand replied, 'anyone can catch a big fish. But how many can then let it go?'

– from *Sixty-six Parables of Wim*

43

from *The Gospel According to Luke*, pp. 378–86

The effects of the burning of the 'Sacred Seed of Wim' were not what he or anyone else expected. Some creatures seemed to be affected primarily by the presence of the plant and were thus mellow and loving, while others seemed to be affected mostly by inhaling the smoke, which meant they became even more of what they already were.

Wim started the fire just after dusk. Within an hour it had drawn half the town's population, beginning with Dr Best and a dozen neighbours, expanding with the arrival of Engine Company 6 of the Maganansett Township Fire Department – eleven men, a dog, two trucks and a lawyer – and growing further with the deployment around the farmhouse and barn of six narcotic agents of the Suffolk County Special Division of Security for the Prevention of the Ingestion of Illegal or Non-therapeutic Drugs. They had meticulously planned their raid for over three weeks in order to first verify the rumours that a million-dollar dope crop disguised as a tree was growing in the barn owned by the son of a moll of reputed South Shore Mafia figure Joe Izzio. They also wanted to make certain that there would be no time for the alleged drugs to be flushed down the outhouse before they were apprehended.

The Society for the Prevention of Cruelty to Animals, in their effort to determine what kind of animal experimentation must be going on in the barn to account for the bizarre behaviour of all the animals in the vicinity, had also deployed three agents, who were quickly convinced that if they could sneak close enough they might discover a grisly animal crematorium.

The Maganansett High School Marching Band and three or four hundred students arrived next, having scheduled at the farmhouse a giant rally in preparation for the next day's graduation, having told their principal of the 'favourable environment' of the barn. New York State police cars 11 and 16 arrived soon after in response to a request from a local householder to eliminate the exuberance of a crowd.

Eastern Airlines flight 401, destination Miami, began circling the old barn at one thousand feet in a tight holding pattern at about 9.30 P.M. and was joined a little later by Delta flight 28, destination Atlanta, holding at seven hundred feet, and after that by TWA flight 666, just in from Rome, holding at thirty-five feet in a close circular pattern. The pilots and co-pilots of each of these planes (three of about sixty in the vicinity which were sucked into the vortex) claimed that 'It just felt better than landing right away,' and 'It made sense to let the passengers get a good look at the barn burning down there,' and 'It reminded me of bonfires when I was a kid so I decided to take her down before heading on to Miami.'

Captain O. R. Williams of TWA flight 666 claimed that he had his plane on automatic pilot and that he and his co-pilot had been sleeping since sometime over the Bay of Fundy when they awoke to find their plane flying at thirty-five feet in a tight circle over a blazing barn with Delta and Eastern only a few hundred feet above them. 'Of course, I was concerned,' Captain Williams reported, 'but since I was ahead of Delta and Eastern for a landing at Kennedy I didn't dare give up my favourable position just because we were mowing somebody's lawn.'

It was only after his plane had run out of fuel that pilot Williams decided to take her off automatic pilot, take control, and essay a landing. His skill at putting the plane down successfully on the eastbound lane of the Southern

State Parkway cannot be diminished by the unfortunate elimination of the twelve toll-booths and their occupants and coins, which brought the big plane to a successful halt.

The US Army Attack Helicopters 'Robert Redford' and 'Xavier Hollander', each carrying ten Green Berets, arrived over the barn a little after ten, responding to a Task Force Alert Grade C, indicating possible guerrilla uprising. The speed of their arrival is a tribute to US defence preparedness, and those who have criticized the degree of military intervention in what turned out to be primarily a civilian disturbance, have forgotten how in the late 1980s it was widely believed that disturbances in Central America might somehow soon lead to an invasion of Queens.

In any case the helicopters maintained an active surveillance of the scene with flares and defoliation grenades until about eleven-thirty when their leader, responding to the combat he was witnessing below, ordered the planes to land and his men to go into action.

The USS *Marlybone*, an attack ship of the US Navy stationed normally in the Atlantic Ocean off Montauk Point, arrived at the headwaters of the Issiwawa Creek in response to an urgent alert signal grade D 'Civil Uprising' at approximately 11.45 P.M. having been held up by the slow pace of the high-speed dredger *Columbo* which had to precede the *Marlybone* the last two miles up the creek.

Neighbours, police, curious citizens and others continued to arrive throughout the evening, with everyone's behaviour leading later critics to refer to this night as the 'Plague of the Potted Plant'. Captain Art Tadwritter of Engine Company 6 not only began exclaiming to everyone of the fire, 'It's beautiful, it's beautiful!', but also, when the flames were dying down, ordered his men to throw kindling and hay on to the embers. Later he ordered his men to set fire to the small shed which until then had remained untouched, crying 'More beauty! Yet more beauty!' and 'Burn, baby, burn!' He also helped out by ordering the fuel siphoned from his firetruck's gas tank and using it to start the fire.

Later, no longer wearing his uniform, he led his men to the Best mansion in order to create yet more beauty, but was hindered in the performance of this task by Wim, Dawn, Billy, Dr Best, and a ferocious man-eating tiger that according to many unreliable sources made an appearance at this time, chasing one fireman high up into a tree.

Agent Ronald Okker of the Suffolk Special Drug Division confiscated a six-and-a-half-foot-long leaf from a high school student and after ingesting a small amount, undoubtedly to determine whether it were a proscribed drug, then proceeded to distribute the remainder in bits and pieces to a hundred or so boys, girls, animals and birds, saying to each boy and girl 'peace', to each dog 'rhgghff', to each cat 'meow', and to the majority of the birds 'tweet, tweet'.

Reports are less reliable that a Mrs Mason of the Suffolk County Chapter of the Society for the Prevention of Cruelty to Animals tried to roast a live rabbit at the end of a pointed stick. Some witnesses claim the animal was a raccoon or a small cat. In any case a large number of animals and birds of a wide variety of species, apparently numbed by the fire and smoke, were picked up and cooked at the end of sticks, golf clubs, and bayonets, and were ingested with no reported opposition from any public official, Mrs Mason herself complaining only that the meat 'hadn't been cooked enough'.

Poor Wim was horrified by the effect the smoke was having on animals and humans alike. Wim and Dawn spent much of the evening trying to gather hundreds of the drowsy birds and animals and hide them in the five-car garage, but were sporadically stopped by officials of the SPCA who claimed that it was illegal to take in a stray animal without the animals first being vaccinated.

The Maganansett High School Marching Band, after playing a Sousa march as they were arriving, shifted quickly to 'Why Don't We Do It in the Road', and, after many of them had finished doing it in the road, the band disintegrated into improvised nude solos whose overall effect was cacophonous. It may have been during the brief searches for illicit drugs that most students were divested of their clothes, although ingesting the handouts from agent Okker probably helped. Some students later claimed that the Green Berets, searching for weapons, ordered them to undress. Many ladies said the heat of the fire became too great for the early spring clothing most wore and that it was purely for reasons of comfort that almost everyone began to go nude. In any case, by 11.00 P.M. most of the students, neighbours, random strangers, parachuting stewardesses, and others at the scene, including the firemen and all but one of the narcotics agents, were naked, and the vast majority of these were engaging in acts of sexual congress, sodomy, statutory rape, forceful rape, fellatio, cunnilingus, masturbation, animal husbandry and corpus delecti. These acts were performed with a degree of abandon which all authorities agree was deplorable, and the active involvement of teachers, bandleaders, cheerleaders, and fire department chiefs was later attributed to the evil power of Wim's plant.

So was their cruelty to animals. Although some moral philosophers claim that the forcible rape of an animal is a much worse crime than burning it on the end of a stick and eating it, others refer to studies at Duke University which indicate that animals in a maze when given the choice prefer rape to a cookout six to one, although of necessity those choosing the cookout route of the maze were a self-delimiting sample. The Duke Study also indicated that roast raccoon is far preferable to roast hamster, and that it is difficult to rape a porcupine.

The USS *Marlybone* didn't start firing until almost midnight, 'an admirable show of restraint', according to the Secretary of the Navy. Commander Ulysses Stoode of the

Marlybone said that when he saw his air cover being removed – referring to the forced landings of the last of the circling commercial aircraft – and then saw the Green Berets being stripped of their uniforms and overwhelmed by hordes of naked protesters, most of them females and thus clearly belonging to guerrilla forces; and when he saw more than fifteen of the naked savages, mostly female, approaching the Issiwawa Creek and the USS *Marlybone* with pointed sticks on which seemed to be impaled baked little children, possibly the children of the Green Berets, he had no other recourse but to open fire. Considering that any gathering of young people in large numbers was in all likelihood to protest something, or worse yet, meant the start of a rock concert, most claim that the *Marlybone's* act is understandable.

The first torpedo apparently exited from Issiwawa Creek a little after midnight, ran irregularly along the ground for one hundred feet and came to an unexplained halt in the exact middle of the now smouldering ruins of the plant and barn. It didn't explode until it was being refuelled on the *Marlybone* two days later. Torpedo number two was more effective. It chased several students over two hundred feet on to the highway before giving up the chase and proceeding down Suffolk County Route 55 at about ten miles an hour, diverting traffic for a mile until it came to a halt in the garage of Mr Lawrence Ingle. It also failed to explode until it was struck by a Porsche from behind when being transported back to the *Marlybone*. The Congressional Military Preparedness Subcommittee that investigated these weapons failures concluded that neither the defence contractors involved nor inadequate maintenance were responsible, but rather 'bad luck', and recommended a larger military budget.

Undeterred by the failure of his initial attack, Commander Stoode ordered his two forward anti-aircraft guns to commence firing over the heads of the guerrillas still molesting the Green Berets, who could be heard moaning all the way up on the bridge, but after expending three hundred rounds that were not even noticed, he ordered his men to hold their fire and thus save ammunition, an order that was perhaps superfluous given the fact that most of his crew, having inhaled too much of the smoke drifting over the ship, had become inspired to join the Green Berets in their hand to hand and leg to leg combat, and abandoned ship. Seeing this, Commander Stoode then climbed down from the bridge, over the rail, waded the twelve feet to the shore, carefully removed his uniform, and advanced into hand to hand entanglement with the guerrillas, male and female, but mostly female, his words the next morning becoming a part of US Navy legend: 'I came, I saw, I came.'

Wim barely survived this 'Night of the Burning Stars'. While he was busy trying to rescue the small helpless creatures, a group of students, confused by his small size, began to try to impale him on a stick for the barbecue, but were hindered by Dawn's fingernail attack. When some other students later began to lynch two narcotics agents for starting the fire that destroyed the plant, Wim intervened and confessed that he himself had started the fire. The students then apologetically removed the ropes from the agents' necks and placed both around Wim's neck, but he was saved by Dawn's distracting them by removing her blouse.

Wim then had to save Dawn from a fate worse than death and did so by releasing some stoned bees he had been taking to the garage into the midst of the male crowd around Dawn.

Wim and Dawn then continued to try to save a few rabbits and pigeons and other creatures whose fate has traditionally been to be eaten and otherwise abused by higher beings. Wim tore the helpless animals out of people's hands and hit and kicked those who resisted. If someone tried to stop him when he carried an armload of animals and birds towards the garage, he would scream so loud the person would leave him alone. He'd learned that trick from

Arf. Neither he nor Dawn seemed to notice the nakedness and love-making – they were too busy carrying animals in a red wagon or bushel baskets or their arms to care.

At some point Billy Best came up to Wim, very pale, and asked what had happened. Wim told him that he had burned down the plant and apologized and told Billy that he agreed that he owed Billy six or seven million dollars and would pay him as soon as he could. Billy just looked at Wim blankly for a long time, sighed and said: 'And to think, I won't even be able to use it as a tax loss.'

When he saw Oscar Broom a half hour later, Oscar was naked and eating the roasted leg of some animal. He told Wim that the plant gave a good high and must have gotten plenty of love. Wim didn't answer, but just kept shovelling the little dazed rabbits into his wagon.

By midnight the barn and plant had been burned to the ground, although the shed was still going good. Wim took Dawn's hand and walked her back towards the garage. They had to be careful not to step on the naked people who were all over the lawn, and men and women kept coming up to them in the dark and trying to pull Dawn away with them, but Wim scared them off either with his scream or by releasing a few bees that were really getting back into beeness. All the animals and birds – those still alive – were gone.

As they entered the garage this time a dozen animals ran out between their legs and twenty or thirty birds fluttered hysterically out over their heads.

Inside the garage the animals that hadn't fled were slaughtering each other. When they saw Wim and Dawn, they too scurried past and out into the night – those still able to move. Left were the dead and dying birds, rabbits, mice, hamsters, lambs, pigs and other less aggressive creatures, and one large Alsatian munching on a chicken. Birds were screeching in terrified circles, and Wim opened a garage door to try to help them escape. Then he took a bloody rat out of the jaws of a bored cat and helped it crawl out into the grass. Within two minutes the five-car garage, which had held hundreds of living creatures before, was empty, except for about three dozen dead or dying birds and little creatures. Wim pushed the Alsatian gently out the door and into the night.

For a while he and Dawn stood at the open door and looked out into the yard at the red coals, all that was left of the plant and barn. Searchlights were sweeping the yard from various police cars. White and black bodies were running around, and there was considerable yelling and screaming. A few members of the marching band tried to play 'Nearer My God to Thee' but without much calming effect. A cold wind was blowing in now from Block Island Sound.

Dawn was crying. Wim's hand alternately squeezed and trembled in hers. Then he turned and looked up at her.

'Let's go,' he said grimly.

'Where ... where are we going?' Dawn asked.

'Away from the sickness.'

WIM AND THE MAD BUDDHAS

'I didn't become happy as a human being,' Wim said one day to his disciples, 'until I suddenly realized, after years of blindness, and after at long last finding old U.T., that instead of myself being a Buddha in a world filled with madmen, I am a – I know not what – moving in a world of genuine, through-to-the-core Buddhas.' Wim paused with a concerned and puzzled frown on his face, and finally added: 'Most of them carefully and fully disguised as madmen.'

– from *Sixty-six Parables of Wim*

44

from *The Gospel According to Luke*, pp. 400–408

The next morning Wim and Dawn were gliding along smoothly at five knots in Wim's twenty-five foot, custom-built day-sailer catamaran. It had cost him eight thousand dollars to have it built back in the days when he was a successful entrepreneur and was now his last and only legal possession on earth. The two sails were filled nicely by a fresh breeze; the sun warmed their bodies; the salt spray spit playfully up over the windward bow, just enough to cool them and give them the illusion of speed and excitement. Only a distant unnoticed rumble of thunder marred what had been an almost perfect day, the first period running over a minute and a half that Wim could remember recently which hadn't been filled with problems. After six hours out on the water the horrors of the night before were beginning to fade.

'You see,' Wim said to Dawn with a sigh, 'the Gods can take away my plant and my money, make me lose the big baseball game with Babylon, make me partly responsible for the slaughter of hundreds of innocent animals, but they can't remove the sun from the sky or the wind from the air, or the water from the sea.'

'Sometimes, Wim,' said Dawn, looking tentatively over at him and taking off her light windbreaker now that the day was warming up, 'you surprise me. After last night I thought you'd never smile again. Yet now you seem to be sailing serenely on.' After glancing around at the horizon – there was no land in sight – she turned back to him with a teasing smile. 'Except for your attacks of lust, your unreliability and your lack of moral concern for the Albanians, you're almost a good man.'

'Goodness has nothing to do with it,' replied Wim, shortening up the jib as he headed up more into the wind. 'Grain-of-Sand taught me that when the Gods frown, the wise man learns to surf on their furrows.'

Dawn smiled.

'But the Gods haven't just been frowning,' she said. 'They've been throwing at you enough bad luck to last the normal man a life–'

'What bad luck?' said Wim. 'A few million dollars, the end of a dream I had about my plant, a lost baseball game – bah. Grain-of-Sand says that the worse things get the better things get. Give me sun, sea and wind and everything is just jim-dan–'

There was a loud 'snap!' and the foresail began flapping and snapping wildly in the wind.

'The jib sheet seems to have parted,' said Wim and he turned the tiller over to Dawn and scrambled forward to try to grab the flailing end of the line which had held the jib in place.

The line cracked and snarled like a bull-whip wielded by an unfriendly slave-driver and, after experiencing two or three lashes across his chest and face, Wim retreated to the mast where he began to try to untie the halyard so he could lower the jib completely. But the loose end of the jib line seemed to pursue him there; as his fingers battled with the knot the bull-whip systematically lashed him back and forth across the thighs and chest. Screaming loudly, Wim crawled back to the boat's cockpit.

'Are you all right?' cried Dawn. 'That was horrible!'

Wim, the welts slowly emerging along twenty-six rows on his body like a system of pimples, didn't comment. Looking back at the flailing jib, he could see the first rips appearing in the sail. In another ten minutes, he knew, it would be a tattered rag.

'It still isn't fixed, is it?' Dawn asked as she emerged from the small cockpit with two tubes of suntan lotion to soothe Wim's wounds. She had to shout over the slapping, whining foresail to add: 'Don't we sail better with the jib?'

'Yes,' said Wim, groaning with the first tender touch of Dawn's fingers on his raw skin, 'but ... but I thought maybe we'd experiment with sailing by mainsail alone.'

'But look, Wim,' said Dawn. 'That sail is being torn to pieces.'

Wim didn't look; he remained hunched over on the cockpit seat groaning as Dawn spread on the lotion.

'Why are you letting it do that?' asked Dawn.

'I need handkerchiefs,' said Wim.

A little later when he heard thunder and noticed a squall heading towards them from the ocean he directed Dawn to bring the boat about and head for home. But after heading for port for about a minute the wind shifted and she had to head off fifteen degrees, then thirty, then sixty, until they were headed back towards the thunderstorm.

'Come about again,' Wim said, but as soon as they changed tack the wind changed too and in no more than a minute they were headed right back out to sea and into the storm. The flailing jib had reduced their speed to three knots and the falling tide was running out to sea at a knot and a half, so that Wim estimated that even if everything went right it would take eighteen hours to return to the harbour they had left only six hours earlier, and if everything went wrong, or rather as it had been going, they would be in Europe within five weeks.

'I'm going to turn on the outboard engine,' said Wim.

The outboard wouldn't start. Wim noted that the fuel tank was empty.

'Go get the gasoline,' said Wim.

'What gasoline?' asked Dawn.

'The gasoline you bought for us at the Mobil station in the red tank.'

'Oh, *that* gasoline,' said Dawn, looking relieved. 'It's in Billy's car.'

There was a loud 'twang' and a steel shroud that supported the mast began swinging in a long lazy arc around the mast.

'Quick,' said Wim. 'Release the mainsail. We've got to lower it before –'

Cra-a-a-a-un-un-KK!

With an informal finality like that of a displeased guest leaving a party, the mast toppled over into the sea. Since, however, the mast and boom and sail were fastened to the boat by stainless-steel shrouds, they settled alongside the catamaran and began banging against it like an irate guest who's forgotten his wallet.

'That shouldn't do that, should it?' suggested Dawn.

The catamaran now lay motionless (actually it was drifting at about two knots away from land and towards the thunderstorm) and noisily (flailing handkerchiefs, boom and mast banging holes in the starboard side of the boat) in the sloppy sea. Wim was now leaning back against the cockpit seat with his eyes closed.

'Shouldn't we do something?' asked Dawn.

'I'm doing it,' said Wim.

'But what are you doing?' asked Dawn.

'I'm doing nothing.'

'But ... but ... how ...'

'Believe me,' said Wim, his eyes still closed. 'It's the most effective thing I've done in a long time.'

For about five minutes they drifted noisily out to sea, the thunder booming closer and closer.

'Wim?' finally said Dawn.

'Yes?'

'Why is the boat leaning?'

Wim slowly opened his eyes.

'Leaning?' he asked.

'See. The boat is leaning to the right.'

'You mean listing to the right.'

'Oh. Listing. What does it mean?'

Wim looked for a few moments at the phenomenon of the right side of the catamaran being approximately two feet deeper into the water than the left and then leaned back against his seat and reclosed his eyes.

'It means the starboard hull is filling with water.'

'Wim!'

'It means we're sinking.'

'Wim!!!'

'It means I won't be able to keep my eyes closed.'

Wim stood up and opened his eyes. His body now resembled a leaning barber pole with red stripes running evenly from his forehead to his shins.

'What are you going to do?' Dawn asked him.

'Grain-of-Sand says when the deluge has covered everything he owns, the wise man learns to love fish.'

'Wim!'

'It's only a proverb. Don't worry, I'm going to set off a few flares and someone will come rescue us.' Wim disappeared into the little portside cabin and reappeared after a minute.

'Where are the emergency flares?' he asked Dawn in a calm, terrified voice.

'Un ... Wim ...'

'Yes, Dawn?'

'You remember the time on Memorial Day weekend you let Billy and me take a sail to shoot off some fireworks?'

'Yes.'

Dawn didn't say anything more.

'I see,' said Wim. He watched the sea beginning to lap over the right side of the boat and slosh around in the cockpit. 'Well,' he went on, 'Grain-of-Sand says that when the mountain falls on you, the wise man learns to sell landfill.'

'What's that mean?'

'It means we put on life preservers, gather fresh water and dried food and assume we're going to sink.'

Nevertheless, while Dawn went below to get life preservers, Wim proceeded to throw overboard everything heavier than water in the hope that then the wooden part of the catamaran would keep them afloat. He unfastened the outboard engine and watched it sink (1,615 dollars 95). He removed the two Danforth anchors (166 dollars 50 and 140 dollars 74 – on sale) and their chains (22 dollars 95 and 18 dollars 95) and watched them sink. He cut and sawed through the shrouds and lines which held the mast, boom and sail (898 dollars, 245 dollars, and 456 dollars 95) attached to the boat and watched them sink, throwing the hacksaw (7 dollars 77) gently in after them.

'It's a good thing you didn't bring that gasoline tank,' he said to Dawn when she emerged from the cabin, 'because then I would have had to throw it overboard.'

'Wim?'

'Yes, Honey.'

'Remember that time you let me and Rocky go sailing last weekend?'

'Yes.'

'Well, we used the life preservers as cushions when we sunbathed on Shelter Island.'

'I see,' said Wim. He sat himself slowly down in the two inches of water on his cockpit seat and noticed that his toes looked bigger when seen through two feet of water. He looked up meditatively at the approaching black clouds.

'Grain-of-Sand says that when the sky falls,' he said slowly, 'and somehow manages to strike only you, it's time to reconsider your position.'

Before Dawn could ask for an interpretation she noticed that the sky was now entirely clouded over and that the thunder squall was almost on top of them.

'Notice,' said Wim, after Dawn had informed him of the closeness of the storm, 'that if we weren't two-thirds sunk we would be blowing out to sea more rapidly.'

'Really?' asked Dawn.

'Absolutely. And notice that when the mast fell it totally failed to strike me on the head.'

'That's true.'

'And that although our engine didn't work, its failure isn't hurting us one bit now because it couldn't push a submerged boat anyway.'

'I suppose not.'

'And that the jib is now so torn to pieces that it is making very little noise.'

'Yes.'

'And that because we have only one mast and two hulls, only one of our hulls has been bashed full of holes by the mast and thus we are still able to float.'

'That's true.'

'And even though we have no flares or life preservers, that single hull should stay afloat and permit us to stay with it until we starve to death.'

'Wim!'

'Thus, when the sky falls and seems somehow to hit only you,' said Wim, almost smiling, 'all you have to do is look a little closer and ...'

'And ...?' asked Dawn.

Wim frowned. 'Look a little closer,' he finally said, 'and you'll see you've probably got a big head.'

'My poor Wim ...'

Just then the squall struck full upon the little half-submerged catamaran, sending rain slashing against their faces and waves breaking over the entire boat, thus permitting Wim and Dawn to be underwater without having to go swimming or even leave the cockpit. Lightning and thunder flashed and crashed about them. As they held on to lifelines and gasped for breath Dawn turned to Wim and shouted above the roar of wind and waves: 'Ah, Wim, I see now your mistake.'

'I was born.'

'This morning you said you could always be happy if you

had the wind, the sun and the sea, but you forgot to mention *land*.'

'Mmmmm.'

'Well, *do* something!'

'Land, land, land,' said Wim sullenly. 'Wind, sea, sun and land.'

But the storm still swept across them like a billion little water particles rioting after a soccer game. For an hour they clung to the boat in the fury of wind, lightning and thunder until suddenly Wim realized, with a fear and joy such as he never remembered experiencing, that the thunder was trying to speak to him. As he wallowed in the debris of his sinking boat, holding Dawn with one arm and a cleat in the floating hull with the other, he abruptly shouted: 'Louder!'

'What!?' shouted Dawn.

'Louder!' shouted Wim to the thunder. 'I can't understand you!'

'I said "what?"' shouted Dawn.

Ignoring her, Wim listened carefully to the Ruddaduddaboom-buddhaboom and *knew* that the thunder was trying to speak to him.

'Speak more slowly!' shouted Wim.

'Wah-uh-ut?' shouted back Dawn.

The thunder said, 'Dahmaddadumbuddhadumbuddhaboomboom dum.'

'Right!' yelled Wim.

'Huh?' interrupted Dawn.

The thunder said, 'Boombuddhatathatadumbuddhadumdhamadadum.'

'Good point!' yelled Wim.

'Land!' yelled Dawn.

The thunder said, 'Damhadatathatabuddhadumdumbuddhaboomboombum.'

'Well, I don't know if I can buy that,' said Wim respectfully.

'Land!' shouted Dawn.

The thunder then paraded out one of its longest sentences in history while Wim, frowning furiously as his bare feet scraped across the barnacles of the rocks against which the remainder of his catamaran began to smash itself to pieces, desperately tried to listen.

'I can stand!' shouted Dawn triumphantly.

Wim discovered that he could too, except for the minor detail that although his feet were firmly on terra firma his head was still four inches under water.

'Glub,' he commented as he took Dawn into his arms and began to stagger with her towards the beach and, when his head had resurfaced, tried to catch the thunder's message. By the time he was kneeling in the sand beside Dawn, the storm seemed to be moving rapidly away and the sound of thunder to be more and more muffled. As Wim watched his beloved catamaran slowly but surely being rebuilt into kindling, he abruptly stood up and shouted skyward over the crashing waves: 'Damn it! The next time you want to get in touch with me, send a telegram!!'

WIM MEETS DEATH

'I met Death once,' Wim said casually.

'You did!' exclaimed several of the disciples. 'Tell us about it!'

'It was during a hurricane in the Atlantic. I was alone aboard a thirty-foot sailboat whose lifeboat had been swept away, whose rudder was broken, engine flooded, mast toppled, sails ripped away, bottom leaking about a bathtubfull a minute, the pumps not functioning, and the wind and waves were pushing us towards an uninhabited reef two miles away. To top it all I was seasick.'

'What happened?'

'All of a sudden, Death appeared in the cockpit beside me. He was a big guy about six foot two, a hundred and ninety pounds with curly red hair and a tattoo on his right arm. I recognized him immediately.

'"It's about time you got here," I said. "What the hell took you so long?"

'For a while he looked at the wrecked boat and the huge seas and my vomit washing back and forth in the cockpit, and finally, looking directly at exhausted, miserable me, he said: "With your luck you didn't expect me to get here when you wanted, did you?"

'"Good point," I said, vomiting neatly into a wave that rolled past under my nose. "But now that you're here, for Christ's sake, hurry up and take me."

'"Shit, no," he replied. "I was just sent here to get a small flying fish that died from water pollution here in the cockpit of your boat."

'"But . . ." I began.

'"When I come for a person," Death went on, "he can't see me." And He began climbing on to the almost submerged cabin top.

'"Hey!" I shouted, feeling worse than ever, "don't leave me!"

'"Sorry. I got a million things to do today." And as Death began fading off fish in hand into the roaring storm, He added: "See you later."'

After Wim had ceased his narration all of the disciples sat quietly in respectful silence until Wim finally commented: 'Death's the sort of guy who's never around when you need him.'

Only after several more minutes was the silence again broken.

'I have no fear of death,' one of the oldest of Wim's disciples then said sombrely. 'I see Death as a friend with whom all men have an appointment.'

'That's true,' said Wim with a frown. Then he suddenly brightened. 'But as for me,' he went on, 'I'm glad I've always been bad at keeping appointments.'

– from *Sixty-six Parables of Wim*

45

As Our Beloved Wim carried Dawn away from the water he realized they had beached on a small round island less than a hundred yards in diameter and with an ancient stone lighthouse in its exact centre. He was still wrestling with what the thunder had told him but was worried about Dawn, who was trembling. As the storm seemed to be passing out into the Atlantic, taking with it the wind, rain and thunder, he set her gently down on to the sand.

'Where are we?' she asked.

'I don't know,' he said, peering through the dusk to see if any other land was nearby.

'Look,' Dawn said through chattering teeth, pointing upwards and looking surprised.

At the top of the lighthouse a dim light seemed to be flickering, casting eerie splinters of light against the ancient glass.

'Let's go in,' Wim said and put his arm around her cold wet waist to guide her through the sand to the opening at the base of the tower. Inside, they climbed an ancient rusting circular staircase towards the hint of light they could see far above. From the cobwebs it didn't seem anyone had been there in centuries.

When they reached the top they entered a tiny round room with a single table upon which was a huge four-foot-high candle with an inch-thick wick, a single shelf with a few cans and potatoes and a two-burner kerosene stove, and a single chair, on which sat the wrinkled, smiling figure of Grain-of-Sand.

'What took you so long?' he asked, looking up calmly, his kindly eyes flicking from Wim to Dawn and back.

'Everything!' Wim answered, both surprised to see him and yet not surprised. Exhausted, he leaned his back up against the stone wall. 'But what are you doing here?'

'I got ordered here by a Vision,' Grain-of-Sand replied, peering at Dawn, 'and steered here by my arthritis. I must say this god of yours has a roundabout way of doing things.'

'I know,' said Wim. 'Have you got a blanket or jacket or something for Dawn? She's freezing.'

Grain-of-Sand stood up, took off his jacket and put it gently round Dawn, motioning her to take his seat.

'Oh, no,' said Dawn. 'Please, you can sit.'

Grain-of-Sand steered her firmly to the chair, where she sank down with a contented sigh.

'Where are we?' Wim asked.

'Near as I can figure, an island ten miles off Montauk Point,' said Grain-of-Sand.

'There is no such island,' Wim countered.

'Oh, well, I wouldn't say that if I were you. You're sitting on it.' Grain-of-Sand began poking around the stove to fix what looked to be hot chocolate.

'But Grain-of-Sand–'

'Near as I can figure this island's been here a long time, but since it ain't got no name, damned geographers never put it on their maps, and since it ain't on the maps, the modern sailor knows it can't possibly be here.'

'But . . .' Wim began, 'but what if I should *name* this island?'

'Then you'd create a dangerous hazard to navigation,' Grain-of-Sand answered amiably, stirring the liquid in the old pot.

'Just by naming it!?'

'Don't exist unless you name it. Once it's here, though, lot of boats going to have to steer around it or get wrecked.'

'What about this lighthouse?' Dawn asked as Grain-of-Sand handed both her and Wim large tin cups filled with hot chocolate, apologizing for stirring both of them with his fingers.

'Of course, that saves a lot of boats from running up here, I admit,' he said.

'But ... where's the light?' Wim asked, utterly bewildered.

'Right in front of you,' snapped Grain-of-Sand, returning to the stove and beginning to slice up potatoes.

'It's just a candle!'

'He who has eyes to see, let him see,' Grain-of-Sand responded, casting Wim a quick glance. When Wim looked back blankly he added, 'You get the message this time?'

'From the thunder? Part of it.'

'What'd you get?'

'Why can't he mail me a letter or something?' Wim asked. 'I'm tir–'

'Tradition,' said Grain-of-Sand. 'Gods never go piddling around with pencils or typewriters. They use fires in bushes and lightning and earthquakes and floods and stone tablets – the things with more flair to 'em.'

'Well, can I put in a request for a stone tablet or a burning bush? This thunderstorm business–'

'Nope. It looks like thunder's your Daddy's trademark. You might as well get used to it. Just remember to always keep galoshes and life preservers handy, and you'll do fine.'

'And can't He learn to speak more clearly?' Wim asked. 'Most of what He says sounds like the rumbling in some monster's bowel system.'

'Now you watch it, Wim,' Grain-of-Sand said, turning his eyes full on Wim. 'You speak respectfully of your Father's bowel system.'

'I'm sorry,' Wim said.

'All right. Ain't everybody whose Daddy even tries to talk to him. You oughta be thankful.'

'I am, Grain-of-Sand,' Wim said. 'I'm sorry.'

'So what did He say?' the old Montauk asked next, squinting at Wim fiercely.

294

'All I got was ... was that I ought to be searching harder for ultimate truth and that I needed to seek out some gurus who might help me.'

'That's all you got!?'

'My boat was sinking!!'

'Great Living Spirit, I never knowed a boy with such bad hearing. You weren't listening at all!'

'I was! There was water in my ears!'

'Why He spoke a whole encyclopedia of stuff and all you got was search for ultimate truth and find some buddhas.'

'And something about Colorado.'

'That's great, just great. Something about Colorado. Even I got more than that.'

'Well, what is it?' Wim asked.

'The thunder spoke in good basic Montauk, so I was able to catch most everything,' Grain-of-Sand explained, handing each of the youngsters a large plate of french fries.

'It spoke in Sanskrit,' Wim countered.

'Montauk, and don't interrupt,' Grain-of-Sand said, motioning him to come up to the table. 'He wants you to get on the stick after old u.t. and gives you a lot of advice 'bout how to do it.'

'I will, I will,' Wim said, trying to look determined but actually feeling a tremendous desire to gobble up the french fries.

'Says you got to go and try to find three great buddhas, and the last one will tell you exactly where to find u.t.'

Wim was stunned. Over the last year his quest had begun to seem like something that would never actually end, and here Grain-of-Sand was telling him that all he had to do was go see some guru and it would all be over.

'That's ... terrific,' he said, feeling a mixture of joy and doubt.

'Yep. All you seem to have to do is go say "howdy" to these three fellas and the whole strange game of your hide 'n' seek with ultimate truth can close up shop.'

'I'll go see them tomorrow. Tonight even. Where are they?'

'Oh, well, 's not that simple. They're in different places.'

'Where?'

'Well, as I got the message, first you got to go try to find a fella called Mayarishi in India.'

'Fine,' Wim said, swallowing another big mouthful of french fries and surprised at what a good cook Grain-of-Sand was. 'I'll just have to borrow some money, hop a plane and go interview him.'

'Not that simple, Wim,' Grain-of-Sand said, holding up a bony hand with a french fry in it. 'Mayarishi's other name is Great Abominable Snowman Sage of the Sky. He lives in the Himalayas.'

'Well, still I can–'

'And this fella has a problem, claims he's been alive now close on to six thousand years, and every winter he needs a little rest. He sort of freezes down into a meditative trance and don't do any talking.'

'Well. I'll simply–'

'And since the Himalayan winter lasts eleven months and two weeks, he's only available for a few days. Rest of the time he's in this great trance and covered with so much ice and snow that when he occasionally walks in his sleep, he scares the icicles off any innocent Sherpa happens to see him.'

'But then–'

'Looks to me like you'll be lucky even to wave "hello" to him, much less chat about old u.t.'

Grain-of-Sand was squinting at Wim again to see how he was taking it all.

'But if I do see him,' Wim asked, 'what comes next?'

'Then you're supposed to go see some monk out in Colorado.'

'That sounds simpler. United Airlines has lots of flights to Denver.'

Grain-of-Sand shook his head slowly, glanced at Dawn, who, like Wim, seemed very hungry, then shook his head again.

'T'aint that simple,' he finally said. 'This Brother Fetticini or Bollajelli fella's a modern monk and the monastery he's 'sociated with don't keep all the old traditions.'

'So?'

'They got transistor radios in every cell, men and women bathing together, and non-organic gardening and the best softball team in the Ecumenical League, and three rock bands –'

'But then why should I have to go see this ... man?'

Grain-of-Sand shook his head again.

'Beats me. I guess this fella must be a buddha. Just that he may hide it real well.'

This time it was Wim's turn to frown.

'And that's gonna be your problem,' Grain-of-Sand went on. 'According to the thunder none of these fellas ever turn out to be what or who you expect them to be.'

'But –'

'Anyway, then the third buddha you got to find is a great black sufi sage from the Sudan.'

'Oh, no. I don't even know where –'

'His name's Narsufin. Used to play basketball for the Detroit Pistons a few years back. His whirling dervish body fakes were 'parently something. Then he went and got enlightened and dropped his stuff shot and is now a great wandering sufi sage.'

'But how will I find him?'

'Oh, he should be the easiest to find. Big guy, six foot nine, but on the slim side. Weighed only about a hundred twenty-eight pounds, fifteen percent of it his sneakers. In a certain slant of light cutting to the basket he was kinda hard to see, sorta disappeared.'

'But –'

'Called him "The Razor". So damn thin. Bill Bradley claimed he got nicked everytime Narsufin bumped him.'

'But what has all this to do with –'

'Narsufin is a Sufi sage,' Grain-of-Sand said sharply in a tone of voice that implied Wim should have known as much. 'The greatest Sufi sage since Sheik El-Ghazali-Rumi, and he and he alone will point you to the very spot you'll find your old u.t.'

'A ... basketball player?'

'He's retired. Damn shame too. He used to have a bag of tricks that drove opponents crazy. He was a master of sounds, you know, mantras or wazifas or whatever they call them, and he used to have a certain low hum that caused Dr J to double-dribble or palm the ball eleven straight times. Had to bench Dr J for some third-stringer who was a little deaf and thus could handle Narsufin.'

'He was a Master of wazifas?' asked Wim. 'I've read that's important.'

'Nonsense,' Grain-of-Sand shot back. 'What's wazifas to a man that went three rounds with Muhammad Ali and beat him.'

'Beat Muhammad Ali!!?'

'Just after the WBA benched Ali for claiming he didn't have nothing against no Cong, Ali was looking to stay in shape and boxed Narsufin in a three-round exhibition for a Muslim charity. Ali didn't land a single punch.'

'"It was like fighting some *mosquito*," Ali claimed after the fight. "Whoever heard a bee able to sting a mosquito. Ain't no way. I AM THE GREATEST! But not against mosquitoes."'

Wim and Dawn were both staring at Grain-of-Sand, baffled by his long dissertation on basketball and boxing.

'But ... but Grain-of-Sand,' Wim asked tentatively. 'How can the Thunder possibly have told you all these things about Narsufin?'

Grain-of-Sand looked a little baffled and embarrassed himself.

'Beats me,' he finally said, shaking his head. 'Damned if I even knew there was a Montauk word for "basketball", much less "stuff shot".'

'But ... but, anyway, where will I find him?'

'Oh you can't never find Narsufin. He hangs out in the Sudan, Egypt, Detroit, Ceylon, Harlem – places like that. He gets around.'

'But –'

'You'll just have to let him find you,' concluded Grain-of-Sand contentedly. 'And when you see Narsufin he'll tell you exactly where you can find ultimate truth.'

'I'll be an old man by that time!' Wim said dejectedly.

'Well, that's the way it usually is. Besides, don't knock old men. I might take it personal.'

'I'm sorry, but how can I possibly manage to find these three great buddhas if it's as hard as you say it is?'

Grain-of-Sand looked at Wim from across the candle, his whole face flickering strangely.

'Beats me,' he suddenly replied and then broke into a brief husky laugh. 'This whole quest of yours is the biggest fuss about nothing I've ever gotten involved in, and I tell you I'm giving serious thought to resigning as navigator.'

'Oh, don't do that, Grain-of-Sand,' Wim said, feeling that he needed him more than any of the three buddhas he was supposed to find.

'It just ain't the way we Montauks are used to doing things,' he complained. 'And the way you go about trying to find your u.t. makes me think the whole quest is some sort of a trick.'

'I'll never find it,' Wim said glumly, pushing his empty plate on to the table and belching from his belly-full of french fries.

'Just gotta keep your eyes open,' Grain-of-Sand said, now looking cheerful again. 'Sooner or later you'll find it.'

'Ultimate truth is like this island,' Wim said, feeling that things were hopeless. 'Nobody can see it except you.'

'That about nails it,' said Grain-of-Sand. 'And most searchers are like you: they sit down with it and belch and claim it don't exist.'

'But ... but –'

'Gotta learn to untie those "buts" of yours, Wim. The way you carry on I figure if the Great Spirit Himself suddenly appeared right here and now and announced "Let there be light", you'd look up at Him respectfully and say, "but ... but."'

Wim couldn't help smiling at Grain-of-Sand.

'I'm not too sure of myself sometimes, am I?' he said.

'I've seen more confidence in a legless centipede,' said Grain-of-Sand, grinning. 'Still, the sickest humans are filled with certainty. At least you're still only stuck in confusion.'

Although through most of Grain-of-Sand's talking about what he had to do Wim had felt heavy and depressed, somehow the phrase 'only stuck in confusion' released him. He felt suddenly excited by what the thunder had told him. Locating three scattered and mostly invisible buddhas somehow seemed no more impossible than the stupid things he'd been doing with his life lately. All the interests and passions of the last four years seemed to fall from him like chainmail shirts, and without having taken a single step towards u.t. he still felt lighter than he had since the last time he'd made himself invisible – six months before. He wouldn't go to college, wouldn't play professional football with Billy, wouldn't become a great physicist, wouldn't do *anything* until he had discovered ultimate truth.

Standing straighter than he had in months he announced proudly: 'I shall *go* to the Himalayas.'

Grain-of-Sand squinted across at him a long time. Finally he said: 'What for?'

46

from *The Gospel According to Luke*, pp. 434–42

When Our Beloved Wim arrived in India that summer with Billy and Dawn and Billy's grant from the Exxon Foundation to dig exploratory holes for u.t., he was filled with excitement. He announced proudly to the Indian customs officials that he was coming to India to seek a guru – it was part of his path to Ultimate Truth. Since Wim was speaking in the last part of the twentieth century, the Indian officials all looked at him blankly. Wim was the first westerner in almost ten years to come looking for a guru. Americans had come in thousands back in the sixties and seventies, but in the eighties, under the guidance of the American president of that era, Ronald Reagan, they had at last discovered total and complete enlightenment. It was called money. In the eighties thousands of Americans still travelled to India each year, but now to start import-export businesses that would provide them even more total and complete enlightenment than they could earn staying in the US.

Dawn told the customs officials she was a tourist, but because she was wearing a light low-cut summer dress and smiling they didn't hear a word she said. Billy declared that he was a businessman interested in exporting to the United States various Indian products which he hadn't yet determined. The product was less important than the producer, Billy explained, who must be skilled, dedicated and above all else connable. Dawn and Billy were passed through customs with smiles, handshakes and pinches, but Wim, after his announcement, was whisked away and strip-searched, given a psychiatric examination, and questioned extensively by an obscure American official, all to determine what his *real* reason for coming to India might be.

'Don't you understand, kid,' the tall, hawk-nosed American finally said to Wim. 'The guru business is dead. What used to be gurus are now just skinny naked Indians who don't work for a living. The Indian government is embarrassed about 'em. They don't want people to think they're a backward country where grownups still wear white diapers and don't eat at McDonalds regular and use nails for mattresses. It's bad for business.'

'I'm sorry,' Wim insisted, 'but that doesn't change why I've come. I'm determined to find the Abominable Snowman Sage in the Sky as part of my quest for Ultimate Truth.'

The hawk-nosed American sighed.

'OK, kid, I believe you. Look, where's this Snowball hang out?'

'In the Himalayas.'

'Fine. Now I like you. It's clear you're too stupid to be a leftist, so here's what we'll do. I want you to go back and tell them custom guys that you're the head of a scientific expedition exploring for ... for u.t., is it?'

'That's terrific!' said Wim, smiling. 'That's just what I'm doing!'

'Right. Businessmen and scientists are always welcome the world over.'

Although Wim was dressed in jeans and a T-shirt that proclaimed 'Brave Men Hide', his explanation of a scientific expedition was greeted with great relief by the customs officials. All he had to do was fill out in triplicate a long questionnaire in which he was asked to give the colour, weight, size, chemical properties, approximate location, and 'precise economic value' of u.t. Fortunately, no one had looked at any of these questionnaires for more than five years, and Wim's vague and whimsical answers therefore disturbed only Wim.

Billy Best handled the travel arrangements. Wim figured

that if Wim made them they'd cost three times as much as for most travellers, but that with Billy making them they'd cost a lot less.

Billy started impressively by discovering an obscure Indian law that no one had bothered to repeal and that permitted holy men to travel free on all Indian railroads on Wednesday and Thursday. Billy announced that Wim was a Montauk holy man, Dawn was his devotee, and he himself his business manager. After long discussions in the New Delhi train manager's office among several well-dressed Indians, it was decided that Wim was indeed a holy man and could go free, that Dawn was indeed a knockout and could go half fare just because she would so improve employee and passenger morale, and that Billy Best was indeed a fraud and would pay double fare – under another obscure Indian law dating back to the 1870s in which anyone unfriendly to the British Empire paid double. Although Billy sang three choruses of 'God Save the Queen', the officials still sensed in him an underlying hostility to the British Empire and charged him double. Billy began to suspect that India might not be the backward country of his dreams.

After a two-day train journey, the three young people arrived in a dingy village in the foothills below the mountain in the Himalayas where they hoped the Great Abominable Snowman Sage of the Sky would soon melt down enough to chat. It was a town so backward, Billy complained, they didn't even sell Kellogg's Sugar Smacks.

Dawn immediately began distributing food she had brought to some of the scrawnier-looking street urchins. After casing the town, Billy began negotiating with a craftsman who took three weeks to create an intricately beautiful wooden jewel box out of local hardwood. Unfortunately, the man was stupidly resisting Billy's offer to buy a hundred jewel boxes at eighty cents apiece.

Meanwhile Wim went alone to find some Sherpa bearers and a guide to take him to find the Mayarishi. The Sherpas lived mostly at the north end of the village in a cluster of ramshackle huts that reminded Wim of some of the places lower-class Montauks lived in. Since Wim spoke fluent Sanskrit and had picked up Hindi on the train, he had no trouble talking to anyone. After meeting a dozen squat muscular men, he found himself drawn to the oldest, a small wizened man with twinkling eyes named Osso. The old Sherpa, who reminded Wim a little of Grain-of-Sand, admitted he could lead Wim to the Great Sage Mayarishi, but wondered why Wim wanted to find him.

'It's part of my quest,' Wim answered, happy to share his search with the little old man. 'Grain-of-Sand had a vision that says I have to see Mayarishi as one of the steps to find ultimate truth.'

Osso was squatting on his haunches in front of his hut smoking a Marlboro. When Wim finished he nodded.

'Ultimate truth ...' Osso echoed in his high sing-songy voice. 'What's that?'

'I don't know,' said Wim. 'That's why I'm looking.'

Osso nodded.

'Always smart to look for things you haven't found,' he said.

'Thank you,' said Wim. 'Will you help me find the Mayarishi?'

Osso took a long drag on his Marlboro.

'Suppose it can't hurt,' he replied after a pause. 'How much do you pay?'

'Oh, I'm not allowed to discuss that,' said Wim. 'Billy Best is my business manager and he handles all my money affairs.'

'Like to meet him,' said Osso. 'Perhaps he will permit me and a few poor bearers to earn enough to avoid starvation.'

'Oh, I'm sure he'll go that high,' said Wim happily.

That evening, while Dawn led Wim through the cold, damp streets looking for an old woman she had met during the day who might benefit from Wim's Montauk herbal medicines, Billy went to old Osso to negotiate an agreement.

The next morning Wim and Dawn were surprised that the three bearers Billy had hired were the three smallest, thinnest and frailest men they'd seen in all of India. Wizened old Osso seemed a giant in comparison. Wim assumed Billy'd gotten them dirt cheap, but when he asked questions about the agreement with Osso, Billy looked unaccustomedly vague and puzzled.

'It's funny,' he said. 'That old Sherpa convinced me last night that those guys were the three toughest men west of the Pacific Ocean. He said because he liked you so much he'd give me a special deal and let us have them at only a third their normal price, which was usually double the normal overweight Sherpa. He gave me a special deal on himself too ... way off his usual fee.'

'That's great!'

'Yeah,' said Billy, looking more puzzled than ever. 'Trouble is, after I'd gotten this great deal – only two hundred dollars a week for all four men – I checked with a big burly Sherpa who was holding up a Volkswagen so someone could rotate the tyres – asked him how much he and three of his weight-lifting buddies would charge per week. He told me they'd do it for five dollars per week per person!'

'Wow!' said Wim.

'Yeah,' said Billy, looking awed. 'I'm paying ten times as much for three guys who look like they'd blow away if I breathe on them too hard.'

'But why?' asked Wim, now looking as puzzled as Billy.

'The best deal I could get,' said Billy in awe. 'The best deal I could get.'

At noon they set off from the village for Mt Ikawandi in the Himalayas. The temperature had fallen below freezing, but Billy had brought along three arctic tents, a month's supply of food, including thirty frozen dinners (lobster, prime sirloin and chicken a la king), and a small portable computer with modem so if he located a telephone on Mt Ikawandi he could check on his stocks. Wim had brought a dozen of his best books about looking for u.t., eight cartons of chocolate chip cookies and a dozen comic books. On the off-chance of beggars on Mt Ikawandi Dawn had brought two suitcases filled with apples. As they trudged upwards along the narrow mountain trail, the three bearers looked to Wim like tiny mice staggering under the carcasses of three elephants.

Osso himself carried only a small handkerchief bundle tied to his waist, explaining that the guide needed to keep his mind unburdened so he could stay on the path.

By the end of the first day Osso told Billy the three Sherpas were so overloaded they were sinking into the earth and thus trudging too slowly and wearing themselves out. He asked that Billy, Wim and Dawn take upon themselves more of the supplies and that a few non-essentials be abandoned.

At the end of the second day Osso convinced Billy that more supplies ought to be abandoned and that because Americans were so much stronger and tougher than the poor Sherpa bearers, they should carry most of the load.

By the end of the third day Billy, Wim and Dawn were each carrying not only all of the few remaining supplies – mostly bread, beans and sleeping bags – but also were each carrying piggyback one of the three frail bearers.

'It's to conserve their energy,' Billy explained to Wim and Dawn as they staggered along together, 'for the push to the top.'

'But I thought it was *us* who were supposed to go on alone to meet the Mayarishi?' said Wim.

'Maybe, but I don't want these guys to break down and become useless later on.'

Wim, carrying twenty pounds of supplies and an eighty-pound Sherpa, wondered when they would need their bearers more than now, but was too pooped to ask.

In the afternoon of the fourth day they finally staggered down into a tiny, decrepit, poverty-stricken village, the first they'd seen. The local population came out to greet them with big smiles and to ask if they'd enjoyed their trip. It was only after Wim had laboriously unloaded his food, sleeping bag and Sherpa that he realized that they had arrived back in the same village they'd left four days before. The big burly Sherpa Billy had spoken to even lowered the Volkswagen long enough to shake hands with them all.

When Billy realized where they were, he turned to Osso, who had pulled from his bundle a pack of Marlboros and, squatting, was lighting up.

'What kind of a guide are you!?' Billy exploded, while the villagers looked on grinning. 'After four days we've had to abandon ninety per cent of our supplies, we've hiked our asses off, carried three of the most useless beings God ever lowered to the face of the earth, and finally, through pluck and luck and your fuckup navigation, arrived right back where we started.'

Osso looked up at Billy's red face with surprise until Billy finished. Then he slowly exhaled cigarette smoke and smiled.

'Oh, no, sir, not true,' he said. 'You much closer now.'

'We're in the same fuckin' spot!!'

'Oh, no, sir, not true,' Osso insisted cheerfully. 'You in very different place from four days ago.'

'The same fuckin' village!!!'

'Same village maybe, but you in very different spot. Much closer to seeing great Mayarishi.'

'I want my money back!'

'Oh, no, sir, no money back,' said Osso with a frown. 'However, because I like your little holy man, I make you another good deal.'

'Another good deal with you and I'll have to declare

bankruptcy!' shouted Billy, and Wim rushed up to comfort him.

The next day Wim, Billy, Dawn and Osso set out again for Mt Ikawandi. As they climbed, Billy whispered to Wim and Dawn that he had conned the old Sherpa into agreeing that for a modest additional cost to them of only ten dollars a day the Americans would no longer have to carry the three Sherpa bearers. When Wim questioned Billy about why they were paying Osso two hundred and seventy dollars a week for *not* taking any supplies and not providing any bearers, Billy grew pale and puzzled and kept muttering that it was the best deal he could get.

An hour later Wim hiked up beside Osso and questioned him about why he'd picked those particular bearers.

'Best men for the job,' Osso answered promptly, not breaking his steady stride upward over the rocks and ice.

Wim hurried after the vigorous little man, who, like Wim himself, seemed almost buried in the mountain of clothing they wore against the Himalayan cold.

'For carrying our supplies?' Wim finally asked.

'Oh, no,' said Osso amiably. 'For dumping them. You would never get to see the Mayarishi with all that stuff. In only four days with my special Sherpa bearers, you threw out almost all of it.'

Wim trudged upwards behind Osso another ten strides.

'Wouldn't it have been simpler just to *tell* us not to take it?' he asked.

'Oh, no,' said Osso, climbing on. 'If I tell you, then even if you leave junk in village you still carry it in your minds. Now, thankyouverymuch to my bearers, you know junk is junk and have thrown it out of your minds too.'

Wim hiked onwards behind Osso for another five minutes, finally drawing abreast of him one more time.

'Still,' said Wim, gasping for breath, 'why did we have to carry the bearers on our backs for almost two days?'

Osso halted and turned to Wim with a big grin.

'Just for the fun of it,' he said, his eyes twinkling out of their slits. 'Just for the fun of it.'

WIM AND THE THREE KITTENS

One day Wim and Billy Best and their old Sherpa guide were hiking in the Himalayas looking for a guru when Wim noticed a cluster of wildflowers nestled against a rock near a tiny spring.

'Look!' said Wim.

'What's up?' asked Billy, stopping several yards ahead of Wim on the steep slope.

'Flowers!' announced Wim.

'So what?' asked Billy.

'They're pretty.'

'So what?'

'Well,' said Wim uncertainly. 'I enjoy seeing them.'

'I thought you had the hots for finding this Mayarishi and your U.T.?'

'I do, I do,' said Wim, 'but –'

'We've come five thousand miles, hiked 200 miles straight up into the air it seems, buttonholed every wise-looking belly button from Calcutta to the top of Everest, and are at last only a few miles from seeing the Great Abominable Snowman Sage of the Sky, and you're standing there looking down at a bunch of colour against a rock.'

Wim's shoulders slumped.

'I don't know what gets into me,' he said apologetically.

'You've no discipline, no sense of purpose, no stick-to-it-iveness,' Billy said sharply. 'Without me you'd probably still be in Maganansett petting kittens.'

'I know, I know,' said Wim. 'Hey! wouldn't that be great!?'

'What's that?'

'If we saw some kittens here.'

'Oh, Jesus,' Billy wailed. 'You're out of your mind.'

'Look!'

Three kittens oozed out from among the cluster of flowers, meowing lazily.

'Kittens!' announced Wim.

Billy squinted down at the black and brown bundles of fur frolicking near the flowers.

'They're optical illusions,' he announced.

'Oh, no, really?' said Wim, his face clouding. 'How can you tell?'

'Real kittens don't live in the Himalayas. They live near litter boxes.'

'They're illusions?' Wim asked uncertainly.

'Absolutely.'

Their old Sherpa guide nodded his head in agreement.

'I bet the flowers are illusions too,' said Wim sadly.

'Probably,' said Billy, and the old Sherpa nodded.

'Still,' said Wim, his face suddenly brightening, 'it could be worse.'

'Yeah?' said Billy.

'We could be seeing illusions of beer cans and used condoms.'

– from *Sixty-six Parables of Wim*

47

from *The Gospel According to Luke* ...

On their third morning of renewed climbing Wim, in his enthusiasm for finding ultimate truth, took the lead and was soon a hundred yards ahead of the other three. Hiking now on top of the snow instead of through it he suddenly saw on the icy plateau above him a huge white creature that towered over any being he had ever seen before.

His heart began to pound with excitement. Wim felt certain this was the Great Abominable Snowman Sage of the Sky, the Most Holy of Yogis, the Greatest of Sages, the Eternal Glacial Guru, the Mayarishi Himself. The first step of his quest was at last about to be completed.

With a feeling of reverence and awe such as he had rarely experienced, Our Beloved Wim began to move humbly towards the Great White Sage, who loomed even bigger than His Reputation. The huge White Being was covered with ice and snow and glared down at Wim with eyes of red fire – just like a zen master looking at his students when their minds wander from their meditations. The Great Sage flexed his foot-long claws like a fighter doing pre-bout callisthenics. From far below, Wim heard a muffled calling from their old Sherpa guide, but he couldn't catch the words.

He advanced a few more humble steps and then prostrated himself on the ice-shelf. Looking up from his knees at the Great White Mass above him, he spoke.

'O Most Honoured of Sages,' he said. 'I bow before your Eternal Wisdom.'

The Great White Father in the Sky raised one white arm

like a bleached Redwood trunk and let out a ferocious howl that so shattered the silence and reverberated along the ridge that it started a small avalanche off to the right.

'Most Mighty of Seers,' Wim said, impressed, and speaking now in Hindi lest there be some misunderstanding, 'I humble myself before your every word.'

The Great Snowman Sage, red eyes ablaze, then lowered his right forearm, claws extended, and in a single swipe flipped Wim thirty yards through the air into a snowdrift.

Wim sensed this was some kind of a test. He knew that the whole secret of finding Ultimate Truth lay in recognizing the One True Guru, and in not being put off by rough exteriors. He struggled up out of the snowdrift, regained his feet, and looked back up at the Great White Abominable Snowman Sage of the Sky.

'Most Mighty of Yogis,' he said loudly, speaking now in careful Sanskrit, lest there be some misunderstanding, 'I acknowledge my presumptuous verbosity. Your blow was like the gentle tap of a zen master's staff, and I honour ...'

The Great White Abominable Sage was ploughing through the snow towards Wim, his huge open drooling mouth revealing a dazzling array of multi-directed teeth, each about half a foot long. The Great White Abominable Father had both arms extended in what might have been affectionate greeting, but Wim was beginning to have doubts. The Great White One picked Wim up in his two huge claws, lifted him sixty feet in the air and held him there a few yards from his friendly fierce tooth-filled red-eyed face. For a long moment the two stared at each other.

'O Most Revered of Saints,' Wim began again, using a combination of Hindi, Sanskrit, and Medieval Latin in a desperate last effort to communicate, 'I place my humble self in Your Hands, recognizing that it is a fearful thing to be in the hands of the Living ...'

The Great White Abomination lowered Wim towards him, opened his gigantic jaws and took a huge chunk of Wim

313

into his mouth and bit it off. Fortunately, Wim's body was very small and was covered with Wim's usual three suits of underwear, six sweaters, four overcoats, three parkas, and a shawl, and although in a trice the Great White Sage had bitten off one-third of Wim, it was all wool.

Wim began softly to remonstrate.

'O Honoured Sir, I would be happy to give you everything I possess, yea, even unto ...'

The huge jaw was chewing irritably and the red eyes seemed to have grown so hot they were steaming in the cold air. Wim stopped speaking to stare into the great revolving jaws, to look at the foot-long claws which encircled him at his waist. Then he looked back sternly into the eyes of the Great Abominable White Sky and spoke firmly in formal Sanskrit.

'I believe, sir, this is a case of mistaken identity.'

Unfortunately, the Beast had stopped chewing and now swallowed. As he did, a look of such pain, nausea and rage passed over his face that Wim concluded instantly it was time to continue his quest elsewhere. As the great jaws opened wide again – like the automatic doors of some huge garage opening to reveal an array of badly arranged chromium bumpers – Wim scrambled quickly out of his thirteen layers of clothing, crawled easily out of the big hole running from his neck to his waist, and dived naked down towards the snow.

It took Dawn and Billy almost an hour after the Great White Beastly Sage had left, to retrieve Wim from where he had jumped. After landing, Wim's naked body had melted the snow down to a depth of eighty feet, so Billy and Osso had to lower Dawn down the tunnel Wim's body had made to get a line around him.

Unfortunately, Dawn discovered that Wim's body was frozen solid, in the form of a perfect swan dive, as solid as the lead statue of Arnold Palmer. Even though his frozen expression of bewildered incredulity looked remarkably life-like, Dawn feared her beloved Wim was dead.

When they'd finally hauled him up, Osso declared that since a fire would thaw Wim out too quickly and give him the bends, Wim's only hope was to get his body immediately against the second hottest thing man could imagine.

Although Dawn worried briefly about the moral implications, her love quickly conquered. Wim's still naked body was stuffed down the back of her layers of clothing against her bare skin, only his frozen swan-dive arms sticking straight out at her neck level. These they wrapped in some of the fragments of Wim's clothing the enraged Great White Abomination had either thrown or vomited at them after Wim's leap to freedom.

So for the next several hours, while a blizzard caused by the Great White Sagely Sky began to swirl around them, Dawn bore him along on her back like a large cross. Osso helpfully pointed out that her carrying a Sherpa bearer for two days turned out to have been good practice. They were headed back down the mountain again, both in fear of the Great White Wisdom of the Snows and in despair of Wim's condition. Dawn would have cried had not her tears frozen so rapidly in her eyes that not a single one could make it out on to her cheek. Not only was Wim dead but she had the horrible feeling that if he was, she might be carrying him around on her back for the rest of her life.

But after three hours of staggering downwards through the blizzard there appeared a hint of hope. It appeared between Dawn's thighs. She became aware of something soft and cold (but becoming harder and warmer) twitching into life at her backside. Halleluya! Wim's resurrection had begun! His penis at least had begun to thaw!

Dawn shouted joyfully to Billy that Wim was alive, but after Billy had checked for breath and chipped with a screwdriver at Wim's face, he had to tell Dawn that her hopes were an illusion.

'That's no illusion poking me!' Dawn shouted back.

As Billy shrugged sadly at Osso, Dawn began chastizing Wim for his indecent behaviour, but after a while, accepting Billy's testimony that the upper half of Wim was not in any condition to take responsibility for the lower part of him, she decided to submit to the indignity. The harder and hotter the thawed part of Wim grew the more poor Dawn was torn between her joy that she might be saving Wim's life and the fear that at any moment she might be losing her honour. Although she knew that neither Wim nor she was morally responsible for anything happening between her thighs she walked with extreme care, and several times asked Billy to adjust Wim's body in order to avoid her being raped.

Four hours later Osso led them into a huge cave, claiming it was a popular tourist stopover for impoverished Sherpa travellers. There was even a supply of wood, and within a few hours they were all seated around a blazing fire. By that time Wim was thoroughly thawed except for the tip of his nose which, tragically, was to remain cold for the rest of his life. He was chatting happily away, apologizing to Dawn for any sin or attempted sin he might have committed, lamenting the fact he didn't remember a thing, when Billy shouted from the back of the cave. He'd gone there in the dark to relieve his bladder and now returned to say that he'd found at the rear of the cave a human body seated in the lotus posture. He was afraid he might have peed on it.

They all followed Billy back into the dark, but this time they brought flashlights. There, sitting in the full lotus posture, clothed only in a single white dhoti, was the most frail, thin and wrinkled body any of them had ever seen. It looked like it had been dead for hundreds of years, but mummified by the cold. There was no sign of breath, heartbeat or pulse.

Back around the fire Wim began arguing that this might

be the Great White Snowman Sage of the Sky. Billy had no opinion on that but declared that it was their scientific duty to carbon-date the skull of the old sunyasi and, as a cross-check on the age of the great sage, saw off a leg and count the number of concentric rings in the thigh bone. Dawn argued that the body should be simply and decently buried untouched by their desecrating inquiries.

Osso didn't comment, spending most of his time grin-ningly surveying Dawn, who, for the first time, was not dressed in the formless arctic clothing but now in only a single layer of woollen thermal longjohns and sweatshirt. He announced that he liked women.

'This is the real Mayarishi,' Wim kept concluding. 'That first thing I met was just a big polar bear with charisma.'

'Even if he is,' countered Billy, 'your great sage is dead. Mummies don't answer questions.'

'Don't you think he's the Mayarishi, Osso?' Wim asked insistently.

'Is possible,' said Osso. 'He certainly holy man.'

'And he'll thaw out just as I did,' said Wim. 'And then I can talk to him and get the scoop about u.t.'

'Is possible,' said Osso. 'He certainly holy man.'

An hour later they got their answer. First, they all noticed the most incredible stink any had ever experienced. Since they all assumed it was intestinal gas from one of the others, no one said anything until all four of them had to make a mad dash for the cave entrance to get fresh air. Returning, they heard noises from the back of the cave. The Great Sage was awakening! And as he did, the gases within him were heated and made their escape by a series of sensational burps and farts that kept Wim at a reverential distance from the Sage for the next two days.

But on the third day Osso reported that the Great Sage was ready to receive visitors. He was eating heartily the three grains of rice and thimble of water which Osso told Wim were his daily intake during the strenuous summer season. Although Osso wouldn't declare for sure that this was the Great Mayarishi, he urged Wim to approach and question the man. Wim, proud and determined, did.

Wim led Billy and Dawn to the back of the cave – now lit by torches – and they all seated themselves cross-legged in a semi-circle in front of the ancient sage. Osso was several yards in their rear playing a game of darts against the cave wall. He was using icicles for darts.

After many minutes of dignified silence, Our Beloved Wim spoke respectfully. 'Honoured Yogi,' he said. 'We have come to receive your wisdom. We are on a pilgrimage. All my life I have been in search of Ultimate Truth.'

For a long time the frail ancient yogi sat staring through half-closed eyes at Wim, who, seated in an identical lotus posture opposite, stared back respectfully.

'I too have looked,' the old man finally said.

Wim trembled to hear the soft spiritual tones of this ancient man.

'And what, O Revered Master, have you found?' he asked.

Several more minutes passed in silence before the yogi replied.

'For almost five thousand years I have spent every moment of every day seeking to purify my mind of every trivial thought which might prevent me from receiving Ultimate Truth. I have visited every yogi or sage who has come within five hundred miles of these mountains for the last three thousand years. I have read every book ever written that might lead me to the light of Ultimate Truth.'

The yogi ceased, and all remained in awed silence.

'O Great Yogi,' Wim asked at last, 'what is it you have found?'

The old sage smiled unevenly through broken lips and revealed his toothless gums.

'I am almost there,' he said.

'You are almost there,' Wim echoed respectfully.

'My mind has been almost totally blank now for over two hundred and eighty-two years. Each day during meditation I experience only eternal, blinding ubiquitous light.'

'Ahhhh,' sighed Wim.

'I am in almost continual bliss.'

'Ahhhh,' sighed Wim.

'I believe I am in almost complete harmony with Ultimate Truth.'

Wim, eyes aglow, turned to look briefly at Dawn and Billy, who were staring in awe and wonder at the old guru. Osso had just scored a bullseye and was too distracted to notice.

There was another long, religious silence until Wim again spoke.

'That is marvellous, O Greatest of Sages, but why do you say "almost complete"?'

This time the old yogi sighed.

'Because in the midst of the eternal, blinding, ubiquitous light, always, sooner or later, sometime during the day, the month or the decade, appears ... appears a thing which is not ... which is not the eternal blinding ubiquitous light.'

'Ahhh,' said Wim.

'I have purified my mind of all but this one thing,' went on the holy man in his soft frail voice. 'When it no longer appears I will have achieved total and complete eternal blinding ubiquitous light. I will be one with Ultimate Truth.'

'Ahhh,' said Wim. For half an hour all sat in respectful, contemplative silence.

'O Most Revered of Masters,' Wim then said, 'tell me what is this thing which sneaks like a snake into your mind to mar the garden of your eternal blinding ubiquitous light.'

The old yogi frowned.

'Each day or month or decade, when I am in perfect bliss, when the whole world is light, when no thought has entered my mind for weeks or months or centuries, there comes from nowhere a clear, precise and unequivocal image.'

They all remained silent for many minutes.

'What is this image, O Most Daring of Divine Seekers?' asked Wim.

The old yogi raised his head a few inches and stared with unblinking serene and honest eyes for a long time into the blinking, troubled and evasive eyes of Wim.

'It is a potato,' he said to Wim.

All were respectfully silent.

'O Most Divine of Holy Men,' said Wim, '... a potato?'

'Each day or month or decade, when I am in perfect bliss, when the whole world is light, when no thought has entered my mind for weeks or months or centuries, there comes from nowhere a clear, precise and unequivocal image of a potato.'

All were respectfully silent for another hour. Finally Wim said: 'How do you interpret this extraordinary image, O Great Sage?'

The old yogi still stared neutrally through half-closed eyes at Wim.

'I am not pure,' he answered. 'Although I have fasted for four thousand two hundred and sixty-one years I am apparently still not free of vile gluttony.'

'Vile gluttony ...' mused Wim cautiously. 'A potato ...'

'Although I have never eaten a potato, never consciously desired a potato, never even knew what a potato was until after I had completed several decades' research to learn what this strange brown round object invading my mind might be, still, it seems clear, that I still lust for food.'

'A potato ...' sighed Wim even more softly.

'But in another century or two, the vile image will be totally wiped out and I will at last have so totally emptied my mind that it will be filled only with Ultimate Truth.'

Wim remained silent opposite the Great White Yogi, moving his lips but one more time in a silent pronunciation of the words 'a potato ...' After almost two hours of a serene joint silence, one in which Wim's mind was filled with twenty-seven thousand thoughts and a hundred thirty-eight desires, and the Great Yogi's mind was filled with only eternal blinding ubiquitous light and an occasionally brown sphere, Wim spoke again.

'O Most Mighty of Meditators,' he said, 'I am but a flea on the face of a flea in the puniness of my knowledge, but may I humbly ask the most stupid of questions?'

The old yogi stared back at Wim for a while and then gave the slightest inclination of his head.

'Well, Great Sir,' began Wim. 'How do we know – I ask this question with prostrate soul, O Most Perfect One – how do we know that ... that in your efforts to empty your mind to receive Ultimate Truth, you have not, in fact, failed to empty it of ... of ... eternal, blinding, ubiquitous light?'

There was a silence of slightly different quality. It lasted for ten minutes. Then an hour. The old yogi finally spoke. 'Beg pardon?' he said.

'In your efforts to empty your mind,' repeated Wim, 'why have you not tried to empty it also of eternal, blinding, ubiquitous light?'

The subsequent silence lasted an hour. A day. Three days. Finally, after a week the old yogi opened his eyes wide for the first time and looked sternly at Wim.

'Who the hell are you?' he asked.

'I am Wim, Seeker from the Montauks.'

The old sage looked at Wim, then at Billy and Dawn and finally at the old Sherpa guide playing with icicles again at the mouth of the cave.

'And those beings behind you?'

'Friends,' replied Wim.

The toothless one sighed.

'When I cleanse my mind of all thoughts,' he said softly, 'my mind is always filled with one of three things: eternal, blinding, ubiquitous light; total darkness; a potato.' He sighed. 'Total darkness comes just before, during, and just after, sleep. Eternal, blinding, ubiquitous light comes whenever I wakefully meditate. The potato just comes ... just comes ... O you, Most Puny of Seekers from the Montauks, which, then, may be Ultimate Truth?'

'I am but a worm in the belly of a worm, O Wisest of Men,' replied Wim, 'and thus do not have the slightest idea. I merely wondered why You had concluded that eternal, blinding, ubiquitous light was related to Ultimate Truth.'

After a long hesitation, the yogi replied: 'Tradition.'

Wim sighed.

'Tradition?'

'Tradition,' repeated the yogi. 'If you think I have been sitting up here in this icebox for close to six thousand years in order to spend eternity staring at a potato, you are less than a flea on a worm in the anus of a worm.'

Billy Best and Dawn both quietly nodded their heads in agreement with the old guru's reply, but Wim frowned.

'But Wise One,' said Wim, 'I ask this question out of the most profound of inherited stupidities – I am but a flea on a flea on a worm in the anus of a worm – what if the potato is It?'

The old one opened his eyes once more and they flashed fiercely out into the room like red laser guns, then set behind the curtains of his eyelids. Even as Wim watched, ice began to form on the yogi's body, then snow. The body grew with incredible speed, getting larger and whiter and colder every minute, until within a half hour the cave was at thirty degrees below zero, their great fire was sputtering helplessly, and the room was almost totally filled with something bearing a striking resemblance to the Great White Abominable Snowman Sage in the Sky, and Wim, and his friends were wrestling their meagre supplies away from the cave as fast as they could.

THE BOAT IS SINKING!

'The boat is sinking, Wim! The boat is sinking!'
  'The boat is always sinking,' replied Wim.
  'But what should we do!? What should we do!?'
  'Sail it 'round the world.'

– from Sixty-six Parables of Wim

48

from 'Fragments of Wim', pp. 222–9
(*being a letter from Wim to Grain-of-Sand*)

Dear Grain-of-Sand,

It was Osso! At least I think it was Osso. Actually I'm still not sure what happened here in India. I guess I must have met the Mayarishi but *when* I met him and who he was and what the Gods think I'm supposed to do with it all is a little confusing.

We were on an ancient train chugging back down out of Nepal towards New Delhi and I was feeling kind of low – no closer to u.t. than I'd been back in Maganansett. Although I was a little disappointed in the old yogi in the cave, Dawn and Billy both thought he was really something. Dawn kept reminding me that he'd been looking fanatically for Ultimate Truth for six thousand years and thus had to be closer to it than someone like me, who'd only been kind of yawningly searching for about a year. The fact that the Mayarishi – if that's who he was – could produce a two thousand watt lightbulb in his mind by meditating and could survive a whole year on maybe only a can of rice, an apple and a loaf of Wonder Bread impressed her too. Billy kept saying that if he could learn the old guy's health programme, he could market it in the US and make a bundle. I told him I thought the old yogi's health programme consisted of being dead ninety-nine per cent of the time, but Billy pointed out that Americans would buy something for an older old age even if they had to live inside their refrigerator and not watch TV as much. Billy also said there was potential in the Mayarishi's personal refrigeration system if Billy could just figure out how he did it.

'Any dude who can lower the temperature in a house-sized cave thirty degrees in thirty seconds,' Billy said, 'must have a helluva effective freon.'

Most of the journey Osso didn't say much. He hadn't been acting in a particularly buddha-like way most of the trip. Ever since he'd seen Dawn without her parka he'd spent most of his time coming on to her pretty strong, but Dawn kept telling him her heart belonged to me. Osso asked about the rest of her, and she said the rest of her was taken too – although, as Billy explained, on a long-term option arrangement.

Osso was on the train with us because he'd somehow convinced Billy that Billy needed a guide to get back to New Delhi. It seemed a little strange to me, but Billy assured me he'd gotten a special deal.

When we were more than halfway to New Delhi to catch our plane back to the US, Billy and Dawn went to the dining-car for dinner, but I was too depressed to eat. Osso had bought some fudge brownies and potato salad in Nepal and wasn't hungry. When Osso and I were alone I suddenly felt I wanted to ask him what he thought about the old yogi in the cave.

'Very holy man,' said Osso, who was seated opposite me dressed in a grimy animal skin of some sort and pants that looked like they'd slid down a mountain of mud and hadn't been cleaned. 'Too bad he can't see.'

'Can't see?'

'Anybody who look for something six thousand years and not find it clearly have eye problem.'

'I guess so,' I said.

'Maybe he look in wrong place.'

'That's what I was thinking.'

'If ultimate truth worth seeing,' said Osso, 'then it must be something everyone can see, even poor people who can't afford caves.'

'That's right,' I said, feeling excited about what Osso was saying. 'If it's a cure, it's got to be available for the masses like me.' I was quiet for a while. 'But that still doesn't tell me where to look.'

'Important thing,' said Osso, beginning to light up a

Marlboro, 'is not to think. Old yogi in cave thinks he knows how and where to look so he blind. You in good shape. You know you're stupid and don't know where to look. Better chance for you to stub your toe on u.t.'

'You think so?'

'Sure thing,' said Osso happily. 'Buddha say if a fool is to become wise he must begin listening only to fools.'

'Wow!' I said, since it sounded neat, but then I had to add: 'But I don't get it.'

'Buddha say if a sick man is to become well he must stop listening to his doctors.'

I thought about this and decided I liked it.

'Except for Grain-of-Sand I've been listening to smart people all my life – that's why I'm stupid.'

(No offence, Grain-of-Sand. It's just you don't *claim* to be smart or know anything.)

'Very good,' said Osso, and then added, squinting at me through his slanted, twinkling eyes, 'best way to find ultimate truth is stop looking.'

'Stop looking!'

'If you're looking, it's because you think you know where to look. Just go find this monkey in Colorapaho the thunder told you about and see what happens.'

'I think it's a monk in Colorado,' I corrected gently, and then did some gloomy thinking. 'I don't know,' I finally went on. 'From what my mentor said, the monk doesn't sound like a holy man to me. There was an article in *People* magazine that made him seem like a jerk.'

'Buddha say that a true Buddha for one man for others only a true jerk.'

'Come on,' I said. 'Buddha didn't say that.'

'Line between Buddha and jerk very thin. Buddha say it usually invisible.'

'Buddha didn't really use the word "jerk", did he?'

'Oh, yes, certainly,' Osso replied, nodding seriously. 'In fact, in *Mayapatha Sutra* Buddha say "Immina pula tathata sanyasi jerk." Three thousand years ago no one understand what this line can mean. Only now in twentieth century buddhist scholars realize "jerk" is English word Buddha accidentally use three thousand years too early.'

I stared at Osso a long time, trying to figure if he was pulling my leg or not, but he just stared back at me looking as innocent and serious as a child playing tic-tac-toe.

'Are you a buddhist?' I finally asked.

'Oh, no. I born in buddhist family but I gave up buddhism many years ago.'

'What are you now?'

'Now I nobody.'

'I mean your religion.'

'I nobody.'

'Are you really just a Sherpa guide?'

Billy and Dawn came back just then, Billy bullying through the crowded aisles, and as they sat down beside us, Osso just stared back at me looking innocent.

'Not even that,' he said.

'You can say that again,' said Billy. 'You're as much a Sherpa guide as I'm a simple blue-collar slob.'

'What you mean?' Osso asked.

'I mean how do you manage to outcon me on all our deals?' Billy persisted, leaning towards Osso from beside me to make his point. 'I've been wheeling and dealing ever since I discovered you needed a penny to buy gum, but you're the first person I consistently end up paying double to get less than I can get free.'

'Oh, I not out-bargain you,' Osso said with a grin. 'You may get very rich from knowing me.'

'Bullshit, fella,' said Billy. 'Another entrepreneurial trip like this one and I'm going to settle down on Long Island where men are men and suckers are born every minute.'

'What's your secret?' I asked, persisting too.

'Oh, well, maybe Billy not used to trading with man who need nothing, want nothing,' said Osso. 'Since I don't care for single dollar I can hold out for two hundred dollar without worry.'

'Yeah, that's it!' said Billy. 'When Osso said he wouldn't take less than two hundred, I could tell he meant it and didn't give a fuck whether I agreed or not. It always seemed he had some inside dope that I didn't that put him in the catbird seat.'

'Yes, but what did he know?' I asked.

'I know I can't lose,' said Osso simply. 'Buddha say man who have nothing and want nothing, tough man to cheat.'

'Will I get that way if I find u.t.?' I asked.

'Anything possible,' said Osso. 'Even for you.'

'Wow.'

'How about me?' asked Billy. 'If I find u.t. would I be able to have all the money I want in six months?'

'Quicker than that,' said Osso. 'Much quicker.'

'Hey, that's terrific,' said Billy. 'If I'd have known this, Wim, I might have gotten interested in u.t. earlier.'

'I'm not interested in riches,' said Dawn. 'Should I be looking for Ultimate Truth too?'

Osso squinted at her.

'If it please you.'

'I'd like to help Wim look.'

Osso shook his head and frowned.

'That bad,' he said. 'Buddha say, "Man who try help person find something he himself never seen not too good a guide."'

'Buddha never said that,' I said, smiling.

'Oh? You know Buddha?' asked Osso.

'No. Do you?' I shot back.

'Oh, yes,' said Osso serenely. 'Buddha good buddy of mine.'

'He get frozen down every winter too?' asked Billy with a sceptical smile.

'Oh, no, my buddha only fifty-five years old.'

'Where does he live?' I asked. 'Maybe I should go visit him.'

'Oh, no, not necessary. I pass along all his good jokes.'

Billy asked: 'Is this the same Buddha who lived three thousand years ago and had a lot of girls and then got upset about people dying and sat under a trée until an apple fell on his head?'

'Same one,' said Osso amiably. 'Except younger.'

Well, the train then pulled into New Delhi, and there was a lot of pushing and shoving as we got off the train. Osso was helping with our luggage – at least I think he was – and the next thing I knew he was gone. No goodbye, no advice, no nothing. Simply gave Dawn a squeeze on her rear and stole Billy's portable computer and modem and disappeared.

Do you think he was really the sage I was sent to India to meet? He seemed so completely at home with himself he reminded me of you. And the nutty things he said reminded me of you too. Do all navigators seem a little stupid?

I miss you and mum, but I'm not going to stop now until I've seen the last buddhas or monks or basketball stars or whatever they are.

Dawn sends her love and tells me to tell you that except when I'm frozen stiff I'm behaving myself. I try to explain to her that you don't care whether I behave myself or not, but she thinks all teachers must be moralists like her, so I don't get far. *She's* a good person, and somehow I think that's good. Maybe because goodness is her special quest. Do you think that might be it?

I rub my nose to yours.

Wim

WIM AND THE MIND

One day Wim announced that every man's mind moves continually from wisdom to madness and then back again in endless oscillation. The disciples found this depressing and asked him to explain.

'It's simple,' said Wim with a big smile. 'A man's mind moves in wisdom whenever it is aware of its basic madness, and moves back into its madness whenever it comes under the illusion of having wisdom.'

'But ... but you seem to be saying the mind is always mad,' persisted one of the disciples.

'Mmmmm.'

'That means that what *you're* saying is mad.'

'Obviously the thought that all my thoughts are madness must itself be madness,' agreed Wim, looking worried.

'Then –'

'Of course there's another way of looking at it,' said Wim, brightening. 'Every thought is a unique, specially-wrapped personal gift of the Supreme Creator of the Universe.'

'Does that mean –'

'We ought, therefore, to treat each other with equal reverence.'

'Then they're not madness?' asked the disciple.

'Oh, they're madness all right. Each and every thought is a unique, specially-wrapped personal gift of insanity from the Supreme Creator – unless we recognize it as such – when it becomes wisdom.'

– from *Sixty-six Parables of Wim*

49

from Grain-of-Sand's *Memoirs of an Old Liar* ...

Wim couldn't make head nor tail of that Catholic place in Colorado. He'd just gotten back from India where you can't get your holy-man badge unless you do all your clothes shopping in an underwear store and can't eat nothing that looks like food, and now he was in this Catholic village where there was shrimp cocktail, Coors Beer, bingo, softball leagues, disco dancing, a ski resort and all sorts of human things that as far as Wim could see didn't have nothing to do with holiness or quests or u.t.

He and Billy and Dawn spent several days trying to get a meeting with this Brother Bodicelli fella but there seemed to be nothing but committee chairman, social chairman, dance chairman, league presidents, ski-lift supervisors, and people like that who always ended up sending Wim to some other chairman. They all said this Bodicelli fella existed, but he really wasn't all that important to the village and they didn't see much of him. They said he was probably busy raising funds over Denver way.

There was a nice new-fangled Catholic Church nestled into the south side of the mountain right in the centre of the town. It had all sorts of slanted roofs and concrete struts. Wim said it looked like a lot of rich men's houses over in Easthampton. The Church had some priests who listened to people tell them all about what things they done during the week that they really got a kick out of and promised not to do next week. The priests also put on a floorshow every morning and a bunch of times on Sunday with music and slow motion movements and refreshments, but Wim said it was dull and skimpy on the servings.

But Billy felt right at home. He was a 'Piscopelian himself. He told Wim 'Piscopelians believed in the salvation of the upper classes through belief that Christ died so that poor people would be satisfied with their lot. Some 'Piscopelians believed in salvation through faith but most believed in salvation through money. Billy quoted a verse from the Bible that said that rich people would get into heaven even easier than a needle through a camel. The verse didn't make much sense to Wim, but when he checked it out in Dawn's Bible the version there made even less sense. Jesus seemed to be saying that *no* rich people could get into heaven. Wim was sure the US government would have outlawed the Bible if it said something like that.

Dawn's daddy had brought her up a Unitarian, but she believed all religions were really the same as long as they talked about God and were hot for goodness and came down hard on badness. She said the Catholic religion was real good at that, but she worried that it didn't seem to have much effect on Catholic guys. A lot of them were hitting on her pretty regular. When Wim said she hadn't complained about Osso's trying a lot of stuff with her, Dawn said Osso didn't count 'cause he wasn't really serious about his lust. She said he was just sort of going through the motions because Dawn was so terrific.

But Wim's search for Brother Bodicelli made him feel like he was trying to wade through molasses. Every day he would go see some chairman or priest and ask about the monk he was looking for and every day they'd send him some place else to someone new who would sooner or later send him back to some place old and someone he'd already talked to twice. He told me he'd read a book once about a guy trying to get into a castle that reminded him of what was happening to him. The guy in the book – Wim liked him 'cause his name was even shorter than Wim's – the guy – K was his name – never did make it into the castle, and Wim said he was pretty sure the same guys K met at the castle were now working in the village.

Well, Wim finally got to have an interview with the priest who everyone said knew Brother Bodicelli better than anybody. Wim said it weren't too good an interview.

Father Cosmo was an old guy, tall and skinny, with pale white skin and wispy white hair. He met Wim in his office in the church, a big room with lots of books and crucifixes and softball league trophies.

'Yes, my son?' Father Cosmo said. 'You wished to see me?'

'Actually, Father,' said Wim, standing in front of the big desk the priest was sitting behind, 'I think I'm supposed to find a Brother Bodicelli, a monk of the Franciscan Order who I thought lived and worked in this village.'

'And why did you wish to speak to Brother Bodicelli?' the old priest asked, making a neat cathedral of his hands.

'I'm on a sort of quest for ultimate truth,' Wim explained, 'and was told that I should see him.'

'Ah, Ultimate Truth,' said Father Cosmo, his eyes lighting up. 'Then you've come to the right place. We would be pleased to help you.'

'You'll take me to him?' Wim asked, taking an excited step nearer the desk.

'There's no need for that, my son,' Father Cosmo countered with a soft smile. 'We have all the Truth you need to have right here in our village.'

Wim hung his head and felt uncomfortable.

'I appreciate that, Father,' he finally said, 'but I was told that I had to see Brother Bodicelli.'

'Brother Bodicelli is a fine man,' said Father Cosmo amiably, 'but a bit out of tune with the village these days. His truth is, shall we say, not as Ultimate as the Church would like. You see how crowded our village is. It is a home for more seekers than any other village around. You should speak to us.'

Wim hung his head and stared down at the plush soft rug under his sneakers.

'I . . . uh . . . Isn't Brother Bodicelli's Franciscan order part of the village?'

'Of course it is, my son,' said Father Cosmo. 'He and men like him are our inspiration.'

'But –'

'An inspiration that we remember always in our prayers.'

'But where can I find him?' Wim persisted.

'But there is no need to find him,' Father Cosmo countered sharply. 'Your quest has brought you to our village and here it can come to an end.'

'I . . . I . . . but Grain-of-Sand and the thunder both made it quite clear –'

'But that was when you were but a child and hadn't come to our village,' Father Cosmo insisted.

Wim stood in front of the desk feeling like he used to when principals used to call him in for a chat. After an embarrassing silence he finally said: 'I'm sorry, Father, but my quest is to find Brother Bodicelli. I've got to do it.' He turned to go.

'Well, if you insist, young man,' Father Cosmo said with a sigh. 'But no matter where you go, sooner or later you'll realize that all roads lead to our village.'

'What about Brother Bodicelli?'

'He, unfortunately, spends most of his time outside the village.'

'Where?' asked Wim at the door.

'On the other side of the mountain.'

'Thank you, Father.'

'Life would be much easier for you if you'd just settle down with us.'

'I'm sure it would be, Father, and I appreciate the offer, but I've got to go.'

WIM MEETS FRANZ KAFKA

One day Our Beloved Wim met Franz Kafka.

'Did you ever get into that Castle?' Wim asked Kafka cheerfully.

'I am still knocking on the gate,' Kafka answered.

Wim frowned sympathetically.

'Still knocking, huh?'

'And recently the gate has been soundproofed so my knock can't be heard,' Kafka continued.

'Mmmmm,' said Wim.

'And the gate is positioned so that my presence outside it cannot be seen from a single vantage point of the Castle.'

'Wow.'

'And all the gatekeepers have been ordered to ignore anyone knocking anyway,' Kafka went on.

'Oh, boy, that's tough.'

'But I still knock,' declared Kafka with a soft smile.

'Wow,' said Wim again and then added: 'I don't blame you, but still...'

'Yes ...?' asked Kafka.

'What if the gate and the gatekeepers and the Castle are actually illusions and there's no one inside to see you?' Wim asked gloomily.

'Oh, yes, I'm sure that's true,' Kafka answered cheerfully. 'That's why I keep knocking.'

– from *Sixty-six Parables of Wim*

50

from *The Gospel According to Luke*, pp. 461–472

When Our Beloved Wim finally gave up finding Brother Bodicelli in the church village, he hiked out of town through the woods, followed a mountain stream several miles, and finally emerged on a back road. After walking six hours he was lost and tired so he decided to hitch-hike. After a few cars had passed him, a new Buick Regal came screeching to a halt fifty feet in front of him. A large, beefy, busty girl with long dark hair got out the passenger's side and held the door open for him.

Wim ended up sitting between Lena, the dark-haired girl, and Patsy, the driver, a gum-chewing redhead, whose long red hair plummeted down from her head and hung from her large chest like a fiery waterfall. Since the front seat wasn't wide, and both women were tall and full-breasted while Wim was short, he soon realized that he couldn't move his face an inch to left or right without his nose being guilty of an obscene act. He tried to stare diligently at the dashboard while holding up his end of the conversation.

'We don't normally pick up hitch-hikers,' Patsy said after she'd introduced them. 'But you being so small and young we figured it'd be – you're not a rapist, are you?'

'No, ma'am,' Wim answered in a small voice.

'Most men are, you know,' Patsy went on promptly, passing a large oil truck. 'It's in their genes.'

'I know,' said Wim.

'But Lena and me, we're on the path now, and learned that even rapists are all just part of the Divine Play.'

'Really?'

'After you been through the discipline of Hors d'Oeuvres you learn to have compassion for the roles people inherit from their society. Isn't that right, Lena?'

'Mmmm,' said Lena, without moving.

'Men got their roles to play, just like we got ours,' Patsy went on. 'Lena and I got big tits so we used to play sexy Patsy and sexy Lena, but we know now that we don't have to play that role or if we do we don't have to take it seriously. Our tits aren't any big thing, you know?'

'Mmmm,' said Wim, feeling that they were certainly big enough, especially for a small, gas-efficient car.

'I mean I used to feel I was hot stuff when men drooled all over my sweater, and I'd get upset if a coupla guys wanted to tie me up or make me eat something dirty that hadn't been washed, but I know now that they got their karma and I got mine and the only freedom is knowing it's all a game.'

Since Patsy was driving at between fifty-five and ninety miles per hour depending on whether the speed limit signs were thirty m.p.h. or fifty-five m.p.h. Wim was having trouble concentrating.

'Take Lena, for instance,' said Patsy. 'Except for her body and the fact that she never talks, she'd be your average down-home girl, but because of her body she became a sex object and hated it and was unhappy until Bobo taught her that being a sex object wasn't all that bad as long as you really wanted to be and if you don't then stop. Right, Lena?'

'Mmmm,' said Lena.

'Then you can go beyond it to something else like treating men as sex objects or becoming a nun or being an even better sex object if that's the game you want to play always understanding it's a game. What games do you play?'

Wim was abruptly aware he'd been asked a question.

'Football,' he said. 'And sometimes baseball.'

'I mean life games,' said Patsy, turning to smile down at him and thus forcing his nose to commit a brief obscene act.

'You know, like sex object or rapist or Joe-know-it-all. Like that.'

Wim thought about it.

'Well, I'm on a quest for ultimate truth,' he replied. 'But it's certainly not a game.'

'Mmmm,' commented Lena.

'Ultimate truth!' exclaimed Patsy, laughing. 'You mean like enlightenment or liberation, right? That's far out. I used to play that one a lot. It used to be more fun than getting screwed.'

'It's not a game,' said Wim.

'Oh, I know,' said Patsy. 'You got to take it seriously. Bobo says you'll never find the pathless path unless you take at least one game seriously.'

'The pathless path?' asked Wim, wanting to hold his breath as they passed a pickup truck. 'What's that?'

'It's Bobo's special way, or not-so-special way as he likes to call it. You ought to come visit with us. Bobo likes to play with seekers like you.'

'I'd like to,' said Wim. 'But actually I've got to find a Brother Bodicelli.'

'But that's him!' exclaimed Patsy. 'That's the same thing!'

'But I'm looking for Brother Bodi-'

'That's Bobo!'

'Bobo is Brother Bodicelli?'

'Or Baba Bobo when we want to tease him. Right, Lena?'

'Mmmm.'

Wim was still too stunned to believe.

'He's a famous Franciscan monk who's studied eastern religions?' Wim persisted, even turning his face to look up at Patsy and risk being accused of sexual assault.

'For sure,' said Patsy, smiling. 'In Japan they used to call him Numero Uno.'

'But I've spent two weeks in the church village and haven't seen any sign of Brother Bodicelli.'

'Of course not,' said Patsy. 'He doesn't go there much –
except when he's being a tourist. Right Lena?'

'Mmmm.'

Patsy swung the car off the road they were on and into an
even narrower dirt road that led upwards through a thick
forest.

'And ... and ... and are there softball leagues and bingo on
this side of the mountain too?' Wim asked.

'Oh, no,' said Patsy, braking the Buick to a halt among a
half-dozen other cars nestled against a solid wall of trees.
'We play other games here.'

They all got out of the car, and though Wim was able to
breathe normally, his neck was locked in the forward
position and he had to turn his whole body to talk to people.

'What sort of games?' he asked.

'Come on, we've got to climb aways,' said Patsy. 'Games
with discipline,' she continued as they entered a path
through the trees and began hiking, Lena trailing them.
'Discipline to overcome the barriers. What Lena and I are
doing now is discipline.'

'What discipline is that?' asked Wim tentatively.

'Take Lena for instance,' Patsy rambled on. 'She used to be
a big dumb Italian broad who talked and talked in a hare-
brained way that made every man wish he'd never seen her
tits. Then she met Baba Bobo and he suggested that she take
a vow of silence for ten minutes and see what happened.
Well, of course she couldn't keep silent for ten minutes. She
just kept blabbing on about how exciting it was to take a vow
of silence. Then Bobo ordered her to be silent for five
minutes and after about thirty seconds she broke into tears
and said she couldn't do it – she was scared. Finally Bobo
ordered her gagged not for ten minutes but for a week.'

Patsy paused to catch a breath and turned to face Wim.

'At the end of the week we took the gag off and we'd
noticed her eyes were glowing most of that time, and when
the gag was off she didn't say a word, just ran to a

342

blackboard and wrote "it works!" She hasn't said a word except "Mmmm" since.'

'Wow!' said Wim.

'Mmmm,' said Lena.

'And me, same thing only opposite. I used to be kinda shy and uncertain and not talk much, and Baba Bobo told me to try talking non-stop all day and I did, and I've been getting better and better at it ever since, although I plan to stop tomorrow at midnight to see what'll happen.'

Brother Bodicelli was meeting privately with other seekers when they arrived, so Wim went with Patsy to a group of tents along a rocky stream. There he was surprised to see dozens of people, mostly young, meditating and doing yoga and pushups. Almost no one was talking or relaxing. Even those just standing around seemed to be kind of spaced out and deeply into their own minds. Patsy continued to chatter away, but it was clear she didn't expect anyone to listen unless it was part of their discipline. Wim sensed that everyone was working hard on overcoming a barrier, but he couldn't quite catch what a barrier was.

It was late afternoon when a scrawny young man came up to Wim where he was sitting by the stream and said simply: 'Your turn,' and began to lead him away. As Patsy followed, Wim marched off up the trail behind the young man.

Twenty minutes later Wim was seated on pine needles in a clearing among the towering trees and staring at Brother Bodicelli, who didn't turn out to look exactly as Wim had pictured a Franciscan monk looking. Instead of being tall and slender and ascetic, Brother Bodicelli was an immense fat giant of a man who overflowed a huge soft easy chair among the pine needles. He was wearing a brown flowing robe and leather sandals and had a large wooden cross hanging from his neck, but his pudgy fingers seemed covered with bright shining rings and the cross was studded with what looked like diamonds. A young woman stood just behind him and was fanning him with an intricately made wooden fan.

Brother Bodicelli greeted Wim with the jolliest, most beautiful smile Wim had ever seen. Three other seekers were seated around him, looking at him with love and admiration.

Wim was so excited at finding his second buddha that he couldn't even absorb what Brother Bodicelli was saying to a young man who turned out to be, to Wim's amazement, Billy Best. And seated on the earth beside Billy was Dawn. She nodded to him seriously, as if they were in church. Wim didn't awaken from his amazement until he realized that Brother Bodicelli had asked him a question.

'Beg pardon?' said Wim, sitting up straighter. Although he was a trifle discouraged by the monk's resembling an Egyptian pharaoh instead of St Francis, he had assumed the full lotus position in order to show what a sincere and serious seeker he was.

'Welcome, Wimsy,' Brother Bodicelli said in a cheerful booming voice.

'Er, thank you, father,' said Wim humbly.

'Brother, Wimsy, brother,' said the fat monk. 'A simple Franciscan friar is called "brother", or by the disrespectful, "Bobo".' When Patsy, who had sat down on one side of Wim, laughed, he shot a wink at her.

'I'm honoured to meet you, Brother Bodicelli,' Wim went on.

'I'm honoured to have you here, Wim,' said the monk. 'I've heard a lot about you.'

'Really?' said Wim, feeling just a hint of pride.

'Patsy has told me you have a nose for keeping out of trouble.'

Wim could only stare at Brother Bodicelli in bafflement, until the monk broke out into a deep bubbling laughter.

'And Dawn tells me you're on a quest for ultimate truth,' the brother went on with sudden seriousness.

'Yes, sir,' said Wim, brightening.

'Why bother?' Brother Bodicelli challenged cheerfully.

Wim was startled.

'Because ... because I'm unhappy when I don't. And when I'm cured I want to keep other humans from being unhappy.'

Brother Bodicelli nodded gravely.

'Extremely noble,' he said. 'Extremely. Aren't you proud of him, Dawn?'

'Yes, I am,' Dawn answered with equal seriousness.

'Can you help me?' Wim asked.

'Absolutely,' said Brother Bodicelli emphatically. 'That's my job here: helping people overcome the ten Great Barriers.'

'The ten Great Barriers?' Wim echoed, hoping the monk might have better luck making sense of them than Patsy had.

'Yeah,' said Billy, who had been looking at Brother Bodicelli with unusual respect, whether for his wisdom or his jewels Wim couldn't yet tell. 'The barriers that prevent a guy from reaching his full potential. If you can overcome them you'll have all the jewels, money, success and fame you want.'

'The ten barriers,' Wim repeated, turning to look back at the monk, who in his brown flowing robe and physical immensity was plopped down like an immense elephant turd.

'The ten distractions which prevent men from becoming empty and seeing ultimate truth,' the huge monk commented, suddenly examining his left arm under the fold of his robe and then holding up a flea pinched between a finger and thumb. 'And here's one of them.' He smiled triumphantly.

'That's one of the ten Great Barriers?' Wim asked doubtfully.

Brother Bodicelli leaned forward and released the flea in the open space between himself and Wim.

'Absolutely,' he said. 'Although one of the easier ones.'

'But what are these ten Great Barriers?' Wim asked.

'There's actually only one,' Brother Bodicelli said, picking up a large pewter jug and taking a long swallow, smacking his lips when he was done. 'But it's tricky. It shows itself in different ways at different times and so ends up getting called different names. Some sages say there are twelve, some only six. My master in Japan taught me that there are ten, one for each finger of his two hands. Though frankly,' Brother Bodicelli went on in a whisper and with a sly grin, 'there are probably more, but it tired my master to have to shift to his toes.'

Wim smiled.

'The hardest for you, Wim,' Brother Bodicelli went on, 'is the Barrier of Enlightenment.'

'The Barrier of Enlightenment!' Wim burst out. 'But that can't be a barrier! It's the means of overcoming barriers!'

'Good point,' said Brother Bodicelli. 'You are filled with your quest, which probably explains why enlightenment's your toughest barrier.'

'But –'

'While for Billy the tough one will probably be Identity,' the monk went on.

'You're wrong there, big fella,' said Billy. 'If there's one thing I know, it's who I am.'

The monk smiled at Billy and nodded.

'Who are you?' he asked cheerfully.

'Billy Best, the valedictorian of my class, leading hitter for three years on the baseball team, leading scorer in basketball, all-County at wide receiver in football, the guy that every girl dreams of dating, the guy who –'

'That's all in the past,' Brother Bodicelli commented. 'Who are you now?'

'Now?' said Billy, looking a little annoyed at his past's

being brushed aside so nonchalantly. 'Now I'm simply the best and the brightest and the boldest and bravest and –'

'No, I mean *right* now,' the monk interrupted gently. 'Right now as you're sitting on the pine needles staring at me. Who are you now?'

Billy was beginning to look a little uneasy.

'Well, I'm the handsomest, strongest –'

'Not your body, Billy,' Brother Bodicelli said, '*you*. Who are *you*?'

'Look, fella,' said Billy irritably. 'I'm the guy who doesn't put up with any shit. Who I am includes my past.'

'What past?' asked Brother Bodicelli.

'*The* past,' Billy answered.

'Since it doesn't exist,' the monk said, smiling, 'if your self depends on the past, then you don't exist either.'

'Doesn't exist!' Billy barked. 'If you'd seen my trophy room you'd know my past exists.'

'Your trophies exist in the present, Billy, and so do your memories of what you call the past. There is no past.'

'I'm me,' Billy declared emphatically. 'Billy Best, the one and only, and all your words don't deflate me one bit.'

'I know that, Billy,' said Brother Bodicelli. 'But until you empty out Billy Best, you'll never get the riches that life has to offer.'

'Don't worry about old Billy. They'll have to bail out Fort Knox before I'm finished.'

'Let's hope so,' said the monk, grinning. Then he turned to Dawn. 'Dawn's toughest barrier will probably be Purpose,' he went on, still with a big smile that implied that he loved all the barriers like old friends. 'All humans, having a sense of self, believing in the past and future, fearing death, are naturally filled with purpose.'

'And proud of it,' said Billy. 'Purpose is what distinguishes man from the lesser beings.'

'I certainly have the purpose to find ultimate truth,' added Wim.

'And my whole purpose in living is to do good,' suggested Dawn shyly, 'and fight evil with all my heart.'

'And I'll be damned if I'm going to stop pursuing success and avoiding failure,' said Billy.

Brother Bodicelli nodded gravely.

'But I'm afraid each of the things you've mentioned is a barrier,' he said, looking like a doctor having to announce a negative prognosis.

'How can success be a barrier?' Billy asked. 'Failure's the barrier.'

'That's true, Billy, failure is the barrier, but unfortunately it can never be separated from success: you can never have the one without the other.'

'Speak for yourself, fella,' Billy said.

'And I'm afraid, Dawn,' Brother Bodicelli went on quietly, 'that you can't have your good without evil, and that together they compose one of the ten Great Barriers. I'm not saying that good is bad, only that pursuing good may be a barrier to your seeing ultimate truth.'

Dawn didn't look too pleased about her pursuit of good being a barrier, but decided that as long as pursuing good was acknowledged as good she could think of it as a good barrier and not get upset with Brother Bodicelli.

'This is getting discouraging,' Wim suddenly burst out. 'Here I am seeking ultimate truth and you say I have to overcome enlightenment, identity, the past, the future, purpose, success, good, and a few other barriers I'm sure I've already forgotten.'

'Like the Barrier of Death,' said Brother Bodicelli jovially.

Wim groaned. 'Aren't there any easy barriers?' he pleaded.

'I suppose pleasure is the easiest,' he said, seeming reluctant to choose from among his lovable barriers.

'I see,' said Wim, scratching his left arm.

'And yet even the easiest of the ten Great Barriers is a

348

mountain so high not one man in a million is ever able to climb it,' the big monk said happily.

'Wow,' said Wim.

'And you, Wim,' Brother Bodicelli went on cheerfully, turning in his big easy chair to face Wim directly. 'You will have to climb them all. You have been sent to earth to overcome the ten Great Barriers in order to empty yourself and see at last what Your Father sent you to earth to find: Ultimate Truth. From this day forth your every waking moment, your every sleeping moment, must be dedicated to your Great Quest.'

'Huh,' said Wim, feeling a little depressed.

'What about me?' asked Billy.

The monk looked at Billy, then for a long time stared in a kind of trance at the earth in front of him, or perhaps at his belly since it blocked his view of the earth. Finally he looked up again at Billy.

'You are one of the lucky ones,' he said.

'How so?' asked Billy.

'You have already arrived,' Brother Bodicelli replied.

Billy beamed.

'Now you're talking,' he said. 'But I think I'll overcome the ten Great Barriers just to stay in shape. Maybe give Wim a hand now and then too.'

'That's very generous of you, Billy.'

'It's nothing,' said Billy. 'Maybe I can help you out with some of your other seekers too.'

'OK,' said Wim cautiously. 'To find old u.t. I've got to climb a few mountains, overcome a few barriers. Let's start right now on the easiest. What was it? Pleasure?'

'Pleasure,' answered the monk.

'Pleasure,' echoed Wim, scratching again at his left arm. 'OK, test me. I can't think of a single pleasure I couldn't stop bingo! just like that if I really wanted to.'

The monk nodded.

'For example,' said Wim, 'I'm thirsty now, but I'm able to resist the desire.'

'That's very good.'

'And after surviving my first years with the bullies of Maganansett there isn't a single pain that bothers me.'

'That's marvellous, Wim,' said Brother Bodicelli. 'Just as an experiment then, why don't you try to deny yourself the pleasure of scratching your left arm.'

'Beg pardon?' said Wim.

'Try giving up the pleasure of scratching your left arm.'

'Oh!' exclaimed Wim, suddenly flushing and throwing his right hand away from where it had been scratching. 'That! Sure. I'll simply stop.'

For several seconds everyone watched Wim's face get redder and redder until with a violent shudder he began vigorously scratching his left arm.

After ten seconds of such scratching Wim's face was more relaxed and he spoke quietly and with confidence.

'Actually,' he said, 'I don't happen to feel like stopping just now, but I'm quite sure that if I really wanted to, I could.' Wim looked hopefully over at Dawn, who looked away.

'OK,' said Wim. 'I see now that a Barrier is a barrier: something I may have to work on a bit.'

'I hope you won't let one little flea discourage you,' said the monk.

'Who's discouraged?' asked Wim, rubbing his left elbow against his side. 'I can stop any time I feel like it.'

'That's true,' said Brother Bodicelli with a smile. 'But, unfortunately, not until then.'

WIM'S IMPOSSIBLE DREAM

When Wim was studying with a Franciscan monk he told the Brother that he wanted to cure the human sickness.

'It's not easy,' said the monk gently.

'I know,' said Wim. 'But if I do nothing else with my life I want to help people stop hurting each other.'

'It's not easy.'

'To help people stop calling other people niggers and commies and Jewboys and dumb Indians and midgets and make them love one another and all be as nice as Dawn.'

'I'm afraid that's even harder.'

'And to cure the madness that makes men waste billions of dollars to build bombs that we'd be even crazier to use.'

'Harder yet.'

'And to cure Billy Best so he's just as happy after he's lost a game as he is when he wins.'

'Ah, Wim,' said the monk with a sigh. '*There* you ask too much of the universe.'

– from *Sixty-six Parables of Wim*

51

from Grain-of-Sand's *Memoirs of an Old Liar*, pp. 456–67

Well, his month with that monk fella was kinda hard on Wim. Since he tackled those ten barriers with all that gungho innocence that made him Wim, he stubbed his toes and banged his head and generally got his come-uppance no matter which way he turned.

The way this Bobo's place worked was that everyone got a barrier to overcome and had to work on it all day. Then he'd go have a chat with Bobo in his study in the monastery to see how he was doing. Bobo had spent five years touring India and Burma and Selma and Tokyo and places like that, and he had a lot of ways of doing things different from that Jesus fella. Seems every time Wim went to Bobo the advice he'd get would make the barrier seem even tougher.

Wim was hot to beat this pleasure barrier that had out-wrastled him earlier in the form of a flea. He decided that since girls were pretty pleasurable, he'd go right to the top and show that he could love 'em or leave 'em. He told Dawn that for the sake of his quest he wanted to do a little kissing and hugging.

Well, Dawn weren't too sure about this idea. She and Wim always did a little kissing and hugging – they was engaged, remember – but it sounded to her like Wim planned to enjoy himself a good deal more than usual so as to make a proper test. She finally said she'd help him all she could, but there was one barrier that he wasn't going to break through, and he better not forget it.

The idea was for Dawn to let Wim get all hot and interested in her and then for Wim to say triumphantly 'no' and walk away having bashed that old pleasure barrier to smithereens.

Well, Wim he didn't produce too many smithereens. Seems every time that afternoon Dawn and him would be getting hot and heavy, and Dawn would barely get herself to gasp out something like 'Your barrier, Wim!', Wim would look even more glassy-eyed than he already was and say 'What barrier?', and Dawn would be pretty glassy-eyed too and have trouble remembering what the hell she was talking about, but then she'd manage to remind him he was supposed to be able to stop right in the middle of things, and he'd say 'I will in a little while,' and sure enough he did in a little while which took half the afternoon.

But there weren't no smithereens. When Wim managed to roll away from Dawn and say 'no more' in a kind of pooped voice, he decided this showed he could beat that old barrier, but the monk weren't too impressed.

And Billy weren't having no luck with overcoming success neither. Bobo give him the job of losing every contest he entered. Billy figured it would be a snap. He played ping-pong with a gal named Lena and he kept smashing every shot up into the pine trees until he was way behind. But damned if when Lena was within five points of winning the game Billy's lips didn't start twitching. When she was within four points of winning his eyes got to blinking real fast, and when she was within three points of winning he accidentally hit a shot that slammed in on her side and almost took her head off. When she was within two points of winning he began to feel tears coming down his cheeks, and when she was within one point of winning and ahead by a score of twenty to one, Billy run off twenty-one straight points and won the game, blubbering the whole time.

Well, that Bobo fella told Billy that all he got to do is think that he is being better than the other guy by purposely losing the game. So the next day Billy plays Wim in ping-pong and purposely loses until the score is twenty to one against him and Wim says 'Boy, wait'll I tell Rocky how I clobbered you in ping-pong,' and Billy began crying again and run off twenty-one straight points and won the game.

He had another chat with Bobo and apologized and said he was sure he could lose, just give him another chance, and the next day he played Wim again and Wim got ahead fifteen to one and Billy was feeling great and knew he could lose this time when Wim realized that he was enjoying winning. Well now, since Wim's barrier was pleasure, he decided he ought to stop enjoying himself and lose, so he began hitting the ball even higher into the pine trees than Billy. And then Billy hit it even higher 'til the last ping-pong ball in Colorado had gone into orbit, and there still weren't no loser.

After a couple of weeks Wim began to get discouraged. He'd been battling with self and pleasure and past and purpose, and every one of 'em kept getting the upper hand. And every time Wim figured he'd finally overcome a barrier, that Bobo fella was able to show him how he'd cheated, and the barrier was still just as big and undefeated as ever.

And when Billy began to make progress against the barriers Wim got even more depressed. According to Billy he was beginning to out-fox Blobbo – as Billy called him. Seems one day the monk asked Billy if he'd discovered his True Self when he was driving a car.

'Sure,' said Billy, feeling he'd begun to pick up Bobo's style. 'Where?'

'Whenever I'm driving my car my True Self is right *there*,' and Billy pointed right at the monk's big belly.

'That's very good, Billy,' said the big guy. 'But then where is my True Self when you are driving your car?'

Well, Billy said that for a moment he was afraid the blobbo had out-foxed him again, but then he answered, '*Your* True Self is right *here*,' and he stabbed a finger into his own chest.

'That's very good,' said the big guy. 'But then how can we tell who is you and who is me?'

Billy smiled triumphantly.

'That's simple,' said Billy. 'You drive a pickup and I drive a Porsche.'

Billy claimed the monk's belly shook pretty good laughing at his answer, but then he asked Billy: 'What is the sound of one hand clapping?'

'Hey, Bobo, you're not getting me with that old staple of guru housewares,' Billy shot back with a confident grin. 'I've been reading up on the subject. The sound of one hand clapping is the Sound beyond sound, the Sound before all sound.'

'Perhaps,' said the monk fella amiably. 'But I don't *hear* anything. What *sound* does it make?'

Billy glared at the monk.

'If you're so smart,' he said, 'what *is* the sound of one hand clapping?'

The big blob shrugged his fat shoulders and then, with amazing agility, shot out a pudgy hand and slapped Billy lightly across the face.

'Splat!'

Billy blinked.

'Wise guy,' Billy said, but he knew he got beat again.

Still, he kept at it. Another time Billy told Wim he'd gone to Bobo's door and knocked.

'Who's there?' boomed out Bobo's voice.

'It's me!' shouted Billy.

'There's no room in here for both you and me,' Bobo shouted back, and the door stayed shut.

Billy bragged that the next time when he went and knocked and the monk asked 'Who's there?'

Billy said: 'It's you!'

And damned if the door didn't get opened.

Well, Wim weren't feeling so cheery about Billy doing so good and him doing so lousy, so he figured he could score a few points with the monk. He went and knocked.

'Who's there?' shouted Bobo.

'It's you!' Wim shouted, feeling pretty cool.

'In that case I'm already inside!' Bobo shouted back, and the door stayed shut.

Just seemed nothing Wim did turned out right.

Finally, he got in to see Bobo and complained that no matter what he did, he seemed to be hopelessly stuck behind all the barriers. Bobo just nodded his six chins and grinned.

'But what should I *do*?' Wim asked.

Bobo was sitting sprawled out on a large couch in the study he received visitors in. 'Whatever it was,' he said, 'you just did it.'

'What's going to happen?'

'It just happened.'

'I think I'm going crazy.'

'Then there's hope,' said Bobo cheerfully.

Wim stared gloomily at the fat cheerful monk.

'Some hope, sir,' he said.

'I think now, Wim,' said Brother Bodicelli with a gentle smile, 'you are ready to pray.'

'Pray?' said Wim, looking up uncertainly. 'I'm afraid I don't have any idea who God is – that's why I'm on my quest.'

'That's fine,' said Brother Bodicelli. 'If you knew who God was you wouldn't need to pray.'

'What should I pray for?'

'Whatever you want.'

Wim thought a while.

'Will God answer my prayers?'

'Depends on whether you already have what you ask for.'

'Beg pardon?'

'If you ask for something you don't have,' explained the monk, 'naturally God won't give it to you.'

Wim groaned.

'So I recommend you pray hard for something you already have.'

Wim, open-mouthed, couldn't speak.

'But –'

'Try it, Wim.'

So Wim went out in the woods and got down on his knees. He felt kind of awkward and self-conscious. Montauks aren't much on praying. I'd taught Wim that asking the Gods to give him something was a mistake, 'cause it gave them a hint of what you wanted so they could work things so you didn't get it. Still, he wanted to pray for some help in finding ultimate truth or overcoming the barriers but remembered Brother Bobo's telling him to pray for something he already had. He thought a bit and then whispered: 'Almighty Spirit, please … please let me be able to run fast.'

Well, the funny thing was it made him feel terrific – being able to run fast seemed like the most precious thing in the world, and God had just given it to him.

'Wow!' said Wim, and after he'd explained to Bobo the next day how he felt, the monk had said simply: 'Now you begin to see the power of prayer.'

Well, for the next few days Wim was as happy as a lark with this prayer business. He said there was nothin' nicer than praying hard that Dawn be alive, and then, sure enough, there she'd be, walking through the woods. It made him glow to have such a beautiful prayer answered. Or he'd pray that Billy be the best at something, and sure enough Billy would show his superiority, and it was wonderful. Or he'd pray hard that the next time he saw Bobo, Bobo would show what a helpless jerk Wim was, and, lo and behold, when his prayer came true he felt wonderful. Seems that when he prayed for something he had, it made that thing seem almost a miracle.

When he was trying to stop hugging Dawn he stopped to pray that she'd be a sweet warm loving sexy gal panting to be made love to, and sure enough, when he looked back down at her, she was. And he felt so glowy about how nice that was that he stopped all his hugging and kissing business, and just sat there beside her and beamed at her – though Dawn got a bit peevish.

358

When he realized that he'd overcome pleasure, he ran to Brother Bobo, and the big guy said that was jimdandy, but now Wim had to give up the pleasure of praying. Wim found that a bummer. Praying had become as much fun as kissing.

'You know,' Wim said to Bobo after the monk had ordered Wim to give up prayer, 'I'm surprised the Catholic Church lets you get away with all this.'

'All what?' asked Bobo with a look as innocent as Wim's.

'All the strange things you order people to do. All those jewels you wear. All those Pepsi Colas you drink. I thought Franciscans were supposed to be poor and pure and dull.'

'We are.'

'What about all those rings on your fingers?'

'They're not mine,' said Bobo, smiling.

'But you wear them,' said Wim.

'No, I don't,' Bobo insisted. 'Franciscans take a vow of poverty – to own nothing, to crave nothing, to need nothing. The obvious fool is the man who's led around by the nose by his unfulfilled desires. But the hidden fool is the man who cuts off his nose and declares himself free. I keep wealth and plenty near me, knowing there's no me to own or enjoy them.'

'How do you know?' Wim asked. 'Maybe you're just like me with the flea.'

Brother Bodicelli began to pull the rings off first his left hand and then his right. When he had all six rings removed, he leaned forward with a loud grunt and handed them all to Wim.

'I want you to give them all to Billy,' Brother Bodicelli said.

'But, Brother Bodi–'

'Jewels aren't one of your barriers so there's no sense my giving them to you. Billy should have an interesting time with them though.'

Wim looked down at the sparkling gems in his hands and then back at Brother Bodicelli.

'And I have to give up prayer?' he said almost to himself.

'Right!'

'And the Pope lets you get away with ordering people to give up prayer or experiment with their sex lives? Doesn't he –'

'Oh, the Pope has received many complaints about my work,' said Brother Bodicelli gravely, 'and the last time I was in Rome the Holy Father called me in for a Special Audience.'

'What happened?'

'The Holy Father was very direct. Before we'd exchanged a single word he said to me: "Do you favour abortion?"

'"No, Father," I said.

'"Are you planning to get married?"

'"No, Father."

'"Are you planning to run for political office?"

'"No, Father."

'"Have you poured blood on any nuclear missiles?"

'"No, Father."

'"Do you advocate that women should be priests?"

'"No, Father."

'"Bless you, my son," the Pope concluded, ending the audience. "Keep up the good work."'

'Wow,' said Wim. 'He let you go.'

'The Lord works in mysterious ways,' said Brother Bodicelli, beaming.

'He sure does,' Wim agreed.

52

from 'Fragments of Wim', pp. 263–70

For a while I was running in place again. If it weren't for Dawn I think I might have given up and left the mountain without getting any clue as to where to find Narsufin. Dawn kept assuring me that since we were all suffering, Brother Bodicelli's teaching methods must be doing us good. I have to admit that though he didn't make us wear hair shirts or sleep on nails or fast for a month, he somehow always managed to uncover the things we most deeply wanted to do or be so that he could order us to give them up. Billy said that Bobo was a sadist who was even better than Billy at making up games that only he could win.

But after I discovered the power of prayer things began to go much easier. Somehow, even after I had to give up praying, losing to the barriers didn't seem so bad any more. One of my last prayers had been that I be able to go a whole day without holding Dawn's hand, and when I finally did break down and hold her hand, it was beautiful – another loss to the barrier – but still, beautiful.

When I asked Bobo about this he grinned and chuckled and told me that when I began not minding losing to the barriers, I was either totally hopeless or getting pretty close to winning.

Dawn and I talked a lot that month about life and love and u.t. and quests and we agreed that we were lucky we were so different from each other since it made it so easy to know we might not be right about everything. Dawn said if it hadn't been for me she might have become a moral fanatic, but with my always breaking her rules she figured there might sometimes be something wrong with her rules. She was willing to try hard to give up doing good because Bobo had convinced her it was good to do so. She said she was even thinking of giving up her virginity since she sensed it might be a barrier. I thought that was a terrific idea, but Bobo told her that her virginity wasn't a barrier, just her special thing that the gods had given her – like a bad complexion. Dawn didn't think the simile was too nice, but she felt he was right.

Billy was a lot better at attacking the barriers than anyone else. He said it was not only because of his natural superiority but also because after eighteen years he'd become the world's expert in game playing, and Bobo's techniques all involved games. He claimed the secret of outwitting Bobo was that losing in his games was winning. Since Billy's first principle was to be the best at everything he did, after a few setbacks he soon became the best loser. It was a little strange hearing Billy brag he'd lost to Patsy arm-wrestling. When he was given six valuable rings by Bobo, he was set back a few hours. Then he concluded that if he kept the rings it would be a victory for the barrier of success and money, but if he gave them to someone, it would be a great victory for Billy Best. So he rushed off to Bobo and gave him back not only the six rings but two of Billy's own.

'Thank you,' said Brother Bodicelli.

'Think nothing of it,' said Billy proudly. 'Just one buddha to another.'

'Exactly,' said Brother Bodicelli. 'And when you *really* overcome the barrier of success and money you'll be able to *keep* all the riches people give you.'

'I will?' asked Billy excitedly.

'Certainly. As soon as you don't want something, it's all yours.'

'Oh,' said Billy gloomily.

But still, on the whole Billy was happier than I'd ever seen him. He was really getting into the quest for u.t.

'Look, Wim,' he said to me one afternoon. 'Did it ever occur to you that U.T. may not be what you think it is?'

'I know it's not what I think it is,' I said. 'If it were, I would have found it already.'

'Exactly,' said Billy confidently. 'Yet, we're sure it's very important, right?'

'It better be, all the time I've put in working to see it.'

'Exactly,' said Billy. 'And all these barriers someone has tossed in to make sure we can't get to it, they show how important it is. And only a few select, secret people have any clue to its whereabouts, right?'

'That's the way I understand it,' I said, wondering what he was driving at. 'And if there are a lot of people who know where old u.t. is and they're not telling me, there are going to be some bloody noses around when I find it.'

'Exactly,' said Billy. 'Now if we add up all these facts what do we have?'

'Confusion,' I said. 'I find whenever I add up all the facts about u.t. that's what I get: confusion.'

'NO!' said Billy. 'We find that U.T. is some sort of magic potion or secret weapon.'

'What!?'

'It's simple,' said Billy, grabbing my arm in his excitement. 'If U.T. were simply some formula for making people a little less stupid or miserable, somebody would publish it in the *New York Review of Books*, and a lot of people would nod their heads and mankind would go quietly on being stupid and miserable. It's utter nonsense to think that someone who *knew* what U.T. was – if it was just something harmless and unimportant like salvation or enlightenment – wouldn't publish it to the world. But they never do. They keep it secret among themselves.' Billy had both my arms now and was staring at me like the ancient mariner. 'Wim, it's time you woke up. U.T. is a magic potion or secret weapon of immense value and the man who finds it and is willing to use it in a modern, reasonable, entrepreneurial, profitable way will be the greatest man in the history of the world.'

I hadn't seen Billy so excited since he scored the winning touchdown in the Sectional Finals the year before.

'I don't think so, Billy,' was all I could say.

'I'll find it, Wim,' Billy declared with that mad gleam in his eye. 'And when I get hold of that potion or weapon, the Russians better fold up their tents and steal away because I'll be one mean dude.' He paused with a far-away look in his eyes. 'And IBM and McDonalds better look out too. With a franchise operation...'

We'd been there almost two months when Bobo called all three of us into his study in the monastery. It was the first time since our first day that he'd seen us together, and we knew it was a special occasion.

He had us sit on the plush rug in front of his couch while he sipped his Pepsi out of his big jug.

'Well, my children,' he began. 'What have you learned so far?'

'I've learned that losing is tougher than winning,' Billy replied promptly. 'And also that losing can be a way of winning.'

'That's very good, Billy,' Bobo said. 'And have you learned who you are?'

'Yeah,' said Billy. 'I'm a speck of something plumped down on a rug.'

Bobo smiled.

'That's very good, Billy,' he said. 'But even now I fear you overestimate yourself.'

Billy squinted up at the mound of flesh who was our teacher and finally shrugged and smiled.

'Never,' he said. 'You can't overestimate Billy Best.'

'How about you, Dawn?' Bobo asked.

Dawn looked pleased that she'd been asked.

'I've learned that doing good is all right,' she said confidently, 'but that trying to be a good person doesn't work.'

'Why not?'

'Because if you worry about being a good person you're worried about yourself which is selfish, which is bad, which is why you shouldn't worry about being a good person.'

'That's very interesting, but then why bother to do good?'

'Doing good is like praying hard for things you already have,' Dawn said, her beautiful face looking even more angelic than usual. 'It makes the world glow a little.'

Brother Bodicelli nodded and smiled and then turned to me.

'And you, Wim?' he asked.

'Well, for one thing I've learned that if I have to overcome all ten Great Barriers before I see ultimate truth, I'm in trouble,' I said.

'What else?'

'That even trying to overcome them somehow makes life ... brighter or something.'

'And ...?'

'That even stuck behind their barriers human beings aren't as bad as I used to think they are.'

'And where is ultimate truth?' Brother Bodicelli asked gently.

'Right here,' I answered, making Dawn and Billy look at me in surprise. 'But I still can't see it.'

'Well,' said Brother Bodicelli with a sigh. 'I'm afraid you're beginning to enjoy yourself here. It's time for you to move on and let your sufi friend have a crack at you.'

'Now!?'

'I thought you were determined to find ultimate truth?'

'I am, but –'

'Well run along then,' said Bobo. 'There are a lot of other folks anxious to learn the power of the flea.'

So we left. The trouble with seeking enlightenment is that as soon as you reach an enjoyable part of the path you can be pretty sure it's not the path.

MESSAGES

And it chanced that the Lord of the Universe, the Divine Creator Himself, did come to send a Message to mankind, a Message which would liberate men from the heavy burdens they had come to encumber themselves with. And He sent the Message to earth and it was spoken and it was written and men did not hear and men did not see.

'How can this be?' asked the Lord of the Universe. 'I have sent the Message that will liberate all men from the burdens they needlessly carry and yet they do not hear it, do not see it.'

All the angels stood in embarrassed silence at the Lord's question except one, Our Beloved Wim, who dared to speak.

'O Mighty Lord,' said Wim. 'In your Infinite Wisdom and Love you have sent men the Message, but they have neither ears to hear it nor eyes to see it.'

'I know,' said the Divine Creator. 'But how can this be?'

'It's simple, Lord,' Wim replied. 'Human beings don't want Messages, they want burdens.'

'But they suffer from their burdens,' said the Lord.

'True, Lord,' replied Our Beloved Wim. 'But not as much as they suffer from Messages.'

– from *Sixty-six Parables of Wim*

53

from *The Gospel According to Luke*, pp. 455–63

'But why Harlem!?' Billy hissed at Wim in a whisper as they emerged from the subway at the corner of 125th Street and Seventh Avenue. 'Why couldn't we look for Narsufin some place safe: like the jungles of darkest Africa?'

The crowded streets he, Wim and Dawn emerged onto looked safe enough, except ninety-nine per cent of the people were coloured black and brown, and Billy had watched a lot of television.

'Because I've got a strong hunch that I'll find Narsufin close to home,' Wim answered, stopping to take Dawn's hand and then peering down the brightly-lit street, filled with milling people even at ten o'clock in the evening. 'Or rather that he'll find me.'

Billy nodded with a nervous smile at two black youths who swaggered past. He edged closer to Wim and Dawn.

'But I thought the only preachers in Harlem,' he went on to Wim in a low voice, 'are Cadillac-driving Baptists and armoured-car-driving black Muslims. No one here's even *heard* of sufis.'

'Neither had you,' Wim countered as they began to move tentatively east on 125th Street.

'But that's expected,' said Billy. 'I'm a businessman. Businessmen have to steer clear of religion – it interferes with profits. Jesus,' he added in a whisper, 'those guys look tough.'

Four or five black men were lounging against a boarded-up store front, smoking and drinking beer. They were staring at the approach of the two young whites and Wim.

'They've never been given a chance,' said Dawn, holding her head high and walking confidently on. 'They're victims of an unjust society.'

'I know,' said Billy. 'But as a member of the oppressing class I find they make me nervous.'

'Excuse me, sir,' said Wim, releasing Dawn's hand and walking up to the largest of the five men standing against the abandoned store. 'I'm looking for a very tall black man named Narsufin.'

All five of the blacks stared at Wim, as stunned as if he were a small poodle who had just spoken.

As they all looked at him blankly, Wim cleared his throat.

'Narsufin,' he repeated. 'Used to play basketball for the Detroit Pistons.'

The big black man, about the size of Rocky Peters but with an expression that suggested that gentleness was not his forte, made a superhuman effort and shoved himself away from the wall.

'Wha' for you wanta see him?' he asked reluctantly.

'He's supposed to help me find u.t.'

'Ain't no dealer 'round here name Nasuffin.'

'Let's get out of here,' Billy hissed from a few feet behind Wim.

'He's not a dealer,' said Wim.

'Then wha' for you wanta see him?'

'U.t. stands for ultimate truth,' Wim explained. 'Narsufin's going to help me find ultimate truth.'

The five black men now looked at Wim as stunned as if he were a small poodle who had not only spoken, but had just shifted from English to Latin.

Being unable to comprehend Wim, they slowly shifted their collective eyes first to Billy, who smiled eagerly, and then Dawn.

'The pussy for sale?' asked a short, thick-set man wearing reflective glasses.

'Er, no,' answered Billy. 'She . . . ah . . . she's a kind of nun.'

Dawn was dressed in jeans and a short-sleeved blouse and looked ravishingly young, sexy and not too nun-like. She smiled at them warmly to show her lack of racial prejudice.

'Yeahhhhhhh,' said the big black man with a widening grin. 'A nun. I like nuns. Hacker here likes nuns too. You her man?'

'Uh, no,' said Billy. 'Although I have no intrinsic objection to entering into an entrepreneurial arrangement of the mode you suggest, providing it is equitable and viable for both parties, in this partic–'

'Shit, man, shutup.'

'Right.'

'Narsufin,' Wim repeated. 'A sufi sage.'

The big man turned back to Wim and leaned to peer down at him.

'Oh,' he said. '*That* Narsufin. Why didn't you say so?'

'You know him!?' Wim asked excitedly.

'Yeah, I know the guy. He's crazy, man.'

'That's OK,' said Wim. 'Where can I –'

'He keeps walking along the street and saying "There! There He is!" and then pointing to some trash-can or bag lady or whore.'

'He does?' said Wim. 'What's he mean?'

'Claims he sees God there,' the big black man answered.

'That's terrific.'

'Shit, man, everybody knows God don't hang out in no bag lady or trash-can.'

'Where can I find him?' Wim asked excitedly.

'How much you want to find him?' the big black man asked slyly, while the other four men began to edge around Wim, Dawn and Billy.

'A million dollars' worth!' Wim exclaimed.

'Er, Wim,' Billy muttered, feeling Wim's bargaining technique left something to be desired.

'Shit, man, I give you a discount on that.'

'Thank you, sir,' said Wim. 'Where can I find Narsufin?'

'Two Ben Franklins gets you lucky.'

'Er, Wim.'

'Oh, I'm lucky without any Ben Franklins,' said Wim. 'Where's Narsufin?'

'A Ben Franklin, General Grant and an Andy,' countered the black man.

'Are you speaking of money?' asked Wim.

'You got it, man,' said the big black. 'You give me money, I give you the *ad*-dress.'

'My friend here handles money matters,' said Wim, 'but I should warn you that I'll probably find Narsufin whether you give me directions or not.'

'You threatenin' me?'

'Er, Wim.'

'No, sir,' said Wim. 'Just speaking truth.'

The black man stared at Wim a long moment and then turned to Billy.

'A Ben Franklin, a General Grant and an Andy.'

'We can't go higher than two Andys and an Alexander,' Billy countered, feeling he was in his element.

'Shit, man, I never heard of an Alexander.'

'An Alexander is an Alexander Hamilton – a ten dollar bill,' Billy explained.

'Fuck, you mean a *dime*!'

'Er, yes. Two Andys and a, er, dime.'

'A Ben, a General and an hour with the fox.'

'Well, maybe a General,' countered Billy, 'two dimes, a nickel and you get to shake hands with the fox, er, the nun, er, Dawn.'

'A Ben, a dime, two joints and ten minutes alone with the nun.'

'Er, Billy,' said Wim.

'Two Andys, a dime, a pack of Merits, and Dawn will talk to you for five minutes.'

'Er, Billy.'

'Two Bens, a carton of Camels, ten lotto tickets, and three minutes alone with the nun.'

'Two Generals, two dimes, half-a-pack of Camels, a six pack –'

When Wim and Dawn left, Billy and the black man were so deeply into negotiating that they didn't notice that their important merchandise was disappearing.

It was twenty minutes later that Billy caught up with Wim several blocks farther east on 125th Street. Breathless, Billy explained that he'd made a marvellous deal, getting the black man to give him Narsufin's whereabouts for only one Ben, two Andys, a dime, Billy's jacket and a night's option on Dawn should she ever go on the street.

'What's the address?' Wim asked, not exactly sharing Billy's enthusiasm for his deal.

'North of 103rd Street,' Billy replied with a scowl.

'Exactly where's that?' asked Wim.

'It's not too exact,' said Billy. 'As far as I can tell it includes all of New York State except for most of Manhattan and the southern half of Long Island.'

'Billy!'

'I asked for my money back, but when the guy began negotiating to see how much I'd have to pay to get my money back and began at a Grover Cleveland and a half-share in Dawn, I knew I was in trouble. Fortunately, I decided that I had wanted to lose to this guy so I emerged victorious anyway.'

'Brother, can you spare a dime?' asked a small, young boy blocking their way.

'Ten bucks!' exclaimed Billy. 'What nerve!' He gave the boy two quarters and was surprised to see the boy look pleased.

'Der He is!!' a loud deep voice suddenly cried from behind them.

As Wim, Billy and Dawn wheeled they saw a tall, skinny

black man dressed in a shabby black suit pointing a long bony finger at Billy.

'I already paid!' Billy shouted back.

'Ain't no way You can hide from me!' the black man shouted, extending his arm directly at Billy and advancing menacingly towards them. 'I *sees* You!'

'I didn't do it!' Billy shouted back, slipping behind Wim. 'Whatever it is I didn't do it!'

'You *der*! I know you der!' proclaimed the preacher. 'Ain't no use hidin' behind no *dis*guise with me.'

'Are you Narsufin?' Wim asked hesitantly, noting the man's extreme height and sensing his meaning.

The skinny black lowered his arm and frowned suspiciously.

' 'Pends who asks.'

'I'm Wim.'

'Who dat?'

'I'm on a quest for ultimate truth,' Wim announced.

'Goody-goody gumdrop for you,' said the man, still peering down suspiciously at Wim, who felt slightly punctured by the reply.

'And Narsufin is the one who will tell me exactly where or how to find it,' he persisted.

'Who dese folks?'

'That's Dawn my always faithful girlfriend and Billy my always . . . my guy friend.'

'Dey lookin' for u.t. too?'

'Damn right,' said Billy. 'Have you ever heard of a black sufi named Narsufin? But I warn you we won't go any higher than two Andys and a lock of Dawn's hair.'

'Ain't no Narsufin in Harlem. He done went and gone to the Sudan.'

'I told you,' said Billy, turning to Wim. 'Let's get out of here.'

'How tall are you?' asked Wim, staring up at the long black-skinned stick that loomed over him.

'Five feet,' the man answered.

'Five feet!' Wim exclaimed.

'Come on, Wim,' said Billy, pulling at Wim's arm. 'The guy's nuts. Let's go.'

'What religion are you?' Wim asked.

'Ain't got no religion.'

'See, come on.'

'You're not a sufi saint?' Wim asked, feeling disappointed.

The skinny black man began a high-pitched cackle totally different from his deep raspy voice, and began slapping his knees.

Reluctantly, Wim turned and followed Billy and Dawn farther east along 125th Street.

The next afternoon Billy and Dawn stayed behind at the hotel so Billy could finish arranging transportation to the Sudan. Wim, still feeling that Narsufin would somehow find him in Harlem, was having his third cup of hot chocolate in a dingy diner on East 125th Street. He wasn't too surprised when the tall, skinny black preacher came into the diner and pointed dramatically at an old man whose face had fallen forward and was buried in a plate of french fries and ketchup.

'I sees You!' the black preacher said. 'One two threesy on You!' He cackled happily and then came over, lifted the man who was sitting on the stool next to Wim into the air and lowered him into a chair in a booth. Smiling, he sat down beside Wim.

'Found it yet?' he asked.

'No, I haven't, Narsufin,' Wim replied. 'Can you help me?'

'Probably. Though you're kind of young for this sort of thing.'

'I know. I'm a little weird.'

'Well, that always helps.' He looked at the dregs of Wim's hot chocolate and then added: 'Can't we go some place where they serve food?'

'Sure,' said Wim, rising to follow Narsufin out. 'The hot chocolate was a little weak.'

'I think they add an M-and-M to lukewarm water and call it a day,' said Narsufin.

Two hours later they had finished dinner at a little restaurant on Lenox Avenue that featured spare-ribs that were black but juicily rare and a beer that was warm with a kick and topless dancers that were both. Wim found he liked Narsufin the most of any of the buddhas he'd met so far. Narsufin told a lot of funny stories about his basketball playing and spiritual questing and the conflict between the two. He kept shifting back and forth from dialect to normal American as easily as most people shift from first gear to second. Dressed in the same shabby black suit and cowboy boots he'd been wearing when Wim first saw him, his most striking features to Wim were his eyes – glittering black pools in the middle of the huge white orbs, eyes that never rested but seemed to dance around the room, throwing out as much light as they took in.

Making an incongruous figure towering in his chair opposite the diminutive Wim, Narsufin interspersed his stories with a series of sleight-of-hand tricks, making spoons disappear and turn up in Wim's glass of ginger ale, or Wim's blue windbreaker disappear and turn up on one of the topless dancers – to the confusion of the young woman and the eventual boos of the few patrons at the bar. Narsufin explained that since everything both existed and didn't exist it wasn't much of a hassle to switch them around all over the place.

But as Wim finished up the last of his dish of vanilla ice-cream – the restaurant had sent out for it as a favour to Narsufin – he realized his new sufi friend still hadn't given Wim the slightest hint that would let him know exactly where to find u.t. So he challenged Narsufin.

'Where can I find u.t.?' he abruptly asked after they'd both finished their ice-cream.

Narsufin, nursing a cup of espresso, raised his thin bony black face and nodded slightly, as if the question were reasonable.

'What you learned so far?' he countered, straightening in his chair and taking out a cigar.

'Well, I don't know,' said Wim after a pause. 'Mostly I keep learning things that I *don't* know.'

Narsufin nodded.

'Do you see u.t. in this room?' he asked Wim.

Wim looked around the restaurant, at the dozen or so customers eating at the tables, the half-dozen men sitting at the bar, at the two fast-moving waitresses, at the slow-moving dancer, and at the various plates of food.

'No,' said Wim.

Narsufin nodded.

'Is it here?' asked Wim.

Narsufin didn't answer.

'Is it?' Wim persisted.

'Hey, fella,' said Narsufin, lighting up his cigar. 'If you don't see it then it ain't here. The only things that exist are what you see.'

'How did you find it, Narsufin?' Wim asked, after it was clear the sufi wasn't going to continue.

'Sheet, man, no trouble at all,' Narsufin answered, changing gears again. 'Just took me twelve years and zap! there it was.'

'Twelve years!' Wim moaned.

'Yeah. You know any cat's done it quicker?'

'Well, no, but –'

' 'Course not. Ain't none. I been zapped fastern Muhammad can say "Jackie Robinson".'

'But *how*?'

'It all started when I was thirteen.'

'Me too!'

'This is my story. You got a story about finding u.t. you get yourself your own agent.'

'I'm sorry.'

'I was living in this backwoods honky village about a hundred miles from the nearest human being.'

'*Honky* village?' Wim interrupted.

'Yeah, honky.'

'There were white people living in your village?'

'Shit no. Honky means "no-account, shiftless, good-for-nothing". Don't necessarily mean white.'

'Oh.'

'I lived in this slow, remote, honky village a hundred miles from nobody and, man, there weren't *nothing* to do.'

'This is in Africa, right?'

'I mean our tribe's trade consist of leaving a bunch of banana at a crossroads de begin of ever' decade and pickin' up a few fish in exchange at de end of it. 'Course de fish a little *ripe* maybe, but our bananas no bargain either. And if some dudes show up from another tribe they don't have to conquer us. We just stare at 'em open-mouthed with big wide eyes until dey's stuck a white flag in all our mouths and we's officially surrendered.'

'They sound like Montauks!'

'Cowards is what I call 'em. De heaviest dude in our tribe's history got famous pushing a stone up against the mouth of a tiny cave and trappin' some dumb squirrel inside and six days later going in with a war-whoop and standing over the corpse.'

'I thought I read that your tribe were head-hunters.'

'No way. Anything that *moves*, our tribe we trained to run, man. If it look like it *might* move, we trained to trot.'

'When I was being brought up by Grain-of–'

'You want to publish your story, go on downtown. You want to find u.t. check out what I say.'

'I'm sorry, Narsufin.'

'You're a regular chatterbox. Surprised you learned a thing so far.'

'I'm listening.'

'Good. Ain't many people made it to old u.t. without learnin' to listen.'

54

Narsufin Tells How He Climbed the Mountain

from *The Gospel According to Luke* . . .

One day I woke up. When I peeked outside my haystack of a house I saw a Mountain, high above the diddly little hills around my village.

Well, soon's as I'd seen it, I says to myself, Narsufin, you got to climb that Mountain.

So I ran to my buddies at the local hangout – a shack where an old guy made beer out of fermented weeds – and said, 'Hey, you motherfuckers, that Mountain is *mine*! Let's go!' I expected them all to give me high five and off we'd go.

They looked at me as if I drunk.

'What mountain?' they all say.

'*That* Mountain,' I said, pointing off beyond our hills where I saw the thing rising up like a great white pyramid against the sky.

They thought I was nuts. Not a single one of 'em saw it. I went tearing around the whole village, and though I found a few others thought maybe they saw it, most of them claimed it was a mirage, or a sham created by a few priestly huckster travel agents looking for a fast buck. They laughed at me. Claimed that the world consisted of hills and valleys, and the cool cat learned to make a comfortable home for himself there without chasing after imaginary mountains.

'If dat mountain really *der*,' the village mayor said to me, 'then why can't I see it?'

'Beats me, brother,' I replied. 'But if dat Mountain don't exist, how come I sees it?'

'Because you crazy, Narsufin,' the Mayor said. 'After all, any cat dat see a mountain where der ain't none, he crazy, right?'

('Is that really how you and the mayor spoke?' Wim asked.

'Bug off, fella,' Narsufin said to Wim. 'You want to be a literary critic, go to Yale. I'm just trying to translate primitive Ungalese into American nigger.')

Anyway, I wanted to climb that old Mountain like nothing I ever wanted before. I decided that the worst that could happen if it didn't exist when I got there was I wouldn't have to climb it. So me and a dozen or so other good-for-nothings got together to start off, but before we even got outside the village, we were all arguing about how the Mountain ought to be climbed.

'Dat ol' Mountain been climbed in the past, and this map proves it,' old Abercrombie Lemon said. He was a crafty old dude who was a big man in the village because of the way he could spit. 'All we got to do is find and follow these old trails, and we're bound to reach the top.'

Well, I was raring to go the way the map said until two other old dudes came up with different maps showing different trails. The Mountain looked a little different on each map, but I decided I liked Abercrombie's map because all the trails were coloured green, which is my favourite colour.

But when I started marching off, a couple of my buddies stopped me and said all the maps were outdated, that the Mountain on those old maps wasn't the same as the one I'd seen. What we got to do, they said, is find a *guide* who knew the way to this new Mountain.

Well, I figured the motherfuckers were right on this one, and sure enough there were three guides listed in the Yellow Pages of the Ungalese Phone Book, and we phoned 'em up and made appointments.

The first one turned out to be white, so we crossed him off the list and went to the second. He was a chunky black guy who wielded a hiking staff as if it were a combination baseball bat, golf club and sword. When he said the fee for his guidance was only one banana, all us climbers figured this was the *man*. But when he mentioned that the path he knew took three years, we decided it might be a good idea to check out the other guide.

The third guide was a fancy dude wearing an elegant robe with a lot of colours and a big hat with plenty of feathers and bones, and he turned out to be our sort of man. He said he'd be happy to guide us to the top of the Mountain. He charged quite a bit, but told us he had all the latest guide equipment – compasses and solar-heated canteens and radar and stuff like that – and the thing that really sold us, he'd get us there in no time. We slapped down our two-dozen bananas and off we went.

Next thing we knew we was in a big carnival with a lot of other climbers, riding roller-coasters, going through the tunnel of love, seeing ourselves all distorted with tricky mirrors, and having a great old time. None of us ever even *heard* of a carnival before, much less been to one, so it was better'n a free pass to a whorehouse. Then I began to notice that we weren't going nowhere. The Mountain was just as far away as ever.

So I managed to drag away three of my buddies, and we left the guide and lit out on our own.

Pretty soon who should we see but old Abercrombie and the guys who were following him and his map. They were looking like they needed a fix – jumpy and depressed. Seems the trail was blocked by an avalanche, and they couldn't figure what to do. Their map only showed this one path to the Mountain and it was blocked. I decided all we could do was look for another trail, and I got a few others to join me.

But after a couple of days of marching through the roughest country east of 155th Street some of the dudes with me decided it was ridiculous to *hike* to the top of the Mountain, they ought to get a job, save some bananas, and rent a helicopter to fly to the top. Or get a plane to fly over the Mountain and drop 'em down by parachute. Well, I couldn't see hiking *away* from the Mountain and I certainly didn't want to work at no job, so when a half-dozen went off to get work and earn bananas so they could fly to the mountaintop I kept on truckin'. What I did was I took one step towards the Mountain and noticed it got closer.

After a while me and the few guys still with me came to a lot of big trees that blocked the sight of the Mountain. A couple of the guys began to get discouraged. Claimed the Mountain wasn't on the other side of the woods at all, maybe didn't even exist. They thought it'd be nicer to hike downhill until they could see the Mountain again. Another guy said it was too bad we weren't Americans 'cause if we were, we could call in the B52s and defoliate it. All of them said we'd get lost in there without a guide.

But I said, yeah, we'd be better off with B52s and a guide, but it was a long hike back to the Yellow Pages, and I went and took one step into those mean-looking trees and noticed that they weren't quite as mean or thick as they looked.

Then I came to a big flooded river with a hundred or so climbers all stuck on the one side and the Mountain clear as day off in the distance on the other. I saw the chunky guide with the big staff with a couple of climbers and even saw one of my buddies who'd gone off to rent an airplane. He told me most who'd gone off to earn bananas had gotten so into their jobs they couldn't see the Mountain any more and weren't interested in it or planes. But when he'd finally earned enough to rent a plane and flown over the Mountain it was the *coolest* thing ever happened to him, but every time he landed again he felt he'd just come down from speed. When he tried parachuting down on top of the Mountain he always got blown off course and ended up landing in some place called Newark.

Well, everybody on the banks of that raging river was down: seemed impossible to cross. A few hiked to look for an easier crossing some place else, but they didn't find one. Some others decided they'd begin looking for an easier mountain to climb. One old man thought we could get the Ungalese government to build a dam upstream so we could cross. I said: 'Fuck the Ungalese government. Let's build a bridge.'

Most the other motherfuckers said that was impossible or would take too long, but I started and a few other good-for-nothings pitched in, and pretty soon a bridge began to grow.

Took us close to a year, but damned if we didn't get one cool bridge across that river. Funny thing, though, after we were done and could cross, a lot of the brothers wanted to keep improving the bridge – make it fancier and prettier or sturdier and things like that. I said, 'Hey, you mother-fuckers, we got a Mountain to climb,' but they said the bridge had to be fixed up first. Those dudes were so into bridge-building they begun building a second bridge across the open field between the river and the Mountain. I said I wasn't too sure we needed a bridge just to cross a field, but they said the bridge had got 'em across the river, hadn't it, and no sense in abandoning a good thing just because we hadn't come to another river yet. 'Bridge building is the *way*, man,' Pete Cooper said. 'We'll just keep building 'em all the way to the top.'

Well, I had nothing against bridges, but I walked on.

Finally me and few others came to the base of the Mountain, and things looked pretty tough. No matter which way I looked, nothing but sheer cliffs. Like standing under a skyscraper. Well, soon as everybody was stuck, the chunky guide with the staff who said it would take one banana and three years showed up. Somehow I now felt that this man was my Guide, so I forked over my banana and began following him. So did about twenty others.

After a while we came to the worst bunch of pricker

bushes you ever saw, and a couple of the climbers said: 'If this dude were a True Guide he wouldn't be leadin' us through no pricker bushes,' so they turned back.

Next we came to a Ice-Cream Cart, and the Guide treated us all to ice-cream cones and fudge. A coupla fellas said: 'If this dude were a True Guide he wouldn't be lettin' us eat no ice-cream and candy,' so they turned back.

When we came to a sheer blank wall, the Guide paused only a second or two and said we could just walk through it. Several of the brothers said: 'Ain't no way anyone can walk through a wall. This dude must be a fake,' and they turned back.

Well, I hung around and when that Guide walked through the wall, I just up and followed him and got through just as neat as I later cut through the Knicks.

After a while we came to a place where there were two trails, and the Guide says, 'You guys take that trail for a while, but I'm gonna take this one. Meet you higher up.'

Well, a coupla brothers say, 'If this dude were a True Guide he wouldn't be deserting us and making us take the steep trail while he loafs along the other,' so after he'd left, they snuck along after him rather than go where he sent 'em, and no one ever heard of 'em again. I took one step along the trail the Guide had pointed to and found it wasn't so steep after all.

Three months later I was still plopping down one foot after the other. I was still with my Guide, though I didn't have to pay much attention to him any more to follow the trail, and the climbing was getting easier and easier. And I began to realize that there was a lot of shacks and huts and people around all along this part of the trail, first we'd seen in years. And then I noticed some other climbers walking along another trail off to my right, and damned if I didn't see the guide with a flowing robe. Seemed like he had half his carnival along with him and a few of his climbers too.

Abercrombie was there, and even the white guide. And on the other side of him I could see some of my old buddies building a bridge across a dried-up stream-bed.

'Look over there,' I said to my Guide, pointing to the travelling carnival. 'You think those dudes will be able to make it to the top too?'

'What do you mean make it to the top?' said the old guide. 'You're already on the top. Where do you think you are?'

And sure 'nuff when I looked around, my Mountain was gone, and the whole fuckin' banana patch of the universe seemed to be spread out beneath me.

'So this is the top of the Mountain,' I said to the Guide, feeling pretty confused. 'It looks ... it looks exactly like life back in my honky village.'

'Exactly the same,' said the Guide.

'And ... and all the other dudes made it to the top too?'

'Everyone's here,' said the Guide.

'It's been three years,' I said dreamily.

'Three years.'

But then I looked again at the village and the people and the whole fuckin' banana patch of the universe stretched out all around me and whoosh! everything lit up like some long-lasting Duracell lightning just struck, and I suddenly *knew* for the first time in my life that I was on the top of the Mountain.

'Hey, man, this is terrific!!' I shouted. 'This is fucking outrageous! This is better than smoking banana peels!'

'Better keep your voice down,' said my Guide, who actually didn't look much like a guide any more – he looked just like everybody else.

'Why!?' I shouted. 'We're all here on top of the Mountain! We should all be shouting and celebrating!'

'Better keep your voice down,' said the Guide.

One of my buddies came up to me and said:

'Hey, how they hanging, Narsi?'

'High! Real high!' I said, grinning and giggling like they just let me out of the loony bin.

'What you on, man?' my buddy asked with a frown.

'This top of the Mountain! Ain't it great?!'

'What top? What mountain? You crazy, man?'

I looked at my motherfucking good-for-nothing buddy and suddenly saw that the guy didn't know where he was. And now that I took a good look at the other folks I saw that most of them didn't know where they were either. I started to shout, but my Guide came up and took me by the arm and led me away, saying again: 'Better keep your voice down.'

'But why don't they know where they are?' I cried.

'They ain't done much hiking,' the Guide said.

'Can't I *tell* them?'

'They won't listen. First they got to see the Mountain.'

'But we're on it!'

'First they got to see an illusion of the Mountain off in the distance and begin going for it.'

'You mean ... I ... the Mountain I thought I saw –'

'An illusion.'

'You mean –'

'You've been there all the time.'

I stared at my Guide a long time, my face being pretty much all eyes, and then I began slowly shaking my head and smiling.

'Sheeeeeet,' I finally said, grinning and giggling and feeling the lightning blazing all around me like the light show at the Apollo. 'I want my banana back.'

*

'That didn't really happen, did it?' Wim asked when Narsufin had ended his story. The restaurant and bar were closing up and almost empty, the last topless dancer sleepwalking through motions that held all the excitement of a girl scout selling cookies.

387

'Who cares?' Narsufin answered, lighting up a cigar. 'I'm not a historian.'

'But, I mean, did you ever see ... a Mountain?'

'Who cares?' Narsufin repeated, drawing in a mouthful of smoke. 'You want a biography go to the New York Public Library. I got better things to do.'

'It was ... a nice story. I liked it,' Wim said dreamily, still somewhat mesmerized.

'Thanks.'

'I think ... I think the message is that –'

'Message!' Narsufin interrupted, yanking the cigar out of his mouth. 'You think I'm some sort of cut-rate Western Union?'

'But –'

'You liked my story, Wim,' Narsufin said, relaxing again and tipping back in his chair. 'Quit while you're ahead.'

'Yes, sir,' said Wim.

PLAYING AT GURU

One of the great zen traditions adopted by Wim was that of the contest where one master or seeker pits his level of enlightenment against that of another. As a result, Wim received repeated challenges through the years, many of which, as we know, he lost.

One day Billy Best challenged Wim, and the two sat on the earth in the middle of a circle of seekers. Billy began by saying: 'The only true path is the one that goes somewhere.'

'The only somewhere worth going to is everywhere,' replied Wim.

'I'd rather climb a mountain,' said Billy, 'than walk to the corner grocery store.'

'Not if you needed a quart of milk,' said Wim.

'If people followed your ideas of detachment and emptiness they'd never get out of bed in the morning.'

'If they were women and I were there, it might not be a bad idea.'

'The simplest way to see the falsity of your way is to look at your life. What have you achieved?'

'Nothing,' replied Wim.

'See!!' announced Billy triumphantly.

'And it took me a long time to do it too,' added Wim.

On another occasion Billy interrupted a discussion Wim was having with some seekers by saying: 'Wim may claim not to believe in success or failure, but you notice he enjoys playing ol' numero uno.'

'You're right, Billy,' Wim said promptly. 'You take over as guru and I'll be one of the seekers.'

'About time,' said Billy with a smile, and he seated himself in the middle of the large group. 'Any questions?' he asked.

'What is Ultimate Truth?' asked someone.

'A lot of baloney that keeps people from eating steak,' replied Billy.

'What is the correct Path?' asked another.

'The correct Path is the long hard road to fame and fortune,' said Billy.

'How can I achieve enlightenment?' asked a third.

'Hard work, consistent effort, clear vision, outstanding ability, special talent, phenomenal energy, total dedication, and you yourself don't have a chance,' said Billy.

'How can we recognize the One True Guru?' asked a fourth.

'I'll mail you my photograph,' replied Billy.

'What is the difference between nirvana and samsara?'

'Nirvana is where you are when you're a success, and samsara is far south of there for you others.'

'Master!' suddenly cried Wim from his position way in the back. 'I have the most crucial question of all!'

'What is it, shrimp?'

'When's it my turn to be guru again?'

– from *Sixty-six Parables of Wim*

55

from *The Gospel According to Luke*, pp. 488-96

Wim spent only a week with Narsufin, who had a fund-raising trip beginning for World Hunger and said a week was all he could spare to get Wim headed for u.t. Most of that time Wim was on a Harlem playground with Billy and Dawn learning how to shoot hook shots.

Each morning Narsufin would meet them off 110th Street and tell them to shoot hook shots from twenty feet away from the basket. Then he'd leave them for most of the day, coming back about four to see how they were doing. Although Billy was a pretty good shooter, basketball was not Wim's sport. He and Dawn were about as accurate with their hook shots as blind monkeys. It didn't help matters that Narsufin's method emphasized their neither looking at the basket nor caring where their shots went.

Being in Harlem was provocation enough for the stunning whiteness of Dawn and Billy without having to compete for hoop space on a teenage playground. As soon as Narsufin left, the black teenagers whose turf the playground was gave the three a rough time. They crowded around, jeering at Billy and Wim and inviting Dawn to participate with them in a little one on one. When Wim explained that they wanted to practise hook shots so that Wim could someday cure the human sickness, they decided that it was no fun to pick on a total loonie, especially one as brown as Wim. So when the white intruders too seemed to be interested in nothing but shooting hook shots, they let them alone. Occasionally they'd insist Billy join one of their games to even up the sides, but mostly they relegated the hook shooters to a side backboard and basket usually used only by girls and kids under six.

Narsufin explained that Wim would find u.t. the same way he'd begin hitting hook shots: by getting in tune with the universe and not having any goal.

'The secret's rhythm, practice and invisibility,' he said to the three of them the first day. 'As soon as you can make the basket, the ball and yourself disappear, you'll have no troubles hitting hook shots.' He was standing at the foul line with his back to the basket, absent-mindedly dribbling the basketball. 'Concentrate on the air. There's a subway tunnel that runs from wherever you are to the basket and all you have to do is let go the ball in that tunnel and the conductor will do the rest.' He idly tossed the ball over his head and it swished through the round metal hoop and loose-hanging cords as if pulled there by a magnet. 'Concentrate on the air,' he concluded.

So Wim concentrated on the air. But all the subway lines he seemed to locate went off behind the backboard or on to Dawn's head or into the wire-mesh fence. Of course, he had to admit that he was usually concentrating on his arm or hand or the ball or the basket rather than the air. And when one of his shots did go through the hoop he'd get so excited that when he was shooting his next shot all he could think of was the basket. His next shot usually went on to 110th Street.

Billy began to have a nervous breakdown. Before he began studying with Narsufin he used to be a good shooter – hitting more than half. After two days of using Narsufin's method he was hitting about one in ten, and that one only because he kept cheating. And by the fourth day he couldn't hit a hook shot even when he cheated.

'My career is ruined!!' he moaned. 'If UCLA hears about what's happened to my hook shot they'll cancel my scholar-ship! All because I simply and humbly want to be the first to find ultimate truth and thus be able to dominate the world!'

It didn't help his morale that Dawn's hook shot was now better than his. Narsufin explained that since Dawn didn't give a fuck about hook shots she was bound to be the best using Narsufin's method. Billy and Wim were goal-oriented and would probably, by the end of the week when Narsufin had to leave, be unable to hit another hook shot for the rest of their lives – unless they tuned into the universe.

On the third day he gave each of them a wazifa to hum as they were shooting. Wim thought it was ridiculous to hum some dumb Arabic word while playing basketball until on the fifth day a strange thing began to happen. He began to get really into the sound of his wazifa and notice that it was very like that of a subway train. Three four five times in a row he was totally absorbed in the sound of the wazifa subway system when Billy slapped him in the face.

'Wake up!' Billy was shouting. 'What happened!?'

'What do you mean what happened?' asked Wim irritably. 'I'm shooting hook shots on to 110th Street.'

'But your last five shots have gone "swish",' Billy cried, his eyes bugging out in terror and envy. 'They somehow didn't even touch the net!'

'Wow! Really?' said Wim.

'And each time the ball bounced off the middle of the steel backboard support and dribbled right back to where you are!'

'How about that?' said Wim, beaming. Then he frowned. 'But it wasn't me. It was the wazifa subway system.'

'The what!?'

'If you concentrate real hard on your wazifa it ends up sounding like a subway train in a tunnel.'

'Not mine,' said Billy. 'My wazifa sounds like a moocow mooing and if you think I can concentrate on hook shooting carrying a damn cow around in my ear you're nuts.'

'What's your wazifa sound like, Dawn?' Wim asked.

'Mine sounds like the voice of some holy man calling everyone to prayer,' Dawn answered.

'Hmmm,' said Wim.

But now that Wim knew he'd made five straight shots he found himself picturing the basket at the end of the subway line and lost his wazifa. His shots went back to being random and inaccurate.

Narsufin nodded when they told the story at four o'clock.

'But how can I concentrate on my wazifa if it sounds like a fucking cow?' Billy complained.

'Look, Bill-Baby,' he said, putting a long arm around Billy's solid shoulders. 'A cow is just as good at carrying the ball to the basket as a fuckin' subway. Just listen, man. Give all your juice to the sound. If it sounds like a cow, groove on the cow. But stop worrying about either the ball or the cow.'

'And Dawn,' he went on. 'Your holy man is both calling the faithful to prayer and calling the ball to the basket. Listen to the sound of his calling, lose yourself in the sound of his calling.'

On the sixth day all hell broke loose. Wim and Dawn had become totally absorbed in their wazifas and from eleven o'clock that morning until three in the afternoon they methodically, with their backs to the basket and without looking, threw up hook shots from twenty-five feet and each one would go 'swish' right through the hoop. By two o'clock there were more than a thousand people gathered around the court watching the bronze little guy who was nuts and the luscious tall blonde who looked like she could barely lift the basketball much less shoot it, both swishing through their long, blind hook shots. Billy had given up and was sitting quietly on the sidelines crying.

'That fuckin' Narsufin done gone and taught a *white* chick to shoot like us,' one of the teenagers complained.

'That little guy got blood,' another insisted hopefully.

'Yeah, but that blonde,' moaned the first. 'Both honky and a girl!'

Narsufin arrived early and put a stop to the exhibition by bringing Wim out of his trance, praising him as the best hook shot artist since Kareem and then ordering him to show the crowd how good he was by hitting a hook from only five feet away from the basket.

Naturally Wim forgot about his wazifa and thought only of the crowd and glory and Kareem and put his shot into a third-storey apartment window.

But when Narsufin told Dawn the same thing, she didn't give a fig for the crowd or Kareem or basketball and she hit her shot from five and then hit one from thirty feet and then four from fifty.

At that point the black crowd was so depressed at a white girl making like Dr J they began to go home. Narsufin tried to comfort Billy by reminding him that at any second the moocow might find the range, but it didn't do much good. Billy begged to be given a different wazifa and Narsufin gave him a new one – this one sounding, Billy announced gloomily, like a long drawn-out fart.

On the seventh day Narsufin announced they could rest. He wanted a final chat with Wim to see if he was ready to find u.t. Billy, depressed but undaunted, insisted on going alone out on the court to see if he could ride the fart sound to victory.

Narsufin, Wim and Dawn sat on a bench nearby to talk and watch.

'The thing to remember,' said Narsufin, crossing his stilt-like legs, 'is that everything's at one and the same time a trap and a trapdoor to freedom. Every event, every guy, every ambition, every lust, can either lock you up for life or open you up to the entire universe. Dawn here may be either snare or salvation. Your listening to me may be either part of your purgatory or your path to paradise. Trap or trapdoor: you're the creator.'

'But how can I be the creator?' asked Wim, 'I haven't found my deep-down central self, so I'm scattered. Sometimes I make traps and sometimes I use a trapdoor.'

'You're scattered because you're looking for something

that doesn't exist,' Narsufin responded quietly. 'There is no centre, Wim.'

'No centre!' Wim said. 'But ... but I thought that's what ultimate truth would be: the *centre*.'.

'When you find ultimate truth you'll know there is no centre.'

'No basic *me*!?'

'No basic you.'

'No ultimate, fundamental, rock-bottom, through-to-the-core purpose for my life?'

'Not one.'

'No ultimate unity?'

'No centre,' Narsufin answered. 'The centre cannot hold because there is no one there to do the holding.'

'There are going to be a lot of disappointed seekers,' Wim concluded, 'when this little item gets around.'

'Oh, no,' said Narsufin. 'Seekers usually find a centre.'

'But you said –'

'They find a centre, all right, but of course it's an illusion,' Narsufin explained, catching one of Billy's wilder shots and tossing it back to him. 'And when they later see it to be an illusion they replace it with another rock-bottom, fundamental, through-to-the-core absolutely basic centre that is equally illusory.'

Wim shook his head.

'I don't know if I trust this universe,' he said.

'When you find your u.t. you'll find you trust in it completely – despite its scattered and chaotic multiplicity.'

'But I'm beginning to doubt I'll ever find u.t.,' said Wim, frowning. 'According to the thunder you were supposed to tell me where to find it, but instead all I've done is develop a hook shot. Or rather discover a subway train that will do the shooting for me.'

'You'll find it,' Narsufin said, smiling one of his rare smiles, the white teeth blazing in the middle of his slender black face. 'Or rather it will find you. Now tell me, what have you learned about u.t. so far?'

Wim nodded and then looked away to watch Billy desperately flinging basketballs in the general direction of a basket. Then he looked at Dawn who was watching him expectantly and finally back to Narsufin.

'I think I've learned that u.t. is right here if I could just get to see it,' he said. 'That we could all see it if ... if somehow our eyes could be opened.'

'Not bad,' Narsufin said, nodding. 'But be careful: that sounds suspiciously like a theory. It may not be here, may not be everywhere.'

'But what more can I do to find it?' Wim asked.

'Nothing,' said Narsufin.

When Wim looked up at him closely, he could see that somehow Narsufin was encouraging him.

'Nothing,' he echoed.

'There's nothing to be done.'

Wim slowly nodded.

'I can go home.'

'Go home.'

Billy Best was suddenly standing in front of them looking dazed and half-ecstatic and half-miserable.

'I did it,' he said in awe of himself. 'The damn fart blew straight to the basket.'

'What?' asked Wim.

'Some black guy said I just sank ten hook shots in a row,' Billy explained dazedly. 'But I wasn't there to enjoy it!!'

'Those are the breaks,' said Narsufin.

'So if I challenge Wim and beat him,' Billy went on gloomily, 'it will be because I've become one with my wazifa fart, and thus I won't be there to enjoy my victory. And if I'm filled with Billy, I'll lose and know it and feel it and be miserable. How could you do this to me, Narsufin?'

'It wasn't easy,' said Narsufin.

'We're going back to Maganansett,' Wim announced, standing. 'I'm going home.'

'What for?' asked Billy, still only half out of his trance. 'I thought Narsufin was going to show you where to find u.t.'

'I think he has,' said Wim. 'I'm going home.'

'But it can't be there,' Billy insisted.

'Good hunting,' said Narsufin, also standing as Wim took Dawn's hand.

'Thank you, Narsufin,' said Wim.

'It's nothing,' he replied.

'It's a lot worse than that,' said Billy bitterly. 'My basketball career's ruined.'

'Cheer up,' said Narsufin, putting a bony hand on Billy's shoulder. 'It could have been worse. I might have taught you how to make money without trying, and then you'd never be around to enjoy your riches.'

'That's right,' said Billy, cheering up. 'I'm still me to enjoy all my other triumphs.'

'But if Wim finds u.t.,' Narsufin reminded him, 'then he'll be able to succeed at everything as he did at his hook shots. Then where will you be?'

'In hell,' said Billy, going gloomy again. 'Let's go, Wim,' he added, turning to Wim. 'Onward to home and u.t.!'

The last Wim saw of Narsufin was when he was about to descend into the subway and looked back. Narsufin was alone at one end of the basketball court, slowly dribbling a basketball. He looked up at the basket only a couple of feet away and then took a stride away from the basket and flung up a hook shot.

It missed.

THE ONE TRUE GURU

'In your own great search for the One True Guru, how, Wim, did you distinguish those yogis who were fakes from those who were real?'

'At first,' Wim replied, 'I found that the fakes had all the answers, while the true Gurus never had answers!'

'I see.'

'But after I finally stumbled upon ultimate truth I realized I'd been wrong.'

'How?'

'Then I knew that every yogi I'd ever been to had been the One True Guru.'

– from *Sixty-six Parables of Wim*

56

from Grain-of-Sand's *Memoirs of an Old Liar*, pp. 500–511

Wim came home.

And it was good to see him. He'd been away half a year chasing down those buddha fellas and life would have been dull without him if it weren't so exciting anyway.

He went to see his mum at her old farmhouse first and give her a hug and kiss and told her all about his summer vacation. Wide Pool was so pleased just to see him and hold him she didn't really hear much of what he said, but she sensed he was changed and was proud. 'Course she was disappointed Wim and Dawn weren't getting married yet, but Wim made up for that by announcing that he'd talked things over with Billy and he was going to leave the Bests and live with Wide Pool again. Since Wim's newest daddy was the town mayor, it looked like he might even be able to stay.

Then he went over to the Bests and shook hands with the doc and his wife. He apologized for taking Billy away from the first six weeks of the football season and ruining his hook shot. When he give 'em the good news that he was moving out, Dr Best scowled. He was worried that there was still an outside chance Wim might somehow beat Billy to u.t. If Wim did get there first it might be a good idea to have Wim part of the family. So he told Wim he was sad to see him go but would stay his foster-parent so Wim wouldn't have to worry about legal hassles. Wim thanked him, promised to clean up his room real good, and left.

Then he come to see me.

I was fishing. It was late fall and chilly and I was standing in the lee of a big boulder casting, when he run up and almost bowled me over trying to give me a hug. Wouldn't be a bit surprised if he cost me a bluefish.

I reeled in my empty line and we took a stroll along the beach. Dawn was with him, and as they walked hand in hand he told me everything that had happened since his last letter. When he was done I asked him where he was gonna hunt for u.t. now that he was home. He said he didn't need to hunt no more. Now that he'd done all the things the buddhas told him to do he was ready, and u.t. would find him. He was just gonna go back to school and finish his senior year.

Well, thinking u.t. would find him was a convenient theory all right and seemed almost like the way Montauks do things, so I was pleased. And the school business didn't bother me 'cause the fact is Wim was different.

I mean Wim was always Wim. No matter how human and miserable he was or how Montauk, he was always polite and bright-eyed and enthusiastic. But that day I noticed that the desperation he'd had since he'd become a human being seemed to have seeped out of him. If he was confused, his confusion didn't seem to bother him. If he wanted to find u.t., he didn't want it in a way that made him unhappy because he hadn't found it yet. If seeing the ashes of the Bests' barn made him remember the way human beings can be humans, he didn't get gloomy or angry because of it.

And Dawn was different too. She'd lost that look she used to have that made a fella feel he hadn't shaved, or his fly was unzipped, or that he'd just said 'shit' when he'd thought he'd said 'tulip'. She looked as sweet and contented and filled with love as the Virgin Mary before Jesus grew up.

They was both Montauks again.

Made me feel like crying. Made me have to admit that maybe, every now and then, the Gods might speak in Sanskrit. Made me remember that black white men like that

Narsufin fella might be Montauks. Or big white slobs like Blobbojelli. Made me happy to be in a universe with Montauks living in disguise all over the place.

'High school, huh?' I said.

'I've missed more than two months, and Coach Cannonball is so furious he's threatened to forbid my calling "X-X-X" on the third,' Wim said with a frown. 'And Mrs Mandleson says I'll probably never be able to pass Social Studies III, but unless seeing u.t. changes things completely, I want to finish.'

'Yep,' I said.

'But I'm not sure about going to UCLA.'

'Yep.'

'After I'm done with high school I might just stay here.'

'Yep.'

'I think first though I'll go down to the old barge and find ultimate truth.'

'Yep,' I said. The nice thing about being navigator to Montauks who are Montauks is you never have to tell 'em anything.

Well, I think it surprised Wim almost as much as it did me and Dawn him saying right out that u.t. was on the barge. He told me later that it just come to him that Narsufin's 'Go home' meant go back to the barge he was born at.

I walked with him towards the barge – he weren't in no hurry – and who should we meet up with but Billy running like a madman towards us.

'Have you found it yet?' he shouted even before he'd come up to us.

'Not yet,' said Wim.

'Thank God,' said Billy, gasping for breath. 'I suddenly realized that now you're home I better stick to you every second.'

'We're going down to my old barge to see it,' Wim announced casually.

'To the barge? It's there!?' cried Billy.

'I think so,' said Wim. 'At least my u.t. I don't know about yours.'

'What do you mean mine and yours?' Billy said, falling into step beside us. 'U.T.'s like an island – first one to find it gets to name it and divide it up into subdivisions and extract the minerals and so on. Of course, in this case I plan to let you have ten per cent rights because of all the help you've been.'

'Thanks, Billy,' said Wim, smiling, 'but I really don't think it works that way. I think u.t. is more like the ocean – if and when you find it, you get to swim in it and sail on it, but it doesn't belong to anyone, and the piece I find may be different from the piece you find.'

As we came into sight of the decrepit old barge, Billy squinted up ahead. I could tell he was itching to run but held himself back.

'In any case,' he said, 'I, uh, promise to share fifty-fifty whatever I discover. Will you do the same?'

'Sure,' said Wim. 'If I can.'

'If you see it, I'll see it,' Billy said confidently. 'If I have to rip out your eyeballs to do it.'

'That's the spirit,' said Wim.

The barge weren't much different than it was the day Wide Pool finished her jumble sale five years before. An old Montauk named Under-the-Rug had been living in it for the last six months, but the only stuff he'd brought was a junky charcoal cooker and an extra pair of socks.

Wim said 'howdy' to Under-the-Rug, who'd been dozing in the sand with his back against the barge, and asked him if we could go in and look around. Naturally that was fine with Under-the-Rug – he loved visitors – and Billy leapt up on the barge and dashed inside the wrecked cabin of the old fishing smack. Wim and Dawn and me stayed to chat with the old Montauk, Wim telling him all about his quest and why he wanted to look in the barge.

'Ain't much in there,' said Under-the-Rug, yawning, 'but

if you find your u.t. you're welcome to it. If u.t. turns out to be my second pair of socks I'll just have to wash these'ns more often.'

'Thanks, Under-the-Rug,' said Wim, and he give Dawn a boost up on to the deck of the barge and climbed up after her. I stayed to compare arthriti with Under-the-Rug, and then we got to chatting about the way the bluefish this year seemed to prefer shiners to lures so I weren't there when Wim found it. He told me all about it later.

Seems by the time he and Dawn went into the cabin of the old fishing smack Billy had ransacked the place and reported it weren't there and dashed out again to search the deck and the bilge. Wim and Dawn walked in, and Wim saw the ancient rocking chair his mom loved to rock in and set in it. Then he looked around for u.t.

As Under-the-Rug said, there weren't much stuff to look at. In the whole cabin there was just the rocking chair, a bed, an old plastic kitchen table with a single chair, two posters, each showing a naked gal fishin' for bluefish, a fishin' pole, a charcoal cooker, a box with a dozen or so pretty seashells in it, and a pair of socks. On the table was a kerosene lamp, a knife, a fork, a jelly glass half-filled with water, a single plate with the remains of some baked potatoes, and a couple of small round green things that looked like pills.

Wim sat there rocking while Dawn eased herself around the room, stopping to admire the shells, and then staring out the cabin window to watch Billy dancing around the deck of the barge.

Wim sat there and he rocked. Says he was thinking of me and Osso and Dawn and Nastuffin and his mum and Miss Lunnigan and for some reason he was feeling pretty good – sort of lovey-dovey towards just about everyone and everything.

Then he remembered his quest. He looked around and looked and looked and suddenly began to get scared. There was absolutely nothing special in the whole room. He wasn't

405

going to find ultimate truth after all. He jumped up out of his chair and begun to run around that room like a rat in a maze with all the doors locked. He weren't going to find it. All the help Osso and Blobbo and Nastuffin give him down the drain.

When he saw Dawn looking at him as if he'd gone mad, Wim collapsed back into the rocker, his eyes sweeping the room one last time, knowing even as he did that there was nothing special to be seen.

Then suddenly, unexpectedly, and accidentally he done went and saw ultimate truth.

He says it hit him like a howitzer shell and sent him sprawling over backwards in that rocker and on to his ass. There he sat, laughing, his face feeling on fire and his body like it was lighter than helium.

When Wim toppled over backwards Dawn screamed and run up to him.

'Are you all right?' she asked, kneeling beside him.

'I love you, Dawn,' Wim said, eyes glowing.

Billy come rushing into the cabin and stared down at Wim who was grinning and giggling and looking suspiciously happy.

'Where is it!? Where is it!?' Billy shouted, his eyes darting around the room, figuring Wim must of seen something pretty interesting.

Smiling like a man already in the middle of making love to Dawn, Wim pointed at the table.

Billy rushed over, but on the table was only those few eating things and the pill-looking things.

'Here!?' Billy asked desperately, turning back to Wim.

Wim was laughing so hard all he could do was nod, while Dawn looked from him to Billy uncertainly.

Billy's eyes were bulging as he stared at the things on the table. Then with a joyful little yip he lifted up the plate of food and there, underneath it, was ... nothin'. Billy groaned and then grabbed the two green pills figuring maybe they was a magic potion. With his eyes glowing triumphantly he popped one of 'em into his mouth. After a while his eyes got sort of dismal again, and he mumbled something like 'clorets' and turned back to Wim.

'Here!!?' Billy pleaded, gesturing desperately at the table. 'Ultimate truth is *here*!?'

Wim staggered dazedly to his feet, touched his nose gently against Dawn's – made 'em both feel good – and floated over to Billy, nodding.

Billy stared some more down at that poor table.

'But *where*!?'

'Billy,' Wim said finally. 'You are the greatest human being I have ever known.'

'I know, I know!' Billy shouted. 'But where's u.t.?'

'You've already got it,' said Wim, smiling and throwing his right arm around Billy to hug him.

'No, I don't!' Billy wailed. 'Or if I do but can't recognize it, it won't do me any good. I want something I can use, promote and sell!'

'But it's right here,' said Wim, grinning down at the table.

'But *where*!?' Billy pleaded.

Wim reached down and picked up a single soggy baked potato.

'Here,' he said simply, holding it up for Billy.

Billy looked at that bedraggled potato and then at Wim and then at the bedraggled potato.

'That's it?' Billy asked in numb awe.

Wim looked at his potato, grinned, then at Billy and frowned. Finally, he nodded.

'That's it.'

'That's ultimate truth?'

'For me,' said Wim. 'It doesn't seem to be too ultimate for you.'

'Oh, shit, shit,' Billy wailed and turned to bang his head against the wooden wall of the old boat cabin.

'Come on, Billy,' Wim said, grabbing him by the arms. 'It's all right.'

Billy turned to Wim.

'I don't mind your finding u.t. first, Wim,' he said. 'It's just I'm going to have such a tough time marketing stale potatoes as the solution to the world's ills.'

'I don't think they have to be stale.'

'You know what I mean.'

'You'll figure an angle,' said Wim, one arm around Billy and the other around Dawn as he led them out of the cabin. 'You're not going to be beaten by a little potato, are you?'

'You're right,' said Billy, brightening. 'Hell, as you say, this is only your u.t. Mine may be more commercially viable.'

'Count on it, Bill,' said Wim. 'Count on it.'

When the three of them come back down off the barge, Wim was glowing a bit and Dawn looked like she couldn't tell if she should cheer or groan. Billy walked as if in a trance.

'Find anything?' I asked.

'Yes, sir,' said Wim. 'But it turned out to be nothing special.'

'Nothing special, huh?' I said. 'I figured. What you gonna do now?'

'I thought I'd like to do some fishing,' said Wim.

'Have to borrow Under-the-Rug's pole, I guess,' I said. 'The way you cast, you ain't using mine.'

'What about ultimate truth?' Dawn asked him. 'Is it the cure for the sickness like you hoped?'

Wim turned to her, thought a bit and nodded.

'Then aren't you going to try to save everyone?' she asked. 'That's what Buddha and Jesus and Muhammad did.'

Wim nodded again and began to smile.

'So what are you going to do?' Dawn asked.

'I'm going to try to save everyone, Dawn,' he answered

her, the smile spreading to fill his whole face. 'And I'm going fishing.'

We didn't catch much that day, though. Wim reeled in a humpback whale, but he threw it back.

The world's greatest novelists now available in paperback from Grafton Books

Doris Lessing
Novels

The Good Terrorist	£2.95	☐
The Grass is Singing	£2.50	☐
The Golden Notebook	£3.50	☐
Briefing for a Descent into Hell	£2.95	☐

'Children of Violence' Series

Martha Quest	£2.50	☐
A Proper Marriage	£3.50	☐
A Ripple from the Storm	£2.50	☐
Landlocked	£2.50	☐
The Four-Gated City	£3.50	☐

'Canopus in Argos: Archives'

Shikasta	£2.95	☐
The Marriages Between Zones Three, Four, and Five	£2.50	☐
The Sirian Experiments	£2.95	☐
The Making of the Representative for Planet 8	£2.50	☐
Documents relating to the Sentimental Agents in the Volyen Empire	£2.50	☐

Non-Fiction

In Pursuit of the English (autobiography)	£1.95	☐
Particularly Cats	£2.50	☐
Going Home	£2.50	☐

Short Stories

Five	£2.95	☐
The Habit of Loving	£2.50	☐
A Man and Two Women	£2.50	☐
Winter in July	£2.50	☐
The Black Madonna	£2.95	☐
This Was the Old Chief's Country (Collected African Stories, Volume 1)	£2.95	☐
The Sun Between Their Feet (Collected African Stories, Volume 2)	£2.95	☐
To Room Nineteen (Collected Stories, Volume 1)	£2.50	☐
The Temptation of Jack Orkney (Collected Stories, Volume 2)	£2.50	☐

To order direct from the publisher just tick the titles you want and fill in the order form.

The world's greatest novelists now available in paperback from Grafton Books

Jack Kerouac

Big Sur	£2.50	☐
Visions of Cody	£2.50	☐
Doctor Sax	£1.95	☐
Lonesome Traveller	£2.50	☐
Desolation Angels	£2.95	☐
The Dharma Bums	£2.50	☐
The Subterraneans and Pic	£1.50	☐
Maggie Cassidy	£1.50	☐
Vanity of Duluoz	£1.95	☐

Norman Mailer

Cannibals and Christians (non-fiction)	£1.50	☐
The Presidential Papers	£1.50	☐
Advertisements for Myself	£2.95	☐
The Naked and The Dead	£2.95	☐
The Deer Park	£2.95	☐

Henry Miller

Black Spring	£2.95	☐
Tropic of Cancer	£2.95	☐
Tropic of Capricorn	£2.95	☐
Nexus	£3.50	☐
Sexus	£3.50	☐
Plexus	£2.95	☐
The Air-Conditioned Nightmare	£2.50	☐

Luke Rhinehart

The Dice Man	£2.95	☐
The Long Voyage Back	£1.95	☐

To order direct from the publisher just tick the titles you want
and fill in the order form.

The world's greatest novelists now available in paperback from Grafton Books

Angus Wilson

Such Darling Dodos	£1.50	☐
Late Call	£1.95	☐
The Wrong Set	£1.95	☐
For Whom the Cloche Tolls	£2.95	☐
A Bit Off the Map	£1.50	☐
As If By Magic	£2.50	☐
Hemlock and After	£1.50	☐
No Laughing Matter	£1.95	☐
The Old Men at the Zoo	£1.95	☐
The Middle Age of Mrs Eliot	£1.95	☐
Setting the World on Fire	£1.95	☐
Anglo-Saxon Attitudes	£2.95	☐
The Strange Ride of Rudyard Kipling (non-fiction)	£1.95	☐
The World of Charles Dickens (non-fiction)	£3.95	☐

John Fowles

The Ebony Tower	£2.50	☐
The Collector	£1.95	☐
The French Lieutenant's Woman	£2.50	☐
The Magus	£2.95	☐
Daniel Martin	£3.95	☐
Mantissa	£2.50	☐
The Aristos (non-fiction)	£2.50	☐

Brian Moore

The Lonely Passion of Judith Hearne	£2.50	☐
I am Mary Dunne	£1.50	☐
Catholics	£2.50	☐
Fergus	£2.50	☐
The Temptation of Eileen Hughes	£1.50	☐
The Feast of Lupercal	£1.50	☐
Cold Heaven	£2.50	☐

To order direct from the publisher just tick the titles you want and fill in the order form.

Outstanding fiction in paperback from Grafton Books

Muriel Spark

The Abbess of Crewe	£1.95	☐
The Only Problem	£2.50	☐
Territorial Rights	£1.25	☐
Not To Disturb	£1.25	☐
Loitering with Intent	£1.25	☐
Bang-Bang You're Dead	£1.25	☐
The Hothouse by the East River	£1.25	☐
Going up to Sotheby's	£1.25	☐
The Takeover	£1.95	☐

Toni Morrison

Song of Solomon	£2.50	☐
The Bluest Eye	£2.50	☐
Sula	£2.50	☐
Tar Baby	£1.95	☐

Erica Jong

Parachutes and Kisses	£2.95	☐
Fear of Flying	£2.95	☐
How to Save Your Own Life	£2.50	☐
Fanny	£2.95	☐
Selected Poems II	£1.25	☐
At the Edge of the Body	£1.25	☐

Anita Brookner

Family and Friends	£2.50	☐
A Start in Life	£2.50	☐
Providence	£2.50	☐
Look at Me	£2.50	☐
Hotel du Lac	£2.50	☐

To order direct from the publisher just tick the titles you want and fill in the order form.

Outstanding fiction in paperback from Grafton Books

Barbara Pym

Quartet in Autumn	£2.50	☐
The Sweet Dove Died	£2.50	☐
Less Than Angels	£1.95	☐
Some Tame Gazelle	£1.95	☐
A Few Green Leaves	£1.95	☐
No Fond Return of Love	£1.95	☐
Jane and Prudence	£2.50	☐
An Unsuitable Attachment	£2.50	☐
Crampton Hodnet	£2.50	☐
A Very Private Eye (non-fiction)	£2.95	☐

Elizabeth Smart

By Grand Central Station I Sat Down and Wept	£2.50	☐

Maggie Gee

Dying, in Other Words	£1.50	☐

Ruth Prawer Jhabvala

A Stronger Climate	£2.50	☐
A New Dominion	£1.95	☐
Like Birds, Like Fishes	£2.50	☐

Clare Nonhebel

Cold Showers	£2.50	☐

To order direct from the publisher just tick the titles you want and fill in the order form.

All these books are available at your local bookshop or newsagent, or can be ordered direct from the publisher.

To order direct from the publishers just tick the titles you want and fill in the form below.

Name _____

Address _____

_____

Send to:
Grafton Cash Sales
PO Box 11, Falmouth, Cornwall TR10 9EN.

Please enclose remittance to the value of the cover price plus:

UK 60p for the first book, 25p for the second book plus 15p per copy for each additional book ordered to a maximum charge of £1.90.

BFPO 60p for the first book, 25p for the second book plus 15p per copy for the next 7 books, thereafter 9p per book.

Overseas including Eire £1.25 for the first book, 75p for second book and 28p for each additional book.

Grafton Books reserve the right to show new retail prices on covers, which may differ from those previously advertised in the text or elsewhere.